THE BEST OF
FANTASY & SCIENCE FICTION
20th series

THE BEST OF

Fantasy

&

Science

Fiction

20th series

Edited by Edward L. Ferman

DOUBLEDAY & COMPANY, INC.
Garden City, New York 1973

Acknowledgments

The editor hereby makes grateful acknowledgment to the following authors and authors' representatives for giving permission to reprint the material in this volume:

Frederik Pohl for *Shaffery Among the Immortals*
Virginia Kidd for *A Different Drummer* by Raylyn Moore
Harlan Ellison for *The Deathbird*—Copyright © 1973 by Harlan Ellison
Phyllis Eisenstein for *Born to Exile*
Phyllis MacLennan for *Thus Love Betrays Us*
Alfred Bester for *The Animal Fair*
Marie Rodell for *Is It The End of the World?* by Wilma Shore
Lurton Blassingame for *The Bear With the Knot on His Tail* by Stephen Tall and *Birdlime* by B. L. Keller
Scott Meredith Literary Agency for *The Problem of Pain* by Poul Anderson
Gary Jennings for *Sooner or Later or Never Never*
Gahan Wilson for the cartoons

Contents

THE BEST OF
FANTASY & SCIENCE FICTION
20th series

*One happy event of 1972 in science fiction was the return of
Fred Pohl to active writing, after almost a decade of serving the
field well as editor and lecturer. One of the first of the new Pohl
stories to be published was this ironic tale of Jeremy Shaffery, an
inept and melancholy astronomer who dreamed wild dreams of a
discovery that would make his name famous and who, one day,
quite by accident, succeeded.*

Shaffery Among
the Immortals

FREDERIK POHL

Jeremy Shaffery had a mind a little bit like Einstein's, although
maybe not in the ways that mattered most. When Einstein first
realized that light carried mass, he sat down to write a friend
about it and described the thought as "amusing and infectious."
Shaffery would have thought that, too, although of course he
would not likely have seen the implications of the Maxwell
equations in the first place.

Shaffery looked a little bit like Einstein. He encouraged the
resemblance, especially in the hair, until his hair began to run
out. Since Einstein loved sailing, he kept a sixteen-foot trimaran
tied up at the observatory dock. Seasickness kept him from
using it much. Among the things he envied Einstein for was

the mirror-smooth Swiss lakes, so much nicer than the lower
Caribbean in that respect. But after a day of poring over pairs of
star photographs with a blink comparator or trying to discover
previously unknown chemical compounds in interstellar space
in a radio trace, he sometimes floated around the cove in his
little yellow rubber raft. It was relaxing, and his wife never
followed him there. To Shaffery that was important. She was a
difficult woman, chronically p.o.'d because his career was so
persistently pointed in the wrong direction. If she had ever
been a proper helpmeet, she wasn't any more. Shaffery doubted
she ever had, remembering that it was her unpleasant comments
that had caused him to give up that other hallmark of the master,
the violin.

At the stage in Shaffery's career at which he had become
Director of the Carmine J. Nuccio Observatory in the Lesser
Antilles, he had begun to look less like Einstein and more like
Edgar Kennedy. Nights when the seeing was good he remorse-
lessly scanned the heavens through the 22-inch reflector, hoping
against hope for glory. Days when he was not sleeping he wandered through the dome like a ghost, running his finger over
desks for dust, filching preserved mushrooms from Mr. Nuccio's
home-canned hoard, trying to persuade his two local assistants to
remember to close the dome slit when it rained. They paid little
attention. They knew where the muscle was, and that it wasn't
with Shaffery. He had few friends. Most of the white residents
couldn't stand his wife; some of them couldn't stand Shaffery
very well, either. There was a nice old-lady drunk out from
England in a tidy white house down the beach, a sort of hippie
commune on the far side of the island, and a New York television
talk-show operator who just flew down for weekends. When
they were respectively sober, unstoned and present, Shaffery
sometimes talked to them. That wasn't often. The only one he
really wanted to see much was the tv man, but there were obstacles. The big obstacle was that the tv man spent most of his
waking time skin diving. The other obstacle was that Shaffery
had discovered that the tv man occasionally laid Mrs. Shaffery. It
wasn't the morality of the thing that bothered him; it was the
feeling of doubt it raised in Shaffery's mind about the other's
sanity. He never spoke to the tv man about it, partly because he

wasn't sure what to say and partly because the man had halfway promised to have Shaffery on his show. Sometime or other.

One must be fair to Shaffery and say that he wasn't a bad man. Like Frank Morgan, his problem was that he wasn't a good wizard. The big score always evaded him.

The Einstein method, which he had studied assiduously over many years, was to make a pretty theory and then see if, by any chance, observations of events in the real world seemed to confirm it. Shaffery greatly approved of that method. It just didn't seem to work out for him. At the Triple A-S meeting in Dallas he read an hour-long paper on his new Principle of Relevance Theory. That was a typical Einstein idea, he flattered himself. He had even worked out simple explanations for the lay public, like Einstein with his sitting on a hot stove or holding hands with a pretty girl. "Relevance Theory," he practiced smiling to the little wavelets of the cove, "only means that observations that don't *relate* to anything don't *exist*. I'll spare you the mathematics because—" self-deprecatory laugh here— "I can't even fill out my income tax without making a mistake." Well, he had worked out the mathematics, inventing signs and operators of his own, just like Einstein. But he seemed to have made a mistake. Before the AAAS audience, fidgeting and whispering to each other behind their hands, he staked his scientific reputation on the prediction that the spectrum of Mars at its next opposition would show a slight but detectable displacement of some 150 angstroms toward the violet. The son of a bitch didn't do anything of the kind. One of the audience was a graduate student at Princeton, hard up for a doctoral thesis subject, and he took a chance on Shaffery and made the observations, and with angry satisfaction sent him the proof that Mars had remained obstinately red.

The next year the International Astrophysical Union's referees, after some discussion, finally allowed him twenty minutes for a Brief Introduction into the General Consideration of Certain Electromagnetic Anomalies. He offered thirty-one pages of calculations leading to the prediction that the next lunar eclipse would be forty-two seconds late. It wasn't. It was right on time. At the meeting of the World Space Science Symposium they told him with great regret that overcommitments of space and time had made it impossible for them to schedule his no doubt valuable contribution, and by the time of the next round of conferences they weren't even sending him invitations any more.

Meanwhile all those other fellows were doing great. Shaffery followed the careers of his contemporaries with rue. There was Hoyle, still making a good thing out of the Steady State Hypothesis and Gamow's name, still reverenced for the Big Bang, and new people like Dyson and Ehricke and Enzmann coming along with all sorts of ideas that, if you looked at them objectively, weren't any cleverer than his, Shaffery thought, except for the detail that somehow or other they seemed lucky enough to find supporting evidence from time to time. It did not strike him as fair. Was he not a Mensa member? Was he not as well educated as the successful ones, as honored with degrees, as photogenic in the newsmagazines and as colorfully entertaining on the talk shows? (Assuming Larry Nesbit ever gave him the chance on his show.) Why did they make out and he fall flat? His wife's theory he considered and rejected. "Your trouble, Jeremy," she would say to him, "is you're a horse's ass." But he knew that wasn't it. Who was to say Isaac Newton wasn't a horse's ass, too, if you looked closely enough at his freaky theology and his nervous breakdowns? And look where he got.

So Shaffery kept looking for the thing that would make him great. He looked all over. Sometimes he checked Kepler's analysis of the orbit of Mars with an adding machine, looking for mistakes in arithmetic. (He found half a dozen, but the damn things all canceled each other out, which proves how hard it is to go wrong when your luck is in.) Sometimes he offered five-dollar prizes to the local kids for finding new stars that might turn out to be Shaffery's Nova, or anyway Shaffery's Comet. No luck. An ambitious scheme to describe stellar ballistics in terms of analogy with free-radical activity in the enzyme molecules fell apart when none of the biochemists he wrote to even answered his letters.

The file of failures grew. One whole drawer of a cabinet was filled with reappraisals of the great exploded theories of the past—*A New Look at Phlogiston*, incomplete because there didn't seem really to be anything to look at when you came down to it; a manuscript called *The Flat Earth Reexamined*, which no one would publish; three hundred sheets of drawings of increasingly tinier and increasingly quirkier circles to see if the Copernican epicycles could not somehow account for what the planet Mercury did that Einstein had considered a proof of relativity. From time to time he was drawn again to attempting to find a scientific basis for astrology and chiromancy, or predicting the paths of charged particles in a cloud chamber by means of yarrow stalks. It all came to nothing. When he was really despairing, he sometimes considered making his mark in industry rather than pure science, wherefore the sheaf of sketches for a nuclear-fueled car, the experiments on smellovision that had permanently destroyed the nerves of his left nostril, the attempt to preserve some of Mr. Nuccio's mushrooms by irradiation in his local dentist's X-ray room. He knew that that sort of thing was not really worthy of a man with all those graduate degrees, but in any event he did no better there than anywhere else. Sometimes he dreamed of what it would be like to run Mount Palomar or Jodrell Bank, with fifty trained assistants to nail down his inspirations with evidence. He was not that fortunate. He had only Cyril and James.

It was not all bad, however, because he didn't have much interference to worry about. The observatory where he was employed, last and least of the string of eleven that had given him a position since his final doctoral degree, didn't seem to mind what he did, as long as he did it without bothering them. On the other hand, they didn't give him much support, either.

Probably they just didn't know how. The observatory was owned by something called the Lesser Antilles Vending Machine Entertainment Co., Ltd., and, so Shaffery had been told by the one old classmate who still kept up a sort of friendship with him, was actually some sort of tax-evasion scheme maintained by a Las Vegas gambling syndicate. Shaffery didn't mind this, particularly, although from time to time he got tired of being told that the only two astronomers who mattered were Giovanni Schiaparelli and Galileo Galilei. That was only a minor annoyance. The big cancerous agony was that every year he got a year older and fame would not come.

At his periodic low spots of despondency (he had even tried linking them with the oppositions of Jupiter, meteor showers,

and his wife's periods, but those didn't come to anything either)
he toyed with the notion of dropping it all and going into some
easier profession. Banking. Business. Law. "President Shaffery"
had the right kind of sound, if he entered politics. But then he
would drag his raft to the water, prop two six-packs of Danish
beer on his abdomen and float away, and by the end of the first
pack his courage would come flowing back, and on the second
he would be well into a scheme for detecting gravity waves by
statistical analysis of 40,000 acute gout sufferers, telephoning the
state of their twinges into a central computer facility.

On such a night he carried his little rubber raft to the shore
of the cove, slipped off his sandals, rolled up his bell-bottoms
and launched himself. It was the beginning of the year, as close
to winter as it ever got on the island, which meant mostly that
the dark came earlier. It was a bad time of the year for him,
because it was the night before the annual Board Meeting. The
first year or two he had looked forward to the meetings as
opportunities. He was no longer so hopeful. His objective for
the present meeting was only to survive it, and there was some
question of a nephew by marriage, an astronomy major at
U.C.L.A., to darken even that hope.
Shaffery's vessel wasn't really a proper raft, only the sort of
kid's toy that drowns a dozen or so nine-year-olds at the world's
bathing beaches every year. It was less than five feet long. When
he got himself twisted and wriggled into it, his back against the
ribbed bottom, his head pillowed against one inflated end, and
his feet dangling into the water at the other, it was quite like
floating in a still sea without the annoyance of getting wet. He
opened the first beer and began to relax. The little waves rocked
and turned him; the faint breeze competed with the tiny island
tide, and the two of them combined to take him erratically away
from the beach at the rate of maybe ten feet a minute. It didn't
matter. He was still inside the cove, with islets, or low sandbanks,
beaded across the mouth of it. If by any sudden meteorological
miracle a storm should spring from that bright-lamped sky, the
wind could take him nowhere but back to shore or near an
island. And of course there would be no storm. He could paddle
back whenever he chose, as easily as he could push his soap dish

around his bathtub, as he routinely did while bathing, which in turn he did at least once a day, and when his wife was particularly difficult as often as six times. The bathroom was his other refuge. His wife never followed him there, being too well brought up to run the chance of inadvertently seeing him doing something filthy.

Up on the low hills he could see the corroded copper dome of the observatory. A crescent of light showed that his assistant had opened the dome, but the light showed that he was not using it for any astronomical purpose. That was easy to unriddle. Cyril had turned the lights on so that the cleaning woman could get the place spotless for the Board Meeting and had opened the dome because that proved the telescope was being used. Shaffery bent the empty beer can into a V, tucked it neatly beside him in the raft, and opened another. He was not yet tranquil, but he was not actively hurting anywhere. At least Cyril would not be using the telescope to study the windows of the Bon Repos Hotel across the cove, since the last time he'd done it he had jammed the elevating gears and it could no longer traverse anywhere near the horizon. Shaffery put aside an unwanted, fugitive vision of Idris, the senior and smartest cleaning lady, polishing the telescope mirror with Bon Ami, sipped his beer, thought nostalgically of Relevance Theory and how close he had come with the epicycles, and freed his mind for constructive thought.

The sun was wholly gone, except for a faint luminous purpling of the sky in the general direction of Venezuela. Almost directly overhead hung the three bright stars of Orion's Belt, slowly turning like the traffic signals on a railroad line, with Sirius and Procyon orbiting headlight bright around them. As his eyes dark-adapted he could make out the stars in Orion's sword, even the faint patch of light that was the great gas cloud. He was far enough from the shore so that sound could not carry, and he softly called out the great four-pointed pattern of first-magnitude stars that surrounded the constellation: "Hey there, Betelguese. Hi, Bellatrix. What's new, Rigel? Nice to see you again, Saiph." He glanced past red Aldebaran to the close-knit stars of the Pleiades, returned to Orion and, showing off now, called off the stars of the Belt: "Hey, Alnitak! Yo, Alnilam! How goes it, Mintaka?"

The problem with drinking beer in the rubber raft was that your head was bent down toward your chest and it was difficult to burp; but Shaffery arched his body up a little, getting in some water in the process but not caring, got rid of the burp, opened another beer, and gazed complacently at Orion. It was a satisfying constellation. It was satisfying that he knew so much about it. He thought briefly of the fact that the Arabs had called the Belt Stars by the name Jauzah, meaning the Golden Nuts; that the Chinese thought they looked like a weighing beam, and that Greenlanders called them Siktut, The Seal Hunters Lost at Sea. As he was going on to remember what the Australian aborigines had thought of them (they thought they resembled three young men dancing a corroboree), his mind flickered back to the lost seal hunters. Um, he thought. He raised his head and looked toward the shore.

It was now more than a hundred yards away. That was farther than he really wanted to be, and so he kicked the raft around, oriented himself by the stars and began to paddle back. It was easy and pleasant to do. He used a sort of splashy upside-down breast stroke of the old-fashioned angel's wing kind, but as all his weight was supported by the raft, he moved quickly across the water. He was rather enjoying the exercises, toes and fingers moving comfortably in the tepid sea, little ghosts of luminescence glowing where he splashed, until quite without warning the fingertips of one hand struck sharply and definitely against something that was resistantly massive and solid where there should have been only water, something that moved stubbornly, something that rasped them like a file. Oh, my God, thought Shaffery. What a lousy thing to happen. They so seldom came in this close to shore. He didn't even think about them. What a shame for a man who might have been Einstein to wind up, incomplete and unfulfilled, as shark shit.

He really was not a bad man, and it was the loss to science that was first on his mind, only a little later what it must feel like to be chopped and gulped.

Shaffery pulled his hands in and folded them on his chest, crossed his feet at the ankles, and rested them on the end of the boat, knees spread on the sides. There was now nothing trailing in the water that might strike a shark as bait. There was, on the other hand, no good way for him to get back to shore. He could yell, but the wind was the wrong way. He could wait till he drifted near one of the islets. But if he missed them, he would be out in the deep ocean before he knew it.

Shaffery was almost sure that sharks seldom attacked a boat, even a rubber one. Of course, he went on analytically, the available evidence didn't signify. They could flip a raft like this over easily enough. If this particular shark ate him off this particular half-shell, there would be no one to report it.

Still, there were some encouraging considerations. Say it was a shark. Say it was capable of tipping the boat or eating him boat and all. They were dull-witted creatures, and what was to keep one hanging around in the absence of blood, splashing, noise, trailing objects or any of the other things sharks were known to take an interest in? It might be a quarter mile away already. But it wasn't, because at that moment he heard the splash of some large object breaking the surface a foot from his head.

Shaffery could have turned to look, but he didn't; he remained quite motionless, listening to the gentle water noises, until they were punctuated by a sort of sucking sound and then a voice. A human voice. It said, "Scared the piss out of you, didn't I? What do you say, Shaffery? Want a tow back to shore?"

It was not the first time Shaffery had encountered Larry Nesbit diving in the cove; it was only the first time it had happened at night. Shaffery twisted about in the raft and gazed at Nesbit's grinning face and its frame of wet strands of nape-length hair. It took a little time to make the transition in his mind from eighteen-foot shark to five-foot-eight TV star. "Come on," Nesbit went on, "what do you say? Tell you what. I'll tow you in, and you give me some of old Nuccio's Scotch, and I'll listen to how you're going to invent antigravity while we get pissed."

That Nesbit, he had a way with him. The upshot of it all was that Shaffery had a terrible hangover the next day; not the headache but the whole works, trotting to the toilet and being able to tolerate only small sips of ginger ale and wishing, or almost wishing, he was dead. (Not, to be sure, before he did the one immortalizing thing. Whatever it was going to be.)

It was not altogether a disaster, the hangover. The next morning was very busy, and it was just as well that he was out of the way. When the Board of Directors convened to discuss the astronomical events of the year, or whatever it is they did discuss in the afternoon session to which Shaffery was definitely not invited, it was always a busy time. They arrived separately, each director with his pair of associates. One after another 40-foot cabin cruisers with fishing tops came up to the landing and gave up cargoes of plump little men wearing crew cuts and aloha shirts. The observatory car, not ever used by any of the observatory personnel, was polished, fueled and used for round trips from the landing strip at Jubila, across the island, to Comray Hill and the observatory. Shaffery laid low in his private retreat. He had never told his wife that he was not allowed in the observatory for the board meetings; so she didn't look for him. He spent the morning in the tar-paper shack where photographic material had once been kept, until he discovered that the damp peeled the emulsion away from the backing. Now it was his home away from home. He had fitted it with a desk, chair, icebox, coffeepot and bed.

Shaffery paid no attention to the activity outside, not even when the directors' assistants, methodically searching the bushes and banana groves all round the observatory, came to his shack, opened the door without knocking, and peered in at him. They knew him from previous meetings, but they studied him silently for a moment before the two in the doorway nodded to each other and left him again. They were not well-mannered men, Shaffery thought, but no doubt they were good at their jobs, whatever those jobs were. He resolutely did not think about the Board Meeting, or about the frightening, calumnious things Larry Nesbit had said to him the night before, drinking the Board Chairman's Scotch and eating his food, in that half-jocular, shafting, probing way he had. Shaffery thought a little bit about the queasy state of his lower abdomen, because he couldn't help it, but what he mostly thought about was Fermat's Last Theorem.

A sort of picayune, derivative immortality was waiting there for someone. Not much, but Shaffery was getting desperate. It was one of those famous mathematical problems that grad students played at for a month or two and amateurs assaulted in vain all their lives. It looked easy enough to deal with. It started with so elementary a proposition that every high-school boy mastered it about the time he learned to masturbate successfully. If you squared the sides of a right triangle, the sum of the squares of the two sides was equal to the square of the hypotenuse.

Well, that was all very well, and it was so easy to understand that it had been used to construct right angles by surveyors for centuries. A triangle whose sides were, say, 3 feet and 4 feet, and whose hypotenuse was 5 feet, had to make a right angle, because $3^2+4^2=5^2$; and it always had, since the time of Pythagoras, five hundred years B.C., $a^2+b^2=c^2$. The hitch was, if the exponent was anything but 2, you could never make the equation come out using whole numbers; a^3+b^3 never equaled c^3, and $a^{27}+b^{27}$ did not add up to any c^{27}, no matter what numbers you used for a, b and c. Everybody knew that this was so. Nobody had ever proved that it *had* to be so, by mathematical proofs, except that Fermat had left a cryptic little note, found among his papers after his death, claiming that he had found a "truly wonderful" proof, only there wasn't enough room in the margin of the book he was writing on to put it all down.

Shaffery was no mathematician. But that morning, waking up to the revolution in his stomach and the thunder in his head, he had seen that that was actually a strength. One, all the mathematicians of three or four centuries had broken their heads against the problem; so obviously it couldn't be solved by any known mathematics anyway. Two, Einstein was weak in mathematics too and had disdained to worry about it, preferring to invent his own.

So he spent the morning, between hurried gallops across the parking lot to the staff toilet, filling paper with mathematical signs and operators of his own invention. It did not seem to be working out, to be sure. For a while he thought of an alternative scheme, to wit, inventing a "truly wonderful" solution of his own and claiming he couldn't find room to write it down in the margin of, say, the latest issue of *Mathematical Abstracts;* but residual sanity persuaded him that perhaps no one would ever find it, or that if it was found it might well be laughed off, and anyway that it would be purely posthumous celebrity and he wanted to taste it while he was alive. So he broke for lunch, came back feeling dizzy and ill and worried about the meeting that was going on, and decided to take a nap before resuming his labors.

When Cyril came looking for him to him the Directors desired his presence, it was dark and Shaffery felt like hell.

Coomray Hill was no taller than a small office building, but it got the mirror away from most of the sea-level dampness. The observatory sat on top of the hill like a mound of pistachio ice cream, hemispheric green copper roof and circular walls of green-painted plaster. Inside, the pedestal of the telescope took up the center of the floor. The instrument itself was traversed as low as it would go any more, clearing enough space for the Directors and their gear. They were all there, looking at him with silent distaste as he came in.

The inner sphere of the dome was painted (by Cyril's talented half-sister) with a large map of Mars, showing Schiaparelli's famous canals in resolute detail; a view of the Bay of Naples from the Vomero, with Vesuvius gently steaming in the background; and an illuminated drawing of the constellation Scorpius, which happened to be the sign of the constellation under which the Chairman of the Board had been born. A row of card tables had been lined up and covered with a green cloth. There were six places set, each with ashtray, note pad, three sharpened pencils, ice, glass, and bottle of John Begg. Another row of tables against the wall held the antipasto, replenished by Cyril after the depredations of the night before, but now seriously depleted by the people for whom it was intended. Six cigars were going and a couple of others were smoldering in the trays. Shaffery tried not to breathe. Even with the door open and the observing aperture in the dome wide, the inside air was faintly blue. At one time Shaffery had mentioned diffidently what the deposit of cigar smoke did to the polished surface of the 22-inch mirror. That was at his first annual meeting. The Chairman hadn't said a word, just stared at him. Then he nodded to his right-hand man, a Mr. DiFirenzo, who had taken a packet of Kleenex out of his pocket and tossed it to Shaffery. "So wipe the goddamn thing off," he had said. "Then you could dump these ashtrays for us, okay?"

Shaffery did his best to smile at his Directors. Behind him he was conscious of the presence of their assistants, who were patrolling the outside of the observatory in loose elliptical orbits, perigeeing at the screen door to peer inside. They had studied Shaffery carefully as he came across the crunching shell of the parking lot, and under their scrutiny he had decided against detouring by way of the staff toilet, which he now regretted.

"Okay, Shaffery," said Mr. DiFirenzo, after glancing at the Chairman of the Board. "Now we come to you."

Shaffery clasped his hands behind him in his Einstein pose and said brightly, "Well, it has been a particularly productive year for the observatory. No doubt you've seen my reports on the Leonid meteorite count and—"

"Right," said Mr. DiFirenzo, "but what we been talking about here is the space shots. Mr. Nuccio has expressed his views that this is a kind of strategic location, like how they shoot the rockets from Cape Kennedy. They have to go right over us, and we want a piece of that."

Shaffery shifted his weight uneasily. "I discussed that in my report last year—"

"No, Shaffery. This year, Shaffery. Why can't we get some of that federal money, like for tracking, for instance?"

"But the position hasn't changed, Mr. DiFirenzo. We don't have the equipment, and besides NASA has its own—"

"No good, Shaffery. You know how much you got out of us for equipment last year? I got the figures right here. And now you tell us you don't have what we need to make a couple bucks?"

"Well, Mr. DiFirenzo, you see, the equipment we have is for purely scientific purposes. For this sort of work you need quite different instruments, and actually—"

"I don't want to hear." DiFirenzo glanced at the Chairman and then went on. "Next thing, what about that comet you said you were going to discover?"

Shaffery smiled forgivingly. "Really, I can't be held accountable for that. I didn't actually say we'd *find* one. I merely said that the continuing *search* for comets was part of our basic *program*. Of course, I've done my very best to—"

"Not good enough, Shaffery. Besides your boy here told Mr.

Nuccio that if you did find a comet you wouldn't name it the Mr. Carmine J. Nuccio Comet like Mr. Nuccio wanted."

Shaffery was going all hollow inside, but he said bravely, "It's not wholly up to me. There's an astronomical convention that the discoverer's name goes on—"

"We don't like that convention, Shaffery. Three, now we come to some really bad things, that I'm sorry to hear you've got yourself into, Shaffery. We hear you been talking over the private affairs of this institution and Mr. Nuccio with that dickhead Nesbit. Shut, Shaffery," the man said warningly as Shaffery started to open his mouth. "We know all about it. This Nesbit is getting himself into big trouble. He has said some very racist things about Mr. Nuccio on that sideshow of his on the TV, which is going to cost him quite a bundle when Mr. Nuccio's lawyers get through with him. That is very bad, Shaffery, and also, four, there is this thing."

He lifted up what had seemed like a crumpled napkin in front of his place. It turned out that it was covering what looked like a large transistor radio.

Shaffery identified it after a moment's thought; he had seen it before, in Larry Nesbit's possession. "It's a tape recorder," he said.

"Right on, Shaffery. Now the question is, who put it in here? I don't mean just left it here like you could leave your rubbers or something, Shaffery. I mean left it here with one of those trick switches, so it was going when a couple of our associates checked the place out and found it under the table."

Shaffery swallowed very hard, but even so his voice sounded unfamiliar to him when he was able to speak. "I—I *assure* you, Mr. DiFirenzo! I had nothing to do with it."

"No, Shaffery, I know you didn't, because you are not that smart. Mr. Nuccio was quite upset about this illegal bugging, and he has already made some phone calls and talked to some people, and we have a pretty good idea of who put it there, and he isn't going to have what he thinks he's going to have to play on his TV show. So here it is, Shaffery. Mr. Nuccio doesn't find your work satisfactory here, and he is letting you go. We got somebody else coming down to take over. We'd appreciate it if you could be out by tomorrow."

There are situations in which there is not much scope for dignity. A man in his middle fifties who has just lost the worst job he ever had has few opportunities for making the sort of terminal remark that one would like to furnish one's biographers.

Shaffery discovered that he was worse off than that; he was frankly sick. The turmoil in his belly grew. The little saliva pumps under his tongue were flooding his mouth faster than he could swallow, and he knew that if he didn't get back to the staff toilet very quickly he would have another embarrassment to add to what was already an overwhelming load. He turned and walked away. Then marched. Then ran. When he had emptied himself of everything in belly, bladder and gut he sat on the edge of the toilet seat and thought of the things he could have said: "Look, Nuccio, you don't know anything about science." "Nuccio, Schiaparelli was all wrong about the canals on Mars." It was too late to say them. It was too late to ask the questions that his wife would be sure to ask, about severance pay, pension, all the things that he had been putting off getting in writing. ("Don't worry about that stuff, Shaffery, Mr. Nuccio always takes care of his friends but he don't like to be aggravated.") He tried to make a plan for his future, and failed. He tried even to make a plan for his present. Surely he should at least call Larry Nesbit, to demand, to complain, and to warn ("Hist! The tape recorder has been discovered! All is lost! Flee!"), but he could not trust himself so far from the toilet. Not at that exact moment. And a moment later it was too late. Half an hour later, when one of the orbiting guards snapped the little lock and peered inside, the man who might have been Einstein was lying on the floor with his trousers around his knees, undignified, uncaring and dead.

Ah, Shaffery! How disappointed he would have been in his *Times* obit, two paragraphs buried under the overhang of a pop singer's final notice. But afterward . . .

The first victim was Larry Nesbit, airsick in his Learjet all the way back to New York, overcome during the taping of his TV show, and dying the next day. The next victims were the Board of Directors, every man. They started home, by plane and boat. Some of them made it, but all of them died: en route or in Las Vegas, Detroit, Chicago, Los Angeles, New York, and Long Branch, New Jersey. Some of the "assistants" died and some were spared. (Briefly.) The reason was not a mystery for very long. The source of the new plague was tracked down quickly enough to Mr. Nuccio's antipasto, and particularly to the preserved mushrooms that Shaffery had borrowed for his experiment.

The botulinus toxin was long recognized as the most deadly poison known to man. The mutated version that Shaffery and his dentist's X-rays had brought into being was not much more deadly, but it had another quality that was new and different. Old, established *Clostridium botulinum* is an organism with a feeble hold on life; expose it to light and air, and it dies. B. shafferia was more sturdy. It grew where it was. In anything. In Mr. Nuccio's antipasto, in a salad in a restaurant kitchen, in Mom's apple pie on a windowsill to cool, in the human digestive tract. There were nine deaths in the first five days, and then for a moment no more. The epidemiologists would not have bothered their heads about so short a casualty list if it had not been for the identities of some of the victims. But the bacteria was multiplying. The stain of vomit under the boardwalk at Long Branch dried; the bacteria turned into spores and were blown on the wind until they struck something damp and fertile. Whereupon they grew. The soiled Kleenex thrown from a Cadillac Fleetwood on the road leading from O'Hare to Evanston, the sneeze between flights at Miami, expectorations in a dozen places—all added to the score. From the urine and feces of the afflicted men, from their sweat, even from their bed linen and discarded clothing, enspored bacteria leaped into the air and were inhaled, eaten, drunk, absorbed into cuts, in every way ingested into the waiting bodies of hundreds, then thousands, ultimately countless millions of human beings.

By the second week Detroit and Los Angeles were declared disaster areas. By the fourth the plague had struck every city in America and had leaped the oceans. If it had any merciful quality at all, it was that it was quick: an upset stomach, a sweat, a few pangs, and then death. None were immune. Few survived. Out of a hundred, three might outlive the disease. But then famine, riot and lesser ills took their toll; and of the billions who lived on the Earth when Shaffery exposed his antipasto in the dentist's office, all but a few tens of millions died in the outbreak that the world will never forget of the disease called Shaffery's Syndrome.

Raylyn Moore's five stories for F&SF over the past couple of years have been of such consistent high quality that we could have comfortably picked any one of them to appear in this anthology. A particular favorite though was this masterly piece of mordant humor about What Happened at the Coltharp Free Children's Center. Progressive preschool education will never be the same.

A Different Drummer

RAYLYN MOORE

My name is Ernestine Coltharp. I am a teacher. Please don't make the mistake of reading into this announcement some hint of apology or self-effacement, for I am not just any teacher but the director of The Coltharp Free Children's Center, of which you may have heard. Not only has it been an enviable financial success—the "free" refers of course not to tuition but to theory— but it has also over the years been the subject of any number of theses and published articles as well as the object of professional visitations by experts from all over the world. All this despite our purposely remote location deep in the motherlode country.

In one important way it is to my advantage to make this statement as brief as possible. However, boredom is also a factor in my present drastic predicament, and when discussing the Free Center I am never bored. I am therefore torn, yet see myself leaning in favor of a certain prolixity. It seems I simply cannot resist including a few details, especially since I may never (it has occurred to me gradually, as the hours pass and the full seriousness of my plight becomes apparent) have another opportunity to express myself. Details such as the secret of my success, for instance.

(It might be argued here by the superficially inclined that "success" has become for me an ironic term in light of what has happened. In the long view, however, I am completely vindicated; my methods of bringing children to their full potential have obviously scored beyond even my own most fanciful projections, as I shall presently show.)

My secret of success, then, has two parts: devotion, and a strong sense of continuity and eclecticism. The question for me is never whether an idea is old or new, but whether or not it works.

The earliest memories I have of myself focus on a jagged, darkgray sheet of slate some three feet at its largest dimension, culled from the refuse bin of the elementary school where my father was janitor. I stood the slate on our back porch and seated my dolls in front of it, along with any younger or weaker children from the neighborhood whom I could impress into the role of pupils. Tirelessly I chalked letters and figures on the board while enunciating rules and fragments of knowledge. "Ernestine is a natural-born teacher," my parents said proudly. I never doubted it.

Later, faced with the conventional choice between career and a love affair or marriage, I hesitated not an instant. In truth my choice was the more clear-cut for my having long since discovered in my character a strong abhorrence for the notion of any other sentient being penetrating my body and attempting to inhabit it with me. Even temporarily, even momentarily. The prospect of male intrusion was horrendous enough; the idea of being host to an alien parasite in the form of a fetus over a long gestation period was absolutely gruesome. Refusing all proposals and propositions indiscriminately, I clove to my studies and the contemplation of my goal: launching a school of my own as soon as I had completed my master's.

Nor did I waste time worrying over my psyche. Never exactly unsophisticated, I was as an education major extremely well read in the sciences leading to self-knowledge and was thus aware that my case was not entirely exceptional among the human race. Also, doing my first practice teaching, I discovered quickly enough that my slight aberration did not extend to a distaste for little boys. On the contrary, I frankly preferred them to little girls.

So much for devotion (that is, until a later incident, with which I shall deal in due course). The eclecticism can be far more simply explained. With the single idea in mind that I wanted to take children into my sole care at two years or younger and turn them out at five absolutely free in mind and body, I carefully selected and adapted to my own purposes the very best insights of Anna Freud, Piaget, Dewey, the indomitable *dottoressa*, the Bank Streeters, A. S. Neill, and the rest of them. To this distillation I gradually added my own original observations and conclusions (later collected under the title, *The Coltharp Method Explained*, Middenstead University Press, 1951), which I shall not attempt to go into here except to say that gestalt therapy and transactional analysis have borrowed much from me, and not given me any credit either.

As for my Free Center, like many another worthwhile ambition it was almost stillborn for lack of early support. On emerging from my own schooling, I discovered that sound theories and academic clouds of glory were not enough. In order to found an institution, I had to have instant money in impossibly large amounts for rental of a plant, insurance, equipment, supplies, and so on.

Banks and loan companies were not noticeably eager to help even though I tried strenuously to put across to them the importance of my plans to the educational world. Personally I had neither money nor prospects. I had been a scholarship student all through college. My parents were by now both dead, and in any case had been very poor.

That left Professor Havelock von Glubok, my graduate school adviser, who according to campus rumor had accumulated a

competent fortune in the old country by black-market manipula-
tion during the war. As an adviser he had been extremely helpful, always sticking strictly to business during the earlier parts of
our many interviews in his stuffy office. The last quarter hour,
however, the professor unfailingly reserved for trying to get his
hand under my skirt. He had never left off trying, and I had
never left off trying to prevent him. At least not until that day I
went to him with my financial troubles.

Rheumy eyes above his Franklin spectacles aglint with lust, he
said glottally, "Bud, my child, do not speeg of *bor*rowinguh. I
vill *giff* you all the money you vand if only—"

Once in Professor von Glubok's bed, I perceived that the
impending experience would be even more ghastly than anything
I had undergone in fancy. I gritted my teeth and squeezed my
eyes shut and at the crunch could not avoid shrieking out, "Don't,
don't, Doctor von Glubok!"

"Gall me 'daddy'," he panted, his oily beard thrust painfully
against my cringing chest. "Zay, 'Don't, don't, *Dad*dy!'"

Instantly I jerked out of his repulsive clutch and sat up in the
welter of sweaty bed linen. "You are profoundly inhibited by an
incest fixation, Doctor," I warned gravely. "You should get help."

In answer he belted me across the mouth.

But enough. I include mention of this depressing scene only
to show the full extent of my dedication to my cause.

With von Glubok's backing I bought twenty secluded moun-
tainous acres, had the property securely enclosed in ten-foot un-
climbable steel-mesh fences to keep meddling civilization at a
distance, and built a magnificent schoolhouse designed down to
the last detail by myself. The next year I added a dormitory with
all furnishings, like those in the school, made to the scale of
young children, and separate living quarters with locks on the
doors for the director. (Though these separate quarters slightly
compromised my ideal of complete freedom of access between
director and students at all times. I found I needed privacy after
all, especially during the weekend visits of the professor.)

I was paying a high price to start at the top, but my maturity
and natural sense of measure saved me from emotional break-
down. And while I never totally adjusted to my former adviser's

loathsome attentions, neither did the relationship affect my essential normality. I still preferred little boys to little girls.

Admittedly it may have been only the fact of Kyle's being a little boy which predisposed me to like him on sight that fateful morning this past summer when I hurried down to the main gate in response to the buzzer and found him standing there alone, his parents, or whoever had delivered him, having already departed.

This fact in itself did not surprise me. The matter of a child's having been "dumped" on me like a foundling, that is. The theory of the Free Center, as I may already have implied, rests on the premise that the entire upbringing of the applicant be left entirely to me. The students remain on the premises for three hundred and sixty-five days a year, holidays not excepted. (Every day is a holiday to the children at the Center.) You would be surprised (or maybe if you are a harassed parent yourself you would not) how many concerned and enlightened people are more than willing to turn over their young to me for a matter of three or four formative years.

But to explain specifically about Kyle, some time ago the Center found itself in a financial position to offer a handful of "scholarships" for use by children from economically depressed situations. Kyle was a scholarship child sent to me from the Love and Peace Society, a commune far back in the wilderness of eastern Oregon, technically eligible because the society has no money; its economy requires none.

My heart had leaped when I discovered Kyle's application in the mail. For like the morticians who see the optimum moment for injecting embalming fluid as "just before actual death sets in," we experimental teachers of the very young would, if we could, claim suzerainty at the instant of conception. (Ah, or even the instant before?) The first few years of life spent in the pure, noncompetitive atmosphere of a group of the stature of the Love and Peace Society seemed to me the next best thing. Not that any outsider really knows what goes on in those communities so long and so cleanly detached from the rest of the world. We can assume, however, from available data however slight, that they enjoy standards exceedingly like my own. Personal freedom within an absolute, naturally evolved democracy.

All this background exposition, however, conveys nothing whatever of Kyle's and my first confrontation on the dusty road. We looked each other over in silence, except for a quiet twittering of insects in the roadside weeds and a soft soughing from the nearby pine tops. My impressions were of a slender yet sturdy body, blond hair, features already partially formed at four years (I had his age from the application) into firm brow, straight nose, chin advancing to a slight underbite. Thin brown legs emerged gracefully from clumsily fashioned lederhosen—all clothing in those communes is handmade, much of it from deerskin or rough homespun—and the large eyes were a level crayon-blue.

Yet even words of description fail in the face of the blinding instant when our glances locked and I knew sudden love, challenge, joyful suspense. For another part of my brain was already ticking off a valid professional, if intuitive, judgment. This Kyle was a *leader*. The happy fact stood out as clearly as if he'd worn a sign. *Was* there also, in that same split-stroke of time, some augury, some fleet vibration too subtle to be apprehended and even by my own sharply attuned and experienced senses?

But again enough. I must yet learn to ration my words, discipline myself to temper the intense happiness of the recent past to the somberness of the present.

In that first meeting, when we finally began to exchange remarks, Kyle seemed instantly responsive. Hands trembling like those of a virgin in the presence of the man she knows will deflower her (and you will excuse the analogy on grounds of what eventually happened), I relocked the heavy gate and on the way up the hill to the compound of buildings elicited easily from Kyle the information that his application had shown no surname because he had none, that within the Love and Peace Society all adults were considered parents to all children. Kyle even indicated, without the slightest hesitation or show of anxiety, that he had never known exactly who his biological father and mother were, a very advanced concept in itself for a four-year-old.

Group interaction of all sorts excites me; after all, it is a large part of my lifework. Hearing these things about the commune, combined with being so near to Kyle, induced a kind of ecstasy. By the time we had reached the dormitory, where I assigned a space to our new arrival, I had a number of times already caressed him. He seemed neither to welcome nor reject these advances. I, in turn, saw in his seeming indifference evidence of superb adjustment; those children who apparently need no attention from adults are not necessarily unaffectionate themselves, but are simply so accustomed to signs of approval that they take them as their due. My assumption on this score seemed further confirmed when within the first twenty-four hours Kyle had completely come to terms with his new environment. He settled in without a ripple, included and accepted by the group with none of the usual painful preliminaries.

At the time—it was August—the children were harvesting the muscats. But again I see a digression is unavoidable, for clarity's sake and despite the alarming build-up of wordage I may soon regret.

You will notice that nowhere in this account have I mentioned assistants or other adult teachers at the Free Center. This is because there are none. One of the most radically innovative tenets of the Coltharp Method is a rejection of the canard that it is of some advantage to have preschool-aged children supervised by one adult per ten or twelve pupils. Nonsense, I say. Such heavy overseeing is only a weak admission of incompetence on the part of a teacher. Our quota at the Center is sixty children and we are always filled, with a long waiting list. I alone serve as their adult guide, making use of common sense.

Really contented children help one another, and share willingly in work they themselves see as necessary. It requires a four-year-old intelligence to wash dishes, a three-year-old intelligence to sweep a floor. The only reason children don't usually take the initiative in such chores is that they are not properly motivated in a cooperative setting.

Of course everything must be kept very basic. No frills like plush carpets or decorative breakables. Wholesome, uncomplicated meals of raw vegetables and fruits are prepared by the children themselves. We even raise our own produce, with the students planting seeds and hoeing out weeds, and later reaping legumes, greens, roots, and sprouts in abundance. We keep several goats and a few laying hens, but raise no meat. The more reliable nutritionists have long assured us children require no animal protein except that in milk and eggs, that one of the worst disasters of this century has been the fraud of the high-protein diet. Too much meat causes, rather than prevents, disease.

However, suffice it here to say we are vegetarians, and almost self-sufficient on our twenty acres. The only food products we require to be shipped to the Free Center are graham crackers and bottled juice, and since I order these only once in eighteen or so months, filling the storeroom each time, some of the children even believe there is a work detail somewhere baking the crackers. (This question has come up a few times at our group-encounter sessions, which are meetings of the full enrollment for the purpose of answering bull session-type questions, and working out problems before they can arise.)

But back now to Kyle and the muscats. I noticed immediately that our new student, predictably, had already, on his first full day in residence and while working with children as much as a year older than himself, taken over as foreman of one of the picking details. Moreover, he had instituted a more efficient system of putting the grapes directly from the vines into the crates as the children came to the ends of the rows, thus saving both time and the extra handling involved when the fruit had to be removed from the picking baskets.

I made no comment of course. To interfere in any interaction within the group is unthinkable unless real strife is apparent. But neither could I take my eyes from Kyle. My musings, I discovered, had an even more violent quality than on the previous day. Did Kyle love me? Had he ever loved any woman before? One of his surrogate mothers in the commune, perhaps? Inevitably, I had been the object on numerous other occasions of the perfect, pure love of little boys, a love uncomplicated by ugly lust, unsullied by the prospect of venery. Coming from Kyle, if I were so fortunate, I could visualize such a love as the apogee of my career, my *raison d'être*. Would I even be able to let him go from the Center once he reached the age of five?

Dazzled by these ruminations, I had involuntarily wandered very near the arbor where Kyle was at work. Which is how I happened to overhear the word he uttered after idly putting a handful of overripe grapes into his mouth and then suddenly, after making a wry face, spitting them out.

In spite of myself, I experienced real shock at his language. If he had used some other word, *any* other, I would have kept silence, for freedom of expression among my pupils is taken for granted. On the other hand, this particular word had never been spoken at the Free Center. Most of the children didn't even know its meaning. I could not allow even my beloved Kyle to undermine our standards.

"Kyle?" I said, "what did I just hear you say? Would you repeat it please?" Yes, it was in the nature of a reprimand, and in front of his peer group. But I was acting on behalf of the greater good.

He answered agreeably enough. "Certainly, Ernestine. I said, 'These grapes are bad'."

"Spoiled," I corrected gently. "You meant, 'These grapes are spoiled.' Or overripe, or rotten, if you like. Wherever did you hear that word 'bad'?"

The blue eyes and full mouth smiled easily, almost mockingly. "Maybe I read it in a book."

"Oh?" I said. "Do you read then?"

"Why would I say I did if it weren't so?" he replied logically.

Had I not been already hopelessly enamored, I would have succumbed at that moment. His maturity was enchanting. He spoke exactly like an adult, yet there he stood in that delicious, diminutive, half-formed body of a little boy.

Now, since I suppose I must say this somewhere, perhaps here is as relevant (or irrelevant) a place as any. As can be seen, I was captivated from the start. My thralldom lasted over a period of two full months. This is the only explanation I can offer as to why the question which should have presented itself immediately simply never occurred to me at all: how was it that the Love and Peace Society, in its fifteen or so years of existence, was only now, for the first time, sending out one of its children for instruction at preschool level?

How indeed.

The temptation at this juncture too, after so much verbiage, seems to be to rush headlong, answering this question and all others, while at the same time sliding over my own many failures of intuition. Nevertheless, a full beginning demands a full ending. So I am obliged instead to proceed step by disheartening step with what happened at the Free Center from the day of the muscats onward, providing this narrative with a filling-in and a rounding-out, even at my own great expense.

But make no mistake; for me the two months were very heaven. (I note here that I seem inclined now and then to Wordsworthian turns of phrase, while Swinburnian would be more apropos, as you will see. Still, who can quibble with the expressions of the unconscious?) For one thing, my daydreams were very soon the most *exalté* I'd ever known, consisting of giddy projections into a future in which Kyle would pass the Harvard entrance exams directly from Coltharp, thus achieving a coup unique in the annals of education. Accompanying him east would be—who else? A new kind of crowning for my life-work which seemed increasingly less like a daydream than a plum within easy reach. We would take an apartment together just off campus; I would exclude all newsmen, charlatans, and curiosity-seekers, giving Kyle hours of uninterrupted study time. Our leisure time, however, would be our own.

Meanwhile, what was going on right under my nose at the Free Center was enough in itself to maintain my ecstatic state. For one of my other dreams was already in fruition. In explanation to those who have not read my book, some years ago a D. Ed. dissertation concerned a project conducted at XYZ School in which two score children, left entirely to their own devices without even a hint of authoritarian regulation from above, drifted naturally into a system of government in which every child had an equal voice in decisions, work was equally divided, and the benignant majority saw to it that the minority were not discriminated against. I myself during my early years of work with children had refined this phenomenon to the nth power, and a vastly improved version of the experiment eventually became part of the Coltharp Method.

On no occasion, however, had I seen the emerging child-society so beautifully operating as it did at the Center after Kyle arrived.

It is my policy, when such projects are running well, not to disturb the mixture, so to speak, by stirring the pot. We all know what happens to the primitive society as soon as the anthropologist appears in its midst, notebook and pen in hand.

My custom is therefore to withdraw to my own apartment for an indeterminate period when one of these governments by the children is being set up or is undergoing changes in leadership. However, I always make it clear I am available for consultation if needed. Oddly, however, during this time no child called on me for anything at all.

Here again one may discern the true depth of my temporary madness. For even in the best run child-development centers hardly half an hour can pass without at least one small participant bursting into tears, gagging on a mouthful of finger paint, stuffing play dough up his nose, or having a bathroom accident. Interpersonal conflicts calling for adult intervention also are common. "Come quick. Danny is urinating all over Sally again," is a rallying cry which will be recognized instantly by preschool teachers everywhere.

However, watching from behind a partially drawn shade over my office window, taking my notes on a pad concealed in my lap, I observed the group's behavior carefully on the day follow-ing the grape harvest and detected no discord. Most of the sixty children first encircled Kyle, sitting down docilely and making Indian legs while he spoke to them at length. Afterward, the large group divided into work details and trudged off in all directions to take care of the routine chores. It was a creditable beginning, I thought. True, I had not seen any voting going on. Kyle had seemed to appoint the work details arbitrarily, though I may have been wrong, I told myself, since I could not hear their actual words.

On the following days the children seemed so self-contained that I even left off watching and began to catch up on the paper work in my office. Once I heard rhythmic sounds and went to the window to discover a marching band, of all things, had been organized. It seemed at once too sophisticated and too con-ventional. I had never encouraged military play of any kind. Still, it was hardly such a departure that I felt I should interpose what might conceivably be my own prejudices.

I shall forego the opportunity for more detail here. Anyone further interested in the day-to-day account of this period at the Free Center may eventually be able to read my notes which, scanty as they were on account of my preoccupation, still exist. Probably. At least I have no evidence they have been destroyed.

Having spoken of my great pleasure in the (at least outward) events of the two months, I must add this was not alone because of my relief at having the direction of the Center virtually lifted from my shoulders. No, it was the night visits from Kyle which caused my cup to overflow. Each evening, after the other students had retired—on stricter curfew under Kyle's leadership than any the group had ever set for themselves previously—he would present himself at my apartment.

There was never any formal discussion about these visits. He appeared as a matter of course, beginning the second night of his residency, and naturally I never discouraged him. I would serve mint tea as we sat together in the library reading. Afterward we would have long discussions. Among other things, these talks made me realize how much I had missed adult company—have I said anywhere that Professor von Glubok, who had become essentially my last link with the grown-up world, though a weak enough one, had died a year or so before this?—for Kyle did prove able to offer mature companionship in every important way, just as I had anticipated.

Reading extremely rapidly, he devoured great piles of my books, showing special interest in a collection, kept as a curiosity, of the work of the most antediluvian educators and theorists, both living and dead. "Who is William H. McGuffey?" he might ask. Or, "What about Dr. Max Rafferty?" Then a long, felicitous conversation would ensue. We talked into the night of Mr. Shaw and Bowes School, of flogging at Eton, the McMillan sisters, private governesses and tutors, the blab schools of pioneer times, rote learning, and corporal punishment.

Kyle was particularly enthusiastic over all the various imaginative forms the latter has taken through the history of education, from "sitting on air" in the classrooms of yesteryear, to the force-feeding of vomitus, said to have been in use as a punishment in a private school in California as recently as this decade. In lovingly recounting for Kyle's edification all the outrages teachers have perpetrated on defenseless children since the beginning of records on such things, I spoke so feelingly and articulately on one occasion that I was immensely sorry not to have thought at the time of turning on my tape recorder, as the material would have done excellently for delivery at an NEA convention sometime.

On several other evenings I also tried, though perhaps not wholeheartedly enough, to divert my visitor's attention to something lighter and more in keeping with his real status as a child. I recall recommending, among other things, Lewis Carroll, who, as you may imagine, occupies a warm spot in my own affections, the good reverend's kinkiness for little girls being a condition I am singularly well equipped to understand. Kyle was not the least interested in Alice's tribulations, however.

Sometimes our sessions lasted until midnight, but never beyond. Though I would not under any circumstances have asked Kyle to leave, he was himself very sensible about getting enough sleep against the demands of the coming day. He did not discuss any of the problems he must surely have been meeting during his running of the children's government, and true to my own ideals I did not venture any suggestion, or even bring up the matter.

After Kyle had left for the night, I usually made the rounds of the compound, seeing what maintenance needed doing, what supplies needed restocking. There was surprisingly little action for me to take, even in these small affairs, so efficient were Kyle's work details. It was on one of these night trips, however, that I discovered the thing that had happened in the dollroom.

Here another word of necessary explanation, though this story is by now growing so unwieldy that the very contemplation of the stacked sheets is a physical agony. I do not exaggerate when I say the manuscript already appears to be over a foot thick!

The dollroom, a popular place for unstructured play, is supplied with a number of extremely life-like dolls arranged in sets of families. In addition to real hair and the skin-like plastic with which they are covered, they have delightfully genuine-looking genitalia. The children endlessly dress and undress these dolls and move them in and out of the split-level, suburban-type dollhouses with two cars and a camper in each garage and a TV aerial on every roof. The nearest things we have to toy weapons at the Free Center are also in this room, a few wooden mallets to be used by the children, if they feel so disposed, on the

parent and sibling dolls, which are of necessity practically in-
destructible.

Imagine my surprise, then, on the evening I walked into the
dollroom and found one of the mommie dolls had been destroyed by a knife, or knife-like implement. That is, both
breasts had been amputated, and the pudenda mutilated by hacking. A quick search of the room disclosed the telltale instrument
jammed into a dollhouse chimney. It was an ordinary table
knife from the dining hall, but I could tell from the signs of
scarification along its edge that the knife had been honed, and
fairly expertly. That presupposed slyness and substantial pre-
meditation on the part of the child involved. Such an incident
had never occurred before at the Free Center.

At first I had misgivings, but quickly enough told myself how
foolish and unprofessional that attitude was. Just because up to
now no child had shown sufficient inventiveness to plan and
perform such an act did not mean the act was in itself inappropriate, I reasoned. After all, that was the function of the
dolls, to serve as aids in working out hostilities. Some child—and
I would never know who, nor would I inquire—had successfully
enacted a psychodrama in the dollroom and was no doubt at this
very minute sleeping the more restfully for the catharsis he or
she had experienced. I decided to think no more about it.

It was the following night that Kyle arrived at my door for his
visit looking extremely tired. I said nothing but thought privately, with considerable concern, that he might be falling ill,
even though children's ailments are one thing we are spared at
the Center because of our organically grown, vegetable diet, as I
have already explained.

My visitor offered to pour out our tea, which I had ready,
and I was charmed anew at this show of graciousness, since he
had taken no initiative about the tea before this.

A brief silence passed, during which Kyle finished with the
tea and took down the volume of Nietzsche he had been affect-
ing to read for the past few evenings. At least I was fairly certain
this latest reading performance was affectation. No one was
more impressed with Kyle's vastly accelerated learning ability
than I, but I felt somehow his sudden interest in archaic philosophy was a posture, perhaps a lover's ploy to impress me or,

knowing Kyle, to tease. (Alas, I still thought in these terms.) So I decided on the instant to chide him, if only to see what would develop.

I took a bracing draught of tea and said, "Oh, Kyle, surely you're not really going to go on with that impossible stuff again tonight?"

He looked at me thoughtfully above the book. "Oh? And what should I read, Ernestine?" Carelessly he closed the Nietzsche and tossed it with a plop onto the floor. He stood with grimy shoes on my sofa to flip down one of the old readers which had so occupied him some weeks earlier. A valuable second-edition Ray's Arithmetic was loosened from the row and crashed to the floor also, taking Kyle's untouched cup of tea with it. I winced but again held my tongue.

Kyle ignored the accident and opened the reader at random. "Is this so much better then? 'The oldest was a bad boy, always in trouble himself and trying to get others into trouble'." He leafed over a page and read, " 'George had a whipping for his folly, as he ought to have had'."

I presumed this was my guest's way of making an overture to one of our dialogues on the evolution of education methods, but no sooner had I begun my careful response than, to my immense joy, I discovered he had leaned his head back against the sofa and immediately fallen asleep.

Though I had prayed for this to happen on Kyle's prior visits, he had never before allowed himself to drowse in my presence. I waited for the slumber to deepen, as it does with young children very quickly, usually in no more than ten minutes. Trembling with anticipation, I laid hasty plans. I would lift him into my bed in the next room, loosen and remove his clothing, and then get in beside him. It would be easily the most thrilling night of my life, a new pinnacle in nonverbal encounter. I had certainly through the years lain down at various times in the cots of little boys in the dormitory, rocked them to sleep, soothed away anxiety, and so on. But this was something else again. I had never had a little boy in my own bed before, nor had I ever felt about any little boy as intensely as I felt about Kyle.

Lovingly I moved him. Tentatively at first. Then I supported his full weight, which is not inconsiderable; he is solid and well muscled. I can only plead that I was out of my mind from the moment I touched his flesh. Perhaps if I hadn't so foolishly left the lamp burning on the dresser? But then an important part of my hoped-for experience was to be the visual element. I wanted to see as well as touch.

Unfortunately he woke prematurely, actually after only about fifteen minutes in bed. He didn't seem surprised to be where he was, only faintly amused. "Well, Ernestine, what now?"

"Do you think, dear," I said, trying to keep my voice from quavering, "that you might be able to bring yourself to call me 'mommie'?"

"What?"

"Only if you *want* to, that is," I choked out. "It would mean a lot to me."

But his attention was now distracted. "Hey, what are *those*, Ernestine?"

Moments before I had impulsively ripped off my dressing gown and was in a state of semi-nakedness. Nearly hysterical with delight at his interest, I was about to explain the function of my breasts when I noted that the crayon-blue gaze was overshooting my body to fasten instead on the far wall of the bedroom. Hanging on that wall was a large assortment of whips, the property of my one-time adviser and late business partner, whose personality disorder had gone far deeper than I suspected when I made my too-hasty analysis during our first roll in the bushes.

There were blacksnakes, cat-o-nine-tails, coach whips, riding crops, flexible-steel lashes, even electric cattle prods and a few branding irons. Having no interest in these implements myself after the passing of my benefactor, I had left them where they were, procrastinating about the day I would get around to packing them away—there had seemed to be no rush, since no one else had visited my bedroom before except von Glubok himself—until the whips had for me taken on the invisibility of the purloined letter.

Now, however, I was terribly chagrined. "Oh, those," I said, striving for a bantering tone but not fooling Kyle, I'm afraid. "Just some souvenirs that once belonged to an old acquaintance of mine."

Slowly Kyle produced his now-familiar smile of worldly comprehension. It had an effect of dissolving even the shattered remnants of my recent joy.

The denouement you must by now have guessed, even though I myself was still unable to predict it at this time. The next morning—or was it two mornings later?—I woke late to the ringing of the telephone at my bedside. It rang once only. Wrong number, I thought sleepily, but I picked it up anyway, fighting off a lethargy which suggested the aftereffects of a strong dose of soporific, though I had taken no pills before retiring. Curiously, the extension in my office had evidently already been picked up and a conversation was going on. Someone speaking in a long-distance voice inquired for me, and the voice next door in my office assured the caller, "Ernestine Coltharp? Yes, this is she."

And it was. The voice was my own, sounding exactly as I do, or as only someone could sound who had over a long period carefully studied and memorized my speech patterns and tonal range. The conversation went on for some minutes, the caller inquiring if an appointment could be made for a group of student teachers to tour the Center, and my voice saying no, it would not be possible, that I was conducting an intricate, long-term experiment in interpersonal relations among very young children and it would preclude all visitations for a period of at least ten months.

I was tempted at several points to interrupt this insane exchange and expose the hoax. Yet my curiosity over what would be said next—more, my admiration for such a work of art as that impersonation—overrode completely my sense of outrage. For I knew who the impersonator must be. Having taken over the children, Kyle must have found it a natural step to enter my office and take it over as well.

As the conversation ended and we all hung up, my eye fell on the far wall of the bedroom where the whips had hung. They were gone.

For lack of space—oh, for a journalist's skill at cutting a whole lifetime down to one narrow paragraph of obituary—I pass over the shock of actually seeing Kyle at my desk, jaw more articulated than ever, blue eyes chill and glittering now, the eyes of a Franco, a Castro, a Che.

The elite corps (I can think of no more accurate term), armed with the whips and honed table silver, arrested me forthwith as a political enemy.

My trial was commendably swift. Kyle was judge and jury. I have been confined ever since in the only other place in the compound with a lock on the door, and that put on by the contractor by mistake: the storeroom. And of course this lock is on the outside.

I shall not starve, nor die of thirst. At least not soon. Before my interest flagged I counted five hundred crates of graham crackers and three hundred cartons of bottled juice.

The court (Kyle) decreed that I was to be taken to the potty three times a day by a whip-and-knife guard and to the shower three times a week. Needless to say, the decree has not been carried out; children are ever forgetful about such matters. However, there happens to be a janitor's closet in the storeroom with running water and a floor-level sink in which to wring out mops. I keep clean as best I can using this facility.

I cannot help worrying from time to time about the effect of the new regime on the children as well as on myself. For I know now how the weepers are controlled, and the spillers at table, and the paint eaters, nose stuffers, and troublemakers of all kinds. Flogging is no doubt one of the milder punishments. I could say, truthfully, that the children are themselves to blame for accepting Kyle so readily, but such criticism applies a thousandfold to myself.

Perhaps I have failed to say that at the encounter sessions where problems are discussed I have often encouraged the children to compose, orally, their life-stories, telling everything they can remember about themselves, using as much free association as they like. And I suppose this custom helped inspire my own sentence, which is a relatively light one. Unless it is changed. (Children are in the end capricious. Who can trust them? I do not for one moment forget what happened to the mommie doll.)

I would have preferred, even welcomed, a sentence calling for flagellation by our Leader. He must apprehend that I yearn even now for some contact with him, however punitive, and purposely stays away. So do they all. I have been alone in this musty, windowless storeroom for seventy-two hours now, which already seem like seventy-two years.

Kyle can no doubt keep stalling people off by telephone indefinitely. How many months before somebody's parents decide finally to storm the barricades and come looking for their little darling? The Love and Peace Society, which, as I think now, expelled Kyle as an incorrigible, a threat to its way of life, can scarcely be expected to come looking for *him*.

But my sentence: I am to write my life-story, in perfect penmanship, using a supply of black crayons and heavy art paper, five thousand times.

At least it is my good fortune never in all these years to have lost my taste for graham crackers.

My name is Ernestine Coltharp. I am a teacher. Please don't make the mistake of reading into this announcement some hint of apology or self-effacement, for I am not just any teacher but . . .

*Many of Harlan Ellison's stories have been called daring or
ambitious, but this one, we feel, goes beyond those two well-worn
adjectives. The author has called it, in some ways, the bottom line
personal statement of all his work. It concerns the depth of love we
should have for ourselves as a species, and yet many will find the
premise outrageous, in that it attempts a transposition of man's
most hallowed beliefs. We think that you'll find it a striking
performance.*

The Deathbird

HARLAN ELLISON

I

This is a test. Take notes. This will count as ¾ of your final
grade. Hints: remember, in chess, kings cancel each other out
and cannot occupy adjacent squares, are therefore all-powerful
and totally powerless, cannot affect one another, produce stalemate. Hinduism is a polytheistic religion; the sect of Atman
worships the divine spark of life within Man; in effect saying,
"Thou art God." Provisos of equal time are not served by one
viewpoint having media access to two hundred million people in
prime time while opposing viewpoints are provided with a soap-
box on the corner. Not everyone tells the truth. Operational
note: these sections may be taken out of numerical sequence:

rearrange to suit yourself for optimum clarity. Turn over your
test papers and begin.

2

Uncounted layers of rock pressed down on the magma pool.
White-hot with the bubbling ferocity of the molten nickel-iron
core, the pool spat and shuddered, yet did not pit or char or
smoke or damage in the slightest the smooth and reflective surfaces of the strange crypt.

Nathan Stack lay in the crypt—silent, sleeping.

A shadow passed through rock. Through shale, through coal,
through marble, through mica schist, through quartzite; through
miles-thick deposits of phosphates, through diatomaceous earth,
through feldspars, through diorite; through faults and folds,
through anticlines and monoclines, through dips and synclines;
through hellfire; and came to the ceiling of the great cavern and
passed through; and saw the magma pool and dropped down; and
came to the crypt. The shadow.

A triangular face with a single eye peered into the crypt, saw
Stack, and lay four-fingered hands on the crypt's cool surface.
Nathan Stack woke at the touch, and the crypt became transparent; he woke though the touch had not been upon his body.
His soul felt the shadowy pressure and he opened his eyes to see
the leaping brilliance of the world-core around him, to see the
shadow with its single eye staring in at him.

The serpentine shadow enfolded the crypt; its darkness flowed
upward again, through the Earth's mantle, toward the crust,
toward the surface of the cinder, the broken toy that was the
Earth.

When they reached the surface, the shadow bore the crypt to
a place where the poison winds did not reach, and caused it to
open.

Nathan Stack tried to move, and moved only with difficulty.
Memories rushed through his head of other lives, many other
lives, as many other men; then the memories slowed and melted
into a background tone that could be ignored.

The shadow thing reached down a hand and touched Stack's

naked flesh. Gently, but firmly, the thing helped him to stand, and gave him garments, and a neck-pouch that contained a short knife and a warming-stone and other things. He offered his hand, and Stack took it, and after two hundred and fifty thousand years sleeping in the crypt, Nathan Stack stepped out on the face of the sick planet Earth.

Then the thing bent low against the poison winds and began walking away. Nathan Stack, having no other choice, bent forward and followed the shadow creature.

3

A messenger had been sent for Dira and he had come as quickly as the meditations would permit. When he reached the Summit, he found the fathers waiting, and they took him gently into their cove, where they immersed themselves and began to speak.

"We've lost the arbitration," the coil-father said. "It will be necessary for us to go and leave it to him."

Dira could not believe it. "But didn't they listen to our arguments, to our logic?"

The fang-father shook his head sadly and touched Dira's shoulder. "There were . . . accommodations to be made. It was their time. So we must leave."

The coil-father said, "We've decided you will remain. One was permitted, in caretakership. Will you accept our commission?"

It was a very great honor, but Dira began to feel the loneliness even as they told him they would leave. Yet he accepted. Wondering why they had selected *him*, of all their people. There were reasons, there were always reasons, but he could not ask. And so he accepted the honor, with all its attendant sadness, and remained behind when they left.

The limits of his caretakership were harsh, for they insured he could not defend himself against whatever slurs or legends would be spread, nor could he take action unless it became clear the trust was being breached by the other—who now held possession. And he had no threat save the Deathbird. A final threat that could be used only when final measures were needed: and therefore too late.

But he was patient. The most patient of all his people.

Thousands of years later, when he saw how it was destined to go, when there was no doubt left how it would end, he understood *that* was the reason he had been chosen to stay behind.

But it did not help the loneliness.

Nor could it save the Earth. Only Stack could do that.

4

1 Now the serpent was more subtil than any beast of the field which the LORD God had made. And he said unto the woman, Yea hath God said, Ye shall not eat of every tree of the garden?

2 And the woman said unto the serpent, We may eat of the fruit of the trees of the garden:

3 But of the fruit of the tree which is in the midst of the garden, God hath said, Ye shall not eat of it, neither shall ye touch it, lest ye die.

4 And the serpent said unto the woman, Ye shall not surely die:

5 (Omitted)

6 And when the woman saw that the tree was good for food, and that it was pleasant to the eyes, and a tree to be desired to make one wise, she took of the fruit thereof, and did eat, and gave also unto her husband with her; and he did eat.

7 (Omitted)

8 (Omitted)

9 And the LORD God called unto Adam, and said unto him, Where art thou?

10 (Omitted)

11 And he said, Who told thee that thou wast naked? Hast thou eaten of the tree, whereof I commanded thee that thou shouldest not eat?

12 And the man said, The woman whom thou gavest to be with me, she gave me of the tree, and I did eat.

13 And the LORD God said unto the woman, What is this

that *thou hast done? And the woman said, The serpent beguiled me, and I did eat.*

14 And the LORD God said unto the serpent, Because thou hast done this, thou art *cursed above all cattle, and above every beast of the field; upon thy belly shalt thou go, and dust shalt thou eat all the days of thy life:*

15 And I will put enmity between thee and the woman, and between thy seed and her seed; it shall bruise thy head, and thou shalt bruise his heel.

GENESIS, Chap. II

TOPICS FOR DISCUSSION
(Give 5 points per right answer.)

1. Melville's *Moby Dick* begins, "Call me Ishmael." We say it is told in the *first* person. In what person is Genesis told? From whose viewpoint?

2. Who is the "good guy" in this story? Who is the "bad guy?" Can you make a strong case for reversal of the roles?

3. Traditionally, the apple is considered to be the fruit the serpent offered to Eve. But apples are not endemic to the Near East. Select one of the following, more logical substitutes, and discuss how myths come into being and are corrupted over long periods of time: olive, fig, date, pomegranate.

4. Why is the word LORD always in capitals and the name God always capitalized? Shouldn't the serpent's name be capitalized, as well? If no, why?

5. If God created everything (see *Genesis,* Chap. I), why did he create problems for himself by creating a serpent who would lead his creations astray? Why did God create a tree he did not want Adam and Eve to know about, and then go out of his way to warn them against it?

6. Compare and contrast Michelangelo's Sistine Chapel ceiling panel of the *Expulsion from Paradise* with Bosch's *Garden of Earthly Delights.*

7. Was Adam being a gentleman when he placed blame on Eve? Who was Quisling? Discuss "narking" as a character flaw.

8. God grew angry when he found out he had been defied. If God is omnipotent and omniscient, didn't he know? Why couldn't he find Adam and Eve when they hid?

9. If God had not wanted Adam and Eve to taste the fruit of the forbidden tree, why didn't he warn the serpent? Could God have prevented the serpent from tempting Adam and Eve? If yes, why didn't he? If no, discuss the possibility the serpent was as powerful as God.

10. Using examples from two different media journals, demonstrate the concept of "slanted news."

5

The poison winds howled and tore at the powder covering the land. Nothing lived there. The winds, green and deadly, dived out of the sky and raked the carcass of the Earth, seeking, seeking: anything moving, anything still living. But there was nothing. Powder. Talc. Pumice.

And the onyx spire of the mountain toward which Nathan Stack and the shadow thing had moved, all that first day. When night fell they dug a pit in the tundra and the shadow thing coated it with a substance thick as glue that had been in Stack's neck-pouch. Stack had slept the night fitfully, clutching the warming-stone to his chest and breathing through a filter tube from the pouch.

Once he had awakened, at the sound of great batlike creatures flying overhead; he had seen them swooping low, coming in flat trajectories across the wasteland toward his pit in the earth. But they seemed unaware that he—and the shadow thing—lay in the hole. They defecated thin, phosphorescent stringers that fell glowing through the night and were lost on the plains; then the creatures swooped upward and were whirled away on the winds. Stack resumed sleeping with difficulty.

In the morning, frosted with an icy light that gave everything a blue tinge, the shadow thing scrabbled its way out of the choking powder and crawled along the ground, then lay flat, fingers clawing for purchase in the whiskaway surface. Behind it, from the powder, Stack bore toward the surface, reached up a hand and trembled for help.

The shadow creature slid across the ground, fighting the winds that had grown stronger in the night, back to the soft place that had been their pit, to the hand thrust up through the powder. It grasped the hand, and Stack's fingers tightened convulsively. Then the crawling shadow exerted pressure and pulled the man from the treacherous pumice.

Together they lay against the earth, fighting to see, fighting to draw breath without filling their lungs with suffocating death.

"Why is it like this . . . what *happened?*" Stack screamed against the wind. The shadow creature did not answer, but it looked at Stack for a long moment and then, with very careful movements, raised its hand, held it up before Stack's eyes and slowly, making claws of the fingers, closed the four fingers into a cage, into a fist, into a painfully tight ball that said more eloquently than words: *destruction.*

Then they began to crawl toward the mountain.

6

The onyx spire of the mountain rose out of hell and struggled toward the shredded sky. It was monstrous arrogance. Nothing should have tried that climb out of desolation. But the black mountain had tried, and succeeded.

It was like an old man. Seamed, ancient, dirt caked in striated lines, autumnal, lonely; black and desolate, piled strength upon strength. It would *not* give in to gravity and pressure and death. It struggled for the sky. Ferociously alone, it was the only feature that broke the desolate line of the horizon.

In another twenty-five million years the mountain might be worn as smooth and featureless as a tiny onyx offering to the deity night. But though the powder plains swirled and the poison winds drove the pumice against the flanks of the pinnacle, thus far their scouring had only served to soften the edges of the mountain's profile, as though divine intervention had protected the spire.

Lights moved near the summit.

7

Stack learned the nature of the phosphorescent stringers defecated onto the plain the night before by the batlike creatures. They were spores that became, in the wan light of day, strange bleeder plants.

All around them as they crawled through the dawn, the little live things sensed their warmth and began thrusting shoots up through the talc. As the fading red ember of the dying sun climbed painfully into the sky, the bleeding plants were already reaching maturity.

Stack cried out as one of the vine tentacles fastened around his ankle, holding him. A second looped itself around his neck.

Thin films of berry-black blood coated the vines, leaving rings on Stack's flesh. The rings burned terribly.

The shadow creature slid on its belly and pulled itself back to the man. Its triangular head came close to Stack's neck, and it bit into the vine. Thick black blood spurted as the vine parted, and the shadow creature rasped its razor-edged teeth back and forth till Stack was able to breathe again. With a violent movement Stack folded himself down and around, pulling the short knife from the neck-pouch. He sawed through the vine tightening inexorably around his ankle. It screamed as it was severed, in the same voice Stack had heard from the skies the night before. The severed vine writhed away, withdrawing into the talc.

Stack and the shadow thing crawled forward once again, low, flat, holding onto the dying earth: toward the mountain. High in the bloody sky, the Deathbird circled.

8

On their own world, they had lived in luminous, oily-walled caverns for millions of years, evolving and spreading their race through the universe. When they had had enough of empire-building, they turned inward, and much of their time was spent

in the intricate construction of songs of wisdom, and the design-
ing of fine worlds for many races.

There were other races that designed, however. And when
there was a conflict over jurisdiction, an arbitration was called,
adjudicated by a race whose *raison d'etre* was impartiality and
cleverness unraveling knotted threads of claim and counter-claim.
Their racial honor, in fact, depended on the flawless application
of these qualities. Through the centuries they had refined their
talents in more and more sophisticated arenas of arbitration until
the time came when they were the final authority. The litigants
were compelled to abide by the judgments, not merely because
the decisions were always wise and creatively fair, but because
the judges' race would, if its decisions were questioned as suspect, destroy itself. In the holiest place on their world they had
erected a religious machine. It could be activated to emit a tone
that would shatter their crystal carapaces. They were a race of
exquisite cricket-like creatures, no larger than the thumb of a
man. They were treasured throughout the civilized worlds, and
their loss would have been catastrophic. Their honor and their
value was never questioned. All races abided by their decisions.

So Dira's people gave over jurisdiction to that certain world,
and went away, leaving Dira with only the Deathbird, a special
caretakership the adjudicators had creatively woven into their
judgment.

There is recorded one last meeting between Dira and those
who had given him his commission. There were readings that
could not be ignored—had, in fact, been urgently brought to the
attention of the fathers of Dira's race by the adjudicators—and
the Great Coiled One came to Dira at the last possible moment
to tell him of the mad thing into whose hands this world had
been given, to tell Dira of what the mad thing could do.

The Great Coiled One—whose rings were loops of wisdom
acquired through centuries of gentleness and perception and
immersed meditations that had brought forth lovely designs for
many worlds—he who was the holiest of Dira's race, honored
Dira by coming to *him*, rather than commanding Dira to appear.

We have only one gift to leave them, he said. *Wisdom. This
mad one will come, and he will lie to them, and he will tell them:*

created he them. *And we will be gone, and there will be nothing between them and the mad one but you. Only you can give them the wisdom to defeat him in their own good time.* Then the Great Coiled One stroked the skin of Dira with ritual affection, and Dira was deeply moved and could not reply. Then he was left alone.

The mad one came, and interposed himself, and Dira gave them wisdom, and time passed. His name became other than Dira, it became Snake, and the new name was despised: but Dira could see the Great Coiled One had been correct in his readings. So Dira made his selection. A man, one of them, and gifted him with the spark.

All of this is recorded somewhere. It is history.

9

The man was not Jesus of Nazareth. He may have been Simon. Not Genghis Khan, but perhaps a foot soldier in his horde. Not Aristotle, but possibly one who sat and listened to Socrates in the agra. Neither the shambler who discovered the wheel nor the link who first ceased painting himself blue and applied the colors to the walls of the cave. But one near them, somewhere near at hand. The man was not Richard *Coeur de Lion*, Rembrandt, Richelieu, Rasputin, Robert Fulton or the Mahdi. Just a man. With the spark.

10

Once, Dira came to the man. Very early on. The spark was there, but the light needed to be converted to energy. So Dira came to the man, and did what had to be done before the mad one knew of it, and when he discovered that Dira, the Snake, had made contact, he quickly made explanations.

This legend has come down to us as the fable of *Faust*.

TRUE or FALSE?

II

Light converted to energy, thus:

In the fortieth year of his five hundredth incarnation, all-unknowing of the eons of which he had been part, the man found himself wandering in a terrible dry place under a thin, flat burning disc of sun. He was a Berber tribesman who had never considered shadows save to relish them when they provided shade. The shadow came to him, sweeping down across the sands like the *khamsin* of Egypt, the *simoom* of Asia Minor, the *harmattan*, all of which he had known in his various lives, none of which he remembered. The shadow came over him like the *sirocco*.

The shadow stole the breath from his lungs and the man's eyes rolled up in his head. He fell to the ground and the shadow took him down and down, through the sands, into the Earth.

Mother Earth.

She lived, this world of trees and rivers and rocks with deep stone thoughts. She breathed, had feelings, dreamed dreams, gave birth, laughed and grew contemplative for millennia. This great creature swimming in the sea of space.

What a wonder, thought the man, for he had never understood that the Earth was his mother, before this. He had never understood, before this, that the Earth had a life of its own, at once a part of mankind and quite separate from mankind. A mother with a life of her own.

Dira, Snake, shadow . . . took the man down and let the spark of light change itself to energy as the man became one with the Earth. His flesh melted and became quiet, cool soil. His eyes glowed with the light that shines in the darkest centers of the planet and he saw the way the mother cared for her young: the worms, the roots of plants, the rivers that cascaded for miles over great cliffs in enormous caverns, the bark of trees. He was taken once more to the bosom of that great Earth mother, and understood the joy of her life.

Remember this, Dira said to the man.

What a wonder, the man thought . . .

. . . and was returned to the sands of the desert, with no remembrance of having slept with, loved, enjoyed the body of his natural mother.

12

They camped at the base of the mountain, in a greenglass cave; not deep but angled sharply so the blown pumice could not reach them. They put Nathan Stack's stone in a fault in the cave's floor, and the heat spread quickly, warming them. The shadow thing with its triangular head sank back in shadow and closed its eye and sent its hunting instinct out for food. A shriek came back on the wind.

Much later, when Nathan Stack had eaten, when he was reasonably content and well-fed, he stared into the shadows and spoke to the creature sitting there.

"How long was I down there . . . how long was the sleep?"

The shadow thing spoke in whispers. *A quarter of a million years.*

Stack did not reply. The figure was beyond belief. The shadow creature seemed to understand.

In the life of a world no time at all.

Nathan Stack was a man who could make accommodations. He smiled quickly and said, "I must have been tired."

The shadow did not respond.

"I don't understand very much of this. It's pretty damned frightening. To die, then to wake up . . . here. Like this."

You did not die. You were taken, put down there. By the end you will understand everything, I promise you.

"Who put me down there?"

I did. I came and found you when the time was right, and I put you down there.

"Am I still Nathan Stack?"

If you wish.

"But *am* I Nathan Stack?"

You always were. You had many other names, many other bodies, but the spark was always yours. Stack seemed about to speak, and the shadow creature added, *You were always on your way to being who you are.*

"But what *am* I? Am I still Nathan Stack, dammit?"

If you wish.

"Listen: you don't seem too sure about that. You came and got me, I mean I woke up and there you were; now who should know better than you what my name is?"

You have had many names in many times. Nathan Stack is merely the one you remember. You had a very different name long ago, at the start, when I first came to you.

Stack was afraid of the answer, but he asked, "What was my name then?"

Ish-lilith. Husband of Lilith. Do you remember her?

Stack thought, tried to open himself to the past, but it was as unfathomable as the quarter of a million years through which he had slept in the crypt.

"No. But there were other women, in other times."

Many. There was one who replaced Lilith.

"I don't remember."

Her name . . . does not matter. But when the mad one took her from you and replaced her with the other . . . then I knew it would end like this. The Deathbird.

"I don't mean to be stupid, but I haven't the faintest idea what you're talking about."

Before it ends, you will understand everything.

"You said that before." Stack paused, stared at the shadow creature for a long time only moments long, then, "What was your name?"

Before I met you my name was Dira.

He said it in his native tongue. Stack could not pronounce it.

"Before you met me. What is it now?"

Snake.

Something slithered past the mouth of the cave. It did not stop, but it called out with the voice of moist mud sucking down into a quagmire.

"Why did you put *me* down there? Why did you come to me in the first place? What spark? Why can't I remember these other lives or who I was? What do you want from me?"

You should sleep. It will be a long climb. And cold.

"I slept for two hundred and fifty thousand years, I'm hardly tired," Stack said. "Why did you pick me?"

Later. Now sleep. Sleep has other uses.

Darkness deepened around Snake, seeped out around the cave, and Nathan Stack lay down near the warming-stone, and the darkness took him.

13

SUPPLEMENTARY READING

This is an essay by a writer. It is clearly an appeal to the emotions. As you read it ask yourself how it applies to the subject under discussion. What is the writer trying to say? Does he succeed in making his point? Does this essay cast light on the point of the subject under discussion? After you have read this essay, using the reverse side of your test paper, write your own essay (500 words or less) on the loss of a loved one. If you have never lost a loved one, fake it.

AHBHU

Yesterday my dog died. For eleven years Ahbhu was my closest friend. He was responsible for my writing a story about a boy and his dog that many people have read. He was not a pet, he was a person. It was impossible to anthropomorphize him, he wouldn't stand for it. But he was so much his own kind of creature, he had such a strongly formed personality, he was so determined to share his life with only those *he* chose, that it was also impossible to think of him as simply a dog. Apart from those canine characteristics into which he was locked by his species, he comported himself like one of a kind.

We met when I came to him at the West Los Angeles Animal Shelter. I'd wanted a dog because I was lonely and I'd remembered when I was a little boy how my dog had been a friend when I had no other friends. One summer I went away to camp and when I returned I found a rotten old neighbor lady from up the street had had my dog picked up and gassed while my father was at work. I crept into the

woman's back yard that night and found a rug hanging on the clothes-
line. The rug beater was hanging from a post. I stole it and buried it.

At the Animal Shelter there was a man in line ahead of me. He had
brought in a puppy only a week or so old. A Puli, a Hungarian sheep
dog; it was a sad-looking little thing. He had too many in the litter and
had brought in this one to either be taken by someone else, or to be put
to sleep. They took the dog inside and the man behind the counter
called my turn. I told him I wanted a dog and he took me back inside to
walk down the line of cages.

In one of the cages the little Puli that had just been brought in was
being assaulted by three larger dogs who had been earlier tenants. He
was a little thing, and he was on the bottom, getting the stuffing knocked
out of him. But he was struggling mightily. The runt of the litter.

"Get him out of there!" I yelled. "I'll take him, I'll take him, get him
out of there!"

He cost two dollars. It was the best two bucks I ever spent.

Driving home with him, he was lying on the other side of the front
seat, staring at me. I had had a vague idea what I'd name a pet, but
as I stared at him, and he stared back at me, I suddenly was put in
mind of the scene in Alexander Korda's 1939 film *The Thief of Bagdad*,
where the evil vizier, played by Conrad Veidt, had changed Ahbhu, the
little thief, played by Sabu, into a dog. The film had superimposed the
human over the canine face for a moment so there was an extraordinary
look of intelligence in the face of the dog. The little Puli was looking at
me with that same expression. "Ahbhu," I said.

He didn't react to the name, but then he couldn't have cared less.
But that was his name, from that time on.

No one who ever came into my house was unaffected by him. When
he sensed someone with good vibrations, he was right there, lying at
their feet. He loved to be scratched, and despite years of admonitions he
refused to stop begging for scraps at table, because he found most of
the people who had come to dinner at my house were patsies unable
to escape his woebegone Jackie-Coogan-as-the-Kid look.

But he was a certain barometer of bums, as well. On any number of
occasions when I found someone I liked, and Ahbhu would have nothing to do with him or her, it always turned out the person was a
wrongo. I took to noting his attitude toward newcomers, and I must admit
it influenced my own reactions. I was always wary of someone Ahbhu
shunned.

Women with whom I had had unsatisfactory affairs would nonetheless return to the house from time to time—to visit the dog. He had an intimate circle of friends, many of whom had nothing to do with me, and numbering among their company some of the most beautiful actresses in Hollywood. One exquisite lady used to send her driver to pick him up for Sunday afternoon romps at the beach.

I never asked him what happened on those occasions. He didn't talk.

Last year he started going downhill, though I didn't realize it because he maintained the manner of a puppy almost to the end. But he began sleeping too much, and he couldn't hold down his food—not even the Hungarian meals prepared for him by the Magyars who lived up the street. And it became apparent to me something was wrong with him when he got scared during the big Los Angeles earthquake last year. Ahbhu wasn't afraid of anything. He attacked the Pacific Ocean and walked tall around vicious cats. But the quake terrified him and he jumped up in my bed and threw his forelegs around my neck. I was very nearly the only victim of the earthquake to die from animal strangulation.

He was in and out of the veterinarian's shop all through the early part of this year, and the idiot always said it was his diet.

Then one Sunday when he was out in the backyard, I found him lying at the foot of the porch stairs, covered with mud, vomiting so heavily all he could bring up was bile. He was matted with his own refuse and he was trying desperately to dig his nose into the earth for coolness. He was barely breathing. I took him to a different vet.

At first they thought it was just old age . . . that they could pull him through. But finally they took X-rays and saw the cancer had taken hold in his stomach and liver.

I put off the day as much as I could. Somehow I just couldn't conceive of a world that didn't have him in it. But yesterday I went to the vet's office and signed the euthanasia papers.

"I'd like to spend a little time with him, before," I said.

They brought him in and put him on the stainless steel examination table. He had grown so thin. He'd always had a pot-belly and it was gone. The muscles in his hind legs were weak, flaccid. He came to me and put his head into the hollow of my armpit. He was trembling violently. I lifted his head and he looked at me with that comic face I'd always thought made him look like Lawrence Talbot, the Wolf Man. He knew. Sharp as hell right up to the end, hey old friend? He knew, and he was scared. He trembled all the way down to his spiderweb legs. This bouncing ball of hair that, when lying on a dark carpet, could be taken for a sheepskin rug, with no way to tell at which end head and which end tail. So thin. Shaking, knowing what was going to happen to him. But still a puppy.

I cried and my eyes closed as my nose swelled with the crying, and he buried his head in my arms because we hadn't done much crying at one another. I was ashamed of myself not to be taking it as well as he was.

"I *got* to, pup, because you're in pain and you can't eat. I *got* to." But he didn't want to know that.

The vet came in, then. He was a nice guy and he asked me if I wanted to go away and just let it be done.

Then Ahbhu came up out of there and *looked* at me.

There is a scene in Kazan's *Viva Zapata* where a close friend of Zapata's, Brando's, has been condemned for conspiring with the *Federales*. A friend that had been with Zapata since the mountains, since the *revolucion* had begun. And they come to the hut to take him to the firing squad, and Brando starts out, and his friend stops him with a hand on his arm, and he says to him with great friendship, "Emiliano, do it yourself."

Ahbhu looked at me and I know he was just a dog, but if he could have spoken with human tongue he could not have said more eloquently than he did with a look, *don't leave me with strangers.*

So I held him as they laid him down and the vet slipped the lanyard up around his right foreleg and drew it tight to bulge the vein, and I held his head and he turned it away from me as the needle went in. It was impossible to tell the moment he passed over from life to death. He simply laid his head on my hand, his eyes fluttered shut and he was gone.

I wrapped him in a sheet with the help of the vet, and I drove home with Ahbhu on the seat beside me, just the way we had come home eleven years before. I took him out in the backyard and began digging his grave. I dug for hours, crying and mumbling to myself, talking to him in the sheet. It was a very neat, rectangular grave with smooth sides and all the loose dirt scooped out by hand.

I laid him down in the hole and he was so tiny in there for a dog who had seemed to be so big in life, so furry, so funny. And I covered him over and when the hole was packed full of dirt I replaced the neat divot of grass I'd scalped off at the start. And that was all.

But I couldn't send him to strangers.

THE END

QUESTIONS FOR DISCUSSION

1. Is there any significance to the reversal of the word *god* being *dog?* If so, what?
2. Does the writer try to impart human qualities to a non-human creature? Why? Discuss anthropomorphism in the light of the phrase, "Thou art God."
3. Discuss the love the writer shows in this essay. Compare and contrast it with other forms of love: the love of a man for a woman, a mother for a child, a son for a mother, a botanist for plants, an ecologist for the Earth.

14

In his sleep, Nathan Stack talked.
"Why did you pick me? Why me . . ."

15

Like the Earth, the Mother was in pain.

The great house was very quiet. The doctor had left, and the relatives had gone into town for dinner. He sat by the side of her bed and stared down at her. She looked gray and old and crumpled; her skin was a soft ashy hue of moth-dust. He was crying softly.

He felt her hand on his knee, and looked up to see her staring at him. "You weren't supposed to catch me," he said.

"I'd be disappointed if I hadn't," she said. Her voice was very thin, very smooth.

"How is it?"

"It hurts. Ben didn't dope me too well."

He bit his lower lip. The doctor had used massive doses, but the pain was more massive. She gave little starts as tremors of sudden agony hit her. Impacts. He watched the life leaking out of her eyes.

"How is your sister taking it?"

He shrugged. "You know Charlene. She's sorry, but it's all pretty intellectual to her."

His mother let a tiny ripple of a smile move her lips. "It's a terrible thing to say, Nathan, but your sister isn't the most likeable woman in the world. I'm glad you're here." She paused, thinking, then added, "It's just possible your father and I missed something from the gene pool. Charlene isn't whole."

"Can I get you something? A drink of water?"

"No. I'm fine."

He looked at the ampoule of narcotic pain killer. The syringe lay mechanical and still on a clean towel beside it. He felt her eyes on him. She knew what he was thinking. He looked away.

"I would kill for a cigarette," she said.

He laughed. At sixty-five, both legs gone, what remained of her left side paralyzed, the cancer spreading like deadly jelly toward her heart, she was still the matriarch. "You can't have a cigarette, so forget it."

"Then why don't you use that hypo and let me out of here."

"Shut up, Mother."

"Oh, for Christ's sake, Nathan. It's hours if I'm lucky. Months if I'm not. We've had this conversation before. You know I always win."

"Did I ever tell you you were a bitchy old lady?"

"Many times, but I love you anyhow."

He got up and walked to the wall. He could not walk through it, so he went around the inside of the room.

"You can't get away from it."

"Mother, Jesus! Please!"

"All right. Let's talk about the business."

"I could care less about the business right now."

"Then what should we talk about? The lofty uses to which an old lady can put her last moments?"

"You know, you're really ghoulish. I think you're enjoying this in some sick way."

"What other way is there to enjoy it."

"An adventure."

"The biggest. A pity your father never had the chance to savor it."

"I hardly think he'd have savored the feeling of being stamped to death in a hydraulic press."

Then he thought about it, because that little smile was on her lips again. "Okay, he probably would have. The two of you were so unreal, you'd have sat there and discussed it and analyzed the pulp."

"And you're our son."

He was, and he was. And he could not deny it, nor had he ever. He was hard and gentle and wild just like them, and he remembered the days in the jungle beyond Brasilia, and the hunt in the Cayman Trench, and the other days working in the mills alongside his father, and he knew when his moment came he would savor death as she did.

"Tell me something. I've always wanted to know. Did Dad kill Tom Golden?"

"Use the needle and I'll tell you."

"I'm a Stack. I don't bribe."

"I'm a Stack, and I know what a killing curiosity you've got. Use the needle and I'll tell you."

He walked widdershins around the room. She watched him, eyes bright as the mill vats.

"You old bitch."

"Shame, Nathan. You know you're not the son of a bitch. Which is more than your sister can say. Did I ever tell you she wasn't your father's child?"

"No, but I knew."

"You'd have liked her father. He was Swedish. Your father liked him."

"Is that why Dad broke both his arms?"

"Probably. But I never heard the Swede complain. One night in bed with me in those days was worth a couple of broken arms. Use the needle."

Finally, while the family was between the entree and the dessert, he filled the syringe and injected her. Her eyes widened as the stuff smacked her heart, and just before she died she rallied all her strength and said, "A deal's a deal. Your father didn't kill Tom Golden, I did. You're a hell of a man, Nathan, and you fought us the way we wanted, and we both loved you more than you could know. Except, dammit, you cunning s.o.b., you do know, don't you?"

"I know," he said, and she died; and he cried; and that was the extent of the poetry in it.

16

He knows we are coming.

They were climbing the northern face of the onyx mountain. Snake had coated Nathan Stack's feet with the thick glue and, though it was hardly a country walk, he was able to keep a foothold and pull himself up. Now they had paused to rest on a spiral ledge, and Snake had spoken for the first time of what waited for them where they were going.

"He?"

Snake did not answer. Stack slumped against the wall of the ledge. At the lower slopes of the mountain they had encountered slug-like creatures that had tried to attach themselves to Stack's flesh, but when Snake had driven them off they had returned to sucking the rocks. They had not come near the shadow creature. Further up, Stack could see the lights that flickered at the summit; he had felt fear that crawled up from his stomach. A short time before they had come to this ledge they had stumbled past a cave in the mountain where the bat creatures slept. They had gone mad at the presence of the man and the Snake and the sounds they had made sent waves of nausea through Stack. Snake had helped him and they had gotten past. Now they had stopped and Snake would not answer Stack's questions.

We must keep climbing.

"Because he knows we're here." There was a sarcastic rise in Stack's voice.

Snake started moving. Stack closed his eyes. Snake stopped and came back to him. Stack looked up at the one-eyed shadow.

"Not another step."

There is no reason why you should not know.

"Except, friend, I have the feeling you aren't going to tell me anything."

It is not yet time for you to know.

"Look: just because I haven't asked, doesn't mean I don't want to know. You've told me things I shouldn't be able to handle . . . all kinds of crazy things . . . I'm as old as, as . . . I don't know *how* old, but I get the feeling you've been trying to tell me I'm Adam . . ."

That is so.

". . . uh." He stopped rattling and stared back at the shadow creature. Then, very softly, accepting even more than he had thought possible, he said, "Snake." He was silent again. After a time he asked, "Give me another dream and let me know the rest of it?"

You must be patient. The one who lives at the top knows we are coming but I have been able to keep him from perceiving your danger to him only because you do not know yourself.

"Tell me this, then: does he *want* us to come up . . . the one on the top?"

He allows it. Because he doesn't know.

Stack nodded, resigned to following Snake's lead. He got to his feet and performed an elaborate butler's motion, after you, Snake.

And Snake turned, his flat hands sticking to the wall of the ledge, and they climbed higher, spiraling upward toward the summit.

The Deathbird swooped, then rose toward the Moon. There was still time.

17

Dira came to Nathan Stack near sunset, appearing in the board room of the industrial consortium Stack had built from the family empire.

Stack sat in the pneumatic chair that dominated the conversation pit where top-level decisions were made. He was alone. The others had left hours before and the room was dim with only the barest glow of light from hidden banks that shone through the soft walls.

The shadow creature passed through the walls—and at his passage they became rose quartz, then returned to what they had been. He stood staring at Nathan Stack, and for long moments the man was unaware of any other presence in the room.

You have to go now, Snake said.

Stack looked up, his eyes widened in horror, and through his mind flitted the unmistakable image of Satan, fanged mouth smiling, horns gleaming with scintillas of light as though seen through crosstar filters, rope tail with its spade-shaped pointed tip thrashing, large cloven hoofs leaving burning imprints in the carpet, eyes as deep as pools of oil, the pitchfork, the satin-lined cape, the hairy legs of a goat, talons. He tried to scream but the sound dammed up in his throat.

No, Snake said, *that is not so. Come with me, and you will understand.*

There was a tone of sadness in the voice. As though Satan had been sorely wronged. Stack shook his head violently.

There was no time for argument. The moment had come, and Dira could not hesitate. He gestured and Nathan Stack rose from the pneumatic chair, leaving behind something that looked like Nathan Stack asleep, and he walked to Dira and Snake took him by the hand and they passed through rose quartz and went away from there.

Down and down Snake took him.

The Mother was in pain. She had been sick for eons, but it had reached the point where Snake knew it would be terminal, and the Mother knew it, too. But she would hide her child, she would intercede in her own behalf and hide him away deep in her bosom where no one, not even the mad one, could find him.

Dira took Stack to Hell.

It was a fine place.

Warm and safe and far from the probing of mad ones.

And the sickness raged on unchecked. Nations crumbled, the oceans boiled and then grew cold and filmed over with scum, the air became thick with dust and killing vapors, flesh ran like oil, the skies grew dark, the sun blurred and became dull. The Earth moaned.

The plants suffered and consumed themselves, beasts became crippled and went mad, trees burst into flame and from their ashes rose glass shapes that shattered in the wind. The Earth was dying; a long, slow, painful death.

In the center of the Earth, in the fine place, Nathan Stack slept. *Don't leave me with strangers.*

Overhead, far away against the stars, the Deathbird circled and circled, waiting for the word.

18

When they reached the highest peak, Nathan Stack looked across through the terrible burning cold and the ferocious grittiness of the demon wind and saw the sanctuary of always, the cathedral of forever, the pillar of remembrance, the haven of perfection, the pyramid of blessings, the toyshop of creation, the vault of deliverance, the monument of longing, the receptacle of thoughts, the maze of wonder, the catafalque of despair, the podium of pronouncements and the kiln of last attempts.

On a slope that rose to a star pinnacle, he saw the home of the one who dwelled here—lights flashing and fllickering, lights that could be seen far off across the deserted face of the planet— and he began to suspect the name of the resident.

Suddenly everything went red for Nathan Stack. As though a filter had been dropped over his eyes, the black sky, the flickering lights, the rocks that formed the great plateau on which they stood, even Snake became red, and with the color came pain. Terrible pain that burned through every channel of Stack's body, as though his blood had been set afire. He screamed and fell to his knees, the pain crackling through his brain, following every nerve and blood vessel and ganglia and neural track. His skull flamed.

Fight him, Snake said. *Fight him!*

I can't, screamed silently through Stack's mind, the pain too great even to speak. Fire licked and leaped and he felt the delicate tissues of thought shriveling. He tried to focus his thoughts on ice. He clutched for salvation at ice, chunks of ice, mountains of ice, swimming icebergs of ice half-buried in frozen water, even as his soul smoked and smoldered. *Ice!* He thought of millions of particles of hail rushing, falling, thundering against the firestorm eating his mind, and there was a spit of steam, a flame that went out, a corner that grew cool . . . and he took his stand in that corner, thinking ice, thinking blocks and chunks and monuments of ice, edging them out to widen the circle of coolness and safety. Then the flames began to retreat, to slide back down the channels, and he sent ice after them, snuffing them, burying them in ice and chill waters.

When he opened his eyes, he was still on his knees, but he could think again, and the red surfaces had become normal again.

He will try again. You must be ready.

"Tell me *everything!* I can't go through this without knowing, I need help!"

You can help yourself. You have the strength. I gave you the spark.

. . . and the second derangement struck!

The air turned shaverasse and he held dripping chunks of unclean rova in his jowls, the taste making him weak with nausea. His pods withered and drew up into his shell and as the bones cracked he howled with strings of pain that came so fast they were almost one. He tried to scuttle away, but his eyes magnified the shatter of light that beat against him. Facets of his eyes cracked and the juice began to bubble out. The pain was unbelievable.

Fight him!

Stack rolled onto his back, sending out cilia to touch the earth, and for an instant he realized he was seeing through the eyes of another creature, another form of life he could not even describe. But he was under an open sky and that produced fear, he was surrounded by air that had become deadly and *that* produced fear, he was going blind and *that* produced fear, he was . . . he was a *man* . . . he fought back against the feeling of being some other thing . . . he was a *man* and he would not feel fear, he would stand.

He rolled over, withdrew his cilia, and struggled to lower his pods. Broken bones grated and pain thundered through his body. He forced himself to ignore it, and finally the pods were down and he was breathing and he felt his head reeling. . .

And when he opened his eyes he was Nathan Stack again.

. . . and the third derangement struck:

Hopelessness.

Out of unending misery he came back to be Stack.

. . . and the fourth derangement struck:

Madness.

Out of raging lunacy he fought his way to be Stack.

. . . and the fifth derangement, and the sixth, and the seventh, and the plagues, and the whirlwinds, and the pools of evil, and the reduction in size and accompanying fall forever through sub-microscopic hells, and the things that fed on him from inside, and the twentieth, and the fortieth, and the sound of his voice screaming for release, and the voice of Snake always beside him, whispering *Fight him!*

Finally it stopped.

Quickly, now.

Snake took Stack by the hand and half-dragging him they raced to the great palace of light and glass on the slope, shining brightly under the star pinnacle, and they passed under an arch of shining metal into the ascension hall. The portal sealed behind them.

There were tremors in the walls. The inlaid floors of jewels began to rumble and tremble. Bits of high and faraway ceilings began to drop. Quaking, the palace gave one hideous shudder and collapsed around them.

Now, Snake said. *Now you will know everything!*

And everything forgot to fall. Frozen in mid-air, the wreckage of the palace hung suspended above them. Even the air ceased to swirl. Time stood still. The movement of the Earth was halted. Everything held utterly immobile as Nathan Stack was permitted to understand all.

19

MULTIPLE CHOICE

(Counts for ½ your final grade.)

1. God is:

   A. An invisible spirit with a long beard.
   B. A small dog dead in a hole.
   C. Everyman.
   D. The Wizard of Oz.

2. Nietzsche wrote "God is dead." By this did he mean:

    A. Life is pointless?
    B. Belief in supreme deities has waned?
    C. There never was a God to begin with?
    D. Thou art God?

3. Ecology is another name for:

    A. Mother love.
    B. Enlightened self-interest.
    C. A good health salad with Granola.
    D. God.

4. Which of these phrases most typifies the profoundest love?

    A. Don't leave me with strangers.
    B. I love you.
    C. God is love.
    D. Use the needle.

5. Which of these powers do we usually associate with God?

    A. Power.
    B. Love.
    C. Humanity.
    D. Docility.

20

None of the above.

Starlight shone in the eyes of the Deathbird and its passage through the night cast a shadow on the Moon.

21

Nathan Stack raised his hands and around them the air was still as the palace fell crashing. They were untouched. *Now you know all there is to know,* Snake said, sinking to one knee as though worshipping. There was no one there to worship but Nathan Stack.

"Was he always mad?"

From the first.

"Then those who gave our world to him were mad, and your race was mad to allow it."

Snake had no answer.

"Perhaps it was supposed to be like this," Stack said.

He reached down and lifted Snake to his feet, and he touched the shadow creature's head. "Friend," he said.

Snake's race was incapable of tears. He said, *I have waited longer than you can know for that word.*

"I'm sorry it comes at the end."

Perhaps it was supposed to be like this.

Then there was a swirling of air, a scintillance in the ruined palace, and the owner of the mountain, the owner of the ruined Earth came to them in a burning bush.

AGAIN, SNAKE? AGAIN YOU ANNOY ME?

The time for toys is ended.

NATHAN STACK YOU BRING TO STOP ME? *I* SAY WHEN THE TIME IS ENDED. *I* SAY, AS I'VE ALWAYS SAID.

Then, to Nathan Stack:

GO AWAY. FIND A PLACE TO HIDE UNTIL I COME FOR YOU.

Stack ignored the burning bush. He waved his hand and the cone of safety in which they stood vanished. "Let's find him, first, then I know what to do."

The Deathbird sharpened its talons on the night wind and sailed down through emptiness toward the cinder of the Earth.

22

Nathan Stack had once contracted pneumonia. He had lain on the operating table as the surgeon made the small incision in the chest wall. Had he not been stubborn, had he not continued working around the clock while the pneumonic infection developed into empyema, he would never have had to go under the knife, even for an operation as safe as a thoractomy. But he was a Stack, and so he lay on the operating table as the rubber tube was inserted into the chest cavity to drain off the pus in the pleural cavity, and heard someone speak his name.

NATHAN STACK

He heard it, from far off, across an Arctic vastness; heard it echoing over and over, down an endless corridor; as the knife sliced.

NATHAN STACK

He remembered Lilith, with hair the color of dark wine. He remembered taking hours to die beneath a rock slide as his hunting companions in the pack ripped apart the remains of the bear and ignored his grunted moans for help. He remembered the impact of the crossbow bolt as it ripped through his hauberk and split his chest and he died at Agincourt. He remembered the icy water of the Ohio as it closed over his head and the flatboat disappearing without his mates noticing his loss. He remembered the mustard gas that ate his lungs and trying to crawl toward a farmhouse near Verdun. He remembered looking directly into the flash of the bomb and feeling the flesh of his face melt away. He remembered Snake coming to him in the board room and husking him like corn from his body. He remembered sleeping in the molten core of the Earth for a quarter of a million years.

Across the dead centuries he heard his mother pleading with him to set her free, to end her pain. *Use the needle.* Her voice mingled with the voice of the Earth crying out in endless pain at her flesh that had been ripped away, at her rivers turned to arteries of dust, at her rolling hills and green fields slagged to greenglass and ashes. The voices of his mother and the mother that was Earth became one, and mingled to become Snake's voice telling him he was the one man in the world—the last man in the world—who could end the terminal case the Earth had become.

Use the needle. Put the suffering Earth out of its misery. *It belongs to you now.*

Nathan Stack was secure in the power he contained. A power that far outstripped that of gods or Snakes or mad creators who stuck pins in their creations, who broke their toys.

YOU CAN'T. I WON'T LET YOU.

Nathan Stack walked around the burning bush crackling impotently in rage. He looked at it almost pityingly, remembering the Wizard of Oz with his great and ominous disembodied head floating in mist and lightning, and the poor little man behind the curtain turning the dials to create the effects. Stack walked around the effect, knowing he had more power than this sad, poor thing that had held his race in thrall since before Lilith had been taken from him.

He went in search of the mad one who capitalized his name.

23

Zarathustra descended alone from the mountains, encountering no one. But when he came into the forest, all at once there stood before him an old man who had left his holy cottage to look for roots in the woods. And thus spoke the old man to Zarathustra.

"No stranger to me is this wanderer: many years ago he passed this way. Zarathustra he was called, but he has changed. At that time you carried your ashes to the mountains; would you now carry your fire into the valleys? Do you not fear to be punished as an arsonist?

"Zarathustra has changed, Zarathustra has become a child, Zarathustra is an awakened one; what do you now want among the sleepers? You lived in your solitude as in the sea, and the sea carried you. Alas, would you now climb ashore? Alas, would you again drag your own body?"

Zarathustra answered: "I love man."

"Why," asked the saint, "did I go into the forest and the desert? Was it not because I loved man all-too-much? Now I love God; man I love not. Man is for me too imperfect a thing. Love of man would kill me."

"And what is the saint doing in the forest?" asked Zarathustra.

The saint answered: "I make songs and sing them; and when I make songs, I laugh, cry, and hum: thus I praise God. With singing, crying, laughing, and humming, I praise the god who is my god. But what do you bring us as a gift?"

When Zarathustra had heard these words he bade the saint farewell and said: "What could I have to give you? But let me go quickly lest I take something from you!" And thus they separated, the old one and the man, laughing as two boys laugh.

But when Zarathustra was alone he spoke thus to his heart: "Could it be possible? This old saint in the forest had not yet heard anything of this, that *God is dead!*"

24

Stack found the mad one wandering in the forest of final moments. He was an old, tired man, and Stack knew with a wave of his hand he could end it for this god in a moment. But what was the reason for it? It was even too late for revenge. It had been too late from the start. So he let the old one go his way, wandering in the forest mumbling to himself, I WON'T LET YOU DO IT, in the voice of a cranky child; mumbling pathetically, OH, PLEASE, I DON'T WANT TO GO TO BED YET. I'M NOT YET DONE PLAYING.

And Stack came back to Snake, who had served his function and protected Stack until Stack had learned that he was more powerful than the God he'd worshipped all through the history of men. He came back to Snake and their hands touched and the bond of friendship was sealed at last, at the end.

Then they worked together and Nathan Stack used the needle with a wave of his hands, and the Earth could not sigh with relief as its endless pain was ended . . . but it did sigh, and it settled in upon itself, and the molten core went out, and the winds died, and from high above them Stack heard the fulfillment of Snake's final act; he heard the descent of the Deathbird.

"What was your name?" Stack asked his friend.

Dira.

And the Deathbird settled down across the tired shape of the Earth, and it spread its wings wide, and brought them over and down, and enfolded the Earth as a mother enfolds her weary child. Dira settled down on the amethyst floor of the dark-shrouded palace, and closed his single eye with gratitude. To sleep at last, at the end.

All this, as Nathan Stack stood watching. He was the last, at the end, and because he had come to own—if even for a few moments—that which could have been his from the start, had he but known, he did not sleep but stood and watched. Knowing at last, at the end, that he had loved and done no wrong.

25

The Deathbird closed its wings over the Earth until at last, at the end, there was only the great bird crouched over the dead cinder. Then the Deathbird raised its head to the star-filled sky and repeated the sigh of loss the Earth had felt at the end. Then its eyes closed, it tucked its head carefully under its wing, and all was night.

Far away, the stars waited for the cry of the Deathbird to reach them so final moments could be observed at last, at the end, for the race of men.

26

THIS IS FOR MARK TWAIN

"YOU KNOW, PHIL, YOU'VE REALLY DONE VERY WELL FOR A WALRUS —"

*Phyllis Eisenstein offers an immensely entertaining tale of a
young minstrel with a talent for teleportation. Mrs. Eisenstein writes,
"I worked my way through the University of Chicago by cutting
meat in a black ghetto grocery store and setting pins in the
Physical Education Department bowling alley, then decided the U
of C Psychology Dept. couldn't teach me to be a science fiction
writer and gave up a year short of graduation. I married, spent
two years in Germany and upper Michigan with my husband, then
in the Air Force; when the USAF released him, we returned home to
Chicago."*

Born to Exile

PHYLLIS EISENSTEIN

The sun of Alaric's fifteenth summer beat down on his head as
he stared at the moat, the drawbridge, and the broad walls of
Castle Royale. A dusty wind swirled about him, adding another
layer of grime to his dark, travel-stained clothes and drying the
rivulets of sweat on his face and neck. He shifted his knapsack
with a shrug, and the lute that was strapped to it twanged
softly.

Presently, a man in light armor came out of the shack on the
near side of the bridge and glared at the boy from under an
enormous, beetle-browed helmet. He held a broadsword at ready.
"Identify yourself."

Alaric swept off his peaked black cap and bowed as much as

his pack permitted. "My name is Alaric, and by trade I'm a minstrel. Having been advised by many that my songs are worthy, I come to offer them to His Majesty and, in short, to become a hanger-on at court."

The guard grunted. "What weapons do you carry?"

Alaric's slender fingers touched his worn leather belt. "None but a paltry dagger, useful for carving fowl and bread. And the feather in my cap, for tickling my enemies to death."

"Empty your pack on the ground and give me that stringed thing."

While Alaric demonstrated that the pack held nothing but a brown cloak, a gray shirt, and four extra lute strings, the guard examined the lute. He shook it, peered into it, rapped it with his knuckles. At last, satisfied that it was nothing dangerous, he returned it to its owner and motioned for the boy to repack his knapsack.

"Gunter!" he shouted. A second man, seeming, in his identically patterned armor, to be a twin to the first, appeared from the shack. "Take him inside and turn him loose in the Great Hall. Seems to be a jester, even if he says he's a minstrel. Don't push the jokes, kid. We already got a jester."

Alaric swung the pack over one shoulder, the lute over the other, and followed Gunter across the bridge. He did not glance back, but in his mind's eye he could see the twisting, turning road that had brought him to this place. How many miles it was, he knew not. For him, it was measured in months, beginning on that gray day in the Forest of Bedham—eight long months and tens of thousands of steps carrying him away from Dall's lonely grave. Eight months through forest and field, asking directions of peasants in hovels and of merchants shepherding their caravans of goods to market; eight months in which he was hardly even tempted to use his witch's power to speed the journey—he needed a clear and precise knowledge of the location of his destination for that, and he had none. He had walked, as normal men did, pretending to be one of them as Dall had always advised, and he had finally arrived at Castle Royale, in search of his fortune.

The ministrel and his escort passed under the portcullis and entered a large courtyard in which a dozen or so well-muscled, half-naked men were practicing various forms of personal combat. Alaric's eyes roamed from swordsmen to wrestlers and boxers, and he was painfully aware of his own slight physique. Battles were not for his untrained hands. His way was to vanish, as he had vanished from beneath his father's whip.

He was seven that day, the day his mother died and his father revealed the fearful secret: that Alaric had been found on a hillside, a helpless newborn babe clothed only in blood. He was obviously a witch child, for a gory hand, raggedly severed just above the wrist, clutched his ankles in a deathlike grasp. The local peasants were frightened, and some wanted to destroy the infant that was surely a changeling or worse, but gentle, barren Mira loved him instantly and took him into her hut. Her husband grumbled sullenly under the lash of Mira's sharp tongue, but he acted the role of a father, albeit distastefully, until she died. And then his strong, gnarled fingers reached greedily for the whip.

Alaric, who had practiced his power in secret, flitting imperceptibly from one tree to another in the nearby wood, backed away in terror. As the vicious leather thong slashed toward him, he pictured a particular tree in his mind, complete to the mushrooms that ringed its trunk and clung to its bark. Suddenly, he stood in its shade and the loamy smell of the forest floor filled his nostrils. He never dared return home.

Gunter led the young minstrel toward a side door of the Palace, the largest building inside the fortress. Just before reaching it, they passed a raised wooden platform where an eight- or nine-year-old boy stood alone and unsheltered under the beating sunlight. He was naked but for a loin cloth, his head and wrists were encased in stocks, and his back was covered with raw wounds and clods of dried mud. Tears stood out in stark relief against his dirty cheeks.

"What's that?" Alaric asked his escort.

Gunter glanced back and shrugged. "A page. He misplaced some silver."

"I didn't take it, Master!" the boy whimpered. "I don't know what happened to it, but I didn't take it!"

Pity welled up in Alaric, not for the boy's innocence but for his stupidity in being caught. Theft was an art a youthful vagabond knew well—theft of money, chickens, and laundry—an art that had kept him alive from the day he left home till the night he met Dall, the minstrel with the silver voice. And the silver coins. The money had been tucked under the straw pallet that served as Dall's bed at the Inn of Three Horses. It was easy for an eleven-year-old boy with slender fingers to slip them out in the middle of the night; it was easy for an eleven-year-old boy with a witch's power to vanish to the safety of the forest. But Dall's voice was too compelling, and morning found Alaric waiting eagerly to listen again.

Dall sat in front of the hearth, strumming his twelve-stringed lute and singing lays of ancient times. When he noticed the child, however, he drew him outside. "I'm not going to hurt you," he said in low tones, "so don't be afraid. If you'd like to learn a song or two, I'll be glad to teach you, but first you must give me back my silver. And then you must tell me who you are and how you come by that vanishing trick."

"What?" the boy muttered. "I haven't any silver."

"You have." The older man lifted Alaric's chin with his index finger and gazed into the boy's eyes. "I saw you enter my room last night, and I saw you leave. What is your name?"

"Alaric."

"Tell me, Alaric." More than his words, the tone of his voice was the key that opened the boy's lips and heart; his story poured out torrentially, beginning with the discovery of his infant self on the hillside and ending half an hour later with his most recent exploit. At that point, he dug deep in his pockets for Dall's silver and returned the coins with trembling, suddenly shy fingers.

"There is no future in this," Dall said. "No matter how careful you are, you have no eyes in the back of your head; someday an arrow or a knife will find you."

"I've managed so far."

"You've already made your first mistake. Anyone but myself would have raised the cry of witch last night. You'd be an outlaw at this moment, and no one gives shelter to an outlaw, on pain of death."

Alaric hung his head and gnawed at his lower lip. "I thought you were asleep."

Dall plucked pensively at the strings of his lute. "I saw you sitting in the corner yesterday. You spent the whole day watching my fingers. Are you interested enough in the lute to learn to play it yourself?"

"Oh, sir, I'd like that very much!"

"Well then, I happen to need an apprentice . . ."

And after that, they traveled together.

Here I am, Dall, Alaric thought. *Where you always planned to go when and if the wanderlust left you. It's all just as you said it would be, cobblestone courtyard and all. You used to tell me we'd sing for His Majesty and find our fortunes here.*

Gunter stopped at a watering trough and let Alaric clean some of the dirt off his face and arms, change into his extra shirt, and stuff his ragged cap into the depths of his knapsack. Then they entered the building that was the Palace proper.

In order to use his power, the minstrel had to be able to visualize his position and his goal, each in relation to the other. Through years of practice—some of them behind Dall's back and against his advice—he had become adept at this. Though other strangers to the Palace might have been hopelessly confused, he was not when, after many twists and branchings, their path gave into an enormous high-ceilinged hall which was filled with voices and the clatter of dishware.

"Just in time for the midday meal," said Gunter. "The King will want entertainment."

On a dais on the other side of the room sat the King—a big man, still on the near side of forty, blond and ruddy-cheeked, dressed in a gold-encrusted red tunic. He was eating a joint of meat and waving it to punctuate booming sentences. To his left sat a handsome, dark-haired, blue-clad boy, and to his right was the most beautiful girl Alaric had ever seen. She resembled the boy enough to be his sister, but where his features were boldly cut, hers were fine and delicate. Her eyes were wide and green, her nose barely turned up, and her thin lips perfectly shaped. Her hair, which was very dark, she wore long and caught in a white lace net that allowed curling tendrils to escape its confines and nestle on her shoulders. Her green linen gown clung to a shapely breast and betrayed a narrow waist with the aid of a heavy girdle of chain.

"A minstrel, you say!" boomed the King's hearty voice. "Sit ye down, boy, and give us a song."

"And if it's good, we'll have you for lunch," said the jester, a wiry, big-headed dwarf who wore the traditional motley and bells and sat at the King's feet playing jacks. "And if it's bad, we'll have you for lunch anyway. Fee fi fo fum!" He turned a handspring and wound up on the floor in front of Alaric, looking curiously into the hole of the lute. "Anybody in there?"

"A silver coin lived there once. Maybe he'll come back, if you put in another so he won't be lonely."

"We'll see whether you're worth a coin after you've sung!" The King motioned to a blue-uniformed man behind him, who called for silence in the room.

Alaric's clear tenor rang out with an old, well-loved ballad.

"Upon the shore of the Northern Sea
Stands a tower of mystery,
Long abandoned, long alone,
Built of weary desert stone
For a purpose now unknown . . ."

Afterward, the King nodded. "I haven't heard that song in years. There was a minstrel who stopped here for a while once and sang that quite well. What was his name?"

"It was Dall, Father," said the girl in green. "Five years ago." She eyed Alaric with half-concealed interest, and when he met her glance she dropped her eyes. She concentrated on a square of green satin in her hands, twisting it and winding it around her fingers as if the action had some use. Alaric was fascinated by the smooth white skin of her hands—untouched by sun, wind, or work—and by her delicate, tapering fingers.

"Ah, yes, Dall," said the King. "He stayed the winter, I remember, and left with the spring thaw. Palace life was too soft for him, I guess."

"He was my teacher," Alaric said.

The King chuckled. "Now I know why you do so well at your trade. He was a master, that fellow. Whatever became of him?"

"He was murdered by bandits eight months ago," Alaric replied.

The Princess gasped, then her left hand flew to cover her mouth, and she turned her face away.

The King frowned sympathetically. "Ah, that's a shame. Were the culprits punished?"

Alaric shook his head. "I . . . I wasn't able to catch them."
The vivid picture of Dall's scarlet blood splashed over the dry
leaves and mold of the forest floor returned once more to haunt
him.

"It's hard to watch someone you love die unavenged. I know,
lad. But at least his place was taken by someone worthy of it.
You're more than welcome here. Join the table." He gestured
toward the left side of the hall, where twenty or thirty brightly
dressed men were eating. At the movement of his hand, the noise
level, temporarily low during and after the song, regained its former height.

Alaric bowed low and went to a vacant seat at one end of a
table, preferring the solitude of his own thoughts and an opportunity for observation to the boisterous conversation of the
courtiers. Taking wine and beef from two passing stewards, he
pretended to be engrossed in eating. Presently, he noticed the
jester wandering through the crowd, joking and capering, but
coming unmistakably in his direction. With a last cartwheel, the
jester was beside him, jarring the bench a trifle with the impact
of his small but solid frame.

"What ho, minstrel!"

"What ho, indeed, motley."

"Here's a silver coin," said the jester, holding out one hand.
"Now show me its brother."

The youth looked at him quizzically for a moment; then he
recognized the reference. "Sorry, that was just a figure of
speech. I haven't even a copper."

"Tch," said the dwarf. "Here I thought you were slyly hinting that you were a magician as well as a singer."

"Not at all. I can make food disappear, but that's my only conjuring trick."

"Then let me try." The jester's empty hand darted toward the
lute that hung over Alaric's shoulder and seemed to pluck a
coin from it. "Both for you, from the King, with his invitation
to stay until he tires of you."

"*You're* the magician, not I," said Alaric.

"Wrong both ways," the jester replied. "The magician is over
there." He pointed across the room to a small, lonely table
occupied by a bearded man in long black robes. "That's

Medron, said to be a cockatrice in disguise. I believe it. Without the beard, he'd turn his own mother to stone. This trick? Nothing, my boy. Medron can pluck gold coins from the King's mouth." The jester cleared his throat. "As long as he's gotten them from the King's purse beforehand."

"He's *not* a magician?"

"So some would say. Myself, I don't look cross-eyed at him. He doesn't have to be a magician to put itching powder in your clothes."

"*My* clothes?"

"What I mean, boy, is that if you *do* know any sleight-of-hand tricks, don't use them. And don't ask me to teach you any. Medron's a *good* wizard. He makes gold out of lead, though I've never seen any of it. But that won't stop him from denouncing you as a witch if he thinks you're competition. And he has lots of little tricks that would convince even *you* of your guilt."

"But the King—"

"Burned three witches last year, just outside the castle walls. Good thing, too. The time before that was inside the courtyard, and the place stank for a week."

Alaric swallowed slowly. "Thanks for the warning. Thanks a lot."

"Nothing at all. I like to keep the ship rolling along smoothly. My last message is from the Princess Solinde: She wants you to sing in her sitting room at sundown. Second stairway on the left, three flights up, the door has gilded birds carved into it." He grinned and did a back-flip off the bench. "Keep your wits about you," he said as he walked away on his hands. "My grandmother was an owl."

Alaric ate mechanically as he watched the dwarf meander back toward the dais, which was now occupied only by the King. The brother and sister had gone.

Toward sunset, blazing torches were scattered around the room, and the twin fireplaces at either end of the hall were loaded up against the approaching chill of night. The courtiers abandoned the tables and clustered around the two hearths, laughing, playing with their huge hunting dogs, and gambling with dice. Alaric plucked idly at his lute for a while, and then he made his way toward the stairway that the jester had indicated. He was stopped at the top of the steps by a blue-uniformed guard who stood beneath a wall-bracketed torch and carried a spear.

"I was invited to sing for the Princess Solinde," Alaric said.

The guard peered into Alaric's knapsack and shook his lute before allowing the boy to walk on, and he pivoted on one foot to watch the minstrel all the way to the door of the carved birds.

Alaric knocked.

The oaken panel swung inward, revealing the beautiful girl and her handsome brother surrounded by giggling, chattering young attendants. The crowd parted in the middle to allow Alaric to enter. He found himself in a small but sumptuously appointed chamber hung with brilliant tapestries depicting opulent, idealized banquet scenes and lit by dozens of large candles hanging in a chandelier. The floor, instead of being strewn with rushes, was covered by an exquisite purple and blue carpet of oval shape and intricate, swirling design. Upholstered chairs of various bright hues were scattered on the rug, and his host and hostess waved Alaric to one of them.

"I am Solinde," said the pale, dark-haired girl. Her lips curved upward in the faintest of smiles—a smile that betokened the poise and confidence of a woman twice her age. "And this is my brother Jeris."

Alaric bowed, not quite certain that he should sit in the presence of royalty, even though the royalty was no older than himself.

"Sit down, for God's sake," said young Jeris. "You made me tired by standing up all through your song for Father this afternoon." The Prince threw himself into the nearest chair, his head resting on one upholstered arm and his legs dangling over the other.

Princess Solinde seated herself on a velvet-covered divan, and the dozen or so young courtiers sank to the floor around her couch. Only then did Alaric perch gingerly on the edge of his chair.

"Dall always sat when he entertained us," said Jeris.

"Did you know him well, Your Highness?" Alaric inquired.

"He was a fine fellow. He used to play hide and seek with us, and draughts, and follow the leader. We always hoped he'd come back sometime."

"Be quiet, Jeris," said his sister. "The minstrel came to entertain *us*, not we him. Do you know any of Dall's other songs?"

"I know all of them, Your Highness."

"Then play us a happy air."

Alaric complied with the amusing tale of the butcher's wife and the magic bull. While he sang, he noticed that the Princess watched him very closely. Her eyes were pale blue, fringed with thick lashes, and they met his boldly now instead of lowering. She looked him up and down until he wondered what she could be searching for.

Jeris whooped at the conclusion of the song, which found the butcher's wife hanging by her heels from the rafters of her husband's shop, waving a cleaver at all the customers. "He never sang us that one, sister. I'll wager he thought it too salty for young children."

"Yes, he did consider us children," she murmured. "Tell us something about his life these last few years."

"How did he die?" Jeris demanded, sitting forward eagerly. "Was it a fair fight, and what were the odds?"

"Oh, Jeris, let's not ask about his death! It's bad enough that he is dead; let's not dwell on the circumstances." She glanced around at the young people gathered about her. "Out! All of you out! I wish to speak to this minstrel privately. Not you, Jeris. How would it look to leave me alone with a stranger? My maid Brynit may also stay."

The room emptied as fast as the youngsters could bow or curtsy and flash through the doorway. The last one out closed the door behind himself.

"Tell us now, Master Alaric," the Princess said breathlessly, leaning forward in her chair, "was his hair still jet black and his manner proud but kindly?"

"Faugh!" muttered Jeris. "She wishes it were he sitting there instead of you. I shall be sick if you speak of him again in *that* way, Solinde."

"Very well, brother. We shall satisfy your curiosity now and mine at some other time." Daintily, she folded her hands in her lap. "Did he suffer much, Master Alaric?"

"No. It was a broad-bladed hunting arrow, and he bled to death quickly." Alaric remembered too much too well: bending over the knapsack to count the gleaming coppers won in the marketplace of Bedham Town, his shoulder brushing Dall's as the two of them knelt by the fire. The smell of burning hickory branches that almost covered the lighter scent of the rich, black earth around them. Crickets chirping a mindless chorus. And then, the snick of an arrow being loosed from a longbow somewhere to his left. Alaric vanished reflexively, without thinking, and found himself at their campsite of the previous night, still clutching the knapsack and a handful of coins. He returned to Dall instantly, but it was too late. The gray-feathered shaft had pierced the singer's chest—a shaft aimed at Alaric, that passed through the space he had suddenly ceased to occupy and struck his friend. Desolated, the boy blamed himself.

"In a sense, it was my fault. The arrow was meant for me, but I moved just before it struck." He felt a tear grow in his eye and petulantly brushed it away. "I'm sorry, Your Highness. I think about it often and bitterly. I loved him as if he were my father."

Solinde sighed and leaned back. "We loved him, too. And we shall always think of you as part of him. I'm glad you came to us, Master Alaric."

"He wanted to return, Your Highness. He spoke of it often. He never told me why, but I see now that it must have been because of you and your brother." Mentally, he crossed his fingers over that white lie. Dall had always said that fortune awaited them at Castle Royale, and now Alaric understood that he had meant the patronage of the heirs to the throne.

"That's . . . very good to know," she murmured. "You had better leave now minstrel; it grows late."

Alaric stood up and bowed deeply. "Good night, Your Highnesses," he said and backed politely to the door. As he slipped out and gently shut the heavy, carved panel, he heard a woman sobbing beyond it and wondered whether it were the Princess herself or her little maid, who had sat silently in a far corner of the salon throughout the interview.

The guard at the top of the stairs gave him leave to descend with a curt nod, and when he reached the main floor and the Great Hall, Alaric found preparations for sleep in progress.

Many of the courtiers who had dined at the long table on the left side of the room had no private apartments in Castle Royale; they were solitary knights and minor nobles without retinues seeking temporary hospitality from their overlord or desiring audiences with him. A few were pilgrims in sackcloth, and these huddled close to one fireplace, as if their very bones were perpetually chilled. A number of maidservants were moving through the throng with quilts and blankets, heaping them over cushions or couches as bedding for the guests. One by one the men settled down, some with their dogs posted beside them, some with more congenial bedmates. Alaric found himself alone with a voluminous, multicolored down-stuffed comforter; he squeezed into a narrow space near the pilgrims, wrapped himself in the coverlet, and lay down with his knapsack as a pillow and the lute under his protecting arm.

The pilgrims were murmuring to each other in low tones.

"Listen to the wind wail," said a bent-backed oldster in a coarse, hooded robe. "It's a night for evil."

"It's a night for rain," replied one of his companions, a younger man with a blond mustache and no eyebrows.

"See the flames flicker and blow? The Dark One himself will be out with his witches tonight," insisted the first.

"How many days before we come to the Holy Well?" asked a third companion, a swarthy, grizzled fellow in his fifties.

"Two more, and not soon enough for me. I feel the Darkness creeping up to strangle me."

"We're safe enough here, uncle," said the fourth member of the group, a beardless youth. "They say Lord Medron has powerful spells wound all around this castle, keeping the Dark Ones always outside."

"I don't know why our good King trusts him. Witches are evil, nephew, every one of them. At night they turn invisible for their foul purposes, and they fly to the ends of the earth for their filthy revels. Darkness oozes from their limbs like honey from a crushed hive."

"I saw nothing oozing from Lord Medron," said the boy.

"After our visit to the Holy Well, perhaps you will see things differently. My old eyes know a witch when they see one." He glanced suspiciously around the room, his eyelids narrowed to slits.

Alaric felt every muscle in his body stiffen as the old man's gaze swept past him. Was there really some unmistakable visual clue to a witch's identity—the color of an eye or the tilt of a nose or the thickness of a brow—that would be apparent to a knowledgeable observer? Alaric had never noticed anything physically special about his body, but that might only mean that he didn't know what to look for. Had that gray-feathered arrow been loosed at him because he possessed a double handful of coppers or because he was obviously a witch who could only be destroyed by stealth and surprise? Would it be best to leave instantly before anyone recognized the power that he always felt glowing softly inside him?

"Perhaps the King has a talisman that binds Medron to his bidding," suggested the grizzled pilgrim.

"Well, our good King is surely a likely person to possess such," the old man muttered, and then he launched into an arcane discussion of talismans and their hypothetical attributes.

Alaric relaxed slowly. The elderly pilgrim had seen his face and not blinked an eye. The man was wrong about Medron, too. Alaric remembered what the jester had said about the court magician being a clever fake. But that in no way lessened the very real danger that the old man presented: He was convinced that he could identify witches, and there was no way of knowing what insignificant action might cause him to raise a cry. More and more, Alaric wondered if he wasn't wrong about seeking his fortune at Castle Royale. One slip, like the reflexive self-defense of that day in Bedham Forest, would mean outlawry and perpetual pursuit. In eight months, he had not used his power once, had steeled himself to forget it existed, but it glowed deep within him still, as strong as ever. He balanced the advantages: acceptance, companionship, physical comfort, and infinite diversion in Castle Royale against the nomadic existence of his childhood. There was no in-between. He was a minstrel, like it or not, and he had no desire to become a farmer or a man-at-arms for some small baron. He had to have a single rich patron or wander from village to village for a few coppers a year. Without a companion, the latter was no pleasant prospect. So he had to take his chances here, stifle the glow, and pretend to be a normal human being. He felt like a bird that had given up the lonely freedom of the skies for the security of a golden cage.

He turned his face away from the whispering pilgrims and drifted to sleep, and the delicate, pale face of Princess Solinde loomed in his dreams.

In the morning, he forced himself to greet the four pilgrims and break fast with them. He inquired after their destination as if had not overheard their conversation the previous night.

"We go to the Holy Well at Canby," said the old man, "to drink and bathe and be cleansed."

"I wish you good speed on your journey," Alaric said.

"And good speed to yourself on your journey through life, minstrel," replied the old man, his gnarled fingers drawing a fleeting holy sign in the air in front of Alaric's nose. "May you and your fine songs, that we heard yesterday, ever be safe from evil."

Alaric watched them troop out of the Great Hall in single file, the old man leading and the boy bringing up the rear. It seemed a good, though ironic, omen that a pilgrim as resolutely holy and evil-hating as the old man should denounce a false witch and bless a real one.

In midmorning, the King strode into the room—having broken fast in private—to judge civil and criminal cases among the nobility. The jester ambled in behind him, trailing a tiny wheeled cart containing variously shaped trinkets. He planted himself at the King's knee and sorted his colored baubles into two piles according to some plan known only to himself. Occasionally, he juggled three or four objects at once while His Majesty deliberated. Alaric watched and listened for a time, but finding the proceedings overlong, complex, and tedious, he drifted away, his lute slung over his shoulder. His pack he left safe in the hands of the Palace Oversteward. Navigating the twisting, branching corridor through which he had first entered the Palace with ease, he returned to the side door that led to the cobblestone courtyard. Outside, in the brilliant summer sunlight, his eyes were dazzled for a moment, and when his vision cleared, he noted that a number of men who had been practicing combat there the previous day were clustered about a pair of fighters in a corner of the yard. One figure about his own size, garbed in quilted gray cloth "armor" and steel helmet, tested his swordsmanship against a heftier man in dirty blue. The two were slashing furiously with wooden swords, and their wooden shields were splintered and cracked. At last the smaller one heaved a strong overhand blow at the heavier man's helm, striking the metal with a loud clunk, and that signaled the end of the match.

"Well struck, my Lord Prince!" exclaimed the man in blue, and he took off his helmet to reveal the ruddy, sweating face and balding pate of a seasoned veteran. "That would have split my head open!"

Prince Jeris removed his own helmet and handed it to a retainer who had stepped forward to receive it. Dark hair was plastered in wet points across his forehead, and he was breathing heavily, but he grinned his satisfaction at his prowess and the compliment.

"Damn, it's hot, Falmar. I've got to get out of this suit!"

A second retainer stepped behind the young prince and deftly began to undo the complex lacings that held the quilted armor together. In a few moments, Jeris was able to shrug off the shirt and kick the leggings aside. Underneath, he wore only abbreviated breeches.

"Ho, it's the minstrel!" he exclaimed, spying Alaric in the throng. "Step aside and sing me a short song while I clear the dust from my throat." Jeris trotted to the scant shade of an overhanging roof, where a table of wines and cheeses was spread for his refreshment. He poured three cups of wine, handed one to his sparring partner, and indicated that the third was for Alaric.

"Thank you, Your Highness."

The Prince tossed down his drink. "You can call me my Lord, minstrel. It feels less formal and far less cumbersome than spouting Your Highness in every sentence. The rest of you can go about your usual business." He waved at the crowd, which immediately dispersed, except for two unobtrusive armed guards who stood a few yards away. Jeris glanced sideways at Alaric. "Were you betting on me?"

"I wasn't aware that wagering was going on, my Lord."

"It was. Father doesn't allow it, but that won't stop them. They think it flatters me."

"And does it, my Lord?"

"Only Falmar's own praise flatters me." He poured himself a second cup of wine and sipped at it. "I see our jester has been thrown out of His Majesty's High Court, as usual." He pointed past Alaric's left shoulder.

The minstrel turned and saw the dwarf skipping across the cobblestones toward them, his little wagon bouncing along behind. He chanted:

"Oh, blue is blue and red is red,

But black and white are gray;

The more you try to take yourself,

The more you throw away!"

He did a flip in midair and landed on his hands in front of the two young men. He peered at them upside down. "A bat may look at a prince," he sang.

Jeris laughed. "What have you done this time, motley?"

The jester lowered his legs, twisting as he did so, until he sat cross-legged on the warm cobblestones. "Baron Eglis . . ." His right hand plucked a blue cube from the pile of gewgaws in his wagon. ". . . who recently had that unfortunate accident which will forever deprive him of the ability to beget a legitimate heir, is suing the King . . ." His left hand chose a red ball. ". . . for permission to make his child by *droit du seigneur* . . ." He transferred ball and cube to one hand and picked up a black pyramid with the other. ". . . which he exercised for an entire week last year . . ." He juggled the three playthings. ". . . heir to the Barony." The pyramid landed on top of his head, and the cube and ball each came to rest on one of his upturned palms. He winked at Jeris. "And so I was cast out of the High Court for being on the wrong side."

"Father ruled that the Barony would revert to the Crown when Eglis dies." The prince turned away, rubbing his cheek with the knuckles of his index finger. "Did you get the names of the child and its mother?"

The dwarf was arranging the contents of his wagon more neatly. "The mother is Dilia, quite a handsome wench, wife of a peasant named Marnit. The baby is Pon, now four months old."

Jeris nodded. "And where is my lovely sister?" he said in a lighter tone.

The jester stepped out of the shade and looked toward the sky speculatively, scanning it from horizon to horizon and up toward the zenith. "There," he said finally, pointing upward.

The Prince leaned into the sunlight and glanced almost straight up, shading his eyes with one hand. He waved broadly toward the sky with the other.

Alaric followed the line of Jeris's gaze up the sheer masonry wall beside him, past two small windows to a third, set in the high tower just a few feet beneath its conical roof.

Princess Solinde leaned from the openings, and her long dark tresses fluttered in the wind.

"Let down your hair!" shouted the jester.

"Foolish dwarf, she can't hear you. And I don't think she'll live long enough for her hair to grow *that* long."

"The lady approves of her brother's prowess with the wooden sword, or else she's letting the wind dry her hair. Who could tell from this distance?"

"Arm yourself, motley knave, and we'll give her a show with sharp-edged steel," Jeris said, leaning indolently against the wall.

The dwarf tapped the Prince's right knee with two fingers. "Why, my Lord King would surely fire me if I caused his son to lose a leg. And where would I find another livelihood so plush?"

Jeris clapped the little man on the head and then picked him up and swung him to a perch on his left shoulder. "The older I grow, the lighter you become, motley."

"And the higher becomes this seat of authority, Your Highness."

The Prince boosted his small companion into the air, where the dwarf executed a series of rolls and landed on his feet on the ground.

"Come with me, my Prince," the jester said, his eyes dancing and his cheeks red. "We will be traveling acrobats and earn our fortunes while seeing the world."

Jeris laughed. "Sometimes I think you're almost serious when you say that. Now, minstrel . . ." He turned abruptly toward Alaric. "I haven't forgotten you standing here so silent. If you have some desire to hold a wooden sword, we can give my curious sister something to watch."

"I know nothing of swordsmanship, Your Highness."

"What, have you never wished to taste the reality of your songs?"

"I never had the opportunity. I am too poor to own a sword."

"What a fate! To sing forever of valorous deeds but never to *do* them. Motley, we must remedy this!"

"I will hold his lute," the jester offered.

"Wait, Your Highness! I'm not at all sure—"

"How did you manage to survive all this time without knowing anything of swordplay?"

"I've never had money worth stealing, I avoid quarrels, and I run away if I must. I'm sure no one will ever write a song about me."

"Well, you might need it sometime, minstrel, and it's best learned early. Come on, we'll get some practical instruction from Falmar, and those wooden swords don't hurt nearly as much as one would think."

In spite of his protests, Alaric soon found himself swaddled in quilting and paired off with a young squire who knew almost as little of the art of swordsmanship as Alaric did. They slashed awkwardly at each other, collected a few bruises, and gave up from exhaustion in a very short while. There was a certain exhilaration to even such a comparatively harmless exchange of blows—Alaric suddenly felt very masculine and self-assured, and these sensations stayed with him after he removed his quilted armor.

"You enjoyed it, didn't you, minstrel," said Jeris.

"Indeed I did, my Lord."

"Practice well, and by spring you'll be able to face me. Ha! It'll be good to see a new nose beyond the other shield."

The midday meal found things much as they had been the previous day: the King sat at a low table on the dais, flanked by his children and the jester. But this day Alaric sat there, too, though at the far end away from the King, who signaled him to play while the others ate. Alaric himself dined afterward.

The Princess wore scarlet today and a white kerchief covering her hair and veiling her forehead. Perhaps it was a trick of the

light, but Alaric thought her eyes were red-rimmed and blood-
shot, as if from weeping. She spoke little and only nodded to
most of the conversational sallies aimed in her direction. She
hardly touched her meal, passing most of it under the table to a
pair of clamoring mastiffs. Her father finally noticed her behavior and remarked that she must be getting ill.

"I'm just not hungry, Father."

"Perhaps you need to be bled."

"No, thank you, Father. I'm all right."

Jeris leaned over and whispered something in her ear.

She shrugged, then nodded. "Father, may I be excused from
the table?" When the King signaled with one hand, she rose and
glided out of the room, her long skirts swishing softly.

"The Moon, you know, Father," Jeris said in an undertone.

"Ah, yes, the Moon, I hadn't thought of it."

"Perhaps some quiet music would soothe her . . ."

"I know you want the minstrel as a playmate, my son." More
loudly, he said, "Another song, Master Alaric, and then you may
accompany the Prince away."

A little later, the two young men passed through the familiar
carved and gilded door. Inside the sitting room, Solinde reclined
upon her velvet divan, her feet tucked under her crimson skirt,
her head and back propped up by a dozen bolsters. In her hands
was a black cloth that she was embroidering with fanciful
flowers of red, purple, and blue. In a nearby chair, her maid
Brynit embroidered in green on a small white glove.

"We've come to cheer you, sister," Jeris said.

"Cheer me, then, with sad songs of love and death," she replied.
She glanced up at Alaric, and when her gaze met his, her busy
fingers fell suddenly still.

Alaric felt a flush of heat sweep through his body, and he
yearned to cool himself in the bottomless oceans of her eyes. He
dropped to one knee, lowering the lute to the rug beside him,
and reached for her hands that lay like nestling birds in her lap.
He touched her slim, white fingers, encircled them with his
own, and drew them to his lips for a brief kiss. "I will always
sing anything you wish, my Lady Princess."

A firm hand touched his shoulder. Jeris. "If someone should
chance to walk in, this would find our minstrel having a very

short career in Castle Royale. Up, Master Alaric, and take a chair."

"Forgive me, Your Highness," Alaric murmured as he moved away from her.

"There is nothing to forgive," she said, and her fingers resumed their embroidery. "We will never speak of this, Brynit."

"Yes, ma'am," the maid replied, bobbing her head.

Safely ensconced in a high-backed chair, the young minstrel sang a song of love and heard the words as if for the first time. They fit her, moved toward her, seemed almost to be composed specifically for *her* hair, *her* eyes, *her* lips. As he sang, he reconsidered Dall's desire to come to Castle Royale someday. He tried to imagine Solinde as Dall had known her: a child of ten or so, not yet budded into womanhood, but promising charm and beauty with her every word, gesture, and expression. Was it only patronage that Dall had expected, or was it something more?

Later that day, the King sent for Alaric to play for two noblemen, who had arrived for an audience and a night's guesting. Still later, the youth slept restlessly by the fire in the Great Hall, and Dall's face haunted his dreams.

The days passed and the weeks passed. On alternate mornings, the minstrel would train with the squires, absorbing the skills of swordplay and horsemanship; at noon he entertained the King's table; after sunset he would often be asked to play in the Great Hall until the torches guttered. Of the time that was his own, he devoted most to Jeris, who took him as a companion for hawking and deer and boar hunting, who taught him the game of draughts, and who secretly split a bottle of His Majesty's finest wine with him. The jester became a friend, too, and in spite of his initial refusal to teach the young man any sleight-of-hand tricks, he deftly demonstrated the palming of coins and other small objects, leaving Alaric to perfect the art on his own.

The only person in the Palace with whom he was not on friendly, or at least neutral, terms was Medron the wizard, that strange, silent, yet baleful figure who dined at a table of his own and only spoke to the King in a whisper inaudible to onlookers. He felt Medron's eyes on the back of his neck sometimes while singing in the Great Hall, and if he turned to test the accuracy of the feeling, he would see the man at his table or skulking in some dim corner. The wizard's eyes were black as pitch and sunk deep into his skull. He never smiled behind his beard but returned every glance with a cold stare. Did he see the *something* that the old pilgrim had spoken of?

The days passed and the weeks passed, and Medron, remaining silent, became part of the background blur of the Palace. Alaric found himself caught up in the routine of Palace life as if he had always been a part of it. He could almost fancy himself a nobleman, playmate of the Prince and Princess from their earliest years. But, of course, there was a line beyond which he dared not go, though often he found himself leaning over it.

One morning when he wasn't training in the courtyard, he sat in the high-backed chair in Solinde's sitting room while she wove on her loom, surrounded by her chattering maids. He sang a plaintive love song, oblivious to the whispers and titters of the girls, seeing only Solinde's flawless profile as she bent over the loom. He had a sudden urge to walk up behind her and kiss the tender nape of her neck, and he almost rose before a loud giggle jarred him back to reality.

His fingers and lips remembered the softness of her hand, and he felt youth racing through his veins like fire. Three maids had already offered him liaisons, but pretty as they were, they faded to drabs beside Solinde. With every day that passed, her image swelled in his mind until it dominated him utterly. She drew his eye as a lodestone draws iron: Whenever she entered a room, a thousand fantasy candles lighted; even though autumn waned, she kept summer in the Palace.

His own new attitude amazed him; previously he had always considered women a momentary diversion. His own songs of yearning and unrequited passion, which he sang so fervently— as Dall had taught him—had never meant anything to him. A woman he couldn't have had always been a woman he didn't want; another just like her waited somewhere beyond the next hill. Peasants or townspeople, they blurred together in his memory: dark-haired and fair, plump bodies and slim.

Somehow, in some way he couldn't recognize consciously, Princess Solinde was different.

She glanced up from her loom. "There is another verse, if I recall correctly."

Alaric strummed a discord. "The lover dies of longing. Too late his lady realizes that she cares for him and now can only strew roses on his grave. You see, Your Highness, why I prefer to leave it off."

"A sad fate, I suppose, if one assumes a person can die of longing."

"Well, if one forgets to eat . . ."

Solinde laughed. "How like Dall you are! That is exactly what I would expect him to say!"

Then, as if her unintentional mention of a subject they had avoided discussing for many weeks jarred the good mood out of her, she bent intensely over her weaving once more. "You may go, minstrel. No doubt my father will soon be requiring your services."

The abrupt dismissal disappointed him—he had thought to remain as long as his voice held out—and he turned and left dejectedly amid a flood of giggling farewells.

Downstairs, a cockfight was in progress, and the Great Hall was filled with shouts as the men crowded around the circle that had been cleared on the floor. The King himself presided and led the wagering. As the morning waned, the defeated roosters were thrown one by one into the pot for dinner. When all but the ultimate victor were dead, the King called on Alaric for some song appropriate to its triumph.

Evening fell at last, the torches were lit, and when his songs were no longer desired, Alaric went out into the courtyard. The air was brisk, and he drew his cloak tightly about his shoulders as he crossed the cobblestones. Above him, the stars shone clear and cold, and the tower which housed the Princess's rooms rose to meet them. A pale yellow light flickered in the window, occasionally dimming as a passing body masked the flame. Alaric imagined it to be Solinde herself, clad only in a translucent nightgown—though in this weather it would more likely be flannel—and he wondered if she would come to the window. How many nights had he stood here like a character from one of his songs, hoping for one last glimpse of her before he slept?

To his right, from a parapet overlooking the yard, came the

metallic sounds of the mailed night guard making his rounds. They ceased as the man leaned into an embrasure to survey the yard.

"Who is there?" he demanded of the dark-cloaked minstrel.

Alaric strummed his lute in reply, improvising a verse about the long, tedious hours of night guard duty, and the watchman walked on.

With a last glance upward, the youth sighed, shivered, and retraced the tortuous route that led to his sleeping place. Halfway there, he was met by Brynit, the Princess's plump little maid, who carried a lit candle stub whose wavering flame she shielded with one cupped palm.

"My Lady's not feeling well this night and wishes a few songs to while away the darkness, minstrel," she said.

Alaric bowed elaborately to conceal his excitement. "If Her Highness wishes, I will sing till the birds begin." He offered the maid his arm, but she turned on her heel and led the way.

The Great Hall had settled down while the minstrel was outside, and only the whispers of the pages assigned to stoke the hearths could be heard above sporadic snores and sleepy mutters. Brynit climbed the stairs quietly, lifting the front of her dress well above her knees; Alaric followed, trying not to tread on her short train. At the top of the stairs, in the puddle of light shed by the wall torch, the guard reclined. One of his knees was bent, the other straight out before him. His spear rested across his lap, and his head lolled forward, bobbing occasionally as he breathed heavily.

"Is he all right?" Alaric whispered, stooping to look at the man's face.

Brynit touched the minstrel's arm and motioned him onward preemptorily. She stepped over the unconscious guard.

Smelling nothing but strong wine, Alaric straightened and gingerly passed the man. He glanced back once before they reached the door of the carved birds, and the scene had not changed.

Inside, the sitting room was transformed by dimness to a tapestry-lined cave. No one was there. Alaric walked toward the chair he usually occupied and started to place his lute upon the seat.

"This way," said Brynit. She stood by the far wall, one plump arm holding aside a hanging to reveal another door. It opened.

The other room was the one with the window, the Princess's bedchamber. It was small and cozy, three walls hung with woolen panels and the fourth, opposite the window, occupied by a fireplace containing a roaring fire that warmed the room considerably more than two hearths warmed the Great Hall. In the center of the chamber, resting on a round brown rug, stood the Princess's bed.

"Good evening, minstrel," said Solinde. She reposed on a cushioned boudoir chair near the fire.

"Is there something else, Your Highness?" asked the maid.

Solinde shook her head.

Brynit curtseyed low and left the room, closing the door behind herself.

"Won't you sit down?" said the Princess.

Alaric glanced around. The only other chair was beside the bed, close to the window. He sat there and shrugged off his cloak. The room was pleasantly warm even though the window shutters were slightly ajar to allow in fresh air.

The Princess stood up and walked around the bed toward him, passing in front of the fire as she did so. Her pale blue gown became translucent for a moment, exposing her youthful contours to Alaric's eye; and as he stopped breathing, he could hear his pulse hammering wildly at his temples. He forced his gaze upward to her face, framed by unbound dark hair over which the flames laced red highlights.

"Am I pretty?" she asked.

"Yes, Your Highness. More than pretty."

She stepped nearer and touched his shoulder with her left hand. "Would you like to kiss me?"

His hand crept up of its own accord and covered her fingers. "What will happen if someone should come here now?" he whispered.

"No one moves at this time of night, not even Father. You saw the guard—he'll wake before dawn and merely think the night unusually short. And Brynit, who has served me faithfully most of my life, is watching the corridor."

"What do you want of me, Your Highness?"

"Nothing. Everything." Her hand moved up his shoulder to the back of his neck, and she was closer, much closer, her body brushing the arm of his chair. "You have no idea of what it's like to be a princess. Everyone very polite, very afraid to offend. No one dares touch me but Father and Jeris and the maids. Yet I've been a woman for four years now, and I want to be touched." Her hand moved over Alaric's close-cropped hair. "*One* would not have been afraid, but he came too early . . . would you like to kiss me, minstrel?" She knelt on the floor beside his chair, and her hand slipped down his arm and came to rest on his knee.

"I've wanted to kiss you for a long time, my Princess." He held her face between his palms and bent forward to press a chaste kiss against her forehead. He breathed in the scent of her hair and felt dizzy. Her cheeks were hot beneath his hands, or perhaps it was his own skin that blazed. He kissed the tip of her nose, and then he saw her lips, upturned, waiting for him like a blossom awaits a butterfly. He tasted them for a long moment—they were cool and soft—and his hands moved back, tangling in her hair.

"Again," she said.

"I can't trust myself again, Your Highness." He forced his hands to let go of her, to push her away gently. He rose, reaching for his cloak and lute.

She clasped him, clinging, staying him with the pressure of breast and hip and thigh. Her arms locked around his waist, and as she tossed her head her hair trapped his upper body in a silken net. "Don't leave me," she whispered.

Their lips met hungrily now, and their tongues fenced. His hands grew bold, caressing her body through the single thin layer of cloth. He bent her back till they lay prone on the bed, and she never pulled away but urged him closer. Soon, her gown was twisted around her waist and he could stroke her naked flesh while she found the lacings of his tunic and breeches.

"Oh, be gentle, my love, I'm a virgin," she whispered, but her body had no fear of violence as it squirmed and thrashed beneath him. For an instant, he felt a slight resistance at the juncture of her thighs, but one abrupt motion allowed him to pierce her maiden head.

"I love you, Solinde," he whispered as they rocked to and fro.

Then a sound penetrated the haze of his pleasure. Voices. Footsteps. The thud of a door swung all the way back on its hinges. He froze, all desire suddenly draining away from his body. He thrust Solinde away from him, rolled across the bed, dived for his boots, cloak, lute . . .

. . . and hit the cold cobblestones hard, bruising his right shoulder. The lute twanged softly as it bumped the ground beside him; he felt it all over till he was sure it was undamaged and until his eyes became accustomed to outdoor blackness. He laced up his awry clothing, slipped into his boots, and wrapped the cloak tightly around his quivering shoulders. Sweat dripping down his neck chilled him, and he wiped it away with the back of one hand. When his eyes were dark-adapted, he looked at the parapet—the guard was out of sight for the moment.

Alaric stood and nearly fell over again. A strip of the Princess's sheet was tangled about his ankles—in his haste to escape, he'd taken it with him. He wadded the fabric up and stuffed it into the hole of his lute.

High above his head, the shutters of Solinde's window were flung wide and the light within flickered wildly as people passed back and forth behind the casement.

Staring upward, he felt dead inside. It was all over. Right at this moment, she was probably confessing everything to her father, if she wasn't in hysterics from his damned show of instinctive self-preservation. Tears brimmed in his eyes for the first time in many weeks; he didn't want to leave and he dared not stay. A single instant would suffice to whisk him to the Forest of Bedham where he could sit by Dall's grave and meditate upon the lovely woman that neither of them could have. But he delayed, looking up toward her window, hoping against hope that she would lean out to let her hair float on the wind, that he might see her one more time.

The shutters closed.

"Still awake, minstrel?" called the night guard.

"Just going in," Alaric replied, and he stepped quickly into the shelter of the doorway, fearing unreasonably that the man was readying his spear. He pressed against the chill stone wall, telling himself over and over that the word could not have spread so quickly.

And still he stayed, tracing the familiar route to the Great Hall. He had a vague desire to get his knapsack from the Oversteward, to be warm again for a little while, to see familiar faces before he bid them farewell forever. Just as he entered the Hall, the King passed through, swiftly and suddenly, clad in his nightwear and a crimson cloak; anger showed on his face, but as he neared Alaric, who was one of the few awake and standing, he nodded a greeting and strode on. The jester trailed after him, and in sudden desperation, Alaric drew the little man aside.

"What's going on? Why is the King abroad so late?"

The dwarf shrugged, grinding sleep out of his eyes with the heel of one hand. "Rumor went out that the Lady Solinde was abed with a man, but the King's righteous wrath went to investigate, the Princess was found abed with herself and no other, peacefully asleep and loath to wake. As who wouldn't be at this ridiculous hour? A certain informant may be finding herself a new job in the laundry before long. Good night, minstrel, before the birds awaken."

Alaric stepped back into the shadows of his usual sleeping place as the royal entourage disappeared from view. His mind was juggling the idea of safety, afraid to accept it, afraid that all that had transpired since he left Solinde was a dream taking place in the split second before he appeared in the courtyard. He pinched his arm, and the pain seemed real. He stamped his foot, and the muttered grumblings of sleepers sounded real.

He had to talk to Solinde. He had to explain himself, defend himself, assure himself that she was as calm and unafraid as the dwarf's words implied. But there was no way; surely a maid would be sleeping in her room now—he dared not take a chance on being discovered now that he seemed so safe.

He found a stray quilt and curled up into a troubled sleep. In his dreams, Solinde alternately screamed and kissed him.

The next morning passed as many mornings did, in mock combat. Alaric did badly, being vanquished more often than usual. He was nervous, and his strokes were wilder than normal, but when the exercise was finished, he felt less tense.

Jeris commented as they were sipping wine in the shade of the overhanging roof, "Did last night's uproar rouse you, too? I thought I'd never get back to sleep."

Alaric nodded.

The Prince chuckled. "Father was rather annoyed at being wakened for nothing."

A clattering on the far side of the courtyard, accompanied by a great outburst of mutters from bystanders, caused the two young men to look in that direction. The magician Medron, flanked by four mailed guards with halberds, approached. His long black robe, embroidered in red and yellow with astrological symbols, swept the cobblestones, raising a cloud of dust. In his outstretched hands he held a short rope twisted of white satin and silver cord. He stopped in front of Alaric and Jeris and made a few passes in the air with the rope while he murmured unintelligibly under his breath. Then he deftly looped a slip knot around the minstrel's left wrist and pulled it tight.

"Alaric the minstrel," he intoned, "in the name of all that is holy, I bind you over to the judgment of the High Court on the charge of witchcraft!"

Outside, dawn was barely breaking over the courtyard, but in the dark depths of Castle Royale, eternal night ruled. Flickering torches cast wild shadows against the walls, and low moans floated in the air like wisps of smoke. Brynit, the Princess's faithful retainer, made her cautious way to the underground alchemical hideaway of Medron the magician. The stone stairs leading downward were slippery with dampness and fungi, and as her fingers trailed the walls for balance, they picked up a slimy coating. At every step, she held her breath and listened, but the loudest sound she heard was the terror-filled beating of her own heart.

At last she reached the massive oaken door to Medron's chambers. A heavy knocker hung at eye level. She grasped it, pulled outward, and allowed it to descend with a muffled clang. Long moments passed, and the door swung slowly inward, revealing Medron himself, swathed in a gray robe spattered with stains of all shapes and colors.

"What do you want?" he said.

Brynit curtseyed nervously. "I need a charm, Lord Medron. A powerful charm against a witch."

He eyed her fiercely. "Come in." He stepped aside to let her enter.

Within was a warm, comparatively dry room of long tables and strangely shaped vessels of ceramic and glass containing colored liquids both cloudy and clear. On the far side of the chamber was a large fireplace that connected somewhere above with one of the hearths in the Great Hall, through which, occasionally, foul smells emanated. A bright blaze filled the fireplace. Overhead, in the corners of the room, were grates through which fresh, cold air entered.

Medron seated himself on one of a pair of stools near the hearth and motioned for Brynit to take the mate. "You must tell me who this witch is and why you fear her."

"*Him,*" said Brynit. "It is Alaric the minstrel. He's bewitched my Lady to love him, and this night she arranged to have him visit her bedchamber after His Majesty slept."

Medron shrugged. "This is nothing but the way of young people."

Brynit twisted her handkerchief unmercifully. "So I thought. I've been my Lady's maid almost since she was born, and she's like a sister to me or even a daughter. I saw this young man and saw her eye on him and I thought, he's well enough made . . . but His Majesty would have my head if I allowed such fancies to go on. The boy is common and low and hardly a fit lover for my Lady. She wheedled and begged and ordered until at last I told her I would help; we gave the stairway guard a sleeping draught my Lady once had for her vapors. The boy came upstairs, and I left them alone together."

Medron plucked at his beard. "And so?"

She squirmed atop the stool and kicked her legs like a bashful child. "There's a chink in the wall between sitting room and bedchamber . . . I've arranged the hangings so that I can see the one from the other. When I was sure that . . . I locked the door and called His Majesty immediately, then returned to watch again." The handkerchief was wound tightly round her white-knuckled fingers by this time. "As the King entered the sitting room, making a great deal of noise, I saw the boy . . . I saw the boy fly out the window!"

Medron stood suddenly. "What?"

"Yes, yes, he flew out the window and my Lady fainted."

The magician began to pace back and forth before the fireplace. "Now, this is a serious charge you bring. Can you recall *exactly* what happened?"

"Oh, yes, *exactly!* The minstrel flew past his cloak and lute, which were lying on the chair beside the bed, grabbed them and went on out the window. When we all entered the bedchamber, he was gone. The King never saw him and of course assumed no one had been there. I didn't dare tell, my Lord Medron, until I got a charm from you. I'm so frightened . . . he'll turn me into a toad if I tell without a charm, won't he?"

"He might." Medron went to the nearest table and stood beside it, tapping his fingers on the smooth surface. "How long ago did this happen?"

"*This very night!* The King has threatened to send me to the laundry for lying, my Lord. Please help me!" She slipped off the stool and fell to her knees before the magician. "I will give you whatever I have. What could I need as a toad? Anything you wish, my Lord!"

Medron looked down at the short, plump, plain woman cringing before him. "Not for you will I do this, silly wench, but for *her*. Come, I will make you a charm to wear about your neck, and you will be able to sleep. In the morning we will bring this matter before the King."

"What's this?" cried Jeris.

Alaric was paralyzed and could only stare at his trapped wrist. The cord meant nothing, of course; he could disappear and take it with him if he chose, or with a little more concentration, leave it hanging limply from Medron's fingers. It was a symbol, though, of the resumption of the wanderer's life which he had wanted so much to leave behind and which he had thought, for a night, he was free of.

"You will accompany me," said the magician.

Alaric glanced at Jeris and shrugged.

"I forbid this!" said the Prince. "State the reasons for your vile accusation!"

"I will do so in the King's Court, and you will do well to hold your tongue while the King's commands are carried out."

Jeris's face reddened, but he fell behind and allowed the magician and the guards to lead Alaric indoors.

Alaric bent to retrieve his lute from the corner in which it rested, but one of the guards snatched it from beneath his fingers and carried it along. Again, the youth shrugged. He thought bleakly of the future; he would wait to see her once more, and then he would vanish in front of the entire court, perhaps taking a section of the floor with him as a parting gesture. He thought longingly of lifting Solinde in his arms and taking *her* along to live in some foreign land, but he knew that was impossible—she would be too well guarded, too well surrounded. Even using his power to get close . . . before he could swing her free of the floor to be sure of taking her whole body along, he would be impaled by a dozen spears. No, alone he would go, and he would have to make this last memory of her worth a lifetime of running from the King.

"And what do you have to say for yourself, witch?" the King shouted as soon as Alaric entered the Great Hall.

"Only that it is not true," the minstrel replied softly when he reached the foot of the throne and bowed.

"Let the second witness be called!"

The guard who had slept at the top of the stairs stepped forward and knelt to the King. "I saw no one pass, Your Majesty. If he entered the Princess's room, he must have been invisible."

"Let the second witness be called!"

The night guard who walked the parapet presented himself. "I saw the minstrel in the courtyard after everyone else slept. He was not there for the space of five rounds; then I heard the lute again and saw a shadowy figure. I called out and his voice answered, and then I saw him go inside."

"Let the third witness be called!"

Brynit stepped forward. She wore a gaudy red and yellow amulet about her neck. "He burst in on us as the Princess readied for bed, Your Majesty. I found myself bewitched, moving backward into the sitting room. Then, the bedchamber door, of its own accord, closed and locked." She pulled herself up to her full height of four and a half feet and glared at Alaric defiantly. "I called out the downstairs guard to rouse His Majesty, our own guard being in some sort of bewitched stupor; and while they dallied I pounded on the door, which did not yield. At last, I remembered a spy-hole which was used when political prisoners were kept in the tower room, and I looked into the Princess's bedchamber. My Lady was helpless, and the witch was working his will on her poor limp body. I screamed and called on the Holy Name, but none of it affected this powerful witch. Then, as Your Majesty arrived," she fingered the amulet, "I saw the witch grab his lute and his cloak and fly out the open window, banging it shut behind him!"

"Oh, Father, this is monstrous!" screamed Solinde as she tore away from the arms of a number of ladies who had held her in an obscure corner behind the throne. She ran across the dais and down the steps, her dark hair flying behind her, her cheeks flaming angrily, until the King caught the sleeve of her blue dress and swung her around. "He is no witch!" she cried.

"Neither are you a virgin," the King replied. "If not last night, when?"

She looked away and her eyes caught Alaric's, scant yards away. "Oh, why have you stayed?" she murmured.

"Hush, child," said the King, jerking her arm sharply. "Your bewitched mind is clouded with false love of this fiend." In a kindlier tone: "Lord Medron shall cure you, my daughter, just as successfully as he has caught and bound this witch." He handed her over to a lady-in-waiting who had come hurrying up. "Now, witch, that tower is sheer; the only way to enter it other than the stairs is by flight, and our faithful Brynit has confessed to *seeing* you fly. Therefore, what say you?"

Alaric still looked at Solinde, etching the vision of her loveliness indelibly on his brain. "I say that faithful Brynit is a liar. I can no more fly than you can."

"The evidence is against you, witch. Have you a final request before I pass sentence?"

For an instant Alaric felt more like laughing than anything else. If a band of roving actors had presented this situation as a farce, Alaric would have helped to boo them off the stage. He sighed. "May I have my lute?"

Medron stepped forward, still holding one end of the white and silver cord attached to Alaric's wrist. "I am most interested in the lute," he said. "The maid has attested that he took the lute as he flew out the window. Might I examine the instrument?"

The King nodded, and Medron slipped the end of the cord into his belt to free both hands to receive the lute. He turned it over, shook it curiously, and then his skinny fingers deftly reached between the strings and plucked white fabric from the hole. He held the wrinkled cloth out for all to see.

"A corner ripped out of my Lady's sheet!" exclaimed Brynit. "It was missing this morning when I straightened the bed!"

"I think we may assume," said Medron, holding the rag gingerly between two fingers, "that this is the object through which he controls the Princess, with the aid of the lute. As part of her cure, I will burn them both."

"And we will do the same for her bewitcher," announced the King, rising to his feet.

Regretting the loss of his lute and riveting his eyes on Solinde, Alaric chose between a number of places he was able to travel to. Yet he hesitated, just to see her face for another moment and another and another.

The jester cartwheeled past him and up onto the dais.

"Away, motley," said the King. "We're to burn a witch today." He stepped past the little man, descended from the dais and stood before Alaric, towering over him. "I am not afraid of you, witch." And he slapped the young man across the mouth.

Alaric fell to his knees, his head spinning and his ears ringing. For a moment, the hot anger that rose in his chest tempted him to take the King's leg with him as he disappeared, leaving only a bloody stump. Or even to spring for the monarch's head and leave a corpse behind. Revulsion for the very thought made him gag, and as his brain cleared, he knew he couldn't do any of it. He had to be satisfied by noting, from the corner of his eye, that Medron, too, had been thrown off balance by the slap, had lost the end of the white and silver cord, and had to scrabble for it frantically.

"If you're going to burn a witch, you'll have to look farther than this room for one," piped the dwarf.

"Quiet, motley," replied the King. "On your feet, witch, and march to your pyre!"

"Your Majesty, I have something here that will certainly interest your pious soul."

The King turned reluctantly. "What is it? Quickly!"

"The device by which our poor minstrel escaped Her Highness's room without relying on the power of flight." The small metal object he handed to the King was a long spike with the blunt end bent into a ring. "It was hammered into the wall outside Her Highness's window. A rope twice long enough to reach from courtyard to window is coiled inside the quilt the minstrel slept in last night. Two guards were with me when these items were found and will gladly vouch for the truth of my statements. Can the faithful maid Brynit say as much?" He turned toward the short, plump woman expectantly.

Brynit shrank back, fingering her amulet and looking at Medron. "It was not bright in the room, but still I know what I saw . . ."

"And she saw him diving through the window to escape by the rope, nothing more," said the dwarf. "He took the lute in order to leave no evidence, and the fragment of sheet is easily explained under the energetic circumstances." The jester cleared his throat noisily and winked at Alaric.

"She lied about everything," Solinde said in a cold voice. "I begged her to help me meet him alone, and she agreed. We mixed a sleeping potion for the guard, and *that* is why he saw nothing. *She* fetched him, and *she* let him into my room, and then she betrayed me. I swear on my mother's grave that all this is true. I spit on you, Brynit. Father, if this woman remains my maid, I will kill her."

The King stepped back and glanced from his daughter to Alaric, who was just climbing unsteadily to his feet. "This becomes another matter entirely."

"Father, I love this man."

"You are young. This love will pass and leave you ready to make a proper marriage."

"I will always love him." She tried to step forward, but the ladies held her back.

"Alaric the minstrel, this is my decision: We will do without your songs from this time forward. I give you a horse and one week to reach the border. After that, you are a dead man in my realm. Go." He whispered to a nearby guard, then strode out of the room.

Alaric dusted himself off and shucked the white and silver rope with a show of distaste. He snatched his lute from Medron, who merely sniffed superciliously and walked away. The Hall emptied quickly; Solinde was dragged away even as she gazed sadly back at him over one shoulder. At length, he was left alone with the jester and the guard to whom the King had whispered.

"I am to give you Lightfoot," said the guard.

"And no doubt to kill him as soon as we enter the stable," commented the dwarf. "You may walk ahead. He will follow at considerable distance."

The guard led the way.

"Well, this is good-by, motley."

"Let's stop with the Oversteward and pick up your knapsack."

They did that.

"I wish I could say good-by to Solinde."

"Perhaps she'll wave from the tower."

But when he looked up toward her room, the window was shuttered.

"I wish . . ."

"That you could undo it all?" supplied the dwarf.

"I don't know. I love her."

"You'll sing your songs much better after this."

"Does it go away—this empty feeling?"

"I don't know."

"Have you ever loved, motley?"

"A few times. A man like me can't really take things like that too seriously."

Alaric glanced at him in surprise and saw a big-headed, funny-looking dwarf and knew he wasn't alone in his despair.

Leading the gray horse, they crossed the drawbridge and stepped onto the dirt road that had brought the minstrel to the castle so many weeks before. It had been deep summer then, but now the wind was chill and winter was near. Dry leaves swirled against their legs.

A clatter of hoofs caused Alaric to glance back once more. It was Jeris, astride a coal-black war horse divested of its heraldic trappings.

"I'll ride a little way with you," he said.

At the dwarf's suggestion, Alaric lifted him up to a perch behind Jeris, and then he mounted his own, smaller nag. In silent companionship, they ambled along the road until the forest closed in and hid the castle from sight, forcing Alaric to stop looking back every few seconds.

"This is as far as I can go," said Jeris when they reached a bend in the road.

Alaric looked up at the Prince, who towered over him much as the King had. He caught the youth's gloved left hand and bowed his head over it. "I'm sorry, my Lord."

Jeris clapped him on the shoulder. "She needed it. And more. We'll miss you, minstrel. She'll plague me with you for a long time, I know. Here, she gave me this for you." From the pouch at his waist he drew a square of black cloth embroidered with fanciful flowers of red, purple, and blue.

"I remember it well. It was for Dall, but now I'm gone, too." He folded it carefully and tucked it inside his lute. "This makes a better favor than a bit of sheeting."

"And from me, I thought you'd find this useful." From the bag on the left side of his saddle, Jeris drew a belt and a sword in a tooled-leather scabbard. "At worst, you can sell it for a reasonable sum." He handed it over.

"And from me," said the dwarf, "this." In his open palm lay the spike that had changed Alaric's fate. "I knew it would be useful someday."

The minstrel drew a deep breath. "You know."

"We know," said Jeris. "Solinde thought your life in danger and confided in us. But I think her fears were groundless—they could never burn you. Am I right?"

Alaric nodded.

"Still, existence as a known which would be unpleasant. As things are, you trail the glory of having seduced a princess, a reputation which will certainly have its advantages." He clasped Alaric's hand. "I want to say that when I am King you'll be welcome here again . . . but Father will probably live a long, long while, and by the time you could return there would be nothing but me and motley to return for. Good luck, my friend, and take care of yourself." He wheeled his horse and galloped away while the jester hung on with one hand and waved with the other.

Alaric pulled his cloak more tightly around his shoulders. A bitter wind was rising.

A colleague once suggested that we use at least one "off-Earth" story in each issue: good advice, except that there are stories that take place off Earth and that read like the rotogravure section of last week's newspaper, so the term is hard to pin down. We know what he meant, but the best way to explain it is to find a story that embodies all the best elements of what is meant by "off Earth," one which is convincingly alien in background and tone and yet which says something very human. To find such a story and point to it and say, "there, that's what we mean!"

Thus Love Betrays Us

PHYLLIS MACLENNAN

It's a strange, sad, lonely world, is Deirdre, forever enshrouded in mists that never lift. There is no day or night. The same dim silvery light seeps always from the pewter sky, casting no shadows and annulling time. The thick, moist atmosphere blots up all sound and muffles the winds into faint-hearted breezes hardly strong enough to sway the pendent branches of the black-barked trees that droop like widows weeping over graves, or rustle the transparent leaves that well from their stems like tears about to fall.

Men have not yet encroached here. Perhaps they never will, but the planet has been charted and described, and research ships have landed. The first of them, the *Magus*, was lost with all hands elsewhere in the system. She stopped at Deirdre before she disappeared and left one man behind, a biologist, her sole survivor; he more than half mad when the search party found him.

When the star Selina was first listed, the *Magus* was ordered to call there for a brief preliminary survey on its way to a more urgent task. Of the system's seven worlds, only one showed life, and Alex Barthold was dropped off to investigate it while the ship made a routine evaluation of the other six.

It was common practice, and he had been left thus before, on worlds more hostile than this one appeared to be. Informed of his assignment, he set up his shelter, checked equipment and supplies, and reported to the captain that everything was in order with the matter-of-factness of habit; nevertheless, when the ship had signed off, he stood at the viewport of the plastic dome to watch her leave with the same involuntary pang of abandonment he had felt the first time and would always feel, no matter how certain he was that he would survive and they would come back for him. The lights on the distant hull glowed faintly through the eternal fog. They were all he could distinguish of the *Magus;* but when the boosters flared, they seared the fog away, and he could see her hoist herself up and squat for a moment on her cushion of flame, like a fat old lady catching her breath before forcing herself into space. She vanished, and the boggy earth quivered beneath his feet in the after-shock like something alive.

He was alone.

He had looked forward to this respite from the cramped quarters of the ship. The dome seemed almost vast in comparison, and there would be relief from the tensions inevitably produced by the confinement and total lack of privacy, the constant noise, the personal frictions that could not be avoided. He would be able to go for long walks, with real gravity tugging at his boots. There would be living things to look at that no man had seen before; and even though the myriad fungus spores that formed the nuclei of the mist droplets forced him to wear a protective suit and filter mask, there was fresh, living air to breathe, untainted by the reek of hot metal, lubricants, and human bodies that no recycling process could ever quite remove. He arranged the few personal belongings he was allowed to bring with him to give the dome an aura of familiarity, put on his suit, stepped through the inner hatch into the lock, and sealed the door behind him with anticipation; but when he opened the outer hatch and stepped onto the virgin soil of Deirdre, it was an anticlimax.

He found no sense of freedom. Fog swallowed him, a milky vagueness in which no object more than ten feet away was clearly seen, which thickened beyond that into a barrier that moved as he moved, walling him in, softly threatening, impenetrable because he could never reach it to test what it was made of. As he stepped forward, dark skeletons of trees flowed into sight. What lurked beyond them? Behind him the outline of the dome was already blurred, as if it melted in the mist. He was suddenly unreasoningly afraid to walk away from it, to leave the reassurance of the warm golden light that beckoned from the viewports. The compass on his gauntlet swung erratically in the weak magnetic field. He dared not depend on it to guide him, but he had the FoolFinder. He bent down and touched the buttons on the heels of his boots. At each step he took, a drop of fluorescent stain would be released to mark his trail. It showed up cold blue-green like insect phosphorescence against the rich tapestry of moss beneath his feet. Only after he had walked around enough to convince the child within him that he could not get lost did he dare move out of visual contact with the shelter.

. . . He did not like Deirdre.

It was not dead. That would have been less disquieting than the waiting stillness that enveloped him. He felt as though something unseen paced him behind the screen of mist, just at the limit of his vision. Drifting on currents beyond his comprehension, the fog thickened and thinned in response to its own will, shaping wraiths of its own substance that seemed solid enough to touch, and then dissolving them as he came closer as if it teased him purposely.

He tried to lose himself in work, but here too Deirdre taunted him. Never had he seen a world so limited in the variety of its flora and fauna. It teemed with life, but most of it was the same. The plants that carpeted the earth in regal splendor were curious forms of algae and lichens, but he could find no true plants. Even the trees were closely related to the mosses, as far as he could tell, and though mosses of such size and toughness were extraordinary, they were all alike. The animal life was equally limited in type—nothing beyond creeping insects, two or three arthropods, and several coelenterates, none larger than a football, and all sluggish enough to make him drowsy watching them.

His specialty was not to have one, to know a little about every aspect of biology; but he did not know any one area of it well enough to make the detailed, exhaustive studies later investigators would undertake, and he came so rapidly to the end of what he was equipped to do that the time he had to wait until the ship returned began to stretch into infinity before him. Bored, restless, increasingly uneasy, he went for long walks, going further and further from the dome in fruitless quest of something new to look at; but Deirdre was everywhere the same. He might have been on a treadmill in some dim, forgotten Limbo. The same dark trees swam up and disappeared behind him, the same fog constantly enshrouded him, the same thick moss sprang back beneath his feet; and in the pale, pearly light, like an eternal dawn, it seemed that Time did not exist. There was only *here, and* now, and the present would never end. He found himself checking his chronometer constantly, but it, too, seemed to have been affected: minutes turned into hours, what seemed like half a day was measured as an hour. The dream-like atmosphere imbued him more and more with a sense of unreality. He blamed it on nerves, on his own more than half illusory sensations; but he could not overcome the developing conviction that something was there, hiding in the mist, just out of sight, seeing him although he could not see it—or them. In the course of his monotonous explorations, he sometimes thought he caught a glimpse of movement from the corner of his eye; but when he turned, there was never anything: a wisp of mist, veils thicker than it had been, but only mist that faded into mist. It frightened him. He grew anxious away from the shelter of the dome, the instruments companionably ticking, the warm, dry air, the light. He ceased to venture out and sealed himself in against the ghostliness of Deirdre to wait for the *Magus'* return.

. . . It was too long. Why did she take so long? They could not have forgotten him. At chronometer noon every twenty-four hours he sent off his I-am-alive-and-well signal. The code-burst acknowledgment came from the computer, he knew; but someone had to log it. If he did not report, if he signaled an emergency, they would notice and come back for him . . . unless something had happened. The ship could be an empty shell, all her crew dead, wandering derelict among the stars. . . . Or perhaps they had never meant to come back for him. Perhaps they had always meant to leave him here alone. There were supplies enough for ten men. Why had they left so much? They always did, he knew that; but still . . . They had told him "ten days to two weeks"; it was ten days by the instruments; and no sign of the *Magus*, no word from her at all.

. . . They couldn't abandon him. He didn't really believe they would. Someone would come for him, eventually; and though, each time he signaled, he was tempted to sound a false emergency that would hurry them, the penalty for that was too severe to risk, as yet.

. . . It was too long. When at last the ship sent back no answer to his daily message, he was not surprised. He had known it wouldn't, he had felt it in his bones, each day the chattering response had startled him more, so sure had he become that it would not be given; and as he tapped his code call out, and repeated it, and repeated it again, and still no answer came, he felt a sick satisfaction now that his fears had been realized. He had suspected that he was somehow doomed to this murky hell of solitude and uncertainty. He had been dropped out of life, shunted aside into nowhere, cursed for crimes committed in the past. . . . What crimes, what misdeeds warranted such punishment? He thought back, and they were many, trival once, but looming larger now: crimes of omission as well as of commission; people he had hurt, unknowing or uncaring; tasks he had slighted; responsibilities he had slid out from under—the list was endless. In this gray, haunted world, his self confronted him and there was no escape. He could not face himself, so naked and alone.

In the back of his head some shred of sanity reminded him that he would not be left here forever, sooner or later another ship would come, no matter what had happened to the *Magus*. He knew that; but, sure as he was of it, he did not believe it.

fMes

The time would come—but there was no Time on Deirdre. Nothing ever ended. He was trapped in an eternal present; the chronometer lied, and not a day had passed since the *Magus* had taken off . . .

But there *would* be a ship. It would materialize out of the fog, and men would step out of it and check the beacon to see how long it had been sending its plaintive cry into the void. Where would he be then? What would he be? Would they know that a man had been left here by himself? Would they think to look for him? He sealed the logs he had kept to date and carried them to the beacon. The FoolFinder would disappear in time. Compass headings would be useless; still he tried to work them out, to devise some way to tell them where to find him. From spare parts he jury-rigged a small homing device for the dome and hooked it into his power pack. Then there was nothing more he could do, except fight to retain his sanity; for he could feel his mind slipping away.

He played films, he played tapes, at high volume, drowning himself in them to shut out awareness of Deirdre—or rather, the realization that there was nothing there, that what he shut out was nothingness, emptiness . . . and looked within himself and saw his soul draw closer and closer in upon itself, shrinking into a hard, bright jewel at the center of his being that not even he could touch, hiding itself away; and he was afraid.

The hemisphere of his shelter was no longer a refuge. It was a trap. There was no safety in it, only a danger greater than any he had known, and of a different kind, harder to fight because it lay within himself, a part of his own essence. Driven to escape, he suited up and fled into the spectral landscape where the fog-figures beckoned. He saw them almost clearly now: pale, childish shadows slipping behind the trees, always just at the limit of his vision, as if they knew he sought them, and mocked him, teasing, whispering, "I am here, but you will never reach me."

They withheld themselves, and he pursued them, surer and surer that they were concrete. They *had* to be. . . . There was one that seemed to wait. He could—not quite—distinguish its slender man-shape, mist-colored, but not mist. As he approached, it drew away, eluding him; yet still it led him on. He followed patiently, keeping his distance so as not to frighten it; and as it seemed to sense that he would not press too closely, its caution lessened. It moved forward stealthily, but with purpose, intent upon some errand of its own, pausing from time to time to look and listen, though its wariness seemed not to be of him. Each time it hesitated, he approached it nearer, until he could see it clearly.

. . . It was beautiful. Under translucent skin, blue-white as watered milk, shapes of internal organs pulsed in faint tints of blue and green and gold. Poised, its back to him, it was a statue carved from living opal; then it turned its head. He shrank away. Such faces he had seen in dreams of ghosts when, child-like, he shuddered at the dark: white; featureless, except for round, fathomless black eyes like peepholes into Hell. It did not fear him. The slight relaxation of its posture told him that, although it still was timid. It was not hostile. If it had been, it would have attacked before. How could he fear it, when it appeared almost to trust him?

It was real. It was alive. It studied him intently, and he marveled that it should be so bold. How must he look to it? A snouted monster nearly twice its size, lumbering blindly through its territory, breath soughing through the filter mask—in its nightmares, if it had them, could it imagine anything so alien?

It was alive, and near him . . . not much less human than an ape. If he could win its confidence, befriend it . . . he would not fear it. He stretched his hands out, palms upward. It slid away, a supple, darting movement like a snake's, putting itself beyond his reach, yet staying with him. It looked at him and turned, as if in invitation. Taking the gesture so, he followed as it wandered through the trees. Watchful, it seemed to scout for enemies, but not to count him one. He felt himself obscurely flattered by this tenuous companionship, like walking with a cat that accompanies because it chooses, not at command. When they came to the village, it had somehow maneuvered him into the lead, so that he entered first and realized with shock just where he was: in an inhabited place.

. . . Or one that had been inhabited. He stared, dumb-struck, at the crude, box-like dwellings huddled around him, for dwellings they must have been. Hacked out of a coarse, fibrous stuff like hardened peat, they had doors, but no windows. He went into one of them and saw scattered on the floor objects designed for uses he could only guess at, and they were real. For a brief panic-stricken moment he had thought himself hallucinating, but these huts were no illusion. As material as his own familiar shelter, they had been constructed by sentients who knew the use of tools; but the builders were no longer there. Where had they gone, and why? When had they left? A lifetime ago, or only as he came? There was no way of knowing.

The being that had led him there stood waiting, as if impatient to go on. He followed once again, wondering where it wished to take him, until they came upon a wide depression in the ground like nothing he had seen before on Deirdre. Scattered pools of condensed moisture dimpled the moss, surrounded by a profusion of large, bulbous lichens quite unlike those he had already found and taken samples of. The mist-child gathered some of these and ate, cramming food into a lipless mouth stretched like a seam across the empty face, continually glancing at the clouded edges of the clearing as if it feared attack. Its suspicion was contagious. Alex found himself peering around, not knowing what he looked for, thinking of predators, and thus unprepared to see another man-thing hurl itself from among the trees upon its feeding victim. On impulse, he thrust himself between the attacker and its prey. It skidded to a stop, and pulled back, snarling. As he advanced on it, it darted toward the trees, then whirled to face him. Something evil glittered in its paw. He had no choice now but to face it down, he raised both arms and roared. It bolted into the secret safety of the fog.

Behind him, the creature he protected crouched huddled in upon itself, head buried in its arms, shivering like a dog expecting to be beaten. He bent and placed his hand upon its back, wanting to reassure it. It shrieked—in fear, or pain?—and oozed flat to the ground as if it deliquesced. What should he do? He dared not leave it. The enemy still watched. He could not see it, but he felt its hating eyes upon him. He waited. The mist-thing sprawled abandoned at his feet, a rag doll waiting to be painted and dressed into a semblance of humanity. Beneath its hide the delicate colors pulsed and wavered, then grew stronger as it returned to consciousness. The outer integument tensed. It flowed upright, peered into the mist, and shuddered.

Alex would have left it then, but as he retraced his course by gleaming flecks of FoolFinder, it slunk behind him as if it found safety in his presence; and when they reached the dome, it sought to interpose itself between him and the hatch so that he could not enter. He motioned it aside. When it refused to move, he stretched out his hand to touch it, and it pulled back, whimpering, far enough for him to reach the release. The hatch irised open. As he stepped inside, the aggressor, who had stubbornly pursued them, slid from the mist and launched itself at them. The mist-thing dashed inside, cowered behind him, moaning in panic, heedless of any but the imminent danger, and Alex slapped the hatch shut, then automatically pulled the lever to turn on the fungicide. Spray hissed from the nozzles all around them, foaming as it struck upon their bodies; and the beast went wild. The lock was barely big enough for two, and as it dashed itself from wall to wall, Alex was forced to seize it to keep it from hurting itself. It turned upon him then. It threw its paws up. Tentacle-digits furled back, and from the center of them, like an ugly flower, a long, sharp tooth flashed forth, serrated on the edges, wickedly pointed. They stood, body to body, frozen an instant, human eyes and Deirdran locked on each other. The spray clicked off, and as if that were a signal, both relaxed. Alex sighed with relief. The thing was as slippery as wet glass—he could not have held it—strong as an octopus and if he had known about its hidden weapons, he would never have dared to touch it.

As he stripped his suit off and draped it on the hooks, the mist-thing pressed its back against the wall and watched, more curious than afraid. Either it was more intelligent than he had suspected, or he was too strange for it to fear him. In either case, now that it was inside and disinfected, he could not open the hatch to let it out without contaminating the lock again; and so he left it there, opened the inner seal, and stepped into the shelter to go about his business, such as it was. He logged the day's events, prepared his meal and ate it, all the while conscious of another presence. Almost transparent, it slipped into the room, an incorporeal substance drifting along the wall like ectoplasm, not quite touching what it studied, lipless mouth half open as if it sniffed or tasted the unfamiliar atmosphere and new, pungent odors. The process of eating over, he slipped a reel of film into the viewer and settled back to watch it—but more to observe the reaction of his visitor. The sounds and the shifting patterns on the screen meant nothing to it, he could see that; but it coiled itself down onto the floor beside him, glancing from the viewer into his face and back, as if it sought some explanation . . .

He hardly dared to hope, but there was nothing lost by trying. He turned the film off, waited a moment, then tapped himself on the chest.

"Alex."

His throat was tight, the word came out half croak, half whisper. He tried again.

"Alex," he repeated, pointing to himself; and—

"Sessiné," it answered.

They were friends.

It was as simple and as natural as that, a relationship that grew from that first small seed of understanding and bound them together in a kind of sharing Alex did not attempt to analyze. There was no need. Sessiné was there. Slowly, in halting steps, he learned to communicate with "him," as, language-bound to sex identification, he thought of his outwardly genderless companion. He had no hope of ever reproducing the half-whispered, bubbling sounds made by the Deirdran, but Sessiné picked up a smattering of Galactic and enriched it constantly as Alex talked to him; and talk he did. In the unmeasured hours they passed together, he confided to this alien being things he had never told to anyone of his own kind, male or female. It listened patiently, deep eyes fixed on his, attentive, whether it knew the meaning of his words or not; and he felt that it did understand, that on an unspoken level it knew his loneliness and shared it, so that he was no longer by himself.

Perhaps the love that grew in him for this inhuman creature was largely based on gratitude. How deep that gratitude was! To hear a voice not his own, pronouncing words that he had not invented, framing thoughts not his; to know a living, sentient presence near him always—although he could not often bring himself to touch it. The texture of its cold, rubbery flesh recalled too sharply how alien it was. He did not wish to be reminded that it was not like him, but made of a different substance, born on a world of which he knew too little. He wanted to learn more, and Sessiné tried to teach him; but much of what the mist-child told him was as far beyond his comprehension as his own maunderings must have been to it. The pattern of life on Deirdre as Sessiné described it baffled him. He wanted to go back to the village, to observe and cross-check some of the apparently conflicting information given him. He could not even guess the level of intelligence. If he could meet others, he might be better able to judge; but Sessiné refused to guide him there, telling him it was useless.

"They are not there," he insisted. "You come, they go. They see . . . these marks—" he pointed to the slight corrugations of the protective suit—"They think are many brands, you are one of those who do not stop to kill. It happens sometimes. But Sessiné comes close when you do *so*—" He imitated Alex collecting specimens—"You look at other things, you do not see Sessiné. I look, and I think that those are not brands on you. You have no brand at all. I know you may not kill, but those others do not know that, and they are afraid."

"Brand?" Alex was puzzled.

"As in the film you showed me. But we are not like those beasts, we go by ourselves to the Place at the Time of Branding, and we are not afraid when the Oldest marks our skin with the water that burns." He held his arm out proudly for inspection. Alex had briefly noted the narrow scar and taken for granted it was the result of accident. He examined it now with more care and saw with revulsion how the gelatinous tissue had been seared away in a deep groove, rough-edged and charred.

"That was done *deliberately?* But . . . why?"

Sessiné was surprised by his reaction.

"It is true I am not big, not strong. I am easy to kill. But—" he groped to express a concept Alex had not taught him words for—"out of myself I made others like me . . . you understand? When that was done, at the next Time of Branding I went to the Place. Now this mark says that I must kill or one will kill me. . . . You do not understand? It is so: with no brand at all, I may not kill, none may kill me. With many brands—*so*—" he indicated that both arms would be stripped from wrist to shoulder—"I do not kill, none may kill me. . . . But Sessiné will not have many brands," he said, apparently resigned to the idea. "At the next Time, one will come to the Oldest to show him this—" he pointed to the scar—"that he has cut from me, and the Oldest will burn on his arm that he has killed this one."

"But *why?*" Alex was horrified. To destroy life was repellent to him. He did it when he had to: for food, if necessary; to collect specimens for research; in self-defense, if there were no other way; but to kill wantonly, merely for the record, as these people seemed to do, was an act that shocked him deeply.

Sessiné was clearly puzzled by his ignorance.

"It must be so. How else could it be?"

They stared at each other in silence, Alex aware as he had not been before of the gulf between them. Sessiné tried to explain; he seemed to sense Alex's repugnance and to want to dispel it.

"It is good so," he urged him to believe. "Those who have killed many times grow tired of the taste of death. They have no wish to kill, and none may kill them. Where they want to go, they go. What they want to do, they do. They lie down to sleep and know that they will awaken. They feed, and if another comes they eat together, they need not run with the food sour inside them. They may be together with another as Sessiné is now with Alex. That is very good. Is it not so?"

"Yes. It is so," Alex admitted. It *was* good to be together with Sessiné, and he was touched and shyly pleased to hear the Deirdran say that it seemed good to him as well. It was a pleasure Sessiné was not likely to survive to enjoy with one of his own kind, he realized. On their excursions to the feeding ground, he noted that Sessiné grew increasingly less cautious, feeling himself secure in Alex's presence; and as his carelessness increased, Alex was compelled to be more watchful.

He knew that they were spied on, that every time they left the dome a hidden enemy trailed them—but never more than one, since only one could claim the brand Sessiné bore. That one must be more brave or else more desperate than its fellows to risk the threat that Alex posed; and, like Sessiné, it might someday conclude that threat was empty. If it should attack . . . he would be forced to kill it. He had no choice. The tight-beam ultrasonic handgun he always carried now was vicious in its effect at full intensity, but he dared not turn it down; for once the thing came at them, he could not give it a second chance. One opening in his suit to let the fungus in would do for him, and Sessiné could never hold his own in battle; he was so sure of this himself that he would submit without struggle to the blades of an assassin. He could not let that happen. If either of them should die, the other was lost.

For Sessiné the matter was simple enough: he would be killed as soon as he lost his protector. For Alex, the prospect was more frightening. He did not like to think about it. . . . A ship would come. Only on Deirdre the present never ended; on other worlds it fled into the past. The silence of the *Magus* would be noted, her course followed until some remnant, some wreckage or survivors had been found. The seekers would trace her path here to the beacon, and they would look for him, his life or death a question they must answer; and when they found him . . . When? If nothing marked the flow of Time, it might as well be never. Without companionship he knew that he could not endure this never-ending *now*.

Those who had lived in the village had not yet been branded, and although Sessiné insisted the huts had been abandoned since he came there, he still had hopes of making contact with some other Deirdrans. He had no trade goods, but he collected a few things he thought might catch their interest: bright, shining wire, gaudy scraps of plastic, a small flashlight, colored pens and paper. He left them in the center of the village and went back now and then to see if they had been touched.

On one such tour of inspection, he decided it would be his last. His trinkets lay as he had left them, the wire corroded, the paper mildewed, mold tracing the convolutions of his fingerprints across the gleaming plastic like an arcane message no one here could read, or wanted to. With disappointment verging on despair, he gave up hope. He would have only Sessiné . . . but where was he? In the brief seconds during which he had let his attention wander the fool had disappeared, probably heading toward the feeding ground alone, so overconfident had he grown of late. Alex swore silently and ran to find his friend, but those few seconds were what the enemy had waited for. As

Alex burst from in between the huts, he saw two figures struggling on the ground. He shouted, fell upon them, tore them
apart and flung one to each side before they knew he was there.
Sessiné lay where he had fallen, cowed, whimpering, arms
wrapped around his head. Not so the attacker. As Alex turned
to face it, it launched itself at him. He saw it vividly as it
hurtled toward him: the opal-hued translucence of its body, its
outstretched arms, one branded to the shoulder, the other almost
to the elbow—and the tooth-daggers, deadly ivory, pointed at
his chest.

He slapped the plastic sheath, the gun leaped to his hand. The
enemy was upon him. He pushed the gun into its belly and fired.
The ultrasonics shook it apart. He pushed it from him. It stood
upright a moment, the tension of its skin still holding it together, its insides shivered into jelly; then it slid shapeless to the
ground, a bag of skin, its substance liquefied inside it.

Sessiné stepped from behind him.

"At the Time of Branding, many will fear me when I show
this."

He bent over the dead creature and with a grunt of satisfaction sliced away the brands that had adorned its arms, when
they were arms.

As his palm-dagger slashed into the skin, the nauseous mess
within gushed forth. Alex had to vomit, he could not control it.
He tore his faceplate open just in time and blurted out the contents of his stomach until dry retching produced no more than
drops of bitter bile. Relieved, the spasms over, he straightened
up and took a deep, clean breath—only to be shocked by a new,
more personal horror: he breathed the raw air of Deirdre, and it
smelled of Death.

Death was the close companion of men who traveled space.
They died predictably, in accidents, and in strange, ugly, painful ways that no one knew of until they happened. But he had
known. Still on the ship, before he had set foot on the planet
itself, he had seen the cultures under their sealed covers swarm
almost instantly with fungi as the voracious spores from the air
samples settled on them. The surface of Deirdre was nothing but
mold, one solid blanket of it. The animals that lived on it were
safe only because their surfaces were too acid for it; but his

skin, his lungs, his mouth and nose and eyes, provided ideal conditions. He had known that, and he had forgotten it, and that was how men died.

Cold sweat broke out all over him, even on his arms and legs, and his knees turned to water. His fingers trembled; he pushed the faceplate home but could not close the catch. There were fungicides and antibiotics in the dome, ample supplies of them for just such an accident as this, but could he reach them? How much time did he have? He was shaking, too weak with fear to walk; but with Sessiné to help, he could still make it. The mist-creature stood several feet away from him, fondling its trophies. He stretched his hands toward it.

"Sessiné!"

It seemed that it did not hear him, that it slid away, starting to fade into the mist.

"Sessiné!"

It heard. It looked at him, blank face unreadable.

"Help me!"

He could hardly breathe, his eyes were filming over—but surely that was his imagination, the fungus could not have taken hold so fast. He felt himself waver, sank to the ground, reaching out . . .

"You are killed."

Its voice was cold and flat; it stated a fact that was of no importance to it.

"No . . . not yet. Not yet! Help me to walk, help me get to the dome. I'll be all right if I get there."

"No. You are killed," it repeated. "Others watch. They see that you are weak; they do not fear you now. If Sessiné stays with you, one will kill him."

"No one will kill you! I will kill them first, I have the gun!"

It lay on the ground where he had dropped it when he started to vomit. He wormed toward it, but even as he spoke Sessiné had seen it and picked it up. The alien handled the small weapon carefully, and Alex could have sworn it smiled.

"With this, Sessiné will kill many. At the next Time of Branding, all will fear him."

"You fool! You don't even know how to use it!"

"It has a button. All your things have buttons to make them do what you want. Sessiné can use it."

It turned away. It really meant to leave him there to die alone. There was no doubt of that.

Alex coughed. His throat felt full of slime, his words pushed bubbling through it.

"You stinking, soulless hunk of protoplasm! Why don't you shoot me while you're at it? You need the practice!"

It didn't even bother to look back at him.

"You have no brand," it stated and vanished in the fog.

Alex stared after it, numb with disbelief. It could not leave him now, it *could* not, when it would take so little effort to save him! . . . But it had done so.

Don't go! Please don't leave me!" he screamed soundlessly. He closed his eyes against the tears that filled them and felt that he dropped through a black, bottomless abyss, desperate, reaching out for something to hold on to; but there was nothing there, nothing to cling to, nobody to save him . . .

. . . Except himself. He would not die, he *would not!* Rage flooded him, and he drew strength from it.

"I'll make it without you, you bastard! Who the hell needs you? You're not even human! Fifty brands I need before they'll talk to me? Then fifty brands I'll have—and yours will be the first!"

It was too hard to struggle to his feet, and if he did he knew that he would fall. But he would make it. On hands and knees, on his belly, if he had to; but he would get there. It wasn't all that far, the fungus couldn't kill him that fast, he wouldn't let it. He only imagined that he suffocated. Although his breath came hard, he still was breathing . . .

He started forward. He and Sessiné had come this way so often, they had begun to leave a trail. Along the shadow of a path drops of FoolFinder still glistened. He would not get lost. He crawled, and as he crawled he talked sometimes to Sessiné in his head, to remind himself that he had something still to live for, something that he must do:

"That gun won't last forever . . . but while it lasts, use it, you son of a bitch—use it, and keep yourself alive until I can come after you. Because I'm going to. I'm going to get you . . . I'm

*going to cut that goddamn brand off you and stuff it down your
miserable throat . . ."*

His lungs were filling, his eyes and nose and mouth, even his
ears were all encrusted. Sick and tired and aching everywhere,
he sank flat to the ground to rest, and he was crying. The hot,
salt tears cleared out his eyes and nose a little. He had not even
tried to close his faceplate—what did it matter now? He forced
himself up as far as he was able and coughed and coughed and
coughed, bringing up great lumps of green slime from his lungs.
He was exhausted, he could not go on . . . He fell back to the
earth and thought of Sessiné, who could have helped him . . .
Flat on his belly, he dug his elbows into the yielding moss, pulled
himself forward, braced his feet, pulled himself forward . . . His
eyes were clouding over, he had to blink and blink again to keep
them clear so he could distinguish the path, he had to stop and
cough from time to time to clear his lungs, but he kept breathing. In his mind's eye, even more clearly than he saw the trail, he
saw a strip of transparent skin and a thin, black scar etched on it.
He crawled to reach it, concentrating on it, blotting out the pain
from his chafed elbows, his tortured lungs. He inched himself
forward, stopped to cough and wipe his burning eyes, inched
himself forward . . .

. . . There was no time, no distance, only slow, hurting movement. It would have been so easy to give up, to sink into the
spongy moss, let it enfold him, wrap itself gently around him
and make him one with it . . . He thought of it; the thought was
sweet; but part of himself watched, as from a distance, and
coldly, detachedly, would not let it happen. God, how he wanted
to die! But he would not.

. . . The dome was there. Warm light streamed from the
viewports, inside were rest and safety and means to kill the
tenacious fibers that wove into his flesh and sucked his
strength away. Three feet above him, on the dull gray plastic
surface, the metal plate to touch to reach that haven twinkled,
remote, unfeeling as a star. He squeezed himself against the
place where the hatch would open, forced his feet under him,
and, remembering Sessiné, pushed himself upward until his hand
lay on it. The hatch irised open to receive him, and he fell
through into the womb that was the lock.

Pain. Fever. Nausea. Delirium.

. . . *He was well and strong. He suited up and left the dome and found the feeding ground. He lay in ambush until Sessine appeared; sprang at him, caught him, choked him, the lipless mouth wide open, screaming, the deep-set eyes popped out like grapes squeezed from their skins . . . But was it Sessine?*

. . . *He found the Place of Branding; it swarmed with Deirdrans weaving in a slow dance like mummies resuscitated by a necromancer. Sessine swaggered forward to be branded, carrying a slimy bundle of fresh trophies. As he stretched his arm out to be honored, Alex let fly at him with a needlegun, and from a thousand tiny wounds his inner stuff spewed out as he sank screaming to the ground . . . But was it Sessine?*

. . . *He found the village. Sessine sat in the central clearing, surrounded by smaller versions of himself, boasting of his exploits. Alex dragged him away, crushed the life from him as he screamed for mercy . . . But was it Sessine?*

They found him screaming in the dome, screaming and screaming. The medic who was with them listened to him for a while, then quietly disposed of the little heap of unspeakable things he found beneath the bunk. There was no need for anyone to know about them, he decided.

Especially not Alex.

"I suppose the least we can do is name the damned thing after poor Dembar."

About nine years ago, Alfred Bester stopped writing fantasy and sf to become an editor at Holiday Magazine. *He didn't cut down; he just stopped. Thus we were both surprised and delighted to get a recent letter from Mr. Bester that began:* "Holiday *has moved to Indianapolis, and after one look at that mighty metrop. I politely refused to go along as Senior Editor. So I've gone back to honest fiction writing . . ."* Indianapolis, we love you.

The Animal Fair

ALFRED BESTER

> I went to the animal fair.
> The birds and the beasts were there.
> By the light of the moon,
> The big baboon,
> Was combing his golden hair.
>
> The monkey he got drunk,
> And climbed up the elephant's trunk.
> The elephant sneezed
> And fell on his knees,
> But what became of the monk?

TRADITIONAL NURSERY SONG

There is a high hill in Bucks County, Pennsylvania, that is called Red Hill because it is formed of red shale, which is a kind of stone. There is an abandoned farm on top of the hill which is called Red Hill farm. It was deserted many years ago when the children of farmers decided that there was more excitement and entertainment in the cities.

Red Hill farm has an old stone house with thick walls, oaken floors and the enormous fireplaces in which the cooking was done two hundred years ago. There is a slate-roofed smokehouse behind it in which hams should be hung. There is a small red barn cluttered with forgotten things like children's sleighs and pieces of horses' harness, and there is a big red barn which is the Big Red Schoolhouse.

Here the ladies and gentlemen who possess the farm in fact, if not in fee simple absolute, hold meetings by day and night to discuss problems of portent and to educate their children. But you must understand that they speak the language of creatures which few humans can hear or understand. Most of us learned it when we were young but lost it as it was replaced by human speech. A rare few can still speak both, and this is our story.

The meetings in the Big Red Schoolhouse are governed by the Chairman, a ring-necked cock pheasant who is all pomp and strut. He is secretly referred to as "The Sex Maniac" because he maintains a harem of five hens. The Professor is a white rat who escaped from the Rutgers university laboratories after three years of intensive education. He believes that he is qualified for a Ph.D. and is considering doing his dissertation "On the Relevance of Hot Water to Science."

George Washington Woodchuck is the peerless surveyor of Red Hill farm. He knows every inch of its forty acres and is the arbiter of all territorial disputes. The Senior Rabbit, who is occasionally called "The Scoutmaster," is the mentor of morality and much alarmed by the freedom and excesses of the Red Hill young. "I will not," he says, "permit Red Hill to become another Woodstock." He also deplores modern music.

There are many other members of the Big Red Schoolhouse— deer, who have darling manners but are really awfully dumb. The intellectuals call them "The debutantes." Moses Mole, who is virtually blind, as all moles are, is pestering the Professor to teach him astronomy. "But how can I teach you astronomy when you can't even see the stars?" "I don't want to be an observing astronomer. I want to be a mathematical astronomer like Einstein." It looks as though the Professor will have to introduce a course in the New Math.

There are a Cardinal and a Brown Thrasher who have mean tempers and are always picking fights. The Cardinal is called "His Eminence," of course, and the Brown Thrasher is nicknamed "Jack Johnson." It's true that Jack Johnson has a rotten disposition but he sings beautifully and conducts regular vocal classes. On the other hand the voice of His Eminence can only be called painful.

The Chaldean Chicken is a runaway from a battery down the road and she's a real mixed-up girl. She's a White Leghorn and had the misfortune at an early age to discover that Leghorn is a place in Italy. Consequently she speaks a gibberish which she believes is fluent Italian. "Ah, *caro mio, come est? Benny*, I hope. *Grazie*. And with *meeyo* is *benny* too." She's called the Chaldean because she's spaced out on astrology, which infuriates the Professor. "Ah, *caro mio*, you will never be *sympathetico* with him. You are Gasitorius and he is Zapricorn."

The cleverest members of the Big Red Schoolhouse are the crows who are witty and talkative and sound like an opening night party at a theatrical restaurant. Unfortunately they are not respected by the Establishment which regards them as "mere mummers" who are likely to try to borrow something (never returned) and who turn serious discussions into a minstrel show. It must be admitted that when two crows get together they begin to behave like Endmen in search of an Interlocutor, convulsing themselves with ancient gags.

"Which do you like, the old writers or the new writers?"

"My brother's got that."

"Got what?"

"Neuritis."

Caw! Caw! Caw!

"How many children do you have?"

"I have five, thank you."

"Don't thank me, friend. Don't thank me."

Caw! Caw! Caw!

It was on an evening in May when the light is long and the shadows even longer that the Chairman entered the Big Red

Schoolhouse attended by his harem. Everyone was there and deeply involved in a discussion of a proposal by the Professor. It was that they should establish an Underground Railroad, something like the Abolitionists, to enable other escapees to reach freedom. Moe Mole, who is rather literal-minded, was pointing out that it would be extremely difficult for him to dig tunnels big enough to accommodate railroad cars. "I saw one once. They're as big as houses." Jack Johnson was needling His Eminence to give flying lessons to all refugees, regardless of race, creed or species. Two black crows were cawing it up. In short, it was a typical Red Barn gathering.

"I call this meeting to order with important news," the Chairman said. "I say, Kaff Kaff, with vital intelligence. Flora, do sit down. Oh, sorry. Frances, do sit— Felicia? Oh, Phyllis. Yes. Quite. Kaff Kaff. Do sit down, Phyllis. This morning a Cadillac drove up the lane leading to Red Hill farm—"

"Two hundred and thirty-five-point-nine yards," Geo. W. Woodchuck said, "bearing east-south-east. Latitude—"

"Yes, yes, my dear George. It was followed by a Volvo containing—"

"Which do you like, a Cadillac or a Volvo?"

"My father's got that."

"Got what?"

"A cadillac condition."

Caw! Caw! Caw!

"Gentlemen! Gentlemen! Please! This is serious. The Cadillac contained a real estate agent. The foreign vehicle contained a man, a woman and an extremely small child, sex as yet undetermined. It is my judgment, Kaff Kaff, I say, my measured opinion that our farm is being shown for sale."

"May is a bad month for buying," the Chaldean Chicken declared. "*Importanto* decisions should be *reservato* for the Sign of Jemimah."

"The word is Gemini," the Professor shouted. "The least you can do is get your superstitions straight."

"You are a male chauvinist rat," Miss Leghorn retorted, "And I am going to form a Chickens' Lib."

"Yes, yes, my dear. And I will be the first to contribute to your worthy cause. Never mind that look, Frances— Oh, Fifi?

There is no need for a Pheasants' Lib movement. You are already liberated. Kaff Kaff. Now, ladies and gentlemen, we are involved in, I say, we are committed to a struggle for the preservation of our property. We must not permit any strangers (I might almost call them Squatters) to invade us. We must make the land as unattractive as possible, and this will demand sacrifices."

"Name one that you'll make," the Professor demanded.

"I will name several. Ladies," here the Chairman addressed himself to the does. "Please do not permit yourselves to be seen. The human animal is always enchanted by your beauty and glamour."

The debutantes giggled prettily.

"My dear Scoutmaster," the Chairman went on to the Senior Rabbit, "the same holds true for yourself and your entire troop. Please disappear until further notice. No more jamborees on the lawns. I, of course, will make a similar sacrifice. I shall conceal my blazing magnificence. Kaff Kaff."

Moe Mole said, "I'm always concealed."

"To be sure. To be sure. But Moses, would it be possible for you to tunnel all the grounds, raising those unsightly mounds? You will have to double your efforts but it would be most helpful."

"I'll get the brothers from Moles Anonymous to lend a hand."

"Splendid. Splendid. Now, George W., I ask this as a special favor. Would you be kind enough to give up your invaluable surveying for the nonce, I say, Kaff Kaff, temporarily, and eat the daffodils?"

"I hate the taste."

"I don't blame him," the Senior Rabbit said. "They're disgusting."

"But so appealing visually to the human eye. You don't have to actually devour them, George; just cut them down and chew a little. I will do the same for the lilacs, under cover of darkness, of course, and my dear ladies will assist."

Jack Johnson said, "What about me and His Eminence?"

"His Eminence will remain out of sight but will sing. You will remain in sight but will not sing."

"I'm as pretty as that Jesuit."

"Yeah? You want to prove it? Step outside."

"Gentlemen. Gentlemen. Please! We are concerting an all-out attack. Now our members of Actors Equity will continue their customary depredations, concentrating on the apple, pear and peach trees."

"We ought to eat the corn, too."

"I'm not going to eat you, friend."

Caw! Caw! Caw!

"Miss Leghorn will remain out of sight. There is nothing more appealing to the human animal than a chicken meditating on a summer day. Oh, and Jack, dear boy, will you try to dispossess the Mocking bird? There is nothing more appealing than a Mocking bird serenading on a summer night."

"Why don't he ever join up?"

"I have solicited him many times and he has always refused. I'm afraid he'll refuse to be drafted now."

"I'll chase him all the way to Canada."

"I shall continue to supervise the campaign from my command post in Freda's—ah, Francie's—ah, from my command post under the lilac bush. I assure you, ladies and gentlemen, we cannot fail. Meeting adjourned."

They failed, of course. Those losers from the Big City took two looks at Red Hill farm and fell in love with it. They saw the miniature hog-backs that Moe Mole had dug and loved them. "Moles have their rights," the husband said. They saw George W. decimating the daffodils. "Woodchucks have their rights," the wife said. "Next year we'll plant enough for us and him." The Kaff Kaff of the Chairman doing his best to destroy the lilacs put them in ecstasies. Flashing glimpses of the does and their fawns hiding in the woods enchanted them. "Do you think they'll all let us live here with them?" the wife asked.

They bought the farm at a high price ($1,000 an acre) with the help of a mortgage, moved in all their possessions and took up residence. Almost immediately there were hammerings and sawings inside the house and flutters of wash outside, hung on a line strung between a couple of oak trees.

They were a family of four. The head of the house was a Burmese cat, all tan and brown with golden eyes, who ruled with an imperious hand. Then there came the husband and wife, and a small boy aged two years who ruled the Burmese. The news of the cat rather disturbed the Big Red Schoolhouse which is not fond of predators. They are all vegetarians, and the Chaldean Chicken has formed an association called OFFO, which stands for Organic Foods For Oll. In the opinion of the Professor Miss Leghorn is ineducable.

"No, it's nothing to worry about," George W. assured the assembled. "She's a right royalty."

"Royalty?"

"I had a long talk with her through the screen door. She's some kind of Burmese Princess, and if the Burmese were ever hunters it's been bred out of her."

"She says. Behind a door."

"No. I helped her get it open and we had a real friendly time until the lady ran out and grabbed her and put her back in the house. She was mad."

"Why?"

"Well, it seems that these Burmese types are very highclass and they don't let them out. They're afraid she'll catch hemophilia or something. The Princess is kind of lonely. We ought to do something for her."

"Hemophilia is not contagious," the Professor said. "It is a congenital characteristic transmitted through the female chromosome."

"So, all right. Leukemia or something."

"What about the family?"

"The Princess says they're a little loose. The name is Dupree. He's Constantine and she's Constance, so they call each other Connie and the Princess never knows where she's at."

"And the kid?"

"He's a boy and he's got six names."

"Six?"

"They call him after some kind of poem, which I think is a pretty rotten scene: James James Morrison Morrison Weatherby George."

"That's four names," the Professor objected.

"But mathematically speaking," Moe Mole began, "it really counts up to—"

"All right. All right. Six. How old is he?"

"Two."

"What does he do?"

"Not much. Just crawls around."

"At two? Arrested. What does the father do?"

"He's an editor."

"What's that?"

"You know those pieces of paper we see sometimes with print on them like; Tomato Ketchup, Net Wt. 32 Oz. or Pall Mall Famous Cigarettes—Wherever Particular People Congregate?"

"Whatever they mean. And?"

"The Princess says somebody has to be in charge of the print. That's an editor."

"What does she do?"

"Who?"

"The other Connie."

"She pastes food on paper."

"She what?"

"That's what the Princess said."

"Pastes food on paper?"

"The Princess says it tastes real good."

"She is not pasting food on paper," the Professor said. "She is making paintings." He turned to Geo. Woodchuck. "In my opinion your friend, the Burmese Princess, is an ass."

"She wants to meet you. Her Connie, the man, went to Rutgers, too."

"Did he, now? Was he Phi Beta Kappa? No matter. Perhaps we can arrange something."

"He doesn't speak our language."

"Too bad. Can he learn? How old is he?"

"Around thirty."

The Professor shook his head. "A Senior Citizen. Too late."

At this point one of the Endmen said, "A funny thing is happening on its way to the barn."

They all stared at him.

"Something's coming," he explained.

They looked through the slit in the barn door. A curious creature, pink and naked, was crawling across the lawn in their direction.

"Where? Where?" Moe Mole asked.

"Bearing south-south-west," George W. told him.

"What is it?"

"It's a Monster!" Miss Leghorn cried.

The Monster crawled through the slit, stopped, rested and panted. Then he looked at the assembly. The assembly examined him.

"It's James James Morrison Morrison Weatherby George," the Woodchuck said. "I saw him hugging the Princess."

"Da," the Monster said pleasantly.

"An obvious illiterate," the Professor said peevishly. "It can't speak. Let's adjourn."

"I can too speak," James said in the creature tongue. "Why are you so mean to me?"

"My dear Monster," the Professor apologized handsomely, "I had no idea. I beg you to forgive me."

"Da," James said.

"But of course," the White Rat explained. "Science always finds the answer. He can speak to us but he can't speak to his own kind."

"Da," James said.

"You've got to speak our language, buddy-boy," Jack Johnson said.

"We think he's cute in any language," the debutantes tittered.

"Ladies," the Monster said. "I thank you for the generous compliment. I am but a simple soul, but I am not impervious to flattery from such glorious females as you. In this hurly-burly world of conflict and confrontation it is a comfort for a lonely creature like myself to know that there are yet a few who are capable of relating and communicating."

"His primitive eloquence goes to the heart," said a fawn, batting her eyes at James.

"Where the hell did you get that fancy spiel?" one of the Endmen demanded.

"From my father's editorials," James grinned. "He reads them out loud to my mother."

"Honest and modest," the Scoutmaster said. "I approve of that."

"Hey, Monster, what's it like living with human types? Is it different?"

"I don't know, sir. I've never lived with anything else."

"What about that Princess? The Burmese type."

"Oh, she's just a flirt. She's visceratonic; that is, she operates from instinctive rather than intellectual motivation."

"Jeez!" Jack Johnson exclaimed.

"One of them editorials?" an Endman asked.

"Yes, sir. What I mean, ladies and gentlemen, is that this is the first chance I've ever had to carry on a rational conversation with anyone."

"Don't your parents talk to you?"

"Oh yes, but when I answer they don't listen."

"That's because you talk Us and they talk Them."

"You know," the Professor said, "I believe this simplistic Monster may have some potential. I think I'll take him on as one of my students in Arts & Science I."

"Here comes one of the two Connies," His Eminence warned.

"Right. Out, Monster. We'll see you tomorrow. Push him through the door, somebody."

James' mother picked him up and started back to the house. "Darling, you had a wonderful exploration. How nice that we don't have to worry about cars. Did you discover anything?"

"As a matter of fact I did," James answered. "There's a brilliant sodality of birds and beasts in the Big Red Barn who made me welcome and have very kindly volunteered to begin my education. They're all characters and most amusing. They call me Monster."

Alas, he was speaking creature language which his mother couldn't hear or understand. So he settled for "Da" in human, but he was extremely annoyed by his mother's failure to hear him, and this is the terrible conflict of our true story.

And so the education of James Dupree began in and around the Big Red Schoolhouse.

"Music achieved its peak in the Baroque Era," Jack Johnson said. "Teleman, Bach, Mozart. The greatest, the guy I dig the most, was Vivaldi. He had muscle. You understand? Right. Now what you have to keep in mind is that these cats made statements.

And you have to realize that you just don't listen to music; you
have to make it, which means that you have to conduct a conversation with the artists. Right? You hear their statement and
then you answer them back. You agree with them or you argue
with them. That's what it's all about."

"Thank you, sir."

"That's all right. Now let's hear you sound your A."

"As we dig deeper and deeper," Moe Mole said, "we find
that, mathematically speaking, the temperature increases one
degree Fahrenheit per foot. But the brothers from the north tell
me that they strike a permafrost layer which is left over from
the Glacial Epoch. This is very interesting. It means that the
last glaciation is not yet finished in the mathematical sense. Have
you ever seen an iceberg?"

"No, sir."

"I would like to dig down to the bottom of an iceberg to
check the temperature."

"But wouldn't it be cold, sir?"

"Cold? Cold? Pah! Cold is better than pep pills."

"Thank you, sir."

"Let me see your hand," Miss Leghorn said. *"Benny. Benny.*
The line of life is strong. Ah, but the line of Venus, of
amourismo, is broken in *multo* places. I'm afraid you will have
an unhappy lovelife, *caro mio.*"

"Repeat after me," the Senior Rabbit said. "On my honor."

"On my honor."

"I will do my best to do my duty."

"I will do my best to do my duty."

"For God and my country."

"For God and my country."

"And to obey the scout law."

"And to obey the scout law."

"I will help other people at all times."

"I will help other people at all times."

"And keep myself physically strong."

"And keep myself physically strong."

"Mentally awake."

"Mentally awake."

"And morally straight."

"And morally straight."

"Good. You are now an official Tenderfoot. We'll start knot-tying tomorrow with the bowline."

"Excuse me, sir. What does morally straight mean?"

"Now watch me," the debutante said. "First you take a step/ And then you take another/And then you take a step/And then you take another/And then, you're doing the Gazpacho. Now you try it."

"But I can't even walk, m'am."

"That's right," the debutante said brightly. "So how can you dance? Shall we sit this one out? Tell me, have you read any good books lately?"

"My professor at Rutgers," the White Rat said, "taught me everything I know. He was a Phi Beta Kappa. He said that we are always faced with problems in the humanities and scientific disciplines and that the most important step is to first decide whether it's a problem of complexity or perplexity. Now, do you know the difference?"

"No, sir. I'm afraid I don't."

"Hmp! Arrested!"

"Sir, what is the difference?"

"George Woodchuck wants to tell you about surveying."

"I can't understand why the Professor said that," Geo. W. said. "Surveying can be an awfully dull line of work. I wouldn't want to wish it on my worst enemy."

"Then why do you do it, sir?"

"I don't know. Maybe, I suppose, because I'm the dull type that enjoys it. But you're not a dull boy; you're very bright."

"Thank you, sir. Why don't you try me and see if I like it, too?"

"Well, all right, provided it's understood that I'm not trying to lay this on you."

"Understood, sir."

"Fair enough. Now, a proper surveying job can't be done unless you've got a fix on latitude and longitude. The altitude of the sun gives you your latitude and time gives you your longitude. Got that?"

"But I can't tell time."

"Of course you can, my boy. You have your biological clock."

"I don't know what that is, sir."

"We all have it. You must have it, too. Quick, now. What time is it?"

"Just before supper."

"No! No! How long since the sun culminated, that is, reached its highest altitude in the sky at noon? Quick, now! In hours, minutes and seconds. Off the top of your head."

"Six hours, seventeen minutes and five seconds."

"It should be three seconds. You'd be out by eight hundred yards." The Peerless Surveyor patted James generously. "You're a brilliant boy and you have your biological clock. Tomorrow we will beat the bounds of the farm."

"Ladies, I say, Kaff Kaff, women are changeable. Never forget that. We can't live with them and we can't live without them. As the great poet wrote: Whenas in silks my pheasant goes, then, then, methinks, how sweetly flows the liquifaction of her clothes. You are, I am afraid, a little too young for the second stanza which is, to say the least, a trifle bawdy."

"Yes, sir."

"Now we come to the matter of the moment," the Chairman said. "I hope you're not colorblind."

"I don't know, sir."

"Color perception is essential for survival. Very well, we'll test you. What is the color of that flower?"

"It's the color of an Iris."

"I know that, but what color? The name? The name?"

"Blue?" James said at a venture.

"It is Marine Purple Navy. And that tulip?"

"Red?"

"It is Cerise. Really, my young friend! Survival! Survival! And the lilacs?"

"Lilac, sir."

"Ah! Now you're exhibiting some perception. Very good. Tomorrow we will study ROYGBIV."

"I don't know what that is, sir."

"They are the initial letters of the colors of the spectrum," the Chairman said severely, and stalked off in a marked manner.

"Hey, kid."

"Yes, your Eminence?"

"Which one is your father?"

"The tall one, sir."

"What does he do?"

"Well, he talks a lot, your Eminence; and I listen a lot."

"What's he talk about?"

"Practically everything. Science and the State of the Nation. Society. Ecology. Books. Ideas. The theater."

"What's that?"

"I don't know, sir. He also does a lot of cooking when he's home; mostly in a foreign language."

"He does, huh? Say, kid, any chance of him putting out some suet for me? I'm queer for suet."

All was not perpetual sweetness and light in the Big Red Schoolhouse; there were unpleasant moments occasionally.

There was the time that James crawled in cranky. He'd had a bad night owing to a surfeit of chocolate pudding w. whipped cream at supper, and was tired and sullen. He rejected the gracious advances of the debutantes. He made faces while the Professor was lecturing. He was quite impossible. He spoke just one word. It wasn't creature, it was human, and it wasn't "Da," it was "Damn!" Then he began to sob. The creatures, who never cry, gazed at him perplexedly.

"What's he doing?"

"He's crying," the voice of the Burmese Princess explained. She entered the barn. "I hope you'll forgive the intrusion, but I managed to get out and came after him. Hello, George. You're looking handsome today. This must be the Professor. James never told me you were so distinguished. The Chairman and His Eminence are magnificent, as usual. I can't tell you how many times I've admired you through the windows."

"Kaff Kaff. I thank your highness."

"You ain't so bad-looking yourself, baby."

"Come on, James, we'll go back to the house."

"But is he sick?" the Professor asked.

"No, just out of sorts. He has a temper, you know, inherited from his mother who is rather Bohemian. Come along, James. Back to the house."

The Princess began to vamp James, tickling him with her cuddly fur but moving off a few steps each time he tried to embrace her for comfort. He crawled after her, out of the Schoolhouse and through the grass toward the house.

"He'll be all right tomorrow," she called. "Charming place you have here. 'Bye, all."

"I told you she was a right royalty," George W. said.

And there was the time when one of the Endmen reeled into the Schoolhouse singing, "How you gonna keep 'em down on the farm after they seen Paree?" He examined the assembly with a bleary eye, rocking slightly. "You're all plastered," he informed them. "You're stoned." Then he was sick.

"What's the matter with our entertaining, I say, thespian friend?" the Chairman inquired.

"The berries on one of the bushes fermented," the other Endman explained, "and I couldn't stop him from eating them. He's blind drunk."

"Actors!" the Senior Rabbit burst out. "Let this be a lesson to you, James. Well, just don't stand there. Somebody get him out of here and walk him around."

"Sir?"

"Yes?"

"The hose is spraying the rose bushes. If we put him under the cold spray . . . ?"

"That is keeping yourself mentally awake. By all means put this clown under the hose. I only hope he sits on a thorn."

"What d'you mean, you can't swim?" the Mallard duck demanded.

"I can't even walk, m'am."

"I am a gentleman."

"I beg your pardon, sir."

"Get into this pond at once. Now!"

"Yes, sir."

"Not too deep. That's fine. Now pay attention."

"Yes, sir."

"Watch my leg action. I'm paddling, see? Now I've only got two legs; you've got four so you ought to do twice as well. Roll over on your front and paddle with all four. Go ahead. Alternately! Alternately! A-one-and-a-two-and-a-three-and-a-four. Keep your head up and breathe through your mouth. Faster! Faster! That's the way. It's the same as crawling except you're crawling through water."

"Am I really swimming, sir?"

"My boy," the Mallard said, "today the pond; tomorrow the English Channel."

"Connie," Constance said to Constantine, "I'm worried about Jamie."

"Why?"

"Shouldn't he be going to pre-school?"

"Why?"

"He seems to be arrested."

"He isn't three yet. What do you want, Connie, some sort of prodigy entering Harvard aged ten and blighted for life? I want James to grow up a healthy normal boy without having his mind forced prematurely."

"If you will permit me, Professor," James said, "I would like to disagree with my learned colleague, Moe Mole, on the Big Bang theory of cosmology."

"Cosmogony," the White Rat corrected shortly.

"Thank you, sir. The idea of a giant protoatom exploding to produce the expanding universe as we know it today is most attractive but in my opinion is pure romance. I believe in the Steady State theory—that our universe is constantly renewing itself with the birth of new stars and galaxies from the primordial hydrogen."

"But what is your mathematical proof?" Moses Mole asked.

"The eternal equation," James answered. "Energy is equal to mass multiplied by the speed of light raised to the second power."

A voice called in human, "James? Jamie? Where are you?"

"Excuse me, Professor," James said politely. "I'm wanted."

He crawled to the crack in the barn door and squirmed through with difficulty. "Da!" he cried in human.

"We'll have to open that door more," the Professor said irritably. "He's grown. Why in the world hasn't he learned how to walk? He's old enough. When I was his age I had grandchildren."

The rabbits and fawns tittered.

"Class dismissed," the Professor said. He glared at Moses Mole. "You and your Big Bang theory! Why can't you help me get microscopes for my biology seminar?"

"I haven't come across any underground," Moe said reasonably. "As a matter of fact I wouldn't know one if I saw it. Could you describe a microscope mathematically?"

"$E=Mc^2$," the Professor snapped and marched off. He was in a terrible state of mind, and his classes were fortunate that they weren't taking examinations just now. He would have flunked every one of his students.

The Professor was deeply concerned about James James Morrison Morrison who was past two years old and should be walking and talking human by now. He felt a sense of impending guilt and went to the duck pond for a searching self-examination.

"Now I am alone," the White Rat said. The Mallard ducks paddled up to have a look at him but he ignored them. Everybody knows that ducks are incapable of appreciating a solemn soliloquy.

"The quality of wisdom is not strained. It droppeth as the gentle rain from heaven, so who are we mere fardels to do battle with the angels? All I ask, James, is that ye remember me. This day is called Father's Day. He who shall outlive this day will stand a tiptoe when this day is named and yearly feast his neighbors. Old men forget, but is it not better to bear the slings and arrows of outrageous fortune?"

Then he began something halfway between a growl and a song:

> My father sent me to old Rutgers,
> And resolved that I should be a man,
> And so I settled down
> In that noisy college town
> On the banks of the Old Raritan.
>
> Her ardent spirit stirred and cheered me
> From the day my college years began
> Gracious Alma Mater mine
> Learning's fair and honored shrine;
> On the banks of the Old Raritan.
>
> I love her flaming far-flung banner,
> I love her triumphs proud to scan,
> And I glory in the fame
> That immortalized her name
> On the banks of the Old Raritan.
>
> My heart clings closer than the ivy
> As life runs out its fleeting span
> To the stately, ancient walls,
> Of her hallowed, classic halls,
> On the banks of the Old Raritan.
>
> On the banks of the Old Raritan, my boys,
> Where Old Rutgers evermore shall stand,
> For has she not stood since the time of the flood
> On the banks of the Old Raritan.

Feeling much better, the Professor returned to the Big Red Schoolhouse to prepare his first lecture on the New Math. "Zero," he said to himself. "One. Ten. Eleven. One hundred. One hundred and one . . ." He was counting in binary arithmetic.

Meanwhile, James James Morrison Morrison had finished his lunch (chicken salad, 1 slice bread w. butter, applesauce and milk) and was upstairs in his cot theoretically having a nap, actually in drowsy conversation with the Princess who had made herself comfortable on his chest.

"I do love you," James said, "but you take me for granted. All you women are alike."

"That's because you love everything, James."

"Shouldn't everybody?"

"Certainly not. Everybody should love me, of course, but not everything. It reduces my rank."

"Princess, are you really a Burmese Princess?"

"I thought you said you loved me."

"But I happen to know you were born in Brooklyn."

"Politics, James. Politics. Daddy, who was also an admiral, was forced to flee Burma at a moment's notice. He barely had time to throw a few rubies into a flight bag and then came to Brooklyn."

"Why Brooklyn?"

"The plane was hijacked."

"What's a ruby?"

"Ask your professor," the Princess snapped.

"Ah-ha! Jealous. Jealous. I knew I'd get you, sooner or later."

"Now who's taking who for granted?"

"Me. Shift up to my neck, Princess. I can't breathe."

"You are a male, chauvinist pig," the Princess said as she obliged. "I'm merely your sex symbol."

"Say, why don't you join Miss Leghorn's Chickens' Lib movement?"

"Me, sir? What have I to do with chickens?"

"I notice you did all right with my chicken salad. Don't pretend you don't know what I'm talking about. I saw you up on the table when mama was loading the dishwasher. I thought the mayonnaise was awful."

"Commercial."

"Can't you teach mama how to make home-made mayo?"

"Me, sir? What have I to do with kitchens? I leave that to the help."

"Ah-ha! Gotcha again."

"I hate you," the Princess said. "I loathe and execrate you."

"You love me," James James said comfortably. "You love me and you're stuck with me. I've got you in my power."

"Are there any cats in the Red Barn?"

"No," James laughed. "You're the one and only Princess on Red Hill."

There was an outlandish noise outside; a snarling and screaming in creature voices.

"What's that?" James exclaimed.

The Princess got to the window in a scamper and returned. "Just a couple of farm dogs playing with George Woodchuck," she reported lazily. "Now, as we were saying about me—"

"Playing? That doesn't sound like playing to me. I'd better see for myself."

"James, you know you can't walk."

"I'm damn well going to walk now."

James James hove himself over the edge of the cot and fell to the floor. He gripped the edge of the bed and pulled himself upright. Then he tottered to the window.

"They aren't playing with George. He's in bad trouble."

James made his way out of the room, clutching at walls and door frames, managed the stairs by sitting down on every tread, butted the screen door open with his head and was out on the soft meadow, trotting, tottering, falling, picking himself up and driving himself toward the Peerless Surveyor who was being torn by two savage mongrels.

They snarled and snapped as James threw himself over George W. and were quite prepared to come in after both of them. James kicked and flailed at them. He also challenged and cursed them in the creature tongue, using language so frightful that it cannot be reported. The display of courage and determination discouraged the mongrels who at last turned and made off jauntily as though it had only been a game all along. James pulled himself to his knees, picked up George, lurched to his feet and began tottering toward the Big Red Barn.

"Thank you," George said.

"Aw, shut up," James replied.

When they reached the Schoolhouse everyone was there. Nothing escapes attention on Red Hill. James James sat down on his fat bottom with the Surveyor still cradled in his arms. The debutantes made sympathetic sounds.

"Hunters! Hoodlums!" the Senior Rabbit growled. "No one is safe from them. It's all the fault of the Bleeding Hearts.

Understand them. Be kind to them. Help them. Help them do what? Kill."

"There is a triangle of Red Hill farm," Geo. W. said faintly, "measuring exactly one point six acres. It extends into the property next door where Paula, the pig, lives. Tell Paula she must respect our— She must— Our boundar—"

"I'll tell her," James said, and began to cry.

They took the body of the woodchuck from his arms and carried it to the woods where they left George exposed to the weather and nature. Creatures do not bury their dead. James was still sitting in the Big Red Schoolhouse, silently weeping.

"The kid's a right guy," one of the Endmen said.

"Yeah, he's got moxie. You see the way he fight them dogs to a Mexican stand-off? Two to one against, it was."

"Yeah. Hey, kid. Kid. It's all over now. Kid, you ever hear the one about the guy who goes into a butcher store, you should excuse the expression?" The Endman poked his partner.

"I'd like a pound of kidleys, please."

"You mean kidneys, don't you?"

"Well I said kidleys, diddle I?"

"Oh, funny! Fun-nee! Huh, kid?"

"He will have to fall into the pond, Kaff Kaff, I say be immersed," the Chairman said. "He is covered with George's blood and the two Commies will ask questions."

"That's Connies."

"No matter. Will our lovely young debutantes be kind enough to convey our valiant friend to the pond and—"

"I can walk now," James said.

"To be sure. To be sure. And push him in. Kaff Kaff. And my apologies to the Mallards who may resent the trespass. May I say, my dear boy, I say, may I state on behalf of us all that we welcome you as a fully accepted member of our commune. It is a privilege to have a specimen of your species, Kaff Kaff, among us. I'm sure my valued friend, the Professor, will agree."

"He's my best pupil," the White Rat admitted grudgingly, "but I'm going to have to work him over if he ever hopes to get into Rutgers."

"Oh, Jamie! You fell into the pond again."

"Da," the hero said.

That night was another bad night for James. He was terribly upset over the murder of George. He was in a quandary about the Scoutmaster's denunciation of dogs because he was as fond of dogs as he was of all creatures.

"There are good dogs and bad dogs," he kept insisting to himself, "and we mustn't judge the good by the bad. I think the Senior Rabbit was wrong, but how can a Scoutmaster be wrong?

"It's a question of the Categorical Imperative. Good acts lead to good results. Bad acts lead to bad results. But can good lead to bad or bad to good? My father could answer that question but I'm damned if I'll ask him in his language. He won't speak ours."

Here, the deep rumbling of the bats began to irritate him. Creature voices are pitched so much higher than human voices that what sounds like a bat squeak to the human ear sounds like a bass boom to the creature ear. This is another reason why most humans can't speak creature. James went to the window.

"All right! All right!" he called. "Break it up and move it out."

One of the bats fluttered to the window screen and hooked on. "What's bugging you, old buddy-boy?" he rumbled.

"Keep it down to a roar, will you? You want to wake up the whole house?"

"They can't hear us."

"I can hear you."

"How come? Not many human types can."

"I don't know, but I can, and you're making so much noise I can't sleep."

"Sorry, old buddy, but we got to."

"Why?"

"Well, in the first place we're night people, you know?"

"Yes. And?"

"In the second place we don't see so good."

"Moe Mole doesn't see either, but he doesn't make a racket."

"Yeah, but Moe is working underground, old buddy. He hasn't got like trees and barns and buildings to worry about. You know? Now the last thing we want to do is crash into something. There'd be a C.A.B. investigation and somebody would lose his license for sure."

"But what's the noise got to do with it?"

"That's our sonar."

"What's sonar?"

"Radar you know about?"

"Yes."

"Sonar is radar by sound. You let out a yell and the echoes come back and you know where everything is."

"Just from the echo?"

"Right on. You want to try it? Go ahead. Wait a minute; no cheating. Close your eyes. Now make with the sonar."

"What should I yell?"

"Anything you feel like."

"WEEHAWKEN!" James shouted. The bat winced. Three echoes returned; Weehawken, Whyhawken and Weehawkee.

"I heard three," James said.

"What were they?"

"Weehawken."

"That was the big barn."

"Whyhawken."

"The smoke house."

"Weehawkee."

"The oak tree. You're getting the hang, old buddy. Now why don't you practice a little? It won't bother us. None of us use place-names except one cracker from the south who keeps hollering Carlsbad."

In addition to the Chickens' Lib and OFFO Miss Leghorn started a Witches' Coven. "In my native Italy," she said, "they still worship paganism. The Establishment concept of *Dio* is *morto*. We must go back to the old gods."

Her only disciple was James James. She had solicited the Burmese Princess who rejected the proposal with revulsion. "Diabolism," her Highness said, "has ruined our reputation for centuries. Is a dog ever a Witches' Familiar? A lamb? A cow? No, it's always a cat. Avaunt!"

So Miss Leghorn held her Covens in the slate-roofed Smokehouse and her Familiar was James. With his help she collected an enormous assortment of herbs; wild garlic, parsley, basil, mint, dried dandelion, bay, sage, fennel, and once James won her undying gratitude by bringing her some bones left over from his

father's Ossobuco Milanese Style. However, he indignantly refused to bring her anything newborn for a sacrifice. They compromised on a tablespoonful of red caviar. James also brought a
handful of kitchen matches to provide the necessary sulphur for
the invocation of Satan.

The plan was to inscribe a pentacle within a circle on the
hearth of the big Smokehouse fireplace, scatter the ingredients of
necromancy over the pentacle, set them on fire and invoke the
Prince of Hell who would, Miss Leghorn said, most assuredly
appear. The only trouble was Miss Leghorn didn't exactly know
what a pentacle was. She couldn't very well ask the Professor
who would have quashed the Coven immediately. All James
could suggest was that he had heard his father mention a
pentagon in Washington, and from the language he used it certainly sounded exactly right for raising the devil. Miss Leghorn
asked James to get the information from his father but James
stubbornly refused to speak Them. However he promised to ask
around and gave his word of honor that he would not consult
with the Professor.

"Sir," he asked Jack Johnson, "do you know what a pentacle
is?"

"Can't say I do, kid, but I can tell you all about the pentatonic
scale."

"What's that, sir?"

"A five-tone scale; the fourth and seventh are omitted and
you reach the octave on the sixth. The Medieval types used it a
lot, but I don't dig it myself."

"Thank you, sir."

"What you up to, kid?"

"I'm trying to get in touch with Hell."

"Jeez!"

"Sir," James asked the Chairman, "do you know what a
pentacle is?"

"Negative, my boy, that is, I say, I haven't the information.
But I came across an interesting reference to a pentarchy in
Robert's Rules of Order."

"What's that, sir?"

"Good Heavens! Everybody must know Robert's Rules of
Order. No meeting can be chaired without thorough familiarity

with formal procedure. How does one rule when a point of order is raised while a motion is before the house but not yet seconded, and—"

"I mean a pentarchy, Mr. Chairman."

"Oh. Ah. That is government by five persons, by five joint rulers."

"Thank you, sir."

"What are you after, my boy?"

"I want to get in touch with one of the five rulers."

"You're speaking to him now, Kaff Kaff."

"Another one, sir."

"Uncle Moe," James said, "do you know what a pentacle is?"

"No I don't," Moses Mole answered. He reflected for a moment. "But visual astronomers use something called a penta-prism."

"What's that, sir?"

"It's a piece of glass with five sides."

"What do they use it for?"

"To tell you the truth, I don't know. I've never seen one. I think they use them on telescopes but I've never seen a telescope either."

"Thank you, sir."

"What are you digging for, James?"

"The Unseen, sir."

"Tenderfoot Dupree reporting, sir."

"The meeting is next Wednesday night."

"With a question, sir."

"Very good. I approve of that," the Senior Rabbit said. "Always come to your Scoutmaster with your problems. What's yours?"

"Is a pentacle a kind of knot?"

The Senior Rabbit thought hard. "No."

"Do you know what a pentacle is, sir?"

"Of course I do. So do you. You've been looking at fifty of them all your life."

"I have? Where?"

The Scoutmaster stood to attention, saluted, and pointed to the American flag which flew over the little barn on various occasions. "There, my boy. Those sacred stars are pentacles.

Each of the five points stands for one of the five virtues; loyalty, leadership, piety, law and order."

"Thank you, sir."

"Are you studying for a merit badge, James?"

"In a way," James said. "I'm studying a sort of piety."

"There is no merit badge for piety."

"A pentacle is a five-pointed star," James told Miss Leghorn. "Like on the flag."

"*Benny! Benny! Multa benny!* You didn't ask the Professor?"

"No. I'm a boy scout so I kept my word of honor. Now we can raise the devil. Incidentally, what is the devil, Miss Leghorn?"

"The Prince of Hell."

"Yes, I know. You told me. But what is hell?"

"You'll find out tonight," the Chaldean Chicken said with sinister gloating and departed from the Smokehouse like Tosca after the murder of Scarpia. James knew because Jack Johnson had acted out the entire opera for the Big Red Schoolhouse one afternoon, singing all the roles. Jack had been particularly impressive in Tosca's second act exit.

So that night while his father was reading his editorial ("Whither Pot: Paradise or Poison?") to his mother, James stole out and joined the witch in the Smokehouse. Between them they managed to scribe a circle and star on the hearth of the fireplace and decorate the diagram with black magic herbs. Then James lit the sulphur matches, everything began to burn noisomely, and Miss Leghorn began her litany which went something like this:

"Satan, come to me! Lucifer, appear! Mephistophales make yourself manifest to your faithful! Belial and Beelzebub, heed my calling! Asmodeus and Apollyon, tempters of evil, tempt me! Prince of Darkness, evil one, foul fiend, devil incarnate, come to your beloved, your adorer, your—" Suddenly Miss Leghorn let out a scream. "He's here! At the window! He's here!" In a panic she actually flew to James' shoulder and perched there, terrified and trembling.

James looked at the window. Reflected in the dim light from the arcane fire was an enormous eye. It disappeared as soon as he saw it and then the Smokehouse door began to creak open. James stood up manfully. Miss Leghorn began to shriek, "I didn't mean it! Go back! Go back!"

An enormous head poked through the door, the head of a horse. "Say," the horse said, "I saw your light and I wanted to ask you. Which way is the Rich farm? I'm kind of lost."

"No, sir, you're not lost," James said. "You're real close. It's just a mile down the road. Go over the hill and you can't miss it."

"Say, thanks," the horse said. Then he inspected Miss Leghorn. "Say, aren't you the hen who ran away from the rooster last year?"

"I am not," Miss Leghorn quavered.

"Sure you are. We're still laughing about it at the Rich farm. A girl afraid of a guy. What are you, some kind of freak? Well, thanks again. Good night."

The horse disappeared into the darkness. Miss Leghorn trembled with indignation.

"Was what he said true?" James asked.

"No!" Miss Leghorn cried. Then, "How dare they laugh at me? A woman has the right to refuse unwelcome advances."

"So it was true."

"All men are beasts."

"You should hear what they say about women."

Miss Leghorn fluttered down from James' shoulder. "How dare you use that sort of vile language to a lady?"

"I'm sorry, Miss Leghorn. I didn't know it was vile. Are we going to make another try at raising the devil tonight?"

"We've already raised him," Miss Leghorn said.

And then James James fell in love. It was a mad, consuming passion for the least likely candidate. Obeying George Woodchuck's dying admonition he went down to the triangle to request Paula, the pig, to respect the boundaries, and it was love at first sight. Paula was white with black patches or black with white patches (Poland China was her type) and she was grossly overweight. Nevertheless, James adored her. He brought her armfuls of apples from the orchard which she ate methodically and without thanks. Nevertheless, James loved her. He was the despair of the Big Red Schoolhouse.

"Puppy love," the Professor snorted.

"He's a set-up for a my-wife-is-so-fat-that joke," one of the Endmen said.

"Marriage is out of the question," the Senior Rabbit said. "She's twice his age."

"And twice his weight."

Caw! Caw! Caw!

"If he dares to bring that woman here," the debutantes said, "we'll never speak to him again."

James dreamed into the barn. "Ready for the biology seminar," he said.

"Mathematics today," the Professor rapped.

"Yes, Paula."

"I am the Professor."

"Sorry, sir."

"We will begin with a review of binary arithmetic. I trust you all remember that the decimal system uses the base of ten. We count from one to ten, ten to twenty, twenty to thirty, and so on. The binary system is based on zero and one. Zero is zero. One is one, but two is ten. Three is eleven. Four is one hundred. What is five, James?"

"One hundred and Paula."

"Class dismissed."

And then James began to skip classes.

"We were supposed to start a dig yesterday," Moe Mole reported, "and he never showed up."

"He cut my oratorio session," Jack Johnson said.

"That boy is turning into a drop-out."

"Have you noticed how he's brushing his hair?" the debutantes inquired.

"Oh, come on!" His Eminence said. "If the kid's got hot pants why can't we—"

"The boy is morally straight," the Scoutmaster interrupted sternly.

"It can't be solved on simplistic terms," the Professor said. "Emotions are involved, and the cerebrum is never on speaking terms with the cerebellum."

Alas, the situation resolved itself on an afternoon when James, carefully combed and brushed, brought another armful of apples to his love. Paula devoured them as stolidly as ever while James sat and watched devotedly. Apparently Paula was extra-hungry this afternoon because when James started to embrace her she started to eat him. James pulled his arm out of her mouth and recoiled in horror and disillusionment.

"Paula!" he exclaimed. "You only love me for myself."

"*Khonyetchna*," Paula grunted in Cyrillic.

James returned to the Big Red Schoolhouse in a gloomy mood. Of course everybody had seen the sad incident and all of them did their best to be tactful.

"Physiology tomorrow," the Professor said. "We will discuss the hydrogen-ion balance in the blood."

"Yes, sir."

"We got to get on to the modern composers, kid."

"Yes, sir."

"You know, shale is an oil-bearing rock," Moses Mole said. "But why isn't there any oil in red shale? There must be a mathematical reason."

"We'll try to find it, sir."

"Stick out your chest and be a man," the Scoutmaster said.

"I'm trying, sir."

"It is better to have loved and lost than never to have loved at all," the Chairman said.

Then a fawn nestled alongside James and whispered, "It's all right. We're sorry you picked the wrong girl, but it has to happen to every man at least once. That's how you find the right girl."

James burst into tears and cried and cried for his lost love while the fawn petted him, but in the end he felt curiously relieved.

"James," the Professor said, "we must have a serious talk."

"Yes, sir. Here?"

"No. Come to the willow grove." They went to the willow grove. "Now we are alone," the Professor said. "James, you must start speaking to your mother and father. I know you can. Why don't you?"

"I'm damned if I will, sir. They won't speak Us. Why should I speak Them?"

"James, they don't know how to speak Us. Aren't you being unfair?"

"They could try."

"And I'm sure they would if they had a clue, but they haven't. Now listen to me. You're our only link between Us and Them. We need you, James, as a diplomatist. Your mother and father are very nice people; no hunting or killing on Red Hill and they're planting many things. We all live together very pleasantly. I admit your mother loses her temper with the Scoutmaster and his troop because they won't get out of her way when she comes out to hang the laundry on the line, but that's because she has a Bohemian disposition. We know what artists are like, unpredictable."

"I won't talk to her," James said.

"Your father is an intellectual of top caliber, and he went to Rutgers. You've brought many of his ideas and speculations to the Schoolhouse, which are stimulating and appreciated. In all fairness you should let him know how grateful we are to him."

"He wouldn't believe me."

"But at least you could speak to him."

"I won't speak to him. He's old, old, old and hidebound. He's a cube. He's trapped in a structured society."

"Where did you get that?"

"From my father."

"Well, then. You see?"

"No, I don't," James said stubbornly. "I won't talk their language to them. They have to try Us first."

"In other words, you have opted for Us?"

"Yes, sir."

"To the exclusion of Them?"

"Yes, sir."

"Then there's nothing more to say."

"Connie," Constance said to Constantine, "we must have a serious talk."

"Now?"

"Yes."

"What about?"

"Jamie."

"What about Jamie?"

"He's a problem child."

"What's his problem?"

"He's arrested."

"Are you starting that again? Now come on, Connie. He's learned to walk. What more do you want?"

"But he hasn't learned to talk."

"Talk! Talk! Talk!" Constantine sounded as though he was cursing. "Words! Words! Words! I've lived my whole life with them and I hate them. Do you know what most words are? They're bullets people use to shoot each other down with. Words are weapons for killers. Language should be the beautiful poetry of communication but we've debased it, poisoned it, corrupted it into hostility, into competition, into a contest between winners and losers. And the winner is never the man with something to say; the winner is always the fastest gun in the west. These are the few simple words I have to say about words."

"Yes, dear," Constance said, "but our son should be shooting words by now, and he isn't."

"I hope he never does."

"He must, and we'll have to take him to a clinic. He's autistic."

"Autism," the Professor said, "is an abnormal absorption in fantasy to the exclusion of external reality. I have known many laboratory victims who have been driven to this deplorable state by fiendish experiments."

"Could you put that in mathematical terms?" Moe asked. "I can't follow your words."

"Ah, yes. Kaff Kaff. I'm having some slight difficulty myself. I'm sure our valued friend will be good enough to simplify."

"All right," the White Rat said. "He won't talk."

"Won't talk? Good heavens! We can't shut him up. Only yesterday he engaged me in a two hour dispute over Robert's Rules of Order, and—"

"He won't talk human."

"Oh. Ah."

"The *questo* is can he?" the Chaldean Chicken said. "Many who are born under the Sign of Torso find it *difficulto* to—"

"Taurus! Taurus! And will you be quiet. He can talk; he just won't."

"What's a fantasy?" Moe asked.

"A hallucination."

"What's that?"

"Something unreal."

"You mean he's not real? But I only saw him yesterday and he—"

"I have no intention of discussing the metaphysics of reality. Those of you who are interested may take my course in Thesis, Synthesis and Antithesis. The situation with James is simple. He talks to us in our language; he refuses to talk to his parents in their language; they are alarmed. The Princess told me."

"Why are they alarmed?"

"They think he's autistic."

"They think he's unreal?"

"No, Moe," the Professor said patiently. "They know he's real. They think he has a psychological hang-up which prevents him from talking human."

"Do they know he talks Us?"

"No."

"Then why don't we tell them? Then everything will be all right."

"Why don't you tell them?"

"I don't know how to talk Them."

"Does anybody here know how? Anybody?"

No answer.

"So much for that brilliant suggestion," the Professor said. "Now we come to the crux of the situation. They're going to send him to a remedial school."

"What's the matter with our school?"

"They don't know about our school, you imbecile! They want him to go to a school where he can learn to speak English."

"What's that?"

"Them talk."

"Oh."

"Well, Kaff Kaff, as our most esteemed and valued scholar,

surely you can have no objections to that program, my dear Professor."

"There's a dilemma," the White Rat said sourly.

"Name it, sir. I say, describe it and we shall, Kaff Kaff, we shall cope."

"He's so used to speaking Us that I'm afraid he won't learn to speak Them."

"But why should he want to, my learned friend?"

"Because he's got Rutgers before him."

"Ah, yes. To be sure. Your beloved Alma Mater. But I still can't quite fathom, I say, perceive the basic difficulty."

"We've got to turn him off."

"I beg your pardon?"

"We've got to stop speaking to him. We've got to break his Us habit so he can learn Them. Nobody can speak both."

"You can't mean Coventry, Professor?"

"I do. Don't you understand? No matter where he goes there will be others of us around. We must break the habit. Now. For his sake." The Professor began to pace angrily. "He will forget how to speak Us. We'll lose him. That's the price. My best pupil. My favorite. Now he may never make Phi Beta Kappa."

The debutantes looked despairing. "We love that boy," they said. "He's a real swinger."

"He is not," the Senior Rabbit stated. "He is trustworthy, loyal, helpful, friendly, courteous, kind, obedient, cheerful, thrifty, brave, clean and reverent."

"He told me all about E equals M C two," Moe said. "It gave me an insight. It will change the world."

"Aquarium," Miss Leghorn said profoundly.

"He is a pest, a bore, a nuisance, a—a human," the Professor shouted. "He doesn't belong in our Schoolhouse. We want nothing to do with him; he'll sell us out sooner or later. Coventry! Coventry!" Then he broke down completely. "I love him, too, but we must be brave. We're going to lose him but we must be brave for his sake. And somebody better warn the Princess."

James James Morrison Morrison shoved the barn door a little wider and swaggered into the Schoolhouse. There was no mistaking his pride in his walk. In an odd way it was a reflection of the Chairman's strut.

"Ladies and gentlemen, good evening," he said, as courteous as ever.

The debutantes sniffled and departed.

"What's the matter with them?" James asked curiously. He turned to the mole. "Uncle Moe, I just heard something up at the house that'll interest you. It seems that the universe may break down. Time is not reversible from the mathematical standpoint, and—"

Here Moe broke down and went underground.

"What's the matter with him?" James asked.

There was no answer. Everybody else had disappeared, too. The long sad silence had begun.

The pheasant strutted, accompanied by his harem, and he ignored James. Martha W. Woodchuck, who had taken on George's surveying duties (she was his daughter-in-law) ignored James. Neither the Professor nor the Scoutmaster were to be seen. The does and the fawns hid in the woods. Moe Mole decided on an early hibernation. Jack Johnson went south for the winter and His Eminence suddenly moved his residence to Paula's territory. The crows could not resist the challenge of an *art noveau* scarecrow on a farm a mile off and left. James James was abandoned.

"Would you like to read my palm?" he asked Miss Leghorn.

"Cluck," she replied.

"Princess," he said, "why doesn't anybody want to talk to me?"

"Aeiou," she replied.

James was abandoned.

"Well, at least he's learned how to walk," Dr. Rapp said, "and that's a favorable prognosis. What beats me is how he can be autistic in such an articulate home. One would think that— Stop. An idea. Is it possible that the home is too articulate; that his autism is a refusal to compete with his betters?"

"But there's no competition in our home," one of the two Connies said.

"You don't grasp the potential of the idea. In our society, if you don't win you have failed. This is our contemporary delusion. James may well be afraid of failure."

"But he's only three years old."

"My dear Mrs. Dupree, competition begins in the womb."

"Not in mine," Connie said indignantly. "I've got the fastest womb in the west."

"Yes. And now if you will excuse me, the first lesson will begin. That door out. Thank you." Dr. Rapp buzzed the intercom. "Sherbet," he said. A chalice of orange sherbet was brought to him.

"James," he said, "would you like some orange ice? Here." He proffered a spoonful. James engulfed it. "Good. Would you like some more? Then tell me what this is." Dr. Rapp held up a striped ball. "It's a ball, James. Repeat after me. Ball."

"Da," James said.

"No more orange ice, James, until you've spoken. Ball. Ball. Ball. And then the goody."

"Da."

"Perhaps he prefers the lemon flavor," Dr. Rapp said next week. He buzzed the intercom. "Lemon sherbet, please." He was served. "James, would you like some lemon ice?" He proffered a spoonful which was absorbed. "Good. Would you like some more? Then tell me what this is. It's a ball, James. Repeat after me. Ball. Ball. Ball."

"Da," James said.

"We'll try ice cream," Dr. Rapp said a week later. "We can't permit him to fall into a pattern of familiarized societal behavior. He must be challenged." He buzzed the intercom. "Chocolate ice cream, please."

James relished the chocolate ice cream but refused to identify the striped ball by name.

"Da," he said.

"I'm beginning to dream that confounded expression," Dr. Rapp complained. "A Roman centurion comes at me, draws his sword and says, 'Da.' Stop. An idea. Is it a phallic symbol? Sexuality begins with conception. Is the child rejecting the facts of life?"

He buzzed the intercom.

"James, here is a banana. Would you like a bite? Feel free. Good. Good. Would you like another? Then tell me what this is. A ball. Ball. Ball. Ball."

"Da."

"I am failing," Dr. Rapp said despondently. "Perhaps I had better go back to Dr. Da for a refresher— What am I saying? It's Dr. Damon. Stop. An idea. Damon and Pythias. A friendship. Can it be that I have been too clinical with James? I shall establish fraternality."

"Good morning, James. It's a beautiful October day. The autumn leaves are glorious. Would you like to go for a drive with me?"

"Da," James said.

"Good. Good. Where would you like to go?"

"To Rutgers," James said, quite distinctly.

"What did you say?"

"I said I would like to go to Rutgers."

"But—good gracious—you're talking."

"Yes, sir."

"Why haven't you talked before?"

"Because I damn well didn't want to."

"Why are you talking now?"

"Because I want to see the banks of the Old Raritan."

"Yes, yes. I see. Or do I?" Dr. Rapp buzzed the intercom. "Please get me Dr. Da, I mean Dr. Damon, on the phone. Tell him I think I've made an important discovery."

"Discovery," James said, "is seeing what everybody else sees but thinking what no one else has thought. What's your opinion? Shall we discuss it on the way to Rutgers?"

So the second summer came. James and his father were strolling the lawns in a hot debate over the bearded irises which, alas, James pronounced Iritheth. He had developed a human lisp. The issue was whether they should be picked and vased or left alone.

James took the position that they were delicate ladies who should not be molested. His father, always pragmatic, declared that flowers had to justify their existence by decorating the house. Father and son parted on a note of exasperation, and the senior Dupree went to inspect the peach trees. James James Morrison Morrison stood quietly on the lawn and looked around. Presently he heard a familiar Kaff Kaff, and the Chairman appeared from under the lilac bush.

"Well, if it isn't my old friend, the Sex Maniac. How are you, sir?"

The cock pheasant glared at him.

"And how are Phyllis and Frances and Felice and all the rest, Mr. Chairman?"

"Their names are, I say, the nomenclature is, Kaff Kaff, Gloria, Glenda, Gertrude, Godiva and—" Here the Chairman stopped short and looked hard at James. "But you're the monster."

"Yes, sir."

"My, how you've grown."

"Thank you, sir."

"Have you learned how to speak Them?"

"Not very well, sir."

"Why not?"

"I've got a lisp. They say it's because I have a lazy tongue."

"But you still speak Us."

"Yes, sir."

"Amazing! I say, unheard of!"

"Did you all think I'd ever forget? I'm the Professor's best pupil, and I'd die for dear old Rutgers. Can we have an emergency meeting right away in the Big Red Schoolhouse, Mr. Chairman? I've got a lot to tell you about the crazy, mixed-up human creatures."

The meeting was attended by most of the regulars plus a few newcomers. There was a Plymouth Rock hen who had become close friends with Miss Leghorn, perhaps because her only reply to the Chaldean harangues was, "Ayeh." The hold-out Mockingbird had at last joined up now that Jack Johnson seemed to be remaining in the Florida keys . . . his (the Mockingbird's) name was Milton. There was one most exotic new member, a little

Barbary ape who was very friendly but extremely shy. James shook hands and asked his name.

"They called me . . . Well, they called me The Great Zunia. Knows All. Does All."

"Who's 'they,' Zunia?"

"The Reeson & Tickel Circus."

"You were in the circus?"

"Well . . . yes. I . . . I did tricks. Knows All. Does All. I was what they . . . what they call a headliner. You know. Rode a motorcycle with the lights on. But I . . . I . . ."

"Yes?"

"But I cracked up when we . . . when we were playing Princeton. Totaled the bike. I got . . . well . . . I split when they were picking up the pieces."

"Why did you run away, Zunia?"

"I . . . I hate to say this . . . Never blow the whistle on another man's act . . . But . . . well . . . I hate show business."

"Zunia, we're all delighted that you're here, and you know you're more than welcome, but there's a problem."

"Well . . . gee . . . Just a little fruit now and then, apples and—"

"Not food. The weather. Winters can be damn cold on Red Hill farm. Don't you think you might be more comfortable farther south?"

"Well . . . If it's all the same to . . . Well, I'd rather stay here. Nice folks."

"If that's what you want, great for us. My parents are going to have fits if they ever see you, so stay under cover."

"I'm a night-type anyway."

"Good. Now stand up, please. All the way up and we'll stand back to back. Professor, are we the same size?"

No answer.

"Professor?"

Moe Mole said, "The Professor is indisposed."

"What?"

"He couldn't come."

"Why not?"

"He's not feeling so good."

"Where is he?"

"Up in his study."

"I'd better go and— No, wait. Are we the same size, Zunia and me? Anybody? Everybody?"

It was agreed that James and Zunia were an approximate match. James promised to pinch some of his sweaters and woolly underwear for Zunia to wear during the winter months.

"If you . . . Well, I'm not asking . . . But I'd love a sweater with Boston on it."

"Boston! Why Boston?"

"Because they hate show business."

James shinnied up one of the rough oak columns that supported the barn roof, walked across the heavy beam above the empty hay loft as casually as a steelworker (his mother would have screamed at the sight), came to a small break in the loft wall and knocked politely.

A faint voice said, "Who is it?"

"It's the Monster, sir. I've come back."

"No! Really? Come in. Come in."

James poked his head through the break. The Professor's study was lined with moss. There were fronds of dried grass and mint leaves on the floor on which the Professor lay. He looked very ill and weak, but his albino red eyes were as fierce as ever.

"Well, James, you've come back," he panted. "I never thought— Do you speak Them?"

"Yes, sir."

"And you still speak Us. I would never— Phi Beta Kappa and cum laude for you. No doubt of it."

"I visited Rutgers, sir."

"Did you? Did you, now? And?"

"It's beautiful, just like you said," James lied. "And they still remember you."

"No!"

"Yes, sir. They can't understand how you escaped. They think you probably bribed the lab attendant, but a few claim you had something on him. Blackmail."

The Professor chuckled, but it turned into a painful hacking.

After the spasm subsided James asked, "What's wrong, sir?"

"Nothing. Nothing. Probably a touch of the Asiatic flu. Nothing serious."

"Please tell me."

The Professor looked at him. "Science is devotion to truth," he said. "I'll be truthful. I'm badly wounded."

"Oh, sir! How?"

"An air-rifle. A couple of farm boys."

"Who are they? From the Rich place? I'll—"

"James! James! There is no room for revenge in science. Did Darwin retaliate when he was ridiculed?"

"No, sir."

"Did Pasteur?"

"N-no, sir."

"Will you be true to what I've taught you?"

"I'll try, sir, b-but those damn boys . . ."

"No anger. Reason always; anger never. And no crying, James. I need your courage now."

"If I have any, sir."

"You have it. I remember George. Now I want you to take my place and continue my classes."

"Oh, Professor, you'll be—"

"I take it you're on speaking terms with your father now. Learn all you can from him and pass it on to Us. That's an order, James."

"Yes, sir. It won't be easy."

"Nothing is ever easy. Now I'm going to ask for an act of great courage."

"Sir?"

"I can't linger like this. It's too painful and it's useless."

"Professor, maybe we can—"

"No, no. I'm hopeless. If you hadn't cut my anatomy classes when you fell in love with Paula, you'd—" He hacked again, even more painfully. At last he said, "James, end this for me, as quickly as possible. You know what I mean."

James was stupefied. At last he managed to whisper, "S-sir . . ."

"Yes. I see you understand me."

"Sir, I c-couldn't."

"Yes you can."

"B-But I wouldn't know how."

"Science always finds a way."

"At least let me ask my—"

"You will ask no one. You will tell no one."

"But you leave me all alone with this."

"Yes, I do. That's how we grow up."

"Sir, I have to refuse. I can't do it."

"No. You just need time to make up your mind. Isn't there a meeting on the floor?"

"Yes, sir. I asked for it."

"Then go to your meeting. Give them my best. Come back quickly. Quickly." The Professor began to tremble and rustle on the dried grass.

"Have you had anything to eat, sir? I'll bring you something, and then we'll talk it over. You have to advise me."

"No dependence," the White Rat said. "You must decide for yourself."

The Chairman was in the full flood of oratory when James climbed down from the loft and seated himself with his friends, the birds and the beasts, but he came to a close fairly promptly and gave the floor to James James who stood up and looked around.

"I'm going to tell you about Them," James began quietly. "I've met Them and lived with Them and I'm beginning to understand Them. We must, too. Many of Them are damned destroyers— we all know that—but what we don't know is that a new breed of Them is rising in revolt against destruction. They're our kind. They live in peace and harmony with the earth, whatever they take from it they return, they do not kill and they fight those who do. But they're young and weak and outnumbered and they need our help. We must help them. We must!

"Now up to now we've done nothing. We hide from the destroyers and use our intelligence to outwit them. We've just been passive victims. Now we must become activists, militant activists. The Professor won't like this; the great scholar still believes in reason and light. So do I, but I reserve reason and light only for those who also are guided by reason and light. For the rest, militant action. Militant!

"I heard my father once tell a story about Confucius, a very wise sage of many years ago. Although he was one of Them he was much like our Professor and may have been almost as wise.

One of his students came to him and said, 'Master, a new wise man named Christ has appeared in the west. He teaches that we must return good for evil. What is your opinion?' Confucius thought and answered, 'No. If we return good for evil what then will we return for good? Return good for good; for evil return justice.' "

James' voice began to shake. "They shot the Professor. You knew that, didn't you. They shot him. He's not indisposed. He's up there and he's hurting. They— We must learn to return militant justice for evil. We can't use this barn as a sanctuary anymore. We must leave it when we graduate and travel and teach. There is a desperate battle being fought for what little remains of our earth. We must all join the fight."

"But how?" Moe Mole asked reasonably.

"That will be the subject of my first lesson tomorrow," James answered. "And now, with the permission of our distinguished chairman, I would like to move that this meeting be adjourned. I have the Professor to look after."

"So moved," the cock pheasant said. "Seconded? Thank you, Miss Plymouth. Moved and seconded. This meeting is adjourned."

"Zunia," James said, "wait here for me, please. I'll need your help. Back in a little while."

James walked to the nearest apple tree, began picking up fallen apples and hurling them into space. His mother glanced out out of the kitchen window and smiled at the sight of a small boy happily lazing away a summer afternoon.

"If I do what the Professor asks it'll be murder," James thought. "They call it mercy killing but I've heard my father say it's murder all the same. He says some doctors do it by deliberately neglecting to give certain medicines. He says that's murder all the same and he doesn't approve. He says religion is against it and if you do it you go to hell, wherever that is. He says life is sacred.

"But the Professor hurts. He hurts bad and he says there's no hope. I don't want him to hurt anymore. I want the boys who shot him to hurt, but not the Professor. I could just bring him a little milk and let him die all by himself, but that could take a long time. It wouldn't be fair to him. So— All right— I'll go to hell."

James returned to the house, lisped courteously to his mother and asked for a small cup of warm milk to hold him until dinnertime. He received it, climbed upstairs to his room and put the cup down. Then he went to his parents' bathroom. He climbed up on the washstand, opened the medicine cabinet which had been declared off-limits for him on pain of frightful punishment, and took a small vial off one of the shelves. It was labeled "Seconal" and was filled with bright orange capsules. James James removed a capsule, returned the vial, closed the cabinet and climbed down from the sink.

"What are you stealing?" the Burmese princess asked.

"Medicine," James answered shortly and returned to his room. He pulled the capsule open and shook its contents into the cup of milk. He stirred gently with his forefinger.

"If that's for me, James, forget it," the Princess said. "I'm not sick and I hate milk. Whatever gave people the idea that cats adore milk? I loathe and execrate it."

"I suppose because you were raised on caviar and champagne."

"Mercy, James, you'll have to put your humor on a diet. It's gaining weight."

"I'm sorry. I'm not feeling funny right now, Princess. In fact I feel damn rotten lousy."

"Why? What's wrong?"

"I can't tell you. I can't tell anybody. Excuse me."

He carried the cup of milk to the Big Red Barn where the Great Zunia was patiently awaiting. "Thanks," James said. "Now look, I've got to shinny up that column and I can't do it and carry this cup. You can, easy. Go up with the cup. Don't spill it. I'll meet you on the beam."

They met on the beam and James received the cup.

"It looks like milk but it tastes funny," Zunia said.

"You didn't drink any!"

"Well, no . . . Just stuck my tongue in . . . You know. Curious. It's . . . well, traditional with us."

"Oh. That's all right. It's medicine for the Professor."

"Sure. Tell him . . . Tell him get well soon."

"He'll be well soon," James promised. Zunia flip-flopped and catapulted himself to another empty loft. James crossed the beam and knocked at the Professor's study. "It's James again, sir."

He could barely hear the "Come in." He poked his head in. The Professor was trembling. "I brought you a little something, sir. Warm milk." James placed the cup close to the Professor's head. "Please drink a little. It'll give you strength."

"Impossible."

"For me, sir. You owe that much to your best pupil. And then we'll discuss your proposal." James waited until he saw the White Rat begin to drink. He withdrew his head, sat down on the beam with his legs dangling and began to chat lightly while tears blurred his eyes.

"Your proposal, Professor, raises an interesting dilemma in the relationship between teacher and pupil. Let me tell you about my lunatic teacher at the remedial school, Dr. Rapp, and my relations with him. I'd value your opinion. How is the milk, sir?"

"Terrible. Did you say lunatic?"

"Drink it anyway. Yes, lunatic. He's a psychiatrist, excessively educated, and—"

"There is no such thing."

"Not for a genius like yourself, sir, but in lesser people too much education produces alienation from reality. That was Dr. Rapp."

"You must be specific," the White Rat said severely.

"Well, sir, let me contrast him with yourself. You always understand the capacity and potential of your students and treat them accordingly. Dr. Rapp was so crammed with education that he never bothered to understand us; he simply tried to fit us into the text book cases he'd read."

"Hmmm. What was his school?"

"I was afraid you'd ask that, sir. You won't like the answer. Abigail college."

"What? What?"

"Abigail college, sir. Finished your milk?"

"Yes, and it was disgusting."

"But you sound stronger already, sir."

"Where is Abigail college?"

"In a state called Kansas."

"Hmp! Fresh water college. No wonder." The Professor's speech began to slur. James began to rock back and forth in agony.

"What would you do if this . . . this Abigail made same proposal to you, James?"

"Oh, sir, that's not a fair question. I don't like or respect Dr. Rapp. I love you."

"No place—f'love—in science."

"No, sir. Always be objective. That's what you taught me."

"Gett'n sleepy . . . James . . . 'bout Zunia."

"What about Zunia, sir?"

"Like him?"

"Very much, sir. You'll enjoy teaching him."

"Don't . . . D'not le'him . . . Came to us f'm Princeton, you know . . . D'nt let'm talk you into going Princeton. Yes?"

"Never, sir. Rutgers forever."

There was a long, long pause. The painful rustling in the study stopped. James poked his head in. The cup of milk was empty. The Professor was peacefully dead. James reached in, picked him up, carried him across the beam and skinned down the oak column with the body in one hand. On the floor he stamped his foot hard, three times. He repeated the signal three times. At last Moe Mole appeared from the depths.

"That you, James?"

"Yes. Please come with me, Uncle Moe. I need your help."

Moe shuffled alongside James James, blinking in the twilight. "Trouble, James?"

"The Professor's dead. We've got to bury him."

"Now that's a shame. And we never started my astronomy lessons. Where's the body?"

"Right here. I'm carrying him." James led Moe to the sundial on the south lawn. "Dig here, Uncle Moe. I want to bury the Professor under the center of the pedestal."

"Easy," Moe said. He tunneled down and disappeared; little flurries of earth sprayed out of the tunnel mouth. Presently Moe reappeared. "All set. Got a nice little chamber dead center. Where is he now?"

James placed the body at the mouth of the tunnel. Moe pushed it before him and was again lost from sight. He reappeared in another flurry of soil. "Just filling in," he explained apologetically. "Got to pack it solid. Don't want any grave robbers nosing around, do we?"

"No," James said. "Bury him for keeps."

Moe finished the job, mumbled a few words of condolence and shambled off. James stared hard at the sundial. "Militant," he said at last and turned away. The weathered bronze plate of the sundial was engraved with a line from the immortal Thomas Henry Huxley: "The great end of life is not knowledge but action."

Exactly two Wilma Shore stories have appeared in the magazine;
both have been anthologized in The Best of F&SF series. Not
that we mean to offer this as evidence that she is a superior writer—
proof enough appears below, in which a sharp-edged and unexpected
drama is played out against the backdrop of a classic sf theme.

Is It the End
of the World?

WILMA SHORE

When Mary looked up from her planting and glimpsed, through
the lilac, Dorene's ankles coming across the lawn, her heart sank,
really dropped in her chest. How *shameful* to feel that way,
when all the child wanted was a lift to Drama Workshop. But
that meant twenty minutes on the freeway, fifteen locked in
downtown traffic; and she had been looking forward to a tranquil
morning with her zinnias, the smell of lilac and damp earth.
When you had three kids there was always something; she just
couldn't bear not having some little bit of time to call her own.

But neither could she bear the tragic face, the familiar tirade:
"You don't *care* if I'm late, all you care about is if I do my

chores, all the worst ones because I'm the oldest, but isn't the oldest entitled to a *few meager privileges . . .*"

"Drama Workshop is a privilege," she said, trying to keep her voice steady. "And you did promise to go by bus."

"I *was,* Mamma, *honestly,* only I had to stop and pick up my *entire record collection, your darling Benny* had them *all over the floor . . .*"

"You should have made her do it," said Mary, but it was an automatic response; she had already gone through the argument in her mind and knew she would end up driving Dorene, not willingly, like a good mother, but in resentment and rage. Dr. Norseman said it was guilt, not love, that made her unable to refuse her children. She jabbed the trowel into the dirt and stood up.

"You *will?*" cried Dorene, and Mary saw that if she had held out one more minute Dorene would have given up and rushed off; now the zinnias would have to go back into the cellar till tomorrow or even Monday. She carried the flat back to the house, set it on the cellar steps, and closed the door over it.

Jack's voice came up through the window: "Hey! I'm working down here!"

Surprised, she cried, "You want a house full of flies?"

He mumbled something. Something disagreeable, even vulgar, or why not say it out loud? Hurt, she lifted the door again. Too bad for the zinnias if the sun came out, but it wasn't likely; it was so damp and still, a *perfect* day for transplanting; the sky . . .

The sky blurred. What was there to cry about? A few dozen zinnias? When she had three wonderful children, a wonderful husband? She ought to get down on her knees every day and thank God, she was that lucky. Instead of just taking it all for granted, as though it had a lifetime guarantee and nothing could possibly ever happen . . .

The sky . . . "Hey, wait a *minute,*" she told Dorene, "I'm not sure you can *go* downtown. Look over there."

"Oh, *Mamma!* Every cloud in the sky you think it's the end of the world. The radio didn't . . ."

"Never mind. I'm going in and look at the terminometer."

Taking long, calm breaths, she walked quickly around the house and into the living room where the terminometer hung. The monoxide needle stood at 340. "Jack!" She rapped on the glass, it jerked on to 343. "Jack!"

Dorene gasped. "How high is it?"

"Oh, now don't start a big melodrama."

"Who's starting a melodrama? *I* didn't holler Jack, Jack!"

"All right, all right," said Jack, pushing them aside. "Let me see."

She waited for him to say, Who's been fooling with the terminometer? . . . but he just rapped on the glass, then turned and looked out the window. Dorene pressed her hands into her cheeks in one of her Gothic poses: *Anxiety.* "How bad is it, Papa?" she said in a hushed voice.

He looked around. "Where's the paper?"

It was on the table, right in front of his eyes. Mary gave it to him and he turned to Atmos-facts. "Is it very bad?" whispered Dorene. "Papa? Will I have to cut Workshop?"

"Oh, really!" exclaimed Mary.

"Yes, but Mamma, you only get three cuts, and I already took one when I had the sore throat—"

"I think I'll call Haskell. He might just know something."

Jack's voice had grown so casual that it was terrifying. Mary called upstairs. "Benny? Benedetta!" She turned to Dorene. "Where is she?"

"*I* don't know. How'm *I* supposed to—"

She ran next door to the Doroskis', Dorene at her heels. David was watching Martha Doroski roll out pie crust. "Benny isn't here? David, time to come home."

Over his head she nodded meaningfully toward the sky, but of course Martha had to open her big mouth. "Will you look at that *sky!*" She wiped her hands on her apron and untied it. "I'm going to pick up my girls at the Y." Too late, she grew nonchalant. "It's nothing, it'll blow over in an hour, but just to be on the safe side. Come by after, Davey; I'll make lemonade."

"Pink or white?" He was a great one for detail. Mary pushed him out, looking all around for Benny. Oh, God, she thought, I know I should keep better track. I will next time, I promise. "Is it an annihilation alert?" cried David keenly. "Is it, Mom? Is it the end of the world?"

"What a *nut!*" Dorene was amused. She began to sing: "Oh,

goody, goody, it's the end of the world! We'll all be blown to beautiful bits! Beautiful, beautiful—"

David kicked out at her. Mary pulled him inside. Jack was shouting into the phone. "Three forty-three! Three—forty— Can't you hear me? Hang up, I'll get another line!"

"Benny come in?" He shook his head. "Dorene, see if she's at Louise's. David, you try Judy's." She ran upstairs to look out the bathroom window. When she passed Benny's room, there she was, sitting in bed with her dolls and blankets, drinking apple juice.

Mary ran in and slapped her backhand across the face. Benny fell sideways, spilling the apple juice, and began to cry. Mary lifted her and held her tight against her shoulder. "Oh, Benny, how could you give me such a fright? Didn't you hear me call?"

Benny sobbed against her neck. "Yes, but I . . . thought you wanted me to practice and I was . . . *busy.*"

She carried her into the bathroom and sponged off the apple juice. Someday we'll laugh about this, she thought, looking out the window to hide her tears. There came David, sauntering along as if he had all day. Turning an innocent, inquiring face as Dorene flew past, hair streaming, eyes wild (*Panic*); the whole thing had slipped his mind. "Mamma!" Dorene called, "She isn't *any*where!"

Mary leaned out. *"Don't scream in the street!"*

Dorene's face closed; she dropped her head and disappeared under the porch. Sitting Benny on her hip Mary ran downstairs to make amends; but she was too late, Dorene stood (*Reverie*) looking at a magazine on the coffee table; her gleaming hair curtained off her face.

Some other time, thought Mary. She sat down on the couch, holding Benny tight against her like a shield, like a hot water bottle. Benny wore an old lace nightgown of Mary's that clung to her plump legs, damp with apple juice. Jack was still on the phone; David stood at his elbow and spoke into his ear. "What about Mousey? And Hammy? And Ratty?"

Jack brushed his ear, as though David were a gnat. *"Yes,* I want that Utah call. Put me through as soon as you can." He hung up and turned to her, bumping David. "It's just some little oxygen shortage. Remember last year? Haskell's not worried. And he's got a dandy terminometer, nearly four hundred dollars second hand."

Then, as always, he spoiled the effect. "At least, he didn't *sound* worried. We had such a rotten connection, I couldn't really hear what he was saying. But hell, it's been 343 before."

"Never," she said.

"It's 349," said David.

"Nonsense," said Jack.

They checked and it was 349. David hooked his thumbs under imaginary suspenders. "You could count on me, der great scientist."

She pulled Benny still closer. "Oh, what should we *do?*"

Jack began to shout. "How the hell do *I* know?"

"I just thought maybe if we went in the cellar," she said reasonably. He was only angry at his own helplessness. Still, why did she always have to be the reasonable one?

"You know it doesn't matter *where* you go, if it's the big one—"

Dorene clutched at Mary. Mary jumped. "Don't *grab* me!"

"Does 349 mean the big one?" said David. "Our book in school says 362—"

"I *didn't* grab, I just feel scary—"

"We *all* feel scary!"

Benny slid down off Mary's lap. "The big *what?*"

In the end Dorene went weeping upstairs and slammed her door and things got a little calmer. Mary found a book to read to David and Benny. Jack pulled the ottoman up to his armchair. "Sitting down?" she said, surprised.

"Why not? You think I'm supporting the world, like Hercules? I'm not supporting anything but my own family. And Dr. Norseman," he added bitterly.

Outrage steadied her voice. "I *thought* you might want to get your mother."

"Oh. Yes, sure," he muttered. "I'll run right over."

She called after him, "Want to take David?" but he didn't seem to hear.

It was getting dark; a strange, sulphury dark. From time to time a car rushed by. David reached behind her and pulled Benny's hair; Benny hit him on the ear. As soon as Mary got them quiet, the alarm began. Oh, wasn't that the story of their marriage? When the world came to an end, when every other man on the block was home with his wife and children, wouldn't he be off getting his mother?

Ah, don't be such a nut, she told herself; you *sent* him for the old lady. "Go *on!*" said Benny, pounding her wrist, and she realized that the sirens were dying down, it was only the noon whistle, not the alarm.

Then Jack and his mother came in. The old lady was worrying about all the things she should have brought, Jack's father's letters, and the canned water, and her diamond brooch . . . "Diamond *brooch?*" said Mary. "What for?"

His mother turned that tight face on her. "We went away and left the house open to the four winds. Anybody could walk in off the street. *I* thought you *prized* that brooch. I left it to you in my will."

"Oh, it's a beautiful brooch," said Mary. She owed it to Dorene at least to keep it in the family.

Poor Dorene! She ought to run up and see how she was. "Where's Dorene?" said the old lady.

"Upstairs."

"People don't believe me when I tell about my wonderful daughter-in-law, so calm, so rational. *I* would have been wild. *I* would have had all my children gathered around me . . ."

The old lady had been making those scorpion remarks for fifteen years, but they still worked; when the tail came around, Mary always got stung. She put the first joint of her index finger between her teeth and bit it. "Oh, Mother," said Jack impatiently, "the alarm hasn't even blown."

"That doesn't mean a thing," said his mother. "They could be delaying it, with all the graft and corruption."

"Absurd," said Jack. But he was beginning to unhitch; he stood up and walked to the window.

"Watch and see if it isn't in the paper tomorrow," said the old lady. "About the alarm being late, an investigation is promised, et cetera."

Jack picked up the phone and dialed. He would check with all his friends; he was so responsible, everybody said; but *she* was the one that got stuck with grandma. "Fix you some tea? A cup of coffee?"

"Oh, I don't want to be a nuisance. Later I'll have a bite of lunch."

"David!" said Mary, "why don't you show grandma how well you read?" and she went briskly into the kitchen as though she had important chores there. *Lunch!* She stared hopelessly into the refrigerator. Hot dogs, but the old lady couldn't eat hot dogs. And if she fixed her something special, she would fuss: *Oh, I hate to give you so much trouble.* What could they all eat? An omelet? They had had eggs for breakfast.

She went to look at the canned goods. Martha Doroski could handle this with her left hand. Some women were big and bountiful, love and food flowing from them, generous, giving. *She* couldn't even fill a shopping cart without getting a headache. Before she started going to Dr. Norseman, she sometimes wept in the supermarket, back in the corner with the dog food.

Oh, well, it wasn't lunch time yet. She stood looking out at the new apricot tulips she had put in last fall, and taking long, slow breaths . . . "Making lunch?" said Jack.

She gave a little scream. "*Already?*"

"Don't bother," he said sharply. "Go inside, I'll take care of everything."

That was how he got when his mother was around, seeing a slight in every remark, every facial expression. "Don't be silly, I'll do it."

"Don't do me any favors!"

"*Oh,* for God's sake!"

Jack's mother appeared in the doorway; they jumped apart as if she had caught them in some illicit embrace. "I just don't know how you young people can be so calm. I'm ready to pop right out of my skin. But I guess it's like anything in life, you get callous. When *I* was your age . . ."

If I have to listen to all that *one more time I'll die*, thought Mary. Oh, God, don't let me be like that in my old age. If I have an old age. "Well, and of course the older you get, the more you feel strain," she said.

It sounded bitchier than she intended. The old lady seemed

to puff slightly, but before she could speak the phone rang. Jack escaped, crying, "I'll take it!" They stood, heads averted, and listened. "Thanks, operator. Haskell?"

David's voice said, "Hey, Dad! It's going down! Dad? It's 341, Dad!"

The old lady took a deep breath. "I'll tell you something, I'm *glad* I'm older. When the oxygen gives out, I won't be around. I'll leave it for the young people. Gasping like a fish, roasting like a leg of—"

"Don't talk like that!" cried Mary.

The old lady seemed more surprised than offended. "You can't tell *me*—"

"Yes, I can!" said Mary, just the way she had always dreamed of doing. "It's my house! You can't talk like that in *my house*, in front of *my children*—"

But then it was all different from her dream. The old lady turned, touching the door frame like a blind person, and went back inside. Why, she's *hurt*, thought Mary, amazed. What should I do? But she just stood there, listening to the voices from the living room.

"Davey, where's grandma's bag?"

"Where you going, Grandma?"

"Home."

"Well, okay, I think it's safe now," said David judiciously.

Why didn't Jack do something? Couldn't he see what was going on? There were loud, old footsteps in the hall and the door slammed. Should she get him off the phone? After all, it was his mother; he was going to be terribly upset. Through the kitchen window she watched the old lady stump down the front walk. She was nearly at the street when Benny went rushing across the lawn, her damp nightgown flapping. "Granny! Granny!"

The old lady turned. Benny clung to her legs; then she took her hand and led her back. The old lady looked uncomfortable; she stopped and picked a flower. That was to explain her running out. Of course it had to be one of the new tulips.

Now that it was over, Mary had begun to shake. She sat down and listened to Benny chattering as they went through the hall and into the living room. "Anyhow it isn't *time* to go, Granny.

I don't *want* you to go yet." Well, she thought, at least I made one good one, able to see, able to love, to act. If one out of three turns out right, I can't be such a nut.

Jack came in. "Haskell says—"

She put her finger on his mouth. "Because you didn't give out the gum yet, Granny," continued the little voice. "You forgot the gum. The gum in your bag! I saw it before. I always like to see what you brought, Granny."

"Oh, well," she said. She got up and leaned against him, and he gripped her shoulders and held her tight. It was all right; it was all all right.

"I *told* you," he said. "Didn't I tell you, some little oxygen shortage?"

Suddenly she felt exhausted. *She* was the reasonable one, and he was always trying to make her look like a hysteric. She pulled away. The phone rang; he rushed in to answer, and she went back to the refrigerator. There was a little sauerkraut in a plastic bag, half a pork chop, white with cold fat, a pinched-looking baked potato. Dorene called down. "Can I go now? It isn't even twelve-thirty!"

"You can come set the table."

"Can I help?" called Jack's mother.

"Dorene will do it!" she called back brightly.

"It's *David's* day!"

"David's reading to grandma." She looked at the soups. Jack hated tomato; Benny hated chicken noodle. It was too sticky for pepper pot. If the world had come to an end, she thought, at least I wouldn't have to decide what to have for lunch.

Dorene hung over the stair rail. "Listen, I miss Workshop just because you're so *nervous*, and then I have to do *his* jobs, because I'm the *oldest*, but the oldest ought to have a *few meager privileges* . . ."

"What are you laughing at?" said Dorene.

She found she was still holding the cellar door. She let it drop onto the supporting post. "Nothing."

"Ah, tell me!" Dorene pleaded, greedily.

"It's a grown-up joke. Run upstairs and get my bag. I'll drive you to the bus, anyhow."

"Ah, you said—"

"To the bus."

To her amazement Dorene turned and scurried inside; she could hear her pounding up the stairs.

"Yes, the public did put up with color TV's radiation, but I think this is really asking an awful lot of them. Even for 3-D."

Stephen Tall is a college professor and sometime fiction writer—
"science fiction mostly now, but I've appeared in magazines as
diverse as Woman's Day *and* Country Gentlemen. *Chronologically,*
put me somewhere between Glen Campbell and Bing Crosby."
This tale of deep-space science fiction is centered about the colorful
crew of a research ship that has been receiving an alien broadcast for
more than a month but has been unable to determine the meaning or
even the source of the transmission.

The Bear With the Knot on His Tail

STEPHEN TALL

We swept in comfortable wide orbit around Earth, thirty thousand miles beyond the Moon. Cap'n Jules Griffin kept us in the
Moon shadow, the umbra, a pleasanter location in which to
drift and listen than out in the raw yellow radiance of Sol. Only
a few degrees away from the Moon's vast shadowy disc the full
Earth hung like a color plate, blue, cloud-shrouded, the most
majestic object I've ever seen from space.

And I've been around. We all have. It's our job.

Ultraspan made us possible. A discovery that must have been
an accident—or almost. How can matter move faster than
energy? Or can it? Ultraspan eliminates time; so our position in
space can be anything Cap'n Jules wills it to be. Not that he

understands what he does. Especially not that. He knows every pulse of the timonium engines that moves us in finite space, but Ultraspan he takes on faith. Like religion. Like magic. Like the things that happen in dreams.

We've tested it. For the past nine years the research ship *Stardust* has done with ease what was not possible before Willoughby's Hypothesis, that strange variant of an Einsteinian concept that divorces space from time. You don't know what I'm talking about? Neither do I—but it works. Harnessed, implemented, it's Ultraspan.

Life aboard the *Stardust* is comfortable, but for me it's not the good life. I really come alive when we drop in, break out of orbit, and drift down to the surface of some unknown world, some planet that from space shows that it will tolerate us long enough for a look-see. And I did say drift down. The searing outpourings of combustion energy that first took us into and out of space are all a part of our history now. Gravity is no longer a problem. If the conditions required it, Cap'n Jules could bring our fifteen-hundred-foot laboratory-home down over any planet surface at ten miles an hour. We have conquered the attraction of mass for mass.

"Dreaming, Roscoe?"

I don't like to be touched or backslapped, but the hand on my shoulder now was a notable exception to that. Especially when the owner slipped around my easy chair and plumped her luscious self into my lap. I put my arms around her, and we both sat watching the wide screen on which the Earth hung in misty glory.

"The Old Homestead," Lindy said. "If I can just see it once in a while, like now, I'm perfectly content with space. But that's the ultimate, that beautiful blue-green marble out there. We can search all our lives and we'll never find anything like it."

"It's a point of view," I admitted. "Statistically, though, probably not defensible. Somewhere in our Galaxy of hundreds of millions of stars, with space only knows how many planets around them, the Earth has to have a twin. We're still babes in the cosmic woods, and already we've come close. You haven't— say you haven't!—forgotten Cyrene?"

She hadn't forgotten. How could she? And the star Cyrene

was a Sol-type sun. Its yellow rays on the surface of its fourth planet could easily have been mistaken for Sol's rays. But Planet Four had had a strange and simple ecology, and life forms so different that they had made me famous. Yes, I'm that Kissinger. *A Different Evolutionary System*, by Roscoe Kissinger. The lettuce-cube-mill-wheel food chain. So now when I'm on Earth, I have to make speeches. And I don't much like to speak. I'm a field ecologist. I like to do.

But that's not why Lindy remembered Planet Four. It was there, after many invitations, that she finally decided that to be Mrs. Kissinger might be a good thing. Maybe it was the home-like atmosphere. For Planet Four of the star Cyrene *was* Earth-like.

Lindy twisted in my lap and faced me, her classic features, green eyes, and red lips not six inches from my more or less Neanderthal visage. So I did what any man in the Galaxy would have done, and when I had finished she was properly breathless.

"Necking again!" Pegleg Williams growled. He came rolling across the lounge, his slight limp accentuated. He does that when he wants to attract attention. He took the chair next ours.

"Don't you two ever fight, like normal couples? You'll both develop space diabetes, living in a sea of sugar like you do."

Lindy giggled. I kept my grin down to respectable proportions.

"You're in good form," I said. "So what's bugging you?"

Pegleg shrugged and hunched down in the chair. After a moment he waved a hand at the screen.

"Ennui!" he said. "Boredom! We've been lying doggo out here in the Moon shadow for a month. We've listened and we've listened—and if anybody has learned anything, they've carefully kept it from me!"

We're used to Pegleg. We wouldn't even like him any way but the way he is. Occasionally he'll put your teeth on edge, but whenever I undertake a field mission where the chips are really down, Pegleg's the other man. We complement each other like salt and vinegar. Pegleg's one of the great geologists—and as an ecologist, I'm not so bad. So I knew what he meant.

"Don't blame it on Mother Earth," I said. "Blame Johnny Rasmussen. He has an itch. You know that. And he's never had one yet where the scratching didn't turn out to be fun."

Pegleg sprawled deeper in the chair. Reflectively he stared at the screen and automatically flexed his plastic knee joint. He does this when he's thinking. It was while we were scratching one of Rasmussen's itches that he lost that leg, bitten off smooth by a plesiosaur-like critter in a little lagoon on a planet I'd just as soon forget. That one had been only partly fun.

But as I said, I knew what he meant. A geologist hasn't got much going for him in space. He's got to have something to set his feet on, rocks to swing his hammer against. And the ecologist is no better off. Oh, I suppose I could get concerned about the space biome. But it's not me. I need my habitats tangible, my biota solid enough to feel and see.

Lindy rolled out of my lap and stood looking down on us both.

"I think," she said casually, "that I've become supernumerary. I recognize the symptoms. You two want to sit and deplore your respective futile situations. You may forget that I, too, am temporarily unemployed."

Lindy's genius with extraterrestrial microforms is such that we wouldn't dare a landing without her. She was Dr. Linda Peterson, microbiologist extraordinary, long before she was Mrs. Roscoe Kissinger. In fact, Johnny Rasmussen has never recognized the marriage, even though he performed the ceremony. He still carries her on the roster as Dr. Peterson.

"Sit down, Lindy," Pegleg said. "We couldn't gripe with effect without you."

"No," said my gorgeous wife. "When discontent's the topic, it's still a man's world. Or should I say universe? I think I'll go run a diabetes test on myself."

Even Pegleg grinned.

But it started then, and almost unwillingly we listened. Not that it was unpleasant. It wasn't at all. It was strange, weird, haunting. The sounds came rolling out of the speakers with a curious lack of rhythm, with no pattern that could be pinned down. In fact, that was what was driving the sound boys out of their skulls.

Here were no pulsars, no monotonously repeated patterns of any of the several types of sound we're getting now from space. Here was infinite sound variety, constantly changing tone and pitch, sometimes like soft music, sometimes raucous, but with a compelling completeness, point and counterpoint. It went from laughter to pleading, from murmur to roar. And yet the overall feel of it was alien. As sophisticated and endlessly changing as it was, no one even considered that it might have human origin. It was from space, from deep space, and no tests that we had yet made could tell us even the direction from whence it came.

I say "we" because that was the way Dr. Johannes Rasmussen regarded every mission the *Stardust* undertook. Each job was a team job. Sitting out here in the Moon shadow, swinging with the Moon in its orbit around Earth, an elaborate organization of explorer specialists, Earth's finest space teams, had only one mandate, one directive. Everyone, regardless of concern or training, was asked to listen to the sounds, to the always different medley our energy dish was picking up from the great disc on the Moon.

At intervals that never varied, nineteen hours and thirteen minutes thirty-seven seconds, the cosmic broadcasts poured from the speakers. They lasted exactly fourteen minutes seven seconds. From the first decibel they had been carefully and completely recorded, and each staff member was urged, in addition to his other duties, to listen to the tapes whenever he had the chance. Since our duties were minimal, to be charitable, we had heard a lot of replays. They hadn't helped a bit.

So we listened now. Lindy dropped back into my lap, and we held hands and sat quietly while the speakers gurgled and cried and moaned.

"They're unhappy," Linda murmured. "They're in danger and frightened and alone. They're begging for help. They're not frantic yet, but they hope we'll hear them. They know they can't help themselves."

"They?" Pegleg and I said it together.

"They!" Lindy said firmly.

" 'One giant step,' " Pegleg quoted. "Have you told Johnny Rasmussen? He'll be delighted. He'll be especially interested in how you know."

Lindy gestured helplessly and squirmed on my lap.

"He'll be like you," she said in disgust. "Literal. Obtuse. But

I *feel* it! That's not just contact. That's urgent contact. They need us!"

Pegleg shifted his gaze to me.

"Your wife makes a nice appearance in public, but she's subject to hallucinations. I hope it doesn't interfere with your home life."

"Helps, really," I deadpanned. "She thinks I'm handsome."

"That proves my point," Pegleg said.

If this dialogue seems out of character to you, just know that it's the way we are. It's the smoke screen behind which we think. We've been doing it our way for years, and in general things have come out all right. See the thick sheaf of research papers under each of our names in any library worthy to be called a library. We've all got oakleaf clusters on our Ph.D.s.

But we weren't trained for this. And the sound boys and the cryptographers and the language experts were beginning to suspect that they weren't either. Especially befuddled were the communications specialists. For the medley of sounds, picked up by the fifty-acre reception disc on the Moon as though it were originating just beyond the next hill, was directionless. After a full month of trying, they still had no clue. The great disc received the sounds equally well whether phased for north or south, east or west; whether focused critically on Polaris, Deneb or Arcturus. And we, hanging in space thirty thousand miles away, found that even their relay was hard to orient.

We listened until the end. As always, there were familiar elements in the broadcast that I felt the cryptographers should have been able to use. But each transmission was different, and since Lindy had suggested it, I fancied that the tone of each was special. Somewhere, beings with an advanced technology were telling a story to the Galaxy. Hoping, hoping, that somewhere there were beings who could hear. These were feelings, too. My feelings. Only the variety, complexity and timing of the broadcasts could be used for support for them. So I kept them to myself.

The last notes of the transmission, a plaintive, appealing series of wails, died away.

Lindy shifted in my arms. She sighed gently.

"The Music of the Spheres," she said.

Pegleg and I were silent. There was nothing to say.

Of the personnel of the *Stardust*, of all the assorted specialists that made up the Earth's most elaborate space organization, one person was never out of a job. Pegleg and I could gripe; Lindy could sigh for new space bugs; Bud Merani could fidget because there was nothing for an archaeologist to explore out there in the Moon shadow. But Ursula Potts was busy.

Ursula was nothing you'd expect to find in a starship. Little, skinny, old, with weasel features and a great bun of gray hair, she looked like her usual mode of transportation ought to be a broom. To see her strolling the corridors in sneakers, knee-length shorts of red or yellow or green, and an old gray sweater that she wore inside or out, hot planet or cold, was enough to make you wonder if it wasn't time for your annual checkup. I mean you, of course. Not us. We knew her well; knew her and respected her, and sometimes were even a little afraid of her.

Ursula painted. Painters are traditionally kooks, and Ursula abused even that privilege, but she also was a mystic—and a genius. Johnny Rasmussen spent more time looking at Ursula's paintings than he did reading my reports. And I didn't resent it. Somehow, Ursula saw things nobody else saw. She pulled together the results of a look-see.

She beckoned to me as I passed her studio door. She didn't do that to everybody. But we'd seen some strange things together, she and Lindy and Pegleg and I. She was with us at Armageddon on Cyrene Four. So I slid back the door and stepped out into the studio; out into the raw depths of space. Or so it seemed.

"What do you see, Roscoe?"

No greeting. No nothing. She didn't even wave at the bib painting on her easel. But that's what she wanted me to look at. Her strange eyes were glinting in a way I recognized. Ursula was excited about something.

A big, decorated star map. That was my first impression of Ursula's painting. Not her usual thing at all. But when I looked closer, I could see what she'd done. It wasn't a star map. Actually, it was a series of isolated sketches on one canvas. They would have been familiar to any schoolchild.

The old constellations. From our postion out there in the Moon shadow, they showed little distortion, and Ursula had simply noted them down, perhaps almost idly, as little dots of yellow and blue and red and white. But then she'd done more. Around the clusters she had sketched the old mythological figures, filling them in as her interest grew, supplying detail and emphasizing it with color until each sketch seemed almost alive.

Old Orion seemed just ready to step off, his club held high, his lion's skin across his shoulder, and the short blade gleaming in his belt. Behind him prowled the Greater and Lesser Dogs, tongues lolling, eyes eager. One was a German shepherd and one was a Great Dane. Pegasus swept his great wings across more than his share of the canvas as he stretched out into what seemed to be a level run, nostrils flared, foam flying from his mouth. In spite of the wings, he wouldn't have been out of place at Churchill Downs.

I chuckled as I skipped from figure to figure. They were clever, done with the technique only a great artist can command, but I couldn't see anything more. They were superficial. I enjoyed them, but that was all.

I looked at Ursula, and her insistent gaze sent me back to the painting again. I was missing something. There sat Cassiopeia on her throne. Draco pushed his ugly head up toward where the northern bears hung with their ridiculous tails pointing to and away from the Pole Star. And then I got it. The Little Bear looked plump and contented, and Ursula had skillfully painted a honeycomb in his mouth. But old Ursa Major was unhappy. He was gaunt and thin. His lips writhed back from his fangs as though in pain. And no wonder! Out near the end of his long, unbear-like tail Ursula had painted a big, livid, and obviously uncomfortable knot.

"I see it," I said. "Why?"

"Don't know," Ursula said. "Just happened. Didn't look right any other way."

I peered at the knot. Two visuals gleamed in the middle of the bruised and purple lump, one yellowish and one white.

"Mizar and Alcor," I said. "Could be three visuals. A little magnification will bring out another one."

"Know it. Put in another one. Didn't look right. Took it out."

"It would scarcely be visible," I protested. "It couldn't make any real difference in the picture, could it?"

"Did, though. Wasn't happy with it in."

I have mentioned stepping out into Ursula's studio. That was literal. When we were in space, Ursula painted in a transparent bubble, a small, room-sized blister that could be extruded from the apparently featureless side of the *Stardust*. There, in radiation-shielded, air-conditioned comfort, Ursula interpreted the Galaxy.

From deep in the umbra of the Moon, the constellations gleamed like on a summer night on Earth, but with far greater scope. The Great Bear literally hung before us. I picked up Ursula's binoculars, a 12x pair she had evidently been using to verify visuals. I focused on Mizar and Alcor, the region of the knot, the Horse and Rider of some mythology. The third visual came faintly into view, just as I remembered.

"It's there," I said. "Hasn't changed a bit."

"Know it," Ursula said. "Still can't put it in. Doesn't feel right."

"And the knot?"

"Belongs. Got to be. Don't know why."

She looked at me for a moment, then suddenly turned back to her easel, her skinny fingers unerringly selecting the right brush from the collection thrust handle-end first into the large gray bun on the back of her head. It was dismissal. But as I slid back the door, she looked up briefly.

"Think about it, Roscoe."

She didn't have to say it. I was thinking.

There hadn't been one for all the time we had spent in the Moon shadow; so when it came, it was overdue. After looking at Ursula's picture, though, I knew I had been expecting it.

"Ladies and gentlemen!" The voice of Stony Price, communications chief, purred sedately out of our speakers. It was evident that he had been given a formal communique and told to stick with it. "Dr. Rasmussen requests the pleasure of the company of all senior and supervisory staff at dinner this evening. Appetizers at 1800. —Be it known I've consulted the cook. It's a good menu!"

The last, of course, was pure Stony Price. He never stuck to a script in his life.

Johnny Rasmussen's dinners were a tradition aboard the *Stardust*. They all had the same format, the same formal lack of formality. That doesn't sound right. But it says what I want. And a dinner always meant more than it appeared to mean. It always preceded a crisis, or a big decision, or with the same deadpan gentility, it occasionally was a celebration. The *rasion d'etre* was never mentioned. Attendance wasn't compulsory. But nobody missed Rasmussen's dinners. They were where big things happened.

"I feel twitchy," Lindy said. "My radar is jumping. This dinner is going to be a weirdy!"

She was selecting a dinner gown, of course. She was busy at that ten minutes after the communique came through.

I knew what she meant. The dinner would be toothsome, as always, the company familiar and comfortable. It was the reason for it that she was talking about.

She strolled back and forth between two creations she had hung on opposite sides of her dressing table. One was gray, a living, almost ominous gray, streaked through with long diagonal flashes of vivid blue. The other was like a flame hung on the wall. And that was the one she turned to, more and more often.

No red-haired, green-eyed woman can wear a blazing red formal and get away with it. False. One can. She did, too; and with her curls piled high in a strange coiffure, a rope of milk pearls across the scenic splendor of her breasts, and a white orchid at her left shoulder, she looked like some barbaric princess on a world we'd just discovered. Actually, that's literary fudging. Since the *Stardust* first passed Pluto, we've found plenty of life, but none of it human or humanoid. Certainly nothing that remotely resembled Lindy.

I seated her proudly, as I always do. The women all tried, and several of them looked pretty spectacular, but I had the queen and everybody knew it. And that's fair to good going for a guy who looks as rough as I do. Even a dinner jacket and a close shave can do only so much for a body like a storage tank, long, thick arms, pillar legs, and black hair showing everywhere hair *can* show except on the top of my head. Add a face that could have been chopped out with a dull hatchet—and you wonder about Lindy. It must be my beautiful eyes.

Dr. Johannes Rasmussen made his entrance, on cue, exactly at 1800 hours. Tall, slender, tanned, immaculate, his mustaches waxed to points, he stood behind his chair and gazed with pleasure down the long table. Then starting at his right, he named names:

"Captain Griffin, Mr. Cheng, Miss Potts, Dr. Kissinger," —on around the table. When he got back to himself he said, "I'm happy to have you here this evening. Won't you please be seated?" He could have done the whole bit in his sleep. And so could most of us.

The men sat, and we all pitched in without ceremony. Utensils clinked. Conversation builded from a polite murmur to a contented waterfall roar, punctuated occasionally by a deep laugh, or perhaps Lindy's high-pitched giggle.

Next to me Ursula Potts dug into her baked fish like a hungry terrier. Ursula loves to eat as well as I do, which is no faint praise. Ursula's dinner dress was a sullen russet, with no ornamentation. Her skinny fingers were heavy with rings. But her wizened face and strange eyes were the same against any backdrop. She flicked those eyes up and down the table and chewed steadily. She wasn't missing a thing.

"Good fish, Ursula," I said. "Must be Friday."

She licked her thin lips.

"Barbaric reference, Roscoe. No connection between food and the days of the week."

"Not to me," I admitted. "I eat anything any day. But a lot of people still connect Friday and fish."

"Day of mourning among the fish," Ursula said drily. "Quit beating around the bush, Roscoe."

"Okay." I shifted my tone. "What's this bash about, Ursula? Any premonitions? Better still, any information?"

Ursula slurped her Chablis with appreciation.

"Don't know. Can guess, though."

"Give!"

"We're going out."

Rasmussen's seating seemed to confirm it. Cap'n Jules Griffin was on his right, and he wasn't there for his sparkling conversation. Cap'n Jules is the dullest man in space. I can't talk to him for five minutes. Usually he sits far down the table. But he's the genius who implements Ultraspan. He gets us where we want to go.

And Moe Cheng sat next to him, a big-nosed, slant-eyed little man who knows more about the Galaxy than any man has ever known. So it *was* logistics! But Ursula was next, and then I. We weren't there by accident either. Johnny never does anything at random.

We ate, and Rasmussen exchanged polite amenities with those of us within range, like the correct, formal English gentleman he is. I did say English. Forget the name. In the nineteenth century he would have been one of the boys. To him, dinner wouldn't taste right if he weren't dressed for it. Dinner jacket. Black tie.

When the coffee arrived, big fragrant cups of it, and delicate shells of good brandy on the side, Johnny unwrapped the baby. Without seeming to do so, he raised his genteel voice, just enough so that the people at the far end of the table could hear him clearly.

"Ladies and gentleman, a brief but important announcement."

He paused, and the talk died.

"Miss Potts has painted a picture."

Again that pause, but this time the silence was from astonishment.

"Well, good for her!" Pegleg's sour voice was low, but it carried. "But that is Miss Potts' business, painting pictures. If Miss Potts had won the high jump, that might be news!"

Rasmussen's eyes twinkled, but he kept the faith. He didn't smile.

"This particular picture is important to all of us," he said. "On the basis of it I have made a decision. Dr. Kissinger, you have seen the picture. Would you describe it, please?"

I was as out of it as anybody, but I can go along with a gag.

"I suppose you mean the knot on the bear's tail," I said.

"Proceed."

So I went over the picture verbally and wound up with gaunt old Ursa Major, with his unhappy look and the painful lump on his caudal appendage. I played it straight, but people began to snicker. Everybody thought it was a yuk. For that matter, so did I.

"I would prefer tangible data," the chief said, "but we don't have them. We tried everything we know. With the help of the Luna Reception Center—the Big Dish, if you will—we have monitored and analyzed and been frustrated by the sounds from space that Dr. Peterson has called the Music of the Spheres. It has been impossible to determine direction of origin."

Johnny had curled his long fingers around his brandy glass, warming it, and now he raised it, barely wetting his lips.

"Miss Potts has sensed a disturbance in Ursa Major. She has even been specific as to location. Now we know that this is not evidence admissible anywhere in any scientific context. But most of us also know that Miss Potts has—shall we say—unique gifts." (What he meant was that the old witch *was* a witch!) "She has been a staff member on every flight of the *Stardust*, and I have never known her painted analyses to be entirely without foundation."

A delicate sip of coffee, then more brandy.

I have therefore notified the International Space Council that the sounds appear to emanate from *zeta Ursae Majoris*, colloquially called Mizar, and have received clearance to proceed there to investigate."

There wasn't even a murmur the entire length of the table.

"The distance is eighty-eight light-years. Captain Griffin has assured me that we have the capacity to span it in seven stages. Mr. Cheng has plotted these stages. For seventy-two hours we will renew supplies at Tycho Base on Luna, during which time R. and R. leave will be granted to all personnel not involved in these activities. If any individual feels disinclined to make this voyage, he may separate without prejudice, and we will understand. That *is* a very angry-looking knot on the bear's tail!"

He couldn't have bound them any closer to the ship if he had put chains on them. And well he knew it.

He rose and stood tall, the brandy glass still in his hand.

"It has been a pleasure to have you here this evening. There will be further refreshment in the main lounge, where the picture is on display for your examination. Good evening!"

The old formula again. He didn't wait to take a bow, just

slipped out the way he always does. And the press toward the lounge was faster than usual. If space people didn't have curiosity, they probably wouldn't be space people.

Well, that was the program, and that's the way it happened. The *Stardust* bestirred herself, swept out of the Moon shadow in a long ellipse and into the bright unfiltered glare of Sol. Cap'n Jules took the scenic route, orbiting the Moon once as we spiraled in to our spot at the Tycho docks.

The landscape below us hadn't changed much. The dome clusters were few and far between. For the most part the long stretches of bleak, jumbled, cratered surface were just as three billion years had left them. I had been over them hundreds of times, but I still took a moment to stand straight and mentally salute two truly brave men in a tiny, flimsy, spider-legged craft who came safely to rest for the first time in that empty wilderness below. Countless messages have come to Earth from space since 1969, but none will ever again have the thrilling impact of the cheerful announcement:

"The Eagle had landed!"

But enough of reminiscence and history. The *Stardust* eased gently into her slip, her thousands of tons completely nullified by her new timonium antigravs. Cap'n Jules brought her in like a feather on a breeze. She lay full length, a vast metal sausage, blunt-nosed, blunt-sterned and featureless. No onlooker could have imagined the variety of handy little gadgets that could be extruded at need from her glistening hide, from jumper platforms to Ursula Pott's studio. Nor was there any hint of the full fifty openings that could be activated; personnel ports, cargo ports, great shutter-like openings that could each discharge a four-man scout-boat into space.

The personnel ports were promptly put to use as all but a handful of our researchers and crew streamed into the pressurized corridors and out into the big-city attractions and fleshpots of Tycho Base. Pegleg and Lindy and I went along. I couldn't have cared less about Tycho's charms, but it did feel good to get my feet back on terra firma once again. I said as much.

"Luna firma," Lindy corrected. "Terra is thataway."

And so it was, hanging resplendent, high in the Lunar northern sky. The great central dome of Tycho arched over the sector of shops and hotels and entertainment places in one graceful, lofty sweep. It filtered out hard radiation and gave a soft, ghost-like quality to the sunlight it allowed to come through. And it changed the celestial view. We looked up at a luminous green Earth, and behind it the northern constellations were picked out in icy dots. The Great Bear was in view. For a moment I could almost see his gaunt, unhappy look, and the swelling knot on his long tail.

We prowled the grass-bordered streets, looked into shop windows, sniffed at the doors of eating places. We sat on the benches in Tycho's famous Aldrin Park, where oaks and beeches and pines and dogwoods pretended, like the people, that they were still on Earth. A mockingbird sang from a holly tree near where we sat. Cardinals and bluebirds flashed as they flew. I wondered what effect the lessened gravity had on their flight. They seemed happy and normal.

It was a pleasant little interlude. Pegleg left us on affairs of his own, which I suspected had to do with a slumberous-eyed, darkhaired little stewardess he knew on one of the shuttle runs to Earth. The nature of man changeth not. I felt smug, for I'd put all that behind me. Or, to put it more correctly, I liked my arrangement better.

Lindy and I had dinner at the Earthview, not Tycho's biggest or grandest restaurant, but I knew from experience that you couldn't beat the food. And that's why I go to eating places. We had oysters Luna, a pale green soup that smelled like a breath of the jungle, reindeer steaks from Lapland, artichokes and spinach from Texas, and three kinds of wine. There were fruits from Malaya, a French dessert, and finally coffee and a heavenly clear liqueur, a specialty of the house. And all served by a blonde goddess six feet tall and magnificently topless!

"Eyes are for looking," Lindy said, "but don't neglect your food. Would you like to bet I couldn't take her job?"

"Why," I asked reproachfully, "would you want to put a poor girl out of work? You already have a job. One that's yours as long as you want it, and when you don't want it any more, I'll close the position out for good. Now may I look?"

Her green eyes danced. She reached across the little table to put a hand on mine.

"Stare away," my wife said. "I don't see how it can hurt you."

If you're thinking that this is irrelevant, that it's all digression, don't you believe it. That little touch of R. and R. was important. We needed the supplies they were loading into the *Stardust*, but no more than we needed that touch of solid ground beneath our feet, the renewed contact with the substrate that periodically we all have to have. Still, the seventy-two hours were enough. When the *Stardust*, herself rested, lifted gently like a living thing from her berth and the Moon dropped away, we were all aboard, and we were all glad.

Earth was in our viewports for a brief while. Then, under full timonium drive we flashed across the Solar System and into deep interstellar space beyond Pluto's orbit. Yet we were simply checking, getting ready for the journey. Light-minutes were nothing, even at the terrific finite speeds of which we were capable. Light-years were ahead of us. Eighty-eight of them. And that meant Ultraspan.

We were in the hands of three unlikely geniuses—they abound on the *Stardust*—and I'm sure I've been more concerned for my life in a Paris taxi.

Moe Cheng planned the stages. Cap'n Jules stood by to implement them, one by one. Johnny Rasmussen structured the patterns at the end of each stage, move by move. This was new space, and we were tracking sounds in a direction not determined by any scientific data. We could never have justified ourselves to any logical inquiry. Still, that didn't disturb me either. Computers can goof, but I'd never known Ursula's weird sixth sense to be entirely wrong.

An Ultraspan stage can't be described. Nevertheless, I'll try. You are conscious in stage, but nothing has either importance or meaning. In effect, according to one school, during the jump you cease to exist as an entity, and the Nirvana-like consciousness is like a shadow projected forward, your id stripped of all concerns and without a home. I don't know. There is a perceptible time-span in stage, and you know it's there. Yet theoretically time does not exist, and with the effect of time suspended, one space is as likely as another. Still, stages can be plotted and the target space occupied. We've been doing it for years.

Lindy and I held hands for the first stage, programmed for ten light-years. I was nothing and she did not exist, yet somehow I knew that we were sitting in our quarters in the *Stardust*, and that we were holding hands. It seemed days and weeks, and yet it seemed only a minute or two. Our view screen showed an alien pattern of stars. My wife's hand was warm in mine. The starship barely had headway, perhaps no more than a thousand miles an hour. We were in pattern after the stage, orienting, checking, verifying. And the life of the ship went on as though it had not been interrupted. Which, indeed, perhaps it had not. We use Ultraspan, but we may never really understand it.

"There'll come a day," Lindy said, "when I won't want to tolerate that any more."

She got up and walked restlessly across the room.

"It's painless," I said.

"Of course. It isn't that. It's—it's just that it seems to take me away from me! You dig? With all my problems solved, all my curiosities satisfied, all my challenges met, maybe sometime I won't want to come back. To go ten light-years in space without time lapse isn't for man. It's—it's ag'in nature!"

"Karma," I said. "Nirvana. Maybe we have found the way. And what, after all, is ag'in nature? What's nature?"

Lindy turned, and suddenly she smiled at me. It was the quick change of mood that all women show. Or I suppose they all do. I could see the strain go out of her face, the confidence return.

"You and me together! That's nature, friend. Pay me no attention, Roscoe. I go gloomy, but I'll always come back."

I rose and started for her. And our speaker rattled, cleared its throat, and the Music of the Spheres poured out of it.

It was different. There was more discord, more harshness, than in any broadcast before. It throbbed and pulsed and wailed. Where before only Lindy could detect urgency, now it seemed to me that anyone could. And I thought I knew why. We were closer. Whatever was impending, whatever motivated those calls to the Galaxy, to whomever or whatever would listen—whatever it was, it was nearer. If we had stayed at our base near Earth, we wouldn't have heard this broadcast for ten years yet.

The signal was no stronger. It came in plainly, though, and here we were dependent on our own sensors. We didn't have the enormous backing of the Big Dish on the Moon. As I listened, conviction grew. We were headed exactly right. We were on the beam.

After an Ultraspan stage, Rasmussen always activated a twenty-four hour pattern. This gave time for a rest period, time for all data to be processed, time for all personnel to adjust. For the feel of one sector of space is not the feel of another. I can't explain that. But it's so.

We staged again, fourteen light-years. There was no star pattern on our view screens then. They were awash with brilliant light, all radiation screens were activated, and not twenty-five million miles away lay the awesome grandeur and tossing energy of a flaring sun. It was as close as we had ever come to a primary energy unit, but it was no mistake. We were where Moe Cheng intended we should be.

The broadcast came through. Fragmented by the roiling radiation, we still picked up most of it. And fourteen years had made a difference. There was panic in the music now, fear, desperation, and the first faint threads of despair. If anyone had doubted that our direction was right, they didn't any more.

Five stage later—five memorable stages—and the *Stardust* drifted at the edge of a spectacular star system. Not large, as such systems go, not as colorful as the red giants are, but with an attraction for us that I suppose was at least partly historical. Since man first had raised his eyes toward the heavens, he had known this little twinkling dot in space. It was a part of the complex by which travelers found their way. Ancients had used it as an eye test. For this was Mizar.

I don't have to instruct you. Any schoolboy knows the double-triple systems of this brighter one of the Alco-Mizar duo. But no schoolboy or anyone else of human origin had ever had our view of them. The first human visitation. And the last.

Our astronomers probed and measured and explored and verified, while we sat impatiently watching the view screens. They made it easy for us. The triple system of Mizar B, three bluish suns, moved slowly along the paths of their complex orbits around their common center in space. From Earth they simply melded to form a dim blue point. But it was Mizar A, the double, that had been our objective, though we had no known it. Here, somewhere here, was the point of origin of the Music of the Spheres.

The smaller component of Mizar A lay far in the distance across the system, a blue-white sun that glimmered cheerily and normally. Its relatively giant twin, a bright yellow on the charts, was no longer that. It hung in space before us, an ominous, shifting, sullen orange, a vast, savage celestial furnace, unstable and threatening. We knew its nature and its fate before the sounds came through once more, exactly on time.

You have listened to a requiem. You know the sounds of a dirge. The Music of the Spheres was still music, but there was in it no hope, no calls for help, no panic and no fear. The time was past for these. Whatever made the music was saying good-bye, was expressing thankfulness for having lived, for the wonders of having been sentient. There was even a gentle speculation that this was not the end after all—that somewhere, in an unimaginable future, there might be something more.

Now I'm not sensitive, as Lindy is. Certainly I have no touch of the mysticism that allowed Ursula Potts to feel crisis across the light-years. And Pegleg is worse. Yet all of us, sitting in the small lounge listening to that broadcast, all of us heard just what I've described. We felt it so plainly that we could put it into words, as I've done here. And there was one thing more we could detect. It was regret. Regret that before life ended it had not known other life, other beings that knew the joys of thought and achievement, beings that it believed existed, and to whom it had sent its music pulsing out among the stars.

Ursula Potts sat small and still in her chair as the broadcast ended, her strange eyes glowing. Tears flowed down Lindy's cheeks. Pegleg twisted uncomfortably as he sat. Automatically he flexed his plastic knee joint. I got up and paced.

"All personnel, attention please!"

Dr. Johannes Rasmussen never speaks on intercom, but they were his cultured tones that came out of the speakers now.

"This is a summary, for your information. The sun Mizar A-1

is in unstable condition, prenova. It will disintegrate in thirty-three hours. It has a single planet. Dr. Frost has recorded all vital physical data; so let it suffice to say that it is appreciably larger than Earth, has an atmosphere, and every evidence of varied and complex life. The music has originated there."

Johnny paused, and I could imagine him sitting, his face calm and apparently untroubled, reflecting on how to phrase his next sentence.

"We have time. We will proceed immediately to the planet, orbit and descend to the surface unless conditions make that impossible. Radiation is already high, many times human tolerance, but far less than the shielding capacities of our ship, or even our spacesuits. Unless the music is mechanically produced, life still exists on the planet's surface. But probably you all detected finality in the last broadcast. Remarkable, really!"

Johnny seemed to be saying the last two words to himself.

"The planet is now on your screens. We will keep it there during approach. Please consider what part you would care to play in our brief reconnaissance. The brevity is occasion for regret, but it is fortunate that we have arrived before the system destroys itself. We will allow ourselves a safety margin of three hours, and we will stage thirty hours from this time. Thank you."

Nobody but Rasmussen could have made the most dramatic experience man had ever known sound as routine as a weather report.

The planet was a small bright dot on our screens as we flashed toward it and toward its glowering sun. It grew steadily, though. Cap'n Jules wasn't wasting time. Before long the dot was a sphere; shadows showed and drifted on its surface; colors glowed. Finally it hung before us in majestic blue-white splendor, suffused over all by the deepening orange light of the sullen sun. Doomed planet!

"What a pity!" Lindy murmured. "What a terrible, horrible, hard-to-understand, unbelievable fate! Roscoe, if I didn't remember Earth, *that* would be the grandest object we've ever seen from space!"

"Location, distance from its primary, rotation rate, revolution rate, light quality and intensity, all ideal," I said. "And there's plenty of water, an oxygen atmosphere, a deep and varied planetary crust. Just the kind of cradle life would have to have."

I had been running down Doug Frost's physical data tables. Like I said, everything was perfect. If you had set out to build a model planet, this was probably how it would have looked when you had finished. Then add countless eons of evolution! The results at least were life forms so sophisticated, so learned, that they could send complicated musical messages far into the Galaxy. How far, we had no way of knowing.

And now the source of its life was sick, stricken with an incurable illness, a slowly progressing loss of balance in its atomic furnaces. In thirty-three hours the story would end. Thirty-one hours, now. We had taken two hours to approach the planet. For the life on that beautiful world out there, thirty-one hours until the end of time!

As we swept into high orbit, three thousand miles above the planet's surface, speakers came alive all over the ship. Johnny Rasmussen was calling the makers of music, and he wanted us all to hear. Every characteristic of the celestial broadcasts had long ago been analyzed. I could imagine the care with which Stony Price was matching element to element, intensity to intensity, frequency to frequency. But it was Rasmussen's voice that was going out. His message was simple. He knew that if it was detected it would not be understood, but his neat soul squirmed if all ends were not carefully tied.

"This is the starship *Stardust*, from the Sol system, eighty-eight light-years from your own. We have come in response to your messages. We see the condition of your sun. We will meet with you if it is possible. Please respond."

The speakers were silent. I probably held my breath for a full minute before I remembered to exhale. But nothing happened. After a brief time lapse Johnny repeated his message. Again nothing. Then he spoke to us, to the personnel of the *Stardust*.

"I had hoped that we might establish the location of the transmitting installations and home directly on them. It was a remote hope, at best. Some hours remain before the next scheduled broadcast, if in fact another ever will be made. A pity. As you may now see from the building complexes on your screens, life has indeed reached a high level here. We have not before encountered any forms so advanced."

He paused, doubtless rearranging his next sentence into a form that pleased him better. He never got a chance to use it.

The music came softly, hesitantly, wonderingly, as if its maker or makers didn't really believe. To our knowledge, they had been sending their calls out across the Galaxy for nearly a hundred years. And now, when time had almost run out, they were answered! The tones deepened, strengthened. We could hear the exultant questions is them: *"Who are you? Where are you? Speak to us again!"*

Pegleg was at our screen, adjusting for a better view, and we all could see the image whirl as the *Stardust* changed direction. Cap'n Jules had shifted course with the first pulse of sound.

"This is the *Stardust*," Rasmussen said. "We hear you. Speak again! Speak again!"

The response poured from the speakers like a hymn of thanksgiving, like the sound of a choir in a great cathedral. I'm no musician, but any field man can sort out sounds. I could tell that that volume came from many sources. Then it died away into soft, happy whispers and only one tone remained, a clear, resonant soloist. That tone went up and down the scale, repeated and doubled back on itself in amazing patterns. And I knew, everybody knew, that it was speech.

The *Stardust* swept down into the atmosphere in a fluid, ever-decreasing glide. She knew where she was going, now. The computer had solved the location of the transmitter in seconds, for the unrelayed sound no longer lacked direction. Clouds briefly blurred the view screens. Then we were cruising smoothly and slowly over a landscape like nothing we had ever seen before. Still, it was familiar. All the elements of cultured, civilized occupancy were there. Only the forms were different.

It was not Earthlike. There were no trees, no grass, no flowers. Color was there, and variety, and I suppose I sorted things out pretty quickly. In the presence of proper stimuli I began to function automatically. If you put food before a hungry animal, it will salivate. Put an ecologist in a new ecosystem and he will start to analyze. Pavlovian. Inevitable.

All over the ship the same thing was going on. Johnny

Rasmussen isued no orders. It wasn't necessary. Every researcher, every team, had gone into a structured behavior pattern, preparing, planning, anticipating. Each knew better than anyone else what his own part should be in this strange, brief, and tragic exploration.

I was in my lab, without remembering how I got there. Lindy undoubtedly was scooping up samples, assaying the life in the atmosphere. Pegleg was readying to go out at first touch down. And there was no doubt that Ursula's studio was extruded and that she was hard at work.

My view screen flickered as the scoutboats went out. Four swishes. Sixteen men. Geographers and meteorologists probably. They would range for hundreds of miles around the mother ship, their cameras recording everything from horizon to horizon, packing in raw data about this world that would be studied and analyzed long after the planet had ceased to be. We knew this. We all faced it. But there was no other thing we could do. Here life had evolved to high level—but all life must end sometime.

I changed into field gear. It wasn't much, just shorts, a jersey, sandals and a gear harness. Outside was going to be awkward and tricky, for we would be in spacesuits. The strange landscape looked tranquil and peaceful, but the radiation was lethal. We'd never worked under such conditions before. The suits anticipated them, though. We had a wide margin of safety.

"Shame about that blasted radiation." Pegleg read my mind. I hadn't even noticed him come into the lab. I was scooting my chair on its track back and forth along the row of sensor consoles that reported and recorded a variety of basic abiotic data. "As you can see, the air is sweet. More oxygen than we're used to."

"I've been checking the sources," I said. "Photosynthesis, as you'd expect from all the green. Funny thing, though. *Everything* seems to be photosynthesizing. Haven't picked up a flicker of what you might call animal life."

"Nothing looks like it either." Pegleg studied my screen. We were cruising at two thousand feet and at fifty miles an hour. First reconnaissance pattern. As eager as we were to contact the dominant life, the makers of music, still Johnny Rasmussen held to the pattern. We had time. We learned as we went. By now we all knew that the transmitter was a thousand miles away, but we'd spend an hour in this pattern, then flash to our destination in minutes. It was midmorning on the land below us, the last midmorning it would ever see.

"Animals are more sensitive to radiation," I suggested. "Could be they're already dead."

"The broadcast boys are still on the ball. Are you hinting that they're plants too?"

"We're shielded," I pointed out. "Why shouldn't they be? Somehow they haven't developed the know-how to escape their planet, but I predict that in many ways they'll be as advanced as we are. We couldn't have sent out the Music of the Spheres."

Pegleg's narrow face had its usual suspicious expression, as though he smelled a dead mouse.

"Smart enough, maybe to take over the *Stardust*, and leave us here in their places to face Eternity in the morning?"

"This is a planet bigger than Earth," I said drily. "The *Stardust* would be just a mite overloaded."

Pegleg snorted.

"Genghis Khan would only have picked a few passengers. Hitler wouldn't have taken everybody. Just a lady friend, maybe, and a few zealots to do the work. Don't be an ass, Roscoe. Even so-called kindly life forms want to keep on living. It's a pretty basic urge. The hand of brotherhood should be backed up by a club, just in case."

"If I know Johnny Rasmussen, it will be. He doesn't look or act as ornery as you do, but I do sometimes get the impression that he's sadly lacking in faith. Taking the *Stardust* would require a gambit we can't even imagine. You know that as well as I do."

"A comforting thought." Pegleg subsided, but he still grumbled. "Just the same, when we finally go, that'll be the reason. 'Love thy neighbor' is an impossible assignment. All it does is to leave the door unlocked so he can knock you on the head or steal you blind."

This was standard Pegleg philosophy, and how much of it he actually believed I suppose I'll never know. What I do know is that if and when I ever do get trapped in a last extremity, there's no man I'd rather have backing me up than Pegleg Williams.

We concentrated on the view screen. The ship was traversing a tremendously wide valley, and in length it seemed to go on and on. There were surfaced roads that swept in sinuous curves, water courses that undulated, and wherever road met river there was a gracefully arching bridge. Everything was curved. There wasn't an angle anywhere.

Nothing seemed to fit the specifications of a town. There were buildings, always in clusters, always piled masses of brightly colored domes. Too big for family dwellings, as we understand families, I still felt that they housed the builders and users of the roads and bridges. The green mounds arranged in orderly curved patterns over wide areas became plants in fields in my thinking. The green was chlorophyll. So the life pattern was below us, at least for this portion of the planet, but never a sign of the dominant forms, never a hint of movement. Either they were already dead from the radiation, or the *Stardust* had spooked them. If they were alive, they must have heard that their space broadcasts had been answered. So I reasoned, but nothing I could see gave much support to my speculations.

The first reconnaissance hour passed. Johnny Rasmussen gave the word, the ship nosed upward slightly, and the land below us began to blur. In an hour we had traveled fifty miles. In the next few minutes we went almost twenty times that far. Then the *Stardust* cut speed and peeled off in a long sweeping glide. The structure we had come eighty-eight light-years to seek spread out ahead of us. It was, it had to be, the transmitter complex, and just to see it was worth the trip.

It rose out of a level plain, row on row and tier on tier of multicolored domes, piled on and against each other in a fashion that looked fearfully unstable, but which must have represented the ultimate in fine engineering. From a distance it looked like an oriental fan or a peacock's tail, spreading outward and upward from a narrow base, the cantilevered domes like beads on strings, thousands and thousands of them, each as large as family dwellings on Earth. Two miles into the sky the great fan spread, the weirdest and most beautiful artifact of my experience.

We swung slowly around it, drifting in a twenty-mile circle. Cameras and sensors were probing and recording the whole improbable complex. My info board also told me that the *Stardust* was enveloped in a force field that would require incredible energy to penetrate. Pegleg needn't have worried. Rasmussen wasn't underestimating anybody—or anything.

Our peerless leader was at his microphone.

"We're here, friends. We're coming in for a landing. Do you see us? Give us a sign! Can you hear us? Give us a sign!"

Perhaps the last was because we had heard nothing since we dropped into the atmosphere. And I found myself wearing a humorless grin. Even in this last extremity, they mistrusted us as well.

The domed dwellings were scattered in patterns outward from the base of the fan, multicolored, brilliant. There were many hundreds of them, and roads curved in from all directions. Everything was there—except the life forms; except the "people."

Cap'n Jules picked the closest empty spot and set the *Stardust* down gently, without a jar. Pegleg and I were suiting up, checking again and again the shielded protective coverings we had never had a chance to use before. Johnny's voice came at intervals from the speakers. No response. Suddenly we were too strange, too alien for the inhabitants of this world, some of whom had to be still alive and watching us at this moment. But they gave no sign.

Rasmussen has imagination. He wasn't getting through and he knew he was being heard. He changed tactics. The next sound that came from the speakers was very familiar and soothing to me. I had heard it under many circumstances, and on at least twenty worlds. Often in my quarters, after a good meal, it relaxes me as nothing else ever could. For Lindy strummed her guitar and sang softly, sang a baby lullaby from old Earth, eighty-eight light-years away.

That did it. Throbbing musical chords broke from the speakers. Sounds ran up the scales and peaked in little questioning tones. Lindy answered with chords of her own, always gentle, always changing. We could feel the answering excitement as the responses caught up each note, elaborated it, and flung it back, every time with the question so plain it was almost in words.

"I wonder what I'm really saying to them," Lindy murmured. "I do hope it's not insulting." She struck a series of soft notes and crooned a paraphrase of an old movie song, a fairy tale from back in the twentieth century: *"Come out, little people, where-ever you are, and see the nice spaceship that came from a star!"*

But the little people did not come out. The musical dialogue continued, but nothing moved. By now, though, we had more information about them. The physiologists had activated their delicate metabolic probes and were searching the dwellings and working their way up and down the fan. There were life forms behind every wall, forms with complicated metabolisms, apparently all one species. They were shy or frightened or suspicious, but they were there.

Pegleg and I were ready. Johnny gave his okay and we went out through the locks, the first human beings to walk on this doomed world. We barely beat out Bud Merani and his team of archaeologists. If Merani can't find ruins, new, strange buildings will do. They swarmed out behind us, spread toward the nearer dwellings. In our bulky white suits and gleaming helmets we may have looked like a pretty formidable invasion, if Lindy's continuing concert wasn't reassuring enough. I rather hoped she wouldn't accidentally say the wrong thing. Undoubtedly the local inhabitants could use energy concentrations, if they chose. We each were protected by a force field, but as you would expect, it was minimal. It would be a minor deterrent, at best.

Pegleg saw them first.

"Roscoe! Bud! Heads up!" Pegleg's communicator was set for universal output; so he rasped in everyone's earphones.

Large oval doors were sliding open all along the base of the transmitter complex. Out of them small cars came rolling, one after another, a veritable fleet of them. Like the houses, their colors glistened. They came steadily toward the starship, falling into lines as the roads fanned out.

We had set down between two wide highways. In a few minutes each was choked with the little vehicles for the entire length of the *Stardust.* There were hundreds, maybe thousands of them, identical except for color, and each with its single occupant. And the reason for that was simple enough. One was all a car could hold. A hitch-hiker would have been out of luck.

Each little car moved on four fat, balloon-like wheels. Each car body was a short, thick flat oval, and the driver fitted down into it like an egg into an eggcup. You'd be surprised how apt that was. The driver *looked* like an egg. Well, maybe not exactly, but they were the same shape. The old idea that intelligent life forms would inevitably be human or humanoid just hasn't panned out for us. We've never found any that *were*. Thinking it over, why should they be?

I walked slowly over to the nearest line of cars, the idea forming in the back of my mind that perhaps the beings couldn't leave their transportation. I could see no limbs, no outgrowths of any sort. They had them, though, as one of them quickly proved. It extended tentacles, pushed itself up out of its nest between the wheels, and climbed down, shooting out extensions wherever it needed them, retracting them again when the need passed. It rolled toward me on multiple outgrowths, each flattening at the tip as weight was put on it.

The thing was perhaps five feet tall. It was a uniform pale olive-green. Longitudinal striations showed on the body surface from top to bottom. Across the upper third of the body, on the side kept toward me, was a conspicuous, eight-inch ribbon-like strip, delicate and glistening and rosy pink in color. It came to a halt six feet away, raised itself up on three stiffened tentacles, tripod-like, and a well-defined oval section in its middle began to vibrate. The flute-like tones were familiar enough. We had been listening to them for many weeks. They were pleasing, varied, and the being produced them in what was evidently a formal manner. We were being welcomed. Or I hoped we were.

"The keys to the city, Roscoe." Pegleg seemed to have the same impression.

I bowed to the egg-like dignity.

"We thank you very much, sir or madam, as the case may be. We understand you're having some trouble with your sun. I regret to say that there's not a blasted thing we can do about it, but we're at your service if you can think of something. Johnny, do you have any suggestions for dealing with our little friends?"

"Play it by ear. You're doing fine!" Rasmussen's voice was in my earphone. The egg couldn't hear him. It was already speaking again. Its voice was rich with overtones and rose and fell with undoubted emotion. Then it paused and stood as high as its tripod would allow, the pink strip across its upper front rippling and intensifying. I suspected that this was an organ of vision, a suspicion later verified.

I bowed again.

"It has made some kind of a profound pronouncement." I spoke clearly. "I think Lindy's guitar can give the best answer. Play something, Lindy." I turned and gestured toward the spaceship.

From twenty speakers Lindy's series of musical chords flooded out. Then, one note at a time, she picked out the first phrase of a simple tune, totally inappropriate and three hundred years out of date:

"Oh, the Moon shines bright tonight along the Wabash!"

Out of date or not, it was a sensation. The beings all swiveled back and forth in their cars, their vision strips rippled, and a whole array of tentacles sprouted and waved and were retracted again.

"Oh, dear!" Lindy sang. "I hope I haven't promised them anything we can't deliver. Would you say they're pleased or angry?"

"If I had a month, I'd be able to tell you." I glanced upward at the savage, sullen sun, and once again was aware of the murderous orange overglow. "This is a shame! To us they look ridiculous, but they know what the problems are. Here's culture and learning and joy of living—and this time tomorrow it will all be gone. They know we know. And they know we can't help. Kismet!"

"In that case," Johnny Rasmussen said in my ear, "they'll find satisfaction in knowing about us. Invite him in!"

A lot of things were happening. Squads of white-suited, helmeted figures were pouring out of the exits as team after special team implemented its investigation pattern. They expected full cooperation from the inhabitants, which had nothing at all to lose, and certainly knew it. There was no time for diplomatic sparring, for evidences of good faith. The only verity was the dwindling time.

The little cars left the roads and scurried like beetles over the fields around the *Stardust*. The featureless hide of the ship changed. Rasmussen opened viewpoints, extruded platforms and a veritable forest of sensors, anything he could make visible without danger from the deadly radiation. I saw a whole circlet of the small vehicles ranged around Ursula's transparent studio, the vision strips of the drivers fixed on the strange figure dabbing away at the big canvas. What they must have thought unfortunately will never be known.

The first of the returning scoutboats circled the transmitter and planed in to ease itself into its slip through a briefly opened orifice. Each boat would be decontaminated as it entered. That the boat caused excited comment from the egg-beings was obvious, for the volume of sound rose and peaked as it came in. They were talking among themselves continuously now, like a vast orchestra tuning up.

Three more beings had left their cars and came rolling across to join the official greeter, if that is what he/she was. I beckoned, waved toward the starship, took a few steps. They got it immediately. They faced each other in a circle, fluted softly back and forth, then turned again to me. I led on and they followed.

As we went through decontamination, I worried. What it would do to them we couldn't even guess. But we were all lethally hot and it had to be done. As it happened, I was wasting my concern. It didn't inconvenience them in the least.

They were more concerned when Pegleg and I shucked our spacesuits and appeared as vastly different creatures emerging, like insects, from our bulky white chrysalides. They twittered and fluted in what was without doubt astonishment. The four of them rolled around and around us, nervously extruding and extending tentacles, almost touching us, but never quite making contact. When the purple all-clear light showed in the little room, we led them through the sphincter into the locker room beyond and then into the corridors of the *Stardust*.

"Bring them up to main."

Rasmussen's voice came from a speaker on the wall, and our guests responded with a series of organ tones. Evidently they recognized the voice. The corridors were empty; the automatic lift opened when we needed it, and there were no sounds. The ship was quiet. Since the egg-beings had no faces, it was pretty hard to read their reactions, but their vision strips were rippling and pulsing wildly, changing from palest pink to cloudy violet.

Dignity is a universal trait. Don't think of it as human. You've seen it in the confident pace of a fine horse, in the gracious, condescending mien of a full-fed lion, in a tabby cat lying in the sun. Dignity projects and demands respect. And our guests or hosts, depending on how you look at it, had it in full measure.

We ushered them into the big main lounge, with its easy chairs scattered as in a retirement club and wide multiview screens everywhere. Just about every chair was occupied. All rose to their feet as we entered. Johnny Rasmussen came forward with the brand of dignity that is *his* special trademark, tall and well-groomed and elegant. And the egg-beings matched him, gesture for gesture, tone for tone. They knew he was The Man.

"Welcome aboard the *Stardust*," the chief said.

The egg-beings responded in unison, a pleasing medley of sounds.

Johnny hesitated for a moment, then lowered himself into the nearest chair. He had nothing comparable to offer to them, but it was an experiment, just the same. It meant: *Let's communicate.* And they weren't at a loss. They ranged themselves in a half-circle before him, retracted all extrusions, flattened themselves on their bases, and sat, after their fashion. They looked like a half-moon of outsized paperweights, motionless except for their rippling vision strips.

Communication, though, wasn't that easy. Somehow, we hadn't been able to stumble on the key that would give meaning to their music. It was reasonable to suppose that they were trying and had had no better luck with our speech. Except for gestures, it was a stalemate. And there was no time.

After a few minutes of unintelligible amenities, Rasmussen made his decision.

"We will show them the ship, Dr. Kissinger." He still seemed to be chatting with his guests. "We'll show them quarters, labs, machinery, communications, libraries. We'll make things work. Project a tape for them. Show them how we prepare food and eat it. Let them look at view screens and through telescopes. Everything we can think of. Many physical principles are universal. They're bound to recognize something. Sooner or later we'll get a common denominator."

I could hear Pegleg's almost inaudible growl beside me. Rasmussen sensed it.

"Don't worry, Dr. Williams. We'll stay alert."

"See that we do, Johnny," Pegleg said. "No dopes built that transmitter out there. They may have us pretty well cased already."

"A possibility," Rasmussen admitted, "and a chance we have to take. You've never been exactly the conservative type, Pegleg."

Johnny *never* uses Pegleg's nickname.

"I'm almost tempted to hope," Pegleg said, "that I get a chance to say 'I told you so!' It doesn't make sense that they will cheerily tell us good-bye and then sit flat on their bottoms like they're doing now and await disintegration. 'Tain't lifelike. 'Tain't human!"

"Neither are they," I said.

We showed them the ship. As we progressed, I could sense the astonishment that they first exhibited give way to keen, understanding scrutiny. I was sure that they grasped the purposes of most equipment we showed them. They twittered and whistled and fluted over each new situation, with an occasional chord thrown in. When I spoke into a microphone and indicated by gestures that my voice was being heard by the thousands outside, they made the connection immediately. As you'd expect. Communication was probably their area of greatest technical competence.

One of them, perhaps the First Greeter, though I never could be sure, rolled before the mike and showed plainly that he wanted to use it.

"Oh, oh!" Pegleg said.

But Johnny waved a hand. The egg-being seemed to swell; his vision strip flickered frantically; and he launched into a long series of clear tones, modulated, muted, and then occasionally ringing. It was quite a speech, and it took him several minutes.

"Complete report," Pegleg said in disgust. "Those boys now know more about how this ship ticks than I do. May I timidly suggest that you don't show them Ultraspan?"

"I always like to hold something back," Rasmussen said drily. "It would take perfect communication even to project the idea of Ultraspan. No, I think we're safe. There was another reason for that speech. Look at them."

The panoramic view screen in the communications room

showed the base of the great transmitter, the roads leading from it, and all the car-packed area between it and the ship. Our four visitors clustered around the screen, flattened their bottoms, and sat watching.

The little cars swirled and circled like colony ants. Many of them swung about and rolled back toward the entrances in the base of the complex. The roads cleared. The traffic departments in some of our Earth cities could have learned a lot from the neatness and dispatch with which they sorted themselves out.

By the time the roads were open, cars were again issuing from the transmitter base. They came slowly, each pulling a small four-wheeled trailer behind it, and each trailer was piled high with multicolored oval packages. Without hesitation they rolled toward the ship and on up to the port through which we had entered.

Our four visitors tried earnestly to explain. Their fluting notes were persuasive and pleading. They extruded more tentacles than we had yet seen, rolled around the communications room, paused to harangue each of us in turn.

"Well, I'll be—!" Pegleg said. "That's a cold-blooded bit. They want to load on supplies and go along. To heck with the peasants!"

Somehow that didn't seem valid to me. Rasmussen, too, looked dubious. Lindy had joined us on our tour of the ship but had stayed in the background. Now she moved forward, her guitar slung into position, her green eyes and bright hair shining. I felt it a shame that our guests had no basis for appreciating her.

They felt her sympathy, though. They clustered around her, all speaking together, a medley of musical frustration. She plucked single, somehow questioning notes. They responded with a flood of sound.

"I don't know what I'm saying," she said, "but maybe it will give them ideas. They make no sense at all out of our vocal sounds. They're more at home with the strings."

She pointed to the loaded trailers on the screen, then to the egg-beings themselves, then swept her hand in a wide arc to indicate the ship. She plucked a single sharp inquiring note on the A string. And the visitors grew completely quiet. There was no way to substantiate it, but to me they seemed appalled.

Suddenly one of them, surely the First Greeter, extruded tentacles in clusters and rolled swiftly to the wall of record files, the rows and rows of cabinets from which we had taken the tapes we had projected. He touched them, rolled to the screen, and pointed to the carts. A single, infinitely dignified tone came from him.

"Records," Lindy said. "They're giving us their history. They're doomed, but they'd like the Universe to know that they've lived, that they've learned and achieved and enjoyed. They're willing to go. They just don't want to be forgotten."

I don't know how she does it. But we all sensed that she was right. The egg-beings sensed it too. They had got through. Their soft medley of sound was thankful and contented.

"Run out a loading belt, bring in a trailer load," Johnny ordered. "We'll have a look."

"A *good* look," Pegleg muttered.

But that's what they were. Many of the bright boxes were filled with tapes, rolls and rolls of them, each inscribed with wavering lines in bewildering and complete confusion. Some were packed with metallic sheets thinner than the thinnest paper, but sturdy and resistant. From edge to edge they were covered with symbols in many colors. Records. The records of a planet. Of a race. Of an evolution. A Galactic treasure beyond imagining.

Rasmussen gave the order; loading belts ran out all along the ship, and hour after hour the little trailers rolled up and discharged their loads onto the endless moving surfaces. We're an explorer ship. We have space for the specimens, the artifacts of an intensive look-see. So storage was no problem. I could imagine how eagerly the archaeologists, the historians, the mathematicians, the cryptologists were eyeing this treasure trove. But it depressed me. When we got down to the point of interpreting them, the beings who had recorded, compiled and packed them would be no more, would be part of a tenuous mass of gas outrushing into the depths of the Galaxy.

"I want to see!" Lindy said. "They'll show me. I'm special. I'm sure they will."

She got it across to them, too. At the screen she pointed to the great fan of the transmitter complex, to them and then to herself.

They fluted with understanding—and beckoned. It was the last thing we could do, and most of the field units took advantage of it. Time remained. Rest and sleep could wait, while a planet lived its last hours.

Spacesuited again, we followed our guests, now our hosts, through the exit ports. Long lines of white-clad members of field teams swarmed out behind us. The egg-beings seemed not to object. There was no possible reason why they should. But we, as Lindy said, were special.

Our four guides climbed back into their little cars, fluted positive notes into the medley of sounds rising from their countrymen, and presto—we had transportation. A car with a trailer ranged alongside each of us, and we were beckoned to climb aboard. The flat trailer beds seemed as soft as sponge rubber, but they held us, one person to a vehicle. Promptly we rolled toward the great fan at a dizzying five miles an hour.

A description of that tour does not belong here. You've read it in Rasmussen's official report (*ISC Annals, Vol. 72, A. D. 2119. The Log of the Stardust*), or you've had it piecemeal in a hundred news media items. It's here only because it's part of a sequence, or an order of happenings, when we had to explore a star system, a planet, and a civilization in less than thirty hours. It's significant because it gave us the beginnings of our understanding of the level of technology which these odd little egg-beings had achieved.

For hours the little cars rolled noisily up the gently sloping ramps, switching back, detouring into lofty chambers packed with mazes of strange machinery, occasionally debouching onto wide outlook window spaces from which the country stretched away to a far horizon. The metallic length of the *Stardust* on the ground below grew smaller and smaller as we climbed, and the tiny cars were beetles swarming around it. We spent half an hour on the highest point, on the very crest of the fan, a flat parking area that might have held a hundred or more of the little cars. And as I think back, we said almost nothing during the whole unreal experience.

The roiling, pulsing, unhappy sun was setting. This world would never see it set again. We watched it for a brief while, then followed our guides back down through the miles of sloping corridors, glowing with multicolored illumination, and finally out into an early darkness sprinkled with an alien canopy of stars.

The night seemed long. The *Stardust* teams worked with the structured efficiency that makes us the best, each team the extended arm of a master scientist. The *Stardust* gleamed like a giant glowworm. The brilliance of magnaflashes lit up the countryside for miles. Scoutboats darted in and away again. And over all, the many colors of the lights of the transmitter complex cast a strange, somber glow. In spite of the seething activity, it all seemed like an enormous wake. Which, in a way, I suppose it was.

I was glad when the night thinned, and finally the sullen orange sun climbed into view. I welcomed Stony Price's solemn announcement on intercom, "Official. Nova minus two hours. Staging minus thirty minutes." A sober Stony Price. No clowning with communiques now.

Outside the little cars still swarmed and scurried about in their thousands. But the last of our people came in. Personnel check was complete. The many checklists were finished and verified. We were ready.

"Staging minus sixty seconds!"

Lindy and I sat side by side, holding hands, watching the second sweep of the chronometer approach the sixty mark, waiting for the antigrav lift that would precede the familiar Nirvana-like state of Ultraspan.

And nothing happened.

Our fingers still clung while the chronometer made another sixty-second circle. The *Stardust* lay inert. No lift. No motion. Then the shaken voice of Stony Price on intercom. "Revision. Staging minus twenty minutes. A small difficulty."

In crisis, I am one of Johnny Rasmussen's four first-line replacements. Any one of us, in emergency, could take over operations and run the ship. Cap'n Jules Griffin, Moe Cheng and Pegleg are the others. I arrived at the control room last, but only by about a couple of seconds.

Cap'n Jules sat in his control chair as always, his square face unchanging. Rasmussen reported.

"There is an energy hold on the antigrav units. We can't lift."

Moe Cheng's slits of eyes gleamed with anger, but Pegleg looked almost happy. Or at least he looked vindicated.

"Outside energy! Applied where it counts! We showed them too much!"

"But why?" I protested. "We have their records. They want them saved. They want the Galaxy to know. I'd swear it!"

"Play-acting," Pegleg said. "If they can't live, why should we? They've analyzed our lift-off mechanism and nullified it. All the while that we've been gathering data, so have they. In an hour and a half, we all go together."

I've never admired Johnny Rasmussen more than at that moment. Impeccably dressed as always, his mustaches newly waxed, he could have been considering a minor detail of operation. His tanned face showed no stress. He seated himself, punched for a brandy from the console alongside. He said nothing until he'd had a sip.

"Cap'n Jules," he said quietly, "I think I know the answer, but why not Ultraspan direct? It has no relation to conventional energy application."

Cap'n Jules shook his white head stolidly.

"We're in contact; so essentially the *Stardust* is a part of the mass of the planet. Even Ultraspan couldn't stage a planet."

"So?"

"We'd disintegrate," the captain said. "Or theory says we would. Never been tried, of course."

"In an hour and twenty minutes we disintegrate anyway. That'll be our last resort, our last experiment. Meanwhile, we try to get them to release us. How, Roscoe?"

"I always get the easy assignments." I tried to keep a calm face, but it was a job to hold my voice steady. "Still, when I'm in deep trouble, I always look in the same direction. This time I think it's practical. Call my wife. Call Lindy—and her guitar."

"Of course." Rasmussen looked like he should have thought of it himself. He made the call. In a few minutes she came into the control room, a quiet, pale Lindy, but with live green eyes sparkling, and a faint wink for me as she passed.

"They're holding us, Dr. Peterson," Rasmussen said. "Somehow they've nullified the antigravs. Do you think you could find out why?"

Lindy looked from face to face. She saw nothing but chagrin and disillusionment, I'm afraid.

"Maybe I can't," she said slowly, "but if they're doing it, there *is* a reason. They don't want us destroyed."

"All the little atoms and ions that used to be me will take satisfaction in that as they blow out across the Universe," Pegleg said.

Lindy's eyes crinkled suddenly, deeply. She turned toward the waiting microphone. Johnny Rasmussen sipped his brandy, and his lean face was faintly quizzical. Pegleg's very sourness had lifted our spirits a little.

Lindy worked. How she worked! Her guitar queried and scolded and pled. The egg-beings crowded around the starship, row on row and rank on rank of little cars. The illusion of the tuning orchestra was more complete than it had ever been. They answered her with flutings and bell tones and deep, majestic chords. But they showed no indication that they understood what she wanted. We couldn't detect any concern that we were overstaying our time. And all the while that time grew shorter.

At nova minus thirty minutes, Rasmussen admitted defeat.

"Thank you, Dr. Peterson. I'm afraid they've won. Our outlook now seems to be the same as theirs. But at nova minus ten we'll try our last experiment. Even in contact with the planet, we'll try Ultraspan."

I don't think Lindy heard the last part of that. Excitedly she grasped Johnny Rasmussen by the arm, almost spilling his brandy. And, even with disintegration staring you in the face, you just don't *do* that!

"That's it!" she cried. "Oh, of course that's it! The one thing we couldn't take away before! They want us to *feel* like they feel, to know what it's like to face the certainty of Eternity! They'll let us go, Johnny! They don't plan for us to die!"

And they proved it for her. Through the packed masses of little cars somehow a roadway opened. A pale blue car came through, hauling a blue trailer. On the trailer sat a large blue casket. The whole blue unit drew up at the location of the port nearest us. That was sealed, of course. No sign of it from outside. But they knew.

A single high clear note came from the thousands of diaphragms, a snaky forest of tentacles sprouted, waved and re-tracted.

"That's for Lindy," I said. I'd heard that note again and again.

Rasmussen gave the order; a loading belt extruded, and the blue casket came aboard. We broke the simple fastenings, and Lindy opened it there in the control room.

For a brief moment the contents of the casket made no sense at all. Then suddenly we knew. Even Cap'n Jules left his chair to join the circle looking down at the smooth, slightly quivering mass of clear gelatin that filled the box to the brim. Embedded in it were rows and rows of tiny green capsules, layer on layer of them. Thousands.

"They don't want to die," Lindy breathed. "They're saying, 'Find us a planet; find us a home with a healthy sun. Let our race and our culture and our knowledge live on.'"

"I don't understand, Dr. Peterson." Cap'n Jules Griffin's heavy, colorless voice was evidence that he didn't. Cap'n Jules is a genius, but he has no imagination whatever.

"These are their spawn, their babies." Lindy looked ready for tears. "Probably the most highly selected genes they could arrange for in a hurry. They themselves will die, of course. But their race is here in this box. We can lift off now, Cap'n Jules. The antigravs are free. They want us to go."

And a moment later the *Stardust* stirred gently, raised herself like a soap bubble on a breeze, and swept slowly in a great circle around the magnificent fan of the transmitter, the thousands of tiny, colorful cars and their occupants dwindling to insect size.

"Nova minus fifteen minutes! Staging minus sixty seconds!" Stony Price sounded vastly relieved.

A sound began and grew and poured from our speakers, a single pure deep organ-tone. Benediction and good-bye!

Lindy and I held hands there in the control room; Pegleg and Rasmussen and Moe Cheng settled into chairs. Our senses blurred into the timeless nothingness of Ultraspan. Then reality returned. The *Stardust* floated in alien space. On our screens, four light-years away, the twin stars of Mizar A gleamed cheerily, although one of them seemed somewhat smudged and murky. But our view was four years old. We all winced when the chronometers swept past nova zero, then sat for a few minutes in a sort of numb sadness.

"They're gone," Lindy said. "Sun and planet snuffed out. Perhaps the other twin rendered unstable by the energy release. But the life and the wisdom it all made possible have escaped." She patted the blue casket.

It was tragedy. We knew them briefly, but they were our friends and we mourned. Yet we knew that such things happened often even in our Galaxy. How much more so across the Universe?

In perspective, this was simply a single blink of the Celestial Eye.

B. (for Beverly) L. Keller is a former journalist, now a free-lance writer whose work has appeared in Cosmopolitan *and* Atlantic. *This was her first story for F&SF; it brings a classic fantasy theme up to date with some hilarious and unsettling results.*

Birdlime

B. L. KELLER

Booba Lawson—the Fabulous Booba, as she was known to her-self—slid loving hands down her sides, rapt gaze ensnared in her mirror. When she bounced on her toes, her new-ripe breasts jiggled merrily under her barely transparent shirt.

With some regret she pulled her poncho over her head, but her disappointment at the eclipse of that enchanting jiggle was swept away in her fascination with the play of light upon the planes of her face as she turned her head this way and that.

Her eyes, twin pools of Maybelline overhung by a sedge of flaxen bangs, narrowed, for she thought she detected a zit erupt-ing on her chin. Leaning forward, soft glossed lips pouting, she became so engrossed in her repertoire of pouts that she had to write herself a tardy note in her mother's hand when she got to school.

Intoxicated by the flowing skill of her forgery, she wrote excuses for three friends who had spent the previous day stoned at the airport, grooving on jet shrieks. She emerged from the girls' rest room with a sycophantic retinue and $4.50 cash.

She moved in triumph through the school day, her sheerest nylon bikini underpanties caught in the cleft between her gulteal globes and peeping from under her wisp of a skirt each time she bent over to pick up any one of the innumerable small objects she found or dropped that day, causing the spillage of more seed than all the agricultural economists in Washington.

Booba had never even heard of Emile Zola.

In the evening she went to a coffee house whose promoters had obtained a license upon their promise to keep the young off alcohol and the streets. A cup of coffee cost more there than a joint, but it was the warmth of togetherness which mattered.

It was not cool for a girl to show up alone. For lack of anybody better, Booba went with her classmate Feebie Frean. Feebie had had her day. The previous year she had been the first eighth-grader to have made a plaster cast of the erectile member of one of the up-and-coming rock stars on the West Coast. But as some of Feebie's peers went on to bigger and better things, even British groups, her trophy became a bore. However, she had other characteristics that made her a desirable companion when nobody better was available—rich parents, an enormous allowance, and a willingness to buy friendship.

The Merdé, a group which had just missed being asked to play with the Stones at that fabulous free Tijuana concert which led to the U.S. occupation of Baja California and the settlement in which we retained Ensenada as a naval base and outlet for factory seconds, was playing. Feebie danced alone until a wispy but bright-eyed youth joined her; they bumped and ground ecstatically, pelvis to pelvis, heads far apart.

Booba, however, was feeling regal. Somebody had told her that afternoon that she dressed like an Hungarian whore, and the compliment had gone to her brain. She stared down the boys who approached her, enjoying their confusion.

An old man was watching her. Dirty old man, she thought,

giggling. He was thirty anyway. Still, there was something fascinating about him. In the first place, he looked like Leonard Nimoy, except for the ears. Tall, pale, sinister, intense, but cool. There was a menace in his gaze, deeper, darker and scarier than what Booba, for want of a better cliché, thought of as naked lust. She felt a throb in her pelvis. No need to question, no need to reason—Booba trusted her finer instincts.

As if monitering her throbs, he made his way to her table.

"Another coffee?"

He looked even older close up. Maybe thirty-two. Would that make him a filthy old man? Booba smiled enchantingly. Feebie had spent her last six dollars just for admission and two Basque mochas, and Booba was starved, having thrown away her $4.50 on incense and horoscopes.

She deigned to blink.

He was hardly wrinkled at all. No pruney old lines. Instead he had grooves down his cheeks like Johnny Cash—not that Johnny Cash was where it's at, but you wouldn't absolutely throw up at the idea of balling Johnny Cash. And he had a black glossy beard that looked like the one on the cat who lay down his cape for old Queen Elizabeth. And he was tall, and thin, and even if his hair cleared his shirt collar, it wasn't sickeningly short. Besides, the shirt itself was absolutely weird, eerie colors and patterns writhing on some strange shimmering cloth.

He said very little. Boys always babbled in an effort to entertain her, and she took a wicked delight in pouting just to watch them sweat. But this man watched her, mostly, and not like any average dirty old man. He reminded her more of her tomcat Genghis contemplating the aquarium. The man didn't even twitch like a tomcat; he seemed more amused than hungry. Her little pelvis throbbed again.

Smiling, eyes as gentle as the Lily Maid's, she let herself drift into rape fantasies. Booba had never been raped herself, but she knew of two girls who claimed to have been.

He was speaking.

Wow! He was saying that if they left right away they could make the Mother Aper's concert. The cheapest seats were $8.50. She'd never seen them once since their lead singer got busted for exposing himself to the studio audience on Ed Sullivan's show.

But did she want to be seen anyplace really groovy with a man this old? What would it do to her image? He was tall and lean and evil looking, but still she was unsure.

Then she saw, really saw, his garments, as if some sudden refulgence had kindled their table. His shirt, that fantastic prismal shirt, was open down to the strange-wrought massive silver buckle of the belt which held up his panne-velvet hip-huggers, the first pubic curls below his hardy belly cosseting the buckle. His opalescent trousers, like latex poured over his lower body, emphasized every muscle, every protuberance. He was not barefoot, but his boots were suitably raunchy. It was his cape that decided it. A great, heavy black cape—was it silk, satin, velvet?—with a lining that must have been woven from an acid freak-out. With that cape he most certainly had the weirdest outfit she had ever seen anywhere.

She realized suddenly that his wonderful beard made it quite impossible to estimate his age exactly. And with those clothes, who would be wondering about his age? The essential thing was that nobody could overlook her when she walked in anyplace, anyplace, with that haberdashery in escort.

"Can you loan me a dime to call my mommy?" she asked.

She told her mother that Feebie had invited her to spend the night, an invitation warmly seconded by Feebie's parents. Booba had employed the most skillful, subtle and unyielding propaganda campaign to convince her mommy that Feebie was a wholesome influence, that the only reason she wasn't in a convent was that the other novices might be a little coarse for her sensibilities. The fact that the Freans had money made it that much easier to sell Booba's mommy on Feebie.

Feebie promised to leave her bedroom window open—her parents would be flaked out on gin as usual, oblivious to what time who or what got in.

He had the grooviest car Booba had ever seen. She began to realize how arresting, virile and intelligent older men were. Gliding down the freeway at homicidal speed, her little pelvis vibrating like a Moog . . .

"Wow! You must have a really groovy pad," she said.

Well, one thing led to another, and there she was in his pad, and it was a trip. His stereo just about split her skull open before she had a thing, and then he brought out some hash straight from Hong Kong, and she wondered what she'd ever seen in younger men.

If she says "groovy" once more, he thought, I will lay a plague of boils on her.

By now she was prattling in imbecile monologue. About foxy dudes and Acapulco gold and Jim Morrison and Mick . . .

He restrained himself. Defaced, she would be of no use to him. And was it not, after all, her very mindlessness, her luscious immaturity, which made her that much more maddening? Wasn't that exactly what he looked for in a girl these days?

On she prattled, drawing from some dank minuscule crease in her glabrous little cerebrum profundities about alienation and the establishment and Huey, sensitivity awareness, truth and meaning. Dear Belial, he thought, this must be the most pompous generation since Cromwell.

His nerve ends hissing and crackling like a short circuit, he fled to his kitchen, where he mixed her a Mai Tai, thinking he might get her inebriated so that she would behave like any mature, disgusting drunk. With more than a little malice, he threw in a pinch of wolfbane, a scrap of mandrake root, a drop of this and that horripilating elixir.

UH! UNNNHHHUH!

The Mai Tai exploded in the sink, dissolving the porcelain in a blinding ebullition.

She had turned up his stereo.

Trembling, he mixed a loathsome, an unspeakable brew, and flavored it with cherry cola.

She was dancing. She had shed her poncho and her little nipples stood out assertively under her membranous shirt.

Turning down the music, he plied her with liquor and flattery, little dreaming how familiar she was with both.

Finally, fixing her with all the dark power of his fathomless gaze, he moved close.

While she snuggled, innocently fingering his belt buckle, he made his pitch. How they were destined to meet. How he had recognized her potential from the moment he saw her. How exquisitely they would work together. What he'd give to have her

join his extended family. She could set her own hours, sleep late
. . . income, furs, diamonds, cars, yachts, adoration, acid, hash,
downers on the house, rock singers, actors, producers. And a
contract guaranteeing that she would be taken care of forever
and ever—one big trip for all eternity.

She listened solemnly, her great luminous eyes all misty with
an appetite the likes of which he'd not seen since the night he
signed up Thais.

But this was not some simple Eastern courtesan. This was not
some impulsive Borgia, some dreary Du Barry. This was Booba,
a child of her time. And Booba knew that she would have everything he offered, and more, without doing a thing, just by the
magic of wanting, because she was her own enchanting, maddening, irresistible Booba. And, being quite unable to think of herself
as anything but lovely, full of juice and estrogen, Booba had no
thoughts about aging, so that eternity interested her not a whit.

He offered her terrible powers, dark mysteries the likes of
which he had uncovered for no mortal. He lowered himself to
the point of wheedling this child.

And then it came out. The irremovable obstacle.

She could never trust anyone over thirty.

Demoralized, reckless in his exhaustion, he took from her
hand the drink he had so irresponsibly concocted, and he drained
it, and the rage this child had roused in him so weakened him
that he, *he*, found himself assailed by what he could not fail to
recognize, a torment he had often fanned in others but never
felt before.

He knew it to be—

LUST

The first rule of his calling was Never Get Involved. Agonized,
tasting the full horror of his disgrace, knowing he was about to
corrupt his profession, his soul, his very style, he seized that enchanting nymph in an embrace more terrible than that of any
leopard, any python, any Tarquin.

They grappled. He might well have ravished her then and
there with her enthused co-operation—for she was terribly curious—but for one thing.

"Oh, wow," she said, her delicate hand pressed firmly over her
crotch. "I'd love to. I mean, I think you're the goooviest. But

I'm having my class picture taken tomorrow, and Feebie says it gives you zits."

"Gives you what?" he shrieked, maddened but unable to turn away from anything that might render this child comprehensible.

"She says balling really screws up your complexion."

With that, she reached with her free hand for his stereo and—
THIS IS THE DAWNING OF THE AGE OF AQUARIUS . . .

One hundred eighty decibels shattering all the aeons of black wisdom enshrined within his head.

He stumbled into his bedroom, calling down fire, flood, gnats, and freeways upon this planet, and cutting off all electricity in the building.

Later, in the darkness and the stillness he found his way back to her side.

"You know what I've been thinking?" she whispered. "I was thinking how I'd love a MacDonald's hamburger. Exercise always makes me hungry."

She devoured two hamburgers, a paper of french fries, and a strawberry shake while he sat behind the wheel of the Maserati, idly increasing the coliform bacteria count in her hamburger even while he knew it was unworthy of him. His fathomless gaze stark and desolate as he stared into the narrow tunnel of time, imagining generations yet to come, he thanked his archenemy that he had not been cursed with the light of foreknowledge.

He let her out at Feebie Frean's, watched her round complacent little behind wriggle as she walked away all unimpressed by the magnitude of her triumph.

Burning, degraded, all that quintessential pride in ruins, he suddenly understood. God help him, he understood. He saw that he had to fail.

For the child had no conception of evil.

Almost mortally wounded, he found the place where it began, as if he could make it come out differently, somehow.

He sat at the table from where he had spied her first.

They were dancing, perhaps a score of them. The musicians were taking a break, but the patrons danced. And were they all,

all of them, in not comprehending evil, quite beyond it? Did this, then, make them innocent?

For a moment he felt again the hot surge of the unthinkable impulse which had brought upon him the deepest defeat of his career. For him, himself, *him*, to be so assailed, so degraded . . .

To give up everything, to grovel, to be enslaved to a mindless, egocentric, babbling bubble of banality. That child . . . these children . . .

FWAAAANNNGGGG

Acned, agued, acrogenic, carnal and androgynous, the Merdé began to play, the lead singer, Dynel wig slipping crazily as he resolutely humped his guitar, lipping wetly at the microphone . . .

Unnnh. UH. UH. Buh-aye-beee. UNNHHH.

In a swirl of black and scarlet the demonic presence fled.

There was not a one of them he'd have as a gift. They'd drive every damned soul in the place up the walls within a week.

Stalking from the coffee house, he called down, in a fit of mere pique, a calamity so hideous upon that place that those within were rendered sober and contemplative beyond their years for the remainder of their natural lives.

He made the next flight to Washington. After a few weeks mending fences, he'd be on to London, then Paris, Berlin, Moscow, Peking, the old territory.

God, he thought, was there ever a time when it all meant something?

Generations, generations. How he despised self-pity.

He accepted another drink from the stewardess who simpered over him. They all did. Breathing estros and Binaca into his face. She'd be easy.

Too easy.

He was sweating under his shirt. A gray Hathaway shirt. A gray man in a gray suit. The gray wings of the aircraft sliced the rain. His gin tasted gray.

His armpits smelled funky. His hair felt nappy.

He saw himself, hung up in a gray bird cutting through a gray drizzle. Riding out there all alone. Out there riding on a shoeshine and a smile.

"BEING THE FIRST ASTRONAUT TO PLAY GOLF ON THE MOON IS ONE THING, MEN, BEING THE FIRST TO SHOOT CRAP IS QUITE ANOTHER!"

*As we said of an earlier contributor, we could have picked any
of Poul Anderson's recent contributions to F&SF for this anthology
and been happy with the choice. What makes Mr. Anderson's
performance in this field so remarkable is the combination of quality
with quantity. As James Blish noted in our Special Poul Anderson
issue, "There may be a few poor stories among his 238-plus, but they
would be hard to find."*

The Problem of Pain

POUL ANDERSON

Maybe only a Christian can understand this story. In that case,
I don't qualify. But I do take an interest in religion, as part of being an amateur psychologist, and—for the grandeur of its language if nothing else—a Bible is among the reels that accompany me wherever I go. This was one reason Peter Berg told
me what had happened in his past. He desperately needed to
make sense of it, and no priest he'd talked to had quite laid his
questions to rest. There was an outside chance that an outside
viewpoint like mine would see what a man couldn't who was
within the faith.

His other reason was simple loneliness. We were on Lucifer,
as part of a study corporation. That world is well named. It will

never be a real colony for any beings whose ancestors evolved amidst clean greenery. But it might be marginally habitable, and if so, its mineral wealth would be worth exploiting. Our job was to determine whether that was true. The gentlest looking environment holds a thousand death traps until you have learned what the difficulties are and how to grip them. (Earth is no exception.) Sometimes you find problems which can't be solved economically, or can't be solved at all. Then you write off the area or the entire planet, and look for another.

We'd contracted to work three standard years on Lucifer. The pay was munificent, but presently we realized that no bank account could buy back one day we might have spent beneath a kindlier sun. It was a knowledge we carefully avoided discussing with teammates.

About midway through, Peter Berg and I were assigned to do an in-depth investigation of a unique cycle in the ecology of the northern middle latitudes. This meant that we settled down for weeks—which ran into months—in a sample region, well away from everybody else to minimize human disturbances. An occasional supply flitter gave us our only real contact; electronics were no proper substitute, especially when that hell-violent star was forever disrupting them.

Under such circumstances, you come to know your partner maybe better than you know yourself. Pete and I got along well. He's a big, sandy-haired, freckle-faced young man, altogether dependable, with enough kindliness, courtesy, and dignity that he need not make a show of them. Soft-spoken, he's a bit short in the humor department. Otherwise I recommend him as a companion. He has a lot to tell from his own wanderings, yet he'll listen with genuine interest to your memories and brags; he's well-read too, a good cook when his turn comes; he plays chess at just about my level of skill.

I already knew he wasn't from Earth, had in fact never been there, but from Aeneas, nearly 200 light-years distant, more than 300 from Lucifer. And, while he's gotten an education at the new little university in Nova Roma, he was raised in the outback. Besides, that town is only a far-off colonial capital. It helped explain his utter commitment to belief in a God who became flesh and died for love of man. Not that I scoff. When he said his prayers, night and morning in our one-room shelter-dome, trustingly as a child, I didn't rag him nor he reproach me. Of course, over the weeks, we came more and more to talk about such matters.

At last he told me of that which haunted him.

We'd been out through the whole of one of Lucifer's long, long days; we'd toiled, we'd sweated, we'd itched and stunk and gotten grimy and staggered from weariness, we'd come near death once: and we'd found the uranium-concentrating root which was the key to the whole weirdness around us. We came back to base as day's fury was dying in the usual twilight gale; we washed, ate something, went to sleep with the hiss of storm-blown dust for a lullaby. Ten or twelve hours later we awoke and saw, through the vitryl panels, stars cold and crystalline beyond this thin air, auroras aflame, landscape hoar, and the twisted things we called trees all sheathed in glittering ice.

"Nothing we can do now till dawn," I said, "and we've earned a celebration." So we prepared a large meal, elaborate as possible —breakfast or supper, what relevance had that here? We drank wine in the course of it, and afterward much brandy while we sat, side by side in our loungers, watching the march of constellations which Earth never saw. And we talked. Finally we talked of God.

"—Maybe you can give me an idea," Pete said. In the dim light, his face bore a struggle. He stared before him and knotted his fingers.

"Mm, I dunno," I said carefully. "To be honest, no offense meant, theological conundrums strike me as silly."

He gave me a direct blue look. His tone was soft: "That is, you feel the paradoxes don't arise if we don't insist on believing?"

"Yes. I respect your faith, Pete, but it's not mine. And if I did suppose that a, well, a spiritual principle or something is behind the universe—" I gestured at the high and terrible sky—"in the name of reason, can we confine, can we understand whatever made *that*, in the bounds of one little dogma?"

"No. Agreed. How could finite minds grasp the infinite? We can see parts of it, though, that've been revealed to us." He drew breath. "'Way back before space travel, the Church decided Jesus had come only to Earth, to man. If other intelligent races need salvation—and obviously a lot of them do!—God will have made His suitable arrangements for them. Sure. However, this does not mean Christianity is not true, or that certain different beliefs are not false."

"Like, say, polytheism, wherever you find it?"

"I think so. Besides, religions evolve. The primitive faiths see God, or the gods, as power; the higher ones see Him as justice; the highest see Him as love." Abruptly he fell silent. I saw his fist clench, until he grabbed up his glass and drained it and re-filled it in nearly a single savage motion.

"I must believe that," he whispered.

I waited a few seconds, in Lucifer's crackling night stillness, before saying: "An experience made you wonder?"

"Made me . . . disturbed. Mind if I tell you?"

"Certainly not." I saw he was about to open himself; and I may be an unbeliever, but I know what is sacred.

"Happened about five years ago. I was on my first real job. So was the—" his voice stumbled the least bit—"the wife I had then. We were fresh out of school and apprenticeship, fresh into mar-riage. Our employers weren't human. They were Ythrians. Ever heard of them?"

I sought through my head. The worlds, races, beings are un-knowably many, in this tiny corner of this one dust-mote galaxy which we have begun to explore a little. "Ythrians, Ythrians . . . wait. Do they fly?"

"Yes. Surely one of the most glorious sights in creation. Your Ythrian isn't as heavy as a man, of course; adults mass around 25 or 30 kilos—but his wingspan goes up to six meters, and when he soars with those feathers shining gold-grown in the light, or stoops in a crack of thunder and whistle of wind—"

"Hold on," I said. "I take it Ythri's a terrestroid planet?"

"Pretty much. Somewhat smaller and drier than Earth, some-what thinner atmosphere—about like Aeneas, in fact, which it's not too far from as interstellar spaces go. You can live there without special protection. The biochemistry's quite similar to ours."

"Then how the devil can those creatures be that size? The wing loading's impossible, when you have only cell tissue to oxidize for power. They'd never get off the ground."

"Ah, but they have antlibranchs as well." Pete smiled, though it didn't go deep. "Those look like three gills, sort of, on either side, below the wings. They're actually more like bellows, pumped by the wing muscles. Extra oxygen is forced directly into the bloodstream during flight. A biological supercharger system."

"Well, I'll be a . . . never mind what." I considered, in delight, this new facet of nature's inventiveness. "Um-m-m . . . if they spend energy at that rate, they've got to have appetites to match."

"Right. They're carnivores. A number of them are still hunters. The advanced societies are based on ranching. In either case, obviously, it takes a lot of meat animals, a lot of square kilometers, to support one Ythrian. So they're fiercely territorial. They live in small groups—single families or extended households—which attack, with intent to kill, any uninvited outsider who doesn't obey an order to leave."

"And still they're civilized enough to hire humans for space exploration?"

"Uh-huh. Remember, being flyers, they've never needed to huddle in cities in order to have ready communication. They do keep a few towns, mining or manufacturing centers, but those are inhabited mostly by wing-clipped slaves. I'm glad to say that institution's dying out as they get modern machinery."

"By trade?" I guessed.

"Yes," Pete replied. "When the first Grand Survey discovered them, their most advanced culture was at an Iron Age level of technology; no industrial revolution, but a lot of sophisticated minds around, and subtle philosophies." He paused. "That's important to my question—that the Ythrians, at least of the Planha-speaking *choths*, are not barbarians and have not been for many centuries. They've had their equivalents of Socrates, Aristotle, Confucius, Galileo, yes, and their prophets and seers."

After another mute moment: "They realized early what the visitors from Earth implied, and set about attracting traders and teachers. Once they had some funds, they sent their promising young folk off-planet to study. I met several at my own university, which is why I got my job offer. By now they have a few spacecraft and native crews. But you'll understand, their tech-

nical people are spread thin, and in several branches of knowledge they have no experts. So they employ humans."

He went on to describe the typical Ythrian: warm-blooded,
feathered like a golden eagle (though more intricately) save for
a crest on the head, and yet not a bird. Instead of a beak, a blunt
muzzle full of fangs juts before two great eyes. The female
bears her young alive. While she does not nurse them, they have
lips to suck the juices of meat and fruits, wherefore their speech
is not hopelessly unlike man's. What were formerly the legs have
evolved into arms bearing three taloned fingers, flanked by two
thumbs, on each hand. Aground, the huge wings fold downward and, with the help of claws at the angles, give locomotion.
That is slow and awkward—but aloft, ah!

"They become more alive, flying, than we ever do," Pete
murmured. His gaze had lost itself in the shuddering auroras
overhead. "They must: the metabolic rate they have then, and
the space around them, speed, sky, a hundred winds to ride on
and be kissed by. . . . That's what made me think Enherrian, in
particular, believed more keenly than I could hope to. I saw him
and others dancing, high, high in the air, swoops, glides, hover-
ings, sunshine molten on their plumes; I asked what they did,
and was told they were honoring God."

He sighed. "Or that's how I translated the Planha phrase,
rightly or wrongly," he went on. "Olga and I had taken a cram
course, and our Ythrian teammates all knew Anglic; but nobody's command of the foreign tongue was perfect. It couldn't
be. Multiple billion years of separate existence, evolution, history—what a miracle that we could think as alike as we did!

"However, you could call Enherrian religious, same as you
could call me that, and not be too grotesquely off the mark. The
rest varied, just like humans. Some were also devout, some less,
some agnostics or atheists; two were pagans, following the
bloody rites of what was called the Old Faith. For that matter,
my Olga—" the knuckles stood forth where he grasped his tum-
bler of brandy—"had tried, for my sake, to believe as I did, and
couldn't.

"Well. The New Faith interested me more. It was new only
by comparison—at least half as ancient as mine. I hoped for a
chance to study it, to ask questions and compare ideas. I really

knew nothing except that it was monotheistic, had sacraments and a theology though no official priesthood, upheld a high ethical and moral standard—for Ythrians, I mean. You can't expect a race which can only live by killing animals, and has an oestrous cycle, and is incapable by instinct of maintaining what we'd recognize as a true nation or government, and on and on— you can't expect them to resemble Christians much. God has given them a different message. I wished to know what. Surely we could learn from it." Again he paused. "After all . . . being a faith with a long tradition . . . and not static but a seeking, a history of prophets and saints and believers . . . I thought it must know God is love. Now what form would God's love take to an Ythrian?"

He drank. I did too, before asking cautiously: "Uh, where was this expedition?"

Pete stirred in his lounger. "To a system about 80 light-years from Ythri's," he answered. "The original survey crew had discovered a terrestroid planet there. They didn't bother to name it. Prospective colonists would choose their own name anyway. Those could be human or Ythrian, conceivably both—if the environment proved out.

"Offhand, the world—our group called it, unofficially, Gray, after that old captain—the world looked brilliantly promising. It's intermediate in size between Earth and Ythri, surface gravity 0.8 terrestrial; slightly more irradiation, from a somewhat yellower sun, than Earth gets, which simply makes it a little warmer; axial tilt, therefore seasonal variations, a bit less than terrestrial; length of year about three-quarters of ours, length of day a bit under half; one small, close-in, bright moon; biochemistry similar to ours—we could eat most native things, though we'd require imported crops and livestock to supplement the diet. All in all, seemingly well-nigh perfect."

"Rather remote to attract Earthlings at this early date," I remarked. "And from your description, the Ythrians won't be able to settle it for quite a while either."

"They think ahead," Pete responded. "Besides, they have scientific curiosity and, yes, in them perhaps even more than in the humans who went along, a spirit of adventure. Oh, it was a wonderful thing to be young in that band!"

He had not yet reached 30, but somehow his cry was not funny.

He shook himself. "Well, we had to make sure," he said. "Besides planetology, ecology, chemistry, oceanography, meteorology, a million and a million mysteries to unravel for their own sakes—we must scout out the death traps, whatever those might be.

"At first everything went like Mary's smile on Christmas morning. The spaceship set us off—it couldn't be spared to linger in orbit—and we established base on the largest continent. Soon our hundred-odd dispersed across the globe, investigating this or that. Olga and I made part of a group on the southern shore, where a great gulf swarmed with life. A strong current ran eastward from there, eventually striking an archipelago which deflected it north. Flying over those waters, we spied immense, I mean immense patches—no, floating islands—of vegetation, densely interwoven, grazed on by monstrous marine creatures, no doubt supporting any number of lesser plant and animal species.

"We wanted a close look. Our camp's sole aircraft wasn't good for that. Anyhow, it was already in demand for a dozen jobs. We had boats, though, and launched one. Our crew was Enherrian, his wife Whell, their grown children Rusa and Arrach, my beautiful new bride Olga, and me. We'd take three or four Gray days to reach the nearest atlantis weed, as Olga dubbed it. Then we'd be at least a week exploring before we turned back—a vacation, a lark, a joy."

He tossed off his drink and reached for the bottle. "You ran into grief," I prompted.

"No." He bent his lips upward, stiffly. "It ran into us. A hurricane. Unpredicted; we knew very little about that planet. Given the higher solar energy input and, especially, the rapid rotation, the storm was more violent than would've been possible on Earth. We could only run and pray.

"At least, I prayed, and imagined that Enherrian did."

Wind shrieked, hooted, yammered, hit flesh with fists and cold knives. Waves rumbled in that driven air, black and green and fang-white, fading from view as the sun sank behind the cloud-roil which hid it. Often a monster among them loomed castle-like over the gunwale. The boat slipped by, spilled into the troughs, rocked onto the crests and down again. Spindrift, icy, stinging, bitter on lips and tongue, made a fog across her length.

"We'll live if we can keep sea room," Enherrian had said when the fury first broke. "She's well-found. The engine capacitors have ample kilowatt-hours in them. Keep her bow on and we'll live."

But the currents had them now, where the mighty gulf stream met the outermost islands and its waters churned, recoiled, spun about and fought. Minute by minute, the riptides grew wilder. They made her yaw till she was broadside on and surges roared over her deck; they shocked her onto her beam ends, and the hull became a toning bell.

Pete, Olga, and Whell were in the cabin, trying to rest before their next watch. That was no longer possible. The Ythrian female locked hands and wing-claws around the net-covered framework wherein she had slept, hung on and uttered nothing. In the wan glow of a single overhead fluoro, among thick restless shadows, her eyes gleamed topaz. They did not seem to look at the crampedness around—at what, then?

The humans had secured themselves by a line onto a lower bunk. They embraced, helping each other fight the leaps and swings which tried to smash them against the sides. Her fair hair on his shoulder was the last brightness in his cosmos. "I love you," she said, over and over, through hammer blows and groans. "Whatever happens, I love you, Pete, I thank you for what you've given me."

"And you," he would answer. *And You,* he would think. *Though You won't take her, not yet, will You? Me, yes, if that's Your Will. But not Olga. It'd leave Your creation too dark.*

A wing smote the cabin door. Barely to be heard through the storm, an Ythrian voice—high, whistly, but resonant out of full lungs—shouted: "Come topside!"

Whell obeyed at once, the Bergs as fast as they could slip on life jackets. Having taken no personal grav units along, they couldn't fly free if they went overboard. Dusk raved around them. Pete could just see Rusa and Arrach in the stern, fighting the tiller. Enherrian stood before him and pointed forward. "Look," the captain said. Pete, who had no nictitating membranes, must shield his eyes with fingers to peer athwart the hurricane. He saw a deeper darkness hump up from a wall of white; he heard surf crash.

"We can't pull free," Enherrian told him. "Between wind and current—too little power. We'll likely be wrecked. Make ready."

Olga's hand went briefly to her mouth. She huddled against Pete and might have whispered, "Oh, no." Then she straightened, swung back down into the cabin, braced herself as best she could, and started assembling the most vital things. He saw that he loved her still more than he had known.

The same calm descended on him. Nobody had time to be afraid. He got busy too. The Ythrians could carry a limited weight of equipment and supplies, but sharply limited under these conditions. The humans, buoyed by their jackets, must carry most. They strapped it to their bodies.

When they re-emerged, the boat was in the shoals. Enherrian ordered them to take the rudder. His wife, son, and daughter stood around—on hands which clutched the rails with prey-snatching strength—and spread their wings to give a bit of shelter. The captain clung to the cabin top as lookout. His yelled commands reached the Bergs dim, tattered.

"Hard right!" Upward cataracts burst on a skerry to port. It glided past, was lost in murk. "Two points starboard—steady!" The hull slipped between a pair of rocks. Ahead was a narrow opening in the island's sheer black face. To a lagoon, to safety? Surf raged on either side of that gate, and everywhere else.

The passage was impossible. The boat struck, threw Olga off her feet and Arrach off her perch. Full reverse engine could not pull free. The deck canted. A billow and a billow smashed across.

Pete was in the water. It grabbed him, pulled him under, dragged him over a sharp bottom. He thought: *Into Your hands, God. Spare Olga,* please, please—and the sea spewed him back up for one gulp of air.

Wallowing in blindness, he tried to gauge how the breakers were acting, what he should do. If he could somehow belly-surf in, he might make it, he barely might. . . . He was on the neck of a rushing giant, it climbed and climbed, it shoved him forward at what he knew was lunatic speed. He saw the reef on which it was about to smash him and knew he was dead.

Talons closed on his jacket. Air brawled beneath wings. The Ythrian could not raise him, but could draw him aside . . . the bare distance needed, and Pete went past the rock whereon his bones were to have been crushed, down into the smother and chaos beyond. The Ythrian didn't break free in time. He glimpsed the plumes go under, as he himself did. They never rose.

He beat on, and on, without end.

He floated in water merely choppy, swart palisades to right and left, a slope of beach ahead. He peered into the clamorous dark and found nothing. "Olga," he croaked. "Olga. Olga."

Wings shadowed him among the shadows. "Get ashore before an undertow eats you!" Enherrian whooped, and beat his way off in search.

Pete crawled to gritty sand, fell, and let annihilation have him. He wasn't unconscious long. When he revived, Rusa and Whell were beside him. Enherrian was further inland. The captain hauled on a line he had snubbed around a tree. Olga floated at the other end. She had no strength left, but he had passed a bight beneath her arms and she was alive.

At wolf-gray dawn the wind had fallen to gale force or maybe less, and the cliffs shielded lagoon and strand from it. Overhead it shrilled, and outside the breakers cannonaded, their rage aquiver through the island. Pete and Olga huddled together, a shared cloak across their shoulders. Enherrian busied himself checking the salvaged material. Whell sat on the hind-bones of her wings and stared seaward. Moisture gleamed on her grizzled feathers like tears.

Rusa flew in from the reefs and landed. "No trace," he said. His voice was emptied by exhaustion. "Neither the boat nor Arrach." Through the rust in his own brain, Pete noticed the order of those words.

Nevertheless—He leaned toward the parents and brother of Arrach, who had been beautiful and merry and had sung to them by moonlight. "How can we say—?" he began, realized he didn't have Planha words, and tried in Anglic: "How can we say how sorry we both are?"

"No necessity," Rusa answered.

"She died saving me!"

"And what you were carrying, which we needed badly." Some energy returned to Rusa. He lifted his head and its crest. "She had deathpride, our lass."

Afterward Pete, in his search for meaning, would learn about that Ythrian concept. "Courage" is too simple and weak a translation. Certain Old Japanese words came closer, though they don't really bear the same value either.

Whell turned her hawk gaze full upon him. "Did you see anything of what happened in the water?" she asked. He was too unfamiliar with her folk to interpret the tone; today he thinks it was loving. He did know that, being creatures of seasonal rut, Ythrians are less sexually motivated than man is, but probably treasure their young even more. The strongest bond between male and female is children, who are what life is all about.

"No, I . . . I fear not," he stammered.

Enherrian reached out to lay claws, very gently and briefly, on his wife's back. "Be sure she fought well," he said. "She gave God honor." (Glory? Praise? Adoration? His due?)

Does he mean she prayed, made her confession, while she drowned? The question dragged itself through Pete's weariness and caused him to murmur: "She's in heaven now." Again he was forced to use Anglic words.

Enherrian gave him a look which he could have sworn was startled. "What do you say? Arrach is dead."

"Why, her . . . her spirit—"

"Will be remembered in pride." Enherrian resumed his work.

Olga said it for Pete: "So you don't believe the spirit outlives the body?"

"How could it?" Enherrian snapped. "Why should it?" His motions, his posture, the set of his plumage added: Leave me alone.

Pete thought: *Well, many faiths, including high ones, including some sects which call themselves Christian, deny immortality. How sorry I feel for these my friends, who don't know they will meet their beloved afresh!*

They will, regardless. It makes no sense that God, Who created what is because in His goodness He wished to share existence, would shape a soul only to break it and throw it way.

Never mind. The job on hand is to keep Olga alive, in her dear body. "Can I help?"

"Yes, check our medical kit," Enherrian said.

It had come through undamaged in its box. The items for human use—stimulants, sedatives, anesthetics, antitoxins, antibiotics, coagulants, healing promoters, et standard cetera—naturally outnumbered those for Ythrians. There hasn't been time to develop a large scientific pharmacopoeia for the latter species. True, certain materials work on both, as does the surgical and monitoring equipment. Pete distributed pills which took the pain out of bruises and scrapes, the heaviness out of muscles. Meanwhile Rusa collected wood, Whell started and tended a fire, Olga made breakfast. They had considerable food, mostly freeze-dried, gear to cook it, tools like knives and a hatchet, cord, cloth, flashbeams, two blasters and abundant recharges: what they required for survival.

"It may be insufficient," Enherrian said. "The portable radio transceiver went down with Arrach. The boat's transmitter couldn't punch a call through that storm, and now the boat's on the bottom—nothing to see from the air, scant metal to register on a detector."

"Oh, they'll check on us when the weather slacks off," Olga said. She caught Pete's hand in hers. He felt the warmth.

"If their flitter survived the hurricane, which I doubt," Enherrian stated. "I'm convinced the camp was also struck. We had built no shelter for the flitter, our people will have been too busy saving themselves to secure it, and I think that thin shell was tumbled about and broken. If I'm right, they'll have to call for an aircraft from elsewhere, which may not be available at once. In either case, we could be anywhere in a huge territory; and the expedition has no time or personnel for an indefinite search. They will seek us, aye; however, if we are not found before an arbitrary date—" A ripple passed over the feathers of face and neck; a human would have shrugged.

"What . . . can we do?" the girl asked.

"Clear a sizable area in a plainly artificial pattern, or heap fuel for beacon fires should a flitter pass within sight—whichever is practicable. If nothing comes of that, we should consider building a raft or the like."

"Or modify a life jacket for me," Rusa suggested, "and I can try to fly to the mainland."

Enherrian nodded. "We must investigate the possibilities. First let's get a real rest."

The Ythrians were quickly asleep, squatted on their locked wing joints like idols of a forgotten people. Pete and Olga felt more excited and wandered a distance off, hand in hand.

Above the crag-enclosed beach, the island rose toward a crest which he estimated as three kilometers away. If it was in the middle, this was no large piece of real estate. Nor did he see adequate shelter. A mat of mossy, intensely green plants squeezed out any possibility of forest. A few trees stood isolated. Their branches tossed in the wind. He noticed particularly one atop a great outcrop nearby, gaunt brown trunk and thin leaf-fringed boughs that whipped insanely about. Blossoms, torn from vines, flew past, and they were gorgeous; but there would be naught to live on here, and he wasn't hopeful about learning, in time, how to catch Gray's equivalent of fish.

"Strange about them, isn't it?" Olga murmured.

"Eh?" He came startled out of his preoccupations.

She gestured at the Ythrians. "Them. The way they took poor Arrach's death."

"Well, you can't judge them by our standards. Maybe they feel grief less than we would, or maybe their culture demands stoicism." He looked at her and did not look away again. "To be frank, darling, I can't really mourn either. I'm too happy to have you back."

"And I you—oh, Pete, Pete, my only—"

They found a secret spot and made love. He saw nothing wrong in that. Do you ever in this life come closer to the wonder which is God?

Afterward they returned to their companions. Thus the clash of wings awoke them, hours later. They scrambled from their bedrolls and saw the Ythrians swing aloft.

The wind was strong and loud as yet, though easing off in fickleness, flaws, downdrafts, whirls and eddies. Clouds were mostly gone. Those which remained raced gold and hot orange before a sun low in the west, across blue serenity. The lagoon glittered purple, the greensward lay aglow. It had warmed up till rich odors of growth, of flowers, blent with the sea-salt.

And splendid in the sky danced Enherrian, Whell, and Rusa. They wheeled, soared, pounced and rushed back into light which ran molten off their pinions. They chanted, and fragments blew down to the humans: "*High flew your spirit on many winds . . . be always remembered. . . .*"

"What *is* that?" Olga breathed.

"Why, they—they—" The knowledge broke upon Pete. "They're holding a service for Arrach."

He knelt and said a prayer for her soul's repose. But he wondered if she, who had belonged to the air, would truly want rest. And his eyes could not leave her kindred.

Enherrian screamed a hunter's challenge and rushed down at the earth. He flung himself meteoric past the stone outcrop Pete had seen; for an instant the man gasped, believing he would be shattered; then he rose, triumphant.

He passed by the lean tree of thin branches. Gusts flailed them about. A nearly razor edge took off his left wing. Blood spurted; Ythrian blood is royal purple. Somehow Enherrian slewed around and made a crash landing on the bluff top just beyond range of what has since been named the surgeon tree.

Pete yanked the medikit to him and ran. Olga wailed, briefly, and followed. When they reached the scene, they found that Whell and Rusa had pulled feathers from their breasts to try staunching the wound.

Evening, night, day, evening, night.

Enherrian sat before a campfire. Its light wavered, picked him red out of shadow and let him half vanish again, save for the unblinking yellow eyes. His wife and son supported him. Stim, cell-freeze, and plasma surrogate had done their work, and he could speak in a weak roughness. The bandages on his stump were a glaring white.

Around crowded shrubs which, by day, showed low and russet-leaved. They filled a hollow on the far side of the island, to which Enherrian had been carried in an improvised litter.

Their odor was rank, in an atmosphere once more subtropically hot, and they clutched at feet with raking twigs. But this was the most sheltered spot his companions could find, and he might die in a new storm on the open beach.

He looked through smoke, at the Bergs, who sat as close together as they were able. He said—the surf growled faintly beneath his words, while never a leaf rustled in the breathless dark—"I have read that your people can make a lost part grow forth afresh."

Pete couldn't answer. He tried but couldn't. It was Olga who had the courage to say, "We can do it for ourselves. None except ourselves." She laid her head on her man's breast and wept.

Well, you need a lot of research to unravel a genetic code, a lot of development to make the molecules of heredity repeat what they did in the womb. Science hasn't had time yet for other races. It never will for all. They are too many.

"As I thought," Enherrian said. "Nor can a proper prosthesis be engineered in my lifetime. I have few years left; an Ythrian who cannot fly soon becomes sickly."

"Grav units—" Pete faltered.

The scorn in those eyes was like a blow. Dead metal to raise you, who have had wings?

Fierce and haughty though the Ythrian is, his quill-clipped slaves have never rebelled: for they are only half alive. Imagine yourself, human male, castrated. Enherrian might flap his remaining wing and the stump to fill his blood with air; but he would have nothing he could do with that extra energy, it would turn inward and corrode his body, perhaps at last his mind.

For a second, Whell laid an arm around him.

"You will devise a signal tomorrow," Enherrian said, "and start work on it. Too much time has already been wasted."

Before they slept, Pete managed to draw Whell aside. "He needs constant care, you know," he whispered to her in the acrid booming gloom. "The drugs got him over the shock, but he can't tolerate more, and he'll be very weak."

True, she said with feathers rather than voice. Aloud: "Olga shall nurse him. She cannot get around as easily as Rusa or I, and lacks your physical strength. Besides, she can prepare meals and the like for us."

Pete nodded absently. He had a dread to explain. "Uh . . . uh . . . do you think—well, I mean in your ethic, in the New Faith—might Enherrian put an end to himself?" And he wondered if God would really blame the captain.

Her wings and tail spread, her chest erected, she glared. "You say that of him?" she shrilled. Seeing his concern, she eased, even made a *krrr* noise which might answer to a chuckle. "No, no, he has his deathpride. He would never rob God of honor."

After survey and experiment, the decision was to hack a giant cross in the island turf. That growth couldn't be ignited, and what wood was burnable—deadfall—was too scant and stingy of smoke for a beacon.

The party had no spades; the vegetable mat was thick and tough; the toil became brutal. Pete, like Whell and Rusa, would return to camp and topple into sleep. He wouldn't rouse till morning, to gulp his food and stumble off to labor. He grew gaunt, bearded, filthy, numb-brained, sore in every cell.

Thus he did not notice how Olga was waning. Enherrian was mending, somewhat, under her care. She did her jobs, which were comparatively light, and would have been ashamed to complain of headaches, giddiness, diarrhea, and nausea. Doubtless she imagined she suffered merely from reaction to disaster, plus a sketchy and ill-balanced diet, plus heat and brilliant sun and—she'd cope.

The days were too short for work, the nights too short for sleep. Pete's terror was that he would see a flitter pass and vanish over the horizon before the Ythrians could hail it. Then they might try sending Rusa for help. But that was a long, tricky flight; and the gulf coast camp was due to be struck soon.

Sometimes he wondered dimly how he and Olga might do if marooned on Gray. He kept enough wits to dismiss that fantasy for what it was. Take the simple fact that native life appeared to lack certain vitamins—

Then one darkness, perhaps a terrestrial week after the shipwreck, he was aroused by her crying his name. He struggled to wakefulness. She lay beside him. Gray's moon was up, nearly full, swifter and brighter than Luna. Its glow drowned most of the stars, frosted the encroaching bushes, fell without pity to show him her fallen cheeks and rolling eyes. She shuddered in his arms; he heard her teeth clapping. "I'm cold, darling, I'm cold," she said in the subtropical summer night. She vomited over him, and presently she was delirious.

The Ythrians gave what help they could, he what medicines he could. By sunrise (an outrageousness of rose and gold and silver-blue, crossed by the jubilant wings of waterfowl) he knew she was dying.

He examined his own physical state, using a robot he discovered he had in his skull: yes, his wretchedness was due to more than overwork, he saw that now; he too had had the upset stomach and the occasional shivers, nothing like the disintegration which possessed Olga, nevertheless the same kind of thing. Yet the Ythrians stayed healthy. Did a local germ attack humans while finding the other race undevourable?

The rescuers, who came on the island two Gray days later, already had the answer. That genus of bushes is widespread on the planet. A party elsewhere, after getting sick and getting into safety suits, analyzed its vapors. They are a cumulative poison to man; they scarcely harm an Ythrian. The analysts named it the hell shrub.

Unfortunately, their report wasn't broadcast until after the boat left. Meanwhile Pete had been out in the field every day while Olga spent her whole time in the hollow, over which the sun regularly created an inversion layer.

Whell and Rusa went grimly back to work. Pete had to get away. He wasn't sure of the reason, but he had to be alone when he screamed at heaven, "Why did You do this to her, why did You do it?" Enherrian could look after Olga, who had brought him back to a life he no longer wanted. Pete had stopped her babblings, writhing, and saw-toothed sounds of pain with a shot. She ought to sleep peacefully into that death which the monitor instruments said was, in the absence of hospital facilities, ineluctable.

He stumbled off to the heights. The sea reached calm, in a thousand hues of azure and green, around the living island, beneath the gentle sky. He knelt in all that emptiness and put his question.

After an hour he could say, "Your will be done," and return to camp.

Olga lay awake. "Pete, Pete!" she cried. Anguish distorted her voice till he couldn't recognize it; nor could he really see her in the yellowed sweating skin and lank hair drawn over a skeleton, or find her in the stench and the nails which flayed him as they clutched. "Where were you, hold me close, it hurts, how it hurts—"

He gave her a second injection, to small effect.

He knelt again, beside her. He has not told me what he said, or how. At last she grew quiet, gripped him hard, and waited for the pain to end.

When she died, he said, it was like seeing a light blown out.

He laid her down, closed eyes and jaw, folded her hands. On mechanical feet he went to the pup tent which had been rigged for Enherrian. The cripple calmly awaited him. "She is fallen?" he asked.

Pete nodded.

"That is well," Enherrian said.

"It is not," Pete heard himself reply, harsh and remote. "She shouldn't have aroused. The drug should've—Did you give her a stim shot? Did you bring her back to suffer?"

"What else?" said Enherrian, though he was unarmed and a blaster lay nearby for Pete to seize. *Not that I'll ease him out of his fate!* went through the man in a spasm. "I saw that you, distraught, had misgauged. You were gone and I unable to follow you. She might well die before your return."

Out of his void, Pete gaped into those eyes. "You mean," rattled from him, "you mean . . . she . . . mustn't?"

Enherrian crawled forth—he could only crawl, on his single wing—to take Pete's hands. "My friend," he said, his tone immeasurably compassionate, "I honored you both too much to deny her her deathpride."

Pete's chief awareness was the the cool sharp talons.

"Have I misunderstood?" asked Enherrian anxiously. "Did you not wish her to give God a battle?"

Even on Lucifer, the nights finally end. Dawn blazed on the tors when Pete finished his story.

I emptied the last few cc. into our glasses. We'd get no work done today. "Yeh," I said. "Cross-cultural semantics. Given the best will in the universe, two beings from different planets—or just different countries, often—take for granted they think alike; and the outcome can be tragic."

"I assumed that at first," Pete said. "I didn't need to forgive Enherrian—how could he know? For his part, he was puzzled when I buried my darling. On Ythri they cast them from a great height into wilderness. But neither race wants to watch the rotting of what was loved, and so he did his lame best to help me."

He drank, looked as near the cruel bluish sun as he was able, and mumbled, "What I couldn't do was forgive God."

"The problem of evil," I said.

"Oh, no. I've studied these matters, these past years: read theology, argued with priests, the whole route. Why does God, if He is a loving and personal God, allow evil? Well, there's a perfectly good Christian answer to that. Man—intelligence everywhere—must have free will. Otherwise we're puppets and have no reason to exist. Free will necessarily includes the capability of doing wrong. We're here, in this cosmos during our lives, to learn how to be good of our unforced choice."

"I spoke illiterately," I apologized. "All that brandy. No, sure, your logic is right, regardless of whether I accept your premises or not. What I meant was: the problem of pain. Why does a merciful God permit undeserved agony? If He's omnipotent, He isn't compelled to.

"I'm not talking about the sensation which warns you to take your hand from the fire, anything useful like that. No, the random accident which wipes out a life . . . or a mind—" I drank. "What happened to Arrach, yes, and to Enherrian, and Olga and you, and Whell. What happens when a disease hits, or those catastrophes we label acts of God. Or the slow decay of us if we grow very old. Every such horror. Never mind if science has licked some of them; we have enough left, and then there were our ancestors who endured them all.

"Why? What possible purpose is served? It's not adequate to declare we'll receive an unbounded reward after we die, and therefore it makes no difference whether a life was gusty or gristly. That's no explanation.

"Is this the problem you're grappling, Pete?"

"In a way." He nodded, cautiously, as if he were already his father's age. "At least, it's the start of the problem.

"You see, there I was, isolated among Ythrians. My fellow humans sympathized, but they had nothing to say that I didn't know already. The New Faith however. . . . Mind you, I wasn't about to convert. What I did hope for was an insight, a freshness, that'd help me make Christian sense of our losses. Enherrian was so sure, so learned, in his beliefs—

"We talked, and talked, and talked, while I was regaining my strength. He was as caught as I. Not that he couldn't fit our troubles into his scheme of things. That was easy. But it turned out that the New Faith has no satisfactory answer to the problem of *evil*. It says God allows wickedness so that we may win honor by fighting for the right. Really when you stop to think, that's weak, especially in carnivore Ythrian terms. Don't you agree?"

"You know them, I don't," I sighed. "You imply they have a better answer to the riddle of pain than your own religion does."

"It seems better." Desperation edged his slightly blurred tone:

"They're hunters, or were until lately. They see God like that, as the Hunter. Not the Torturer—you absolutely must understand this point—no, He rejoices in our happiness the way we might rejoice to see a game animal gamboling. Yet at last He comes after us. Our noblest moment is when we, knowing He is irresistible, give Him a good chase, give Him a good fight.

"Then He wins honor. And some infinite end is furthered. (The same one as when my God is given praise? How can I tell?) We're dead, struck down, lingering at most a few years in the memories of those who escaped this time. And that's what we're here for. That's why God created the universe."

"And this belief is old," I said. "It doesn't belong just to a few cranks. No, it's been held for centuries by millions of sensitive, intelligent, educated beings. You can live by it, you can die by it. If it doesn't solve every paradox, it solves some that your faith won't, quite. This is your dilemma, true?"

He nodded again. "The priests have told me to deny a false creed and to acknowledge a mystery. Neither instruction feels right. Or am I asking too much?"

"I'm sorry, Pete," I said, altogether honestly. It hurt. "But how should I know? I looked into the abyss once, and saw nothing, and haven't looked since. You keep looking. Which of us is the braver?

"Maybe you can find a text in Job. I don't know, I tell you, I don't know."

The sun lifted higher above the burning horizon.

"O.K., THEY'VE SIGNED THE RELEASE."

From Gary Jennings: "Born in Virginia, spent most of life in New York City, now live blissfully in flower-clad Mexican mountain town. Worked for ten years as an ad man, finally split with Madison Avenue to devote full time to free-lance writing. Since then, have published six books of non-fiction plus short stories, articles in almost all American magazines. The occasional fantasy story is my release valve, or sanity valve, between bouts of more nuts-and-bolts type writing." We guaranteed in the magazine introduction to this story that it would be the funniest piece you've read in a long time, and we haven't heard any complaints yet.

Sooner or Later or Never Never

GARY JENNINGS

"The Anula tribe of Northern Australia associate the dollar-bird with rain, and call it the rain-bird. A man who has the bird for his totem can make rain at a certain pool. He catches a snake, puts it alive into the pool, and after holding it under water for a time takes it out, kills it, and lays it down by the side of the creek. Then he makes an arched bundle of grass stalks in imitation of a rainbow, and sets it up over the snake. After that all he does is to sing over the snake and the mimic rainbow; *sooner or later the rain will fall.*"

—Sir James Frazer
The Golden Bough

The Rt. Rev. Orville Dismey
Dean of Missionary Vocations
Southern Primitive Protestant College
Grobian, Virginia

Most Reverend Sir:

It has been quite a long time since we parted, but the attached
Frazer quotation should help you to remember me—Crispin
Mobey, your erstwhile student at dear old SoPrim. Since it occurred to me that you may have heard only a sketchy account of
my activities in Australia, this letter will constitute my full report.

For instance, I should like to refute anything you may have
heard from the Primitive Protestant Pacific Synod about my
mission to the Anula tribe having been less than an unqualified
success. If I helped a little to wean the Anulas away from
heathen sorceries—and I did—I feel I have brought them that
much closer to the True Word, and my mission was worth its
cost.

It was also, for me, the realization of a lifelong dream. Even as
a boy in Dreer, Virginia, I saw myself as a future missionary to
the backward and unenlightened corners of the world, and comported myself in keeping with that vision. Among the rougher
hewn young men of Dreer I often heard myself referred to, in a
sort of awe, as "that Christly young Mobey." In all humility, I
deplored being set on such a pedestal.

But it wasn't until I entered the hallowed halls of Southern
Primitive College that my previously vague aspirations found
their focus. It was during my senior year at dear old SoPrim
that I came upon Sir James Frazer's twelve-volume anthropologi-
cal compendium, *The Golden Bough,* with its account of the
poor deluded Anula tribe. I investigated, and discovered to my
joy that there still was such a tribe in Australia, that it was just
as pitiably devoid of Salvation as it had been when Frazer wrote
about it, and that no Primitive Protestant mission had ever been
sent to minister to these poor unsaved souls. Unquestionably (I
said to myself) the time, the need, and the man had here con-
joined. And I began agitating for a Board of Missions assignment
to the overlooked Anulas.

This did not come easily. The Regents complained that I was dismally near failing even such basic ecclesiastic subjects as Offertory Management, Histrionics and Nasal Singing. But you came to my rescue, Dean Dismey. I remember how you argued. "Admittedly, Mobey's academic grades tend toward Z. But let us in mercy write a Z for zeal, rather than zero, and grant his application. It would be criminal, gentlemen, if we did *not* send Crispin Mobey to the Outback of Australia."

(And I believe this report on my mission will demonstrate that your faith in me, Dean Dismey, was not misplaced. I will say, modestly, that during my travels Down Under, I was often referred to as "the very picture of a missionary.")

I would have been perfectly willing to work my passage to Australia, to claw my way unaided into the Outback, and to live as primitively as my flock while I taught them The Word. Instead, I was surprised to discover that I had at my disposal a generous allocation from the Overseas Mission Fund; overgenerous, in fact, as all I intended to take with me was some beads.

"Beads!" exclaimed the Mission Board bursar, when I presented my requisition. "You want the entire allocation in *glass beads?*"

I tried to explain to him what I had learned from my research. The Australian aborigines, I had been given to understand, are the most primitive of all the peoples living on earth. An actual remnant of the Stone Age, these poor creatures never even got far enough up the scale of evolution to develop the bow and arrow.

"My dear boy," the bursar said gently. "Beads went out with Stanley and Livingstone. You'll want an electric golf cart for the chief. Lampshades for his wives—they wear them for hats, you know."

"The Anulas never heard of golf, and they don't wear hats. They don't wear anything."

"All the best missionaries," the bursar said rather stiffly, "swear by lampshades."

"The Anulas are practically cavemen," I insisted. "They don't even have spoons. They have no written language. I've got to educate them from ape on up. I'm just taking the beads to catch their fancy, to show I'm a friend."

"Snuff is always appreciated," he tried as a last resort.

"Beads," I said firmly.

As you have no doubt deduced from the invoices, my allocation bought a tremendous lot of colored glass beads. I really should have waited to buy them in Australia and avoided the excessive transportation bill; they filled one entire cargo hold of the ship which took me from Norfolk that June day.

Arriving at Sydney, I transferred the beads to a warehouse on the Woolloomooloo docks, and went to report immediately to PrimPro BisPac Shagnasty (as Bishop Shagnasty likes to style himself; he was a Navy chaplain during the war). I found that august gentleman, after some search and inquiry, at the local clubhouse of the English-Speaking Union. "A fortress, a refuge," he called it, "among the Aussies. Will you join me in one of these delicious Stingarees?"

I declined the drink and launched into the story behind my visit.

"Going to the Anulas, eh? In the Northern Territory?" He nodded judiciously. "Excellent choice. Virgin territory. You'll find good fishing."

A splendid metaphor. "That's what I came for, sir," I said enthusiastically.

"Yes," he mused. "I lost a Royal Coachman up there on the River Roper, three years back."

"Mercy me!" I exclaimed, aghast. "I had no idea the poor heathens were hostile! And one of the Queen's own chauf—!"

"No, no, no! A trout fly!" He stared at me. "I begin to understand," he said after a moment, "why they sent you to the Outback. I trust you're leaving for the North immediately."

"I want to learn the native language before I get started," I said. "The Berlitz people in Richmond told me I could study Anula at their branch school here in Sydney."

Next day, when I located the Berlitz office, I discovered to my chagrin that I would have to learn German first. Their only teacher of the Anula language was a melancholy defrocked priest of some German Catholic order—a former missionary himself—and he spoke no English.

It took me a restless and anxious three months of tutorage in the German tongue (while storage charges piled up on my beads) before I could start learning Anula from the ex-priest,

Herr Krapp. As you can imagine, Dean Dismey, I was on guard against any subtle Papist propaganda he might try to sneak into my instruction. But the only thing I found odd was that Herr Krapp's stock of Anula seemed to consist mainly of phases of endearment. And he frequently muttered almost heartbrokenly, in his own language, *"Ach, das liebenswerte schwarze Madchen!"* and licked his chops.

By the end of September Herr Krapp had taught me all he knew, and there was no reason for me to delay any longer my start for the Outback. I hired two drivers and two trucks to carry my beads and myself. Besides my missionary's KampKit (a scaled-down revival tent), my luggage consisted only of my New Testament, my spectacles, my German-English dictionary, a one-volume edition of *The Golden Bough*, and my textbook of the native language, *Die Gliederung der australischen Sprachen*, by W. Schmidt.

Then I went to bid farewell to Bishop Shagnasty. I found him again, or still, at the English-Speaking Union refreshment stand.

"Back from the bush, eh?" he greeted me. "Have a Stingaree. How are all the little blackfellows?"

I tried to explain that I hadn't gone yet, but he interrupted me to introduce me to a military-looking gentleman nearby.

"Major Mashworm is a Deputy Protector of the Aborigines. He'll be interested to hear how you found his little black wards, as he never seems to get any farther Outback than right here."

I shook hands with Major Mashworm and explained that I hadn't yet seen his little black wards, but expected to shortly.

"Ah, another Yank," he said as soon as I opened my mouth.

"Sir!" I said, bridling. "I am a *South*erner!"

"Quite so, quite so," he said, as if it made no difference. "And are you circumcised?"

"Sir!" I gasped. "I am a *Christ*ian!"

"Too right. Well, if you expect to get anywhere with a myall abo tribe, you'll have to be circumcised or they don't accept you as a full-grown bloke. The abo witch doctor will do it for you, if necessary, but I fancy you'd rather have it done in hospital. The native ceremony also involves knocking out one or two of your teeth, and then you have to squat out in the bush, twirling a bullroarer, until you're jake again."

Had I heard about this when I first heard of the Anulas, my zeal might have been less. But having come this far, I saw nothing for it but to submit to the operation. Still, someone might have told me earlier; I could have been healing while I was studying languages. As it was, I couldn't delay my start North. So I had the operation done that very night at Sydney Mercy—by an incredulous doctor and two sniggering nurses— and got my little caravan on the road immediately afterward.

The trip was sheer agony, not to say a marathon embarrassment. Convalescence involved wearing a cumbersome contraption that was a cross between a splint and a truss, and which was well-nigh impossible to conceal even beneath a mackintosh several sizes too large for me. I won't dwell on the numerous humiliations that beset me at rest stops along the way. But you can get some idea, reverend sir, if you imagine yourself in my tender condition, driving in a badly sprung war-relic truck, along a practically nonexistent road, all the way from Richmond to the Grand Canyon.

Everything in the vast interior of Australia is known roughly as the Outback. But the Northern Territory, where I was going, is even out back of the Outback, and is known to the Aussies as the Never Never. The territory is the size of Alaska, but has exactly as many people in it as my hometown of Dreer, Virginia. The Anula tribal grounds are situated in the far north of this Never Never, on the Barkly Tableland between the bush country and the tropical swamps of the Gulf of Carpentaria—a horrible 2,500 miles from my starting point at Sydney.

The *city* of Cloncurry (pop. 1,955) was our last real glimpse of humankind. By way of illustrating what I mean, the next town we touched, Dobbyn, had a population of about 0. And the last town with a name in all that Never Never wilderness, Brunette Downs, had a population of minus something.

That was where my drivers left me, as agreed from the start. It was the last possible place they might contrive to hitchhike a ride back toward civilization. They showed me the direction I should take from there, and I proceeded on my pilgrim's progress into the unknown, driving one of the trucks myself and parking the other in Brunette Downs for the time being.

My drivers said I would eventually come upon an Experimental Agricultural Station, where the resident agents would have the latest word on where to find the nomadic Anulas. But I arrived there late one afternoon to find the station deserted, except for a few languid kangaroos and one shriveled, whiskery little desert rat who came running and whooping a strange cry of welcome.

"Cooee! What cheer? What cheer? Gawdstrewth, it's bonzer to see a bloody newchum buggering barstid out here, dinkum it is!"

(Lest this outburst has horrified you, Dean Dismey, allow me to explain. At first, I blushed at the apparent blasphemies and obscenities commonly employed by the Australians, from Mashworm on down. Then I realized that they use such locutions as casually and innocently as punctuation. And, their "Strine" dialect being what it is, I never knew *when* to blush at their real deliberate cuss-words, because I couldn't tell which they were. Therefore, rather than try here to censor or euphemize every sentence uttered, I shall report conversations verbatim and without comment.)

"Set your arse a spell, cobber! The billy's on the boil. We'll split a pannikin and have a real shivoo, what say?"

"How do you do?" I managed to get in.

"What-o, a Yank!" he exclaimed in surprise.

"Sir," I said with dignity, "I am a Virginian."

"Strewth? Well, if you're looking to lose it, you've come to one helluva place for gash. There ain't a blooming sheila inside three hundred mile, unless you're aiming to go combo with the Black Velvet."

This made no sense whatever, so to change the subject I introduced myself.

"Garn! A narky Bush Brother? Should of known, when you announced you was cherry. Now I'll have to bag me bloody langwidge."

If he "bagged" his language, it was to no noticeable degree. He repeated one obscene-sounding proposal several times before I interpreted it as an invitation to have a cup of tea ("go snacks on Betty Lee") with him. While we drank the tea, brewed over a twig fire, he told me about himself. At least I suppose that's what he told me, though all I got out of it was that his name was McCubby.

"Been doing a walkabout in the woop-woop, fossicking for wolfram. But my cuddy went bush with the brumbies and I found meself in a prebloody-dicament. So I humped my bluey in here to the Speriment Station, hoping I'd strike a stock muster, a squatter, anybody, even a dingo-barstid jonnop. But no go, and I was bloody well down on my bone when you showed your dial."

"What do you do out here?" I asked.

"I toldjer, I was fossicking for wolfram."

"Well, you've got so many unfamiliar animals here in Australia," I said apologetically. "I never heard of a wolf ram."

He peered at me suspiciously and said, "Wolfram is tungsten ore. Fossicking is prospecting."

"Speaking of Australian fauna," I said, "can you tell me what a dollar-bird is?"

(The dollar-bird, you will recall, sir, is the totem agent mentioned in Frazer's account of the rain-making ceremony. I had come this far without being able to find out just what a dollar-bird *was*.)

"It ain't no fawn, Rev," said McCubby. "And you can be glad it ain't. That was a dollar-bird which just took a dump on your titfer."

"What?"

"I keep forgetting you're a newchum," he sighed. "Your titfer is your hat. A dollar-bird just flew over and let fly."

I took off my hat and wiped at it with a tuft of dry grass.

"The dollar-bird," McCubby said pedantically, "is so called because of a silvery-colored circular patch on its spread wings."

"Thank you," I said, and started to explain how the bird had inspired my mission to the aborigines—

"To the abos! Strike me blind!" blurted McCubby. "And here I thought you was out to preach at the buggering snoozers up at Darwin. I presoom the whole rest of the world is already gone Christian, then, if Gawd's scraping the barrel for blackfellow converts."

"Why, no," I said. "But the abos have as much right as any-body else to learn the True Word. To learn that their heathen gods are delusive devils tempting them to hell fire."

"They're looking forward to hell fire, Rev," said McCubby, "as an improvement on the Never Never. Ain't they got enough grief without you have to inflict religion on 'em?"

"Religion is a sap," I said, quoting William Penn, "to penetrate the farthest boughs of the living tree."

"Looks to me like you're bringing the Bingis a whole bloody cathedral," said McCubby. "What kind of swag you got in the lorry, anyway?"

"Beads," I said. "Nothing but beads."

"Beans, eh?" he said, cocking an eye at the huge truck. "You must be more than meejum fond of flute fruit."

Before I could correct his misapprehension, he stepped to the rear of the vehicle and unlatched both gate doors. The entire van was loaded to the ceiling with beads, dumped in loose for convenience. Of course he was instantly engulfed in a seething avalanche, while several more tons of the beads inundated about an acre of the local flatlands, and rivulets and droplets of them went twinkling off to form a diminishing nimbus around the main mass. After a while, the mound behind the truck heaved and blasphemed and McCubby's whiskery head emerged.

"Look what you've done," I said, justifiably exasperated.

"Oh my word," he said softly. "First time beans ever dumped *me.*"

He picked up one of the things, tried his teeth on it and said, "These would constipate a cassowary, Rev." He took a closer look at it and staggered through the pile toward me, dribbling beads from every fold of his clothes. "Somebody has give you the sweet but-all, son," he confided. "These ain't beans. They're glass."

I'm afraid I snapped at him. "I know it! They're for the natives!"

He looked at me, expressionless. He turned, still expression-less, and looked slowly around the glittering expanse that spread seemingly to the horizon in all directions.

"What religion did you say you're magging?" he asked cau-tiously.

I ignored him. "Well," I sighed. "No sense trying to pick them all up before nightfall. Mind if I camp here till morning?"

I was awakened several times during the night by a hideous crunching noise from the perimeter of our glass desert, but, since McCubby didn't stir, I tried not to let it perturb me.

We arose at sunup, our whole part of the world gleaming "like the buggering Land of Hoz," as McCubby put it. After breakfast I began the Herculean task of regathering my stock, with a rusty shovel I found in a tumbledown station outbuilding. McCubby left me for a while, to go slithering across the beads to their outer reaches. He came back beaming happily, with an armload of bloody scraps of fur.

"Dingo scalps," he chortled. "Worth a quid apiece in bounties. Rev, you may have spragged the curse of this whole blunny continent. Out there's just heaped with the corpses of dingos, rabbits and dunnikan rats what tried to make a meal off your bijous. Oh my word!"

He was so pleased at the sudden windfall that he hunted up another shovel and pitched in to help me scoop beads. It was night again by the time we had the truck loaded, and, at that, half its content was topsoil. The territory around the Experimental Station still looked like Disneyland.

"Oh, well," I said philosophically. "Good thing I've got another truckful waiting at Brunette Downs."

McCubby started, stared at me, and went off muttering in his beard.

The next morning I finally set forth on the last lap of my mission of mercy. McCubby told me he had encountered the Anula tribe on his trek in to the station. They were camped in a certain swale of acacia trees, he said, scratching for witchetty grubs and irriakura bulbs, the only available food in this dry season.

And it was there I found them, just at sundown. The whole tribe couldn't have numbered more than seventy-five souls, each of them uglier than the next. Had I not known of their crying need of me, I might have backtracked. The men were great broad-shouldered fellows, coppery-black, with even blacker beards and hair brushed around their low foreheads, sullen eyes and bone-pierced flat noses. The women had more hair and no beards, and limp, empty breasts that hung down their fronts like a couple of pinned-on medals. The men wore only a horsehair rope around their middles, in which they stuck their boomerangs, music sticks, feather charms, and the like. The women wore *nagas*, fig newton-sized aprons of paperbark. The children wore drool.

They looked up dully as I brought the truck to a halt. There was no evidence either of welcome or hostility. I climbed onto the truck hood, waved my arms and called out in their language, "My children, come unto me! I bring tidings of great joy!"

A few of the tots crept closer and picked their noses at me. The women went back to rooting around the acacias with their yamsticks. The men simply continued to do nothing. They're all bashful, I thought; nobody wants to be first.

So I strode boldly into their midst and took a wizened, white-bearded oldster by the arm. I leaned into the truck cab, opened the little hatch that gave access to the van, and plunged the old gaffer's resisting hand inside. It came out grasping a fistful of dirt and one green bead, at which he blinked in perplexity.

As I had hoped, curiosity brought the rest of the tribe around.

"Plenty for everybody, my children!" I shouted in their language. Pulling and hauling, I forced them one by one up to the cab. They each obediently reached through the hatch, took one bead apiece and drifted back to their occupations as if thankful the ceremony was over.

"What's the matter?" I asked one shy young girl, the last of the procession and the only one who had taken *two* beads. "Doesn't anybody like the pretty-pretties?" She flinched guiltily, put back one of the beads and scurried away.

I was flabbergasted at the lack of enthusiasm. As of now, the Anulas had one tiny bead apiece, and I had about six hundred billion.

Beginning to suspect what was amiss, I went and stood among them and listened to their furtive, secretive talk. *I couldn't understand a word!* Horrors, I thought. Unless we could communicate, I had no hope of making them accept the beads . . . or me . . . or The Gospel. Could I have stumbled on the wrong tribe? Or were they deliberately misunderstanding me and talking in gibberish?

There was one way to find out, and that without more ado.
I turned the truck around and drove pell-mell back for the
station, hoping mightily that McCubby hadn't left yet.

He hadn't. The wild dogs were still committing suicide en
masse by dining on my beads, and McCubby wasn't about to
leave until the bounty business petered out. I reached the station
at sunrise again, when he was out collecting the night's scalps. I
leapt from the truck and blurted out my problem.

"I don't understand them and they don't understand me. You
claim you know most of the abo tongues. What am I doing
wrong?" I reeled off a sentence and asked anxiously, "Did you
understand that?"

"Too right," he said. "You offered me thirty pfennig to get
my black arse in bed with you. Cheap barstid," he added.

A little rattled, I pleaded, "Never mind what the words *said*.
Is my pronunciation bad or something?"

"Oh, no. You're mooshing perfect Pitjantjatjara."

"What?"

"A considerably different langwidge from Anula. Anula has
nine noun classes. Singular, dual, trial and plural are expressed
by perfixes in its pronouns. Transitive werbs incorporate the
object pronouns. The werbs show many tenses and moods and
also a separate negative conjugation."

"What?"

"On the other hand, in Pitjantjatjara, the suffixes indicating
the personal pronouns may be appended to the first inflected
word in the sentence, not merely to the werb root."

"What?"

"I don't like to bulsh on your linguistic accomplishments,
cobber. But Pitjantjatjara, although it *has* four declensions and
four conjugations, is alleged to be the simplest of all the bloody
Australoid langwidges."

I was speechless.

"How much," McCubby asked at last, "is thirty pfennig in
shillings and pence?"

"Maybe," I murmured thoughtfully, "I'd better go and minister to the Pitjantjatjara tribe instead, as long as I know their
language."

McCubby shrugged. "They live way the hell the other side

of the Great Sandy. And they're no myall rootdiggers like these Anulas. They're all upjumped stockriders and donahs now, on the merino stations around Shark Bay. Also, them boongs would prob'ly wind up converting *you*, and that's the dinkum oil. They're staunch Catholics."

Well, that figured. And I was beginning to suspect why Herr Krapp had been defrocked.

My next move was obvious: to hire McCubby as my interpreter to the Anulas. At first he balked. My expense fund was so depleted by now that I couldn't offer enough to tempt him away from his booming business here in dingo scalps. But finally I thought to offer him all the beads in the second truck—"Enough to kill every dingo in the Outback." So he rolled up his swag and took the wheel (I was dead tired of driving), and we headed again for the Anula country.

On the way, I told McCubby how I intended to introduce the blackfellows to modern Primitive Protestantism. I read aloud to him Sir James Frazer's paragraph on rainmaking, which concludes, " 'After that all he does is to sing over the snake and the mimic rainbow . . .' "

"*All* he docs!" McCubby snorted.

" 'Sooner or later the rain will fall.' " I closed the book. "And that's where I step in. If the rain doesn't fall, the natives can plainly see that their sorcery doesn't work, and I can turn their clearer eyes toward Christianity. If the rain *should* fall, I simply explain that they were actually praying to the true, Protestant God without realizing it, and the rain-bird had nothing to do with it."

"And how do you cozen 'em into doing this rain-bird corroboree?"

"Heavens, they're probably doing it all the time. The good Lord knows they need rain. This whole country is burned crisp as paper."

"If it do come on to rain," McCubby muttered darkly, "my word, *I'll* fall down on me knees." What that signified, I (unfortunately) didn't surmise at the time.

The reception at the Anula camp was rather different this time. The abos swarmed to greet McCubby; three of the younger females in particular appeared to rejoice at his arrival.

"Ah, me cheeky little blackgins," he said affectionately. Then, after a colloquy with the tribe's elders, he said to me, "They want to offer you a lubra, too, Rev."

A lubra is a female, and I had expected this hospitality, knowing it to be a custom of the Anulas. I asked McCubby to explain my religious reasons for declining and went to work to set up my tent on a knoll overlooking the native camp. As I crawled into it, McCubby asked, "Going to plow the deep so early?"

"I just want to take off my clothes," I said. "When in Rome, you know. See if you can borrow one of those waist strings for me."

"A nood missionary?" he said, scandalized.

"Our church teaches that the body is nothing," I said, "but a machine to carry the soul around. Besides, I feel a true missionary should not set himself above his flock in matters of dress and social deportment."

"A true missionary," McCubby said drily, "ain't got the crocodile hide of these Bingis." But he brought me the horsehair rope. I tied it around my waist and stuck into it my New Testament, my pocket comb, and my spectacles case.

When I was ready, I felt very vulnerable and vaguely vulgar. For one as modest and introverted as I, it was painful to think of stepping out there—especially in view of the females—in my stark white nakedness. But after all, I consoled myself, I wasn't quite as stark as my flock. On the Sydney doctor's orders, I would have to wear my bandage contrivance for another week.

I scrambled out of the tent and stood up, dancing delicately as the ground stubble jabbed my bare feet. My, all those white eyeballs in all those black faces! McCubby was staring just as intently and unbelievingly as everyone else. He worked his mouth for a while before he spoke.

"Crikey! No wonder you're virginian, poor cove."

The abos began to crowd around the point and babble and measure the apparatus as if they contemplated getting copies to wear. Finally, a trifle annoyed, I asked my still-goggling interpreter why they were making so much fuss.

"They think you're either bragging or humbugging. Dinkum, so do I."

So I told him about my operation, that I had endured it because it was an Anula custom. McCubby repeated this to the mob. The blackfellows nodded knowingly at each other, jabbered even more furiously, and came one by one to pat me on the head.

"Ah, they approve, do they?" I said with great satisfaction.

"They think you're crazy as a kookaburra," McCubby said flatly. "It's supposed to bring good luck to fondle a zany."

"What?"

"If you'll take a pike at the men of your flock," he suggested, "you'll note that the custom of circumbloodycision must of went out of style some time back."

I looked, and it was so. I found myself mentally composing some un-Christian remarks to make to Major Mashworm. So, to elevate my thoughts, I proposed that we try again to distribute my gift of beads. I don't know what McCubby told the black-fellows, but the whole tribe trooped off eagerly to the truck and came back with a double handful of beads apiece. Several of them made two or more trips. I was pleased.

The brief tropical dusk was on us now; the Anulas' cooking fires began to twinkle among the acacias. I wouldn't be able to accomplish anything more today; so McCubby and I set our own billy on a fire. We had just settled down to our tucker when one of the abos came up smiling and handed me a slab of bark heaped with some kind of native food. Whatever it was, it quivered disgustingly, and, looking at it, so did I.

"Emu fat," said McCubby. "Their favorite delicacy. It's in return for them beads."

I was ever so delighted, but the dish was nauseatingly difficult to get down. It was like eating a bowlful of lips.

"I'd wolf the stuff if I was you," McCubby advised, after a visit to the natives' fires. "They're likely to come and take it back, when they give up on the beads."

"What?"

"They've been boiling 'em for two hours, now, and it seems they still taste gritty."

"They're *eating* the *beads?*"

He saw my consternation and said, almost kindly, "Rev, all these boongs live for is to eat for to live for to eat. They don't have houses and they don't wear pockets, so they got no use for propitty. They know they're ugly as the backside of a wombat, so they got no use for pretties. In this crook country, finding food is cruel hard. If anything new comes along, they try it for food, in hopes."

I was too weary even to worry; I crept into my tent desiring only to "plow the deep," in McCubby's phrase. As it turned out, though, I got precious little sleep. I had to keep evicting a procession of young black girls who, I presume, had a childish desire to sleep under canvas for a change.

I arose quite late in the morning, to find all the Anulas still huddled, groaning, in their *wagga* rugs. "You won't see any rain-debbil corroboree today," McCubby told me. "Them rumbustious beads has got 'em all just about keck-livered."

Now I *was* worried. Suppose they all died like the dingos!

"I wouldn't do this for any ruggerlugs but you, Rev," said McCubby, digging into his swag. "But I'll squander some of my lollies on 'em."

"What?"

"Chawnklit. It's what *I* use for trading and bribing the Bingis. They like it a buggering sight better than beads."

"But that's Ex-Lax!" I exclaimed when he brought it out.

"That's what they like about it. A pleasure at both ends."

The events of the rest of that day are indescribable. But the setting sun picked bright glints from little heaps of beads here and there throughout the rolling land in the locality. And I was having troubles of my own; I had begun to itch intolerably, all over. McCubby wasn't surprised.

"Meat ants," he theorized, "or sugar ants, white ants, buffalo flies, marsh flies, blow flies. We also got anopheles mosquitos. I tell you, Rev, missionaries ain't got the hide for cavorting bare arse." Not too regretfully, I abandoned my idea of living as primitively as my horny-skinned flock and went back to wearing clothes.

That day was not an entire waste, however. I reminded McCubby that we required a pool of water for the upcoming ritual, and he led me to the Anulas' tribal oasis.

"T'ain't much of a billabong in the Dry," he admitted. The waterhole was respectably wide and deep, but it contained only a scummy, fetid expanse of mud, through which meandered a sullen greenish trickle of water, the thickness of a lead pencil. "But come the Wet and it'd faze Noah. Anyhow, I figure it must be the one in your Golden Bow-Wow. It's the only water inside a hundred mile."

I wondered how, if Frazer's hero had been desperate enough to try conjuring up a rain, he had been provided with a pool to do it at. But I muttered, "Well, dam it, that's all."

"Rev, I'm surprised at your intemperate bloody langwidge!"

I explained. We would throw up a temporary dam across the lower end of the billabong. By the time the Anulas recovered from their gastrointestinal malfunctions, the water should have attained a level sufficient to our purpose. So that's what we did, McCubby and I: hauled and stacked up stones, and chinked their interstices with mud, which the fierce sun baked to an adobe-like cement. We knocked off at nightfall, and the water was already as high as our ankles.

I awoke the next morning to a tumult of whoops, shrills and clangor from the direction of the Anulas' camp. Ah, thought I, stretching complacently; they've discovered their new and improved waterworks and are celebrating. Then McCubby thrust his bristly head through my tent flap and announced excitedly, "War's bin declared!"

"Not with America?" I gasped—his report had sounded rather accusatory—but he had as suddenly withdrawn. I dragged on my boots and joined him on the knoll, and realized he had meant a tribal war.

There were about twice as many blacks down there as I had remembered, and every one of them was ululating loud enough for two more. They milled about, whacking at one another with spears and yamsticks, flinging stones and boomerangs, and jabbing brands from the cooking fires into each other's frizzy hair.

"It's their neighbor tribe, the Bingbingas," said McCubby. "They live downstream on the creek, and this sunup they found their water turned off. They're blaming the Anulas for deliberate mass murder, so as to take over their yam grounds. If this ain't a fair cow!"

"We must do something!"

McCubby rummaged in his swag and brought out a toy-like

pistol. "This is only a pipsqueak .22," he said. "But they ought to nick off home when they see white man's weapons."

We pelted together down the slope and into the fray, McCubby ferociously pop-popping his little revolver in the air, and I brandishing my New Testament to proclaim that Right was on our side. Sure enough, the invading Bingbingas fell back from this new onslaught. They separated out of the confusion and withdrew carrying their wounded. We chased them to the top of a nearby hill, from which vantage they shook their fists and shouted taunts and insults for a while before retiring, defeated, in the direction of their home grounds.

McCubby circulated through the Anula camp, dusting athlete's-foot powder—the only medicament he carried—on the more seriously wounded. There were few casualties, actually, and most of these had suffered only bloody noses, lumped skulls or superficial depilations where hair or whiskers had been yanked out. I played battlefield chaplain as best I could in dumb show, pantomiming spiritual comfort at them. One good thing. All the Anulas appeared to have recovered utterly from their bead-diet prostration. This early-morning exercise had helped.

When things had calmed down, and after some breakfast tucker and tea, I dispatched McCubby to search through the tribe for an unoccupied male of the clan which claimed the dollar-bird for its *kobong*, or totem. He did find a young man of that persuasion and, overcoming his stubborn unwillingness, brought him to me.

"This is Yartatgurk," said McCubby.

Yartatgurk walked with a limp, courtesy of a stiff Bingbinga kick in the shin, and was bushily bearded only on the left side of his face, courtesy of a Bingbinga firebrand. The rest of the tribe came and squatted down expectantly around the three of us, as if eager to see what new and individual treat I had in store for their young man.

"Now we must recapitulate the procedure," I said, and began to read *The Golden Bough*'s description of the ceremony, McCubby translating phrase by phrase. At the conclusion, young Yartatgurk stood up abruptly and, despite his limp, commenced a vigorous heel-and-toe toward the far horizon. All the other

Anulas began muttering among themselves and tapping their foreheads with a forefinger.

When McCubby fetched the struggling Yartatgurk back, I said, "Surely they all must be familiar with the ceremony."

"They say, if you're so buggering thirsty as to go through all that taradiddle, it'd've been just as easy to lug an artesian drill in here as all them beads. Too right!"

"That's not the point," I said. "According to Frazer, the belief is that long ago the dollar-bird had a snake for a mate. The snake lived in a pool and used to make rain by spitting up into the sky until a rainbow and clouds appeared and rain fell."

This, translated, sent the Anulas into a regular frenzy of chattering and head-tapping.

"They say," McCubby interpreted, "you show them a bird mating with a snake and they'll get you all the water you want, if they have to hump the bloody Carpentaria Gulf down here by hand."

This was depressing. "I'm quite sure a reputable anthropologist like Frazer wouldn't *lie* about their tribal beliefs."

"If he's any kin to the Frazer I used to cobber with—old Blazer Frazer—he'd lie about which is his left and right hand."

"Well," I said unquenchably, "I've come twelve thousand miles to repudiate this custom, and I won't be put off. Now tell Yartatgurk to stop that screeching, and let's get on with it."

McCubby managed, by giving Yartatgurk a large slab of Ex-Lax, to convince him that the ceremony—idiotic as he might ignorantly think it—wasn't going to hurt him. The three of us went first to check on the billabong, and found it gratifyingly abrim with repulsive brown water, wide and deep enough to have submerged our truck. From there, we headed into the endless savanna.

"First," I said, "we need a snake. A live one."

McCubby scratched in his whiskers. "That might be a wowser, Rev. The boongs have et most of the snakes within hunting range. And they sprag 'em from a cautious distance, with boomerang or spear. The wipers out here in the Never Never, you don't want to meet 'em alive."

"Why?"

"Well, we got the tiger snake and the death adder, which

their wenom has been measured twenty times as wicked as the bloody cobra's. Then there's the taipan, and I've seen meself a horse die five minutes after it nipped him. Then there's—"

He broke off to make a grab for Yartatgurk, who was trying to sneak away. McCubby pointed into the bush and sent the blackfellow horizonward with explicit instructions. Yartatgurk limped off, looking about him nervously and sucking moodily on his chunk of chocolate. McCubby didn't look any too happy himself, as we followed after the native at a distance. "I wish it was your buggering Frazer we was sending on this chase," he muttered spitefully.

"Oh, come," I said encouragingly. "There must be *some* nonpoisonous variety that will serve our purpose."

"Won't help our purpose none if we tread on one of the others first," growled McCubby. "If this ain't the most nincompoop—"

There was a sudden commotion out ahead of us, where we had last seen Yartatgurk creeping, hunched over, through the tussocky grass.

"He's got one!" I shouted, as the blackfellow rose up into view with a strangled cry. He was silhouetted against the sky, toiling desperately with something huge and lashing, a fearsome sight to behold.

"Dash me rags!" breathed McCubby, in awed surprise. "I ain't never seen a Queensland python this far west before."

"A python!"

"Too bloody right," said McCubby, in unfeigned admiration. "Twenty feet if he's a hinch."

I gaped at the lunging, Laocoön-like tableau before us. Yartatgurk was almost invisible inside the writhing coils, but he was clearly audible. I wondered momentarily if we might not have bitten off more than we could chew, but I sternly laid that specter of uncertainty. Manifestly, the good Lord was following Frazer's script.

"Yartatgurk is inquiring," McCubby said quietly, "who we're rooting for."

"Do you suppose we'll spoil the magic if we lend a hand?"

"We'll spoil the blackfellow if we don't. Look there."

"Mercy on us, he's spouting blood!"

"T'ain't blood. If you'd just et a quarter of a pound of Hex-Lax and then got hugged by a python, you'd spout, too."

We fought our way into the squirming tangle and finally managed to peel the creature loose from Yartatgurk. It took the utmost strength of all three of us to straighten it out and prevent its coiling again. Yartatgurk had turned almost as white as I, but he bravely hung onto the python's tail—being lashed and tumbled about, sometimes high off the ground—while McCubby, at its head, and I, grasping its barrel-like middle, manhandled it toward the billabong.

By the time we made it to the pool bank, all three of us were being whipped through the air, back and forth past each other, and occasionally colliding.

"Now," I managed to gasp out, between the snake's convulsions. "He's got to—hold it under—*oof!*—the water . . ."

"I don't think," said McCubby, on my left, "he's likely to agree," said McCubby, from behind me. "When I yell *go*," said McCubby, on my right, "dowse him and the snake both," said McCubby, from overhead. "*Cooee!*—Go!!!"

At the command, he and I simultaneously swung our portions of the python out over the water and let go. It and the wretched Yartatgurk, flapping helplessly along like the tail of a kite, disappeared with a mighty splash. Instantly the billabong was roiled into a hissing brown froth.

"Pythons," panted McCubby, when he could get his breath, "hates water worse'n cats do."

The entire Anula tribe, I now noticed, had come down to cluster on the opposite side of the billabong, and were attentively following the proceedings with eyes like boiled onions.

"Was you to ask me," said McCubby, when we had rested a while, "I'd be hard put to say who was holding who under."

"I guess it's been long enough," I decreed.

We waded waist-deep into the pool and, after being knocked about a bit, managed to grab hold of the slithery loops and haul the reptile back onto the bank. Yartatgurk, we were pleased to see, came along clenched in a coil of the python's tail.

Somewhere along about here, our handmade dam collapsed. Its mud chinking had been gradually eroded as the water backed up behind it during the night and morning. Now the agitation of the billalong toppled the weakened structure, and all the collected water drained out with a swoosh. This would probably gratify the thirsty Bingbingas downstream, I reflected, if it didn't drown them all in that first grand flood-wave.

The submersion had taken some of the fight out of the snake, but not a great deal. McCubby and I sustained numerous bruises and contusions during this stage of the struggle, while we fought to immobilize the forepart of the thing. Yartatgurk was not much help to us, as he had gone quite limp and, clutched by the freely thrashing tail of the serpent, was being batted like a bludgeon against the surrounding trees and terrain.

"It's time for him to kill it," I shouted to McCubby.

As the blackfellow whisked to and fro past us, McCubby listened to his barely audible mumblings and finally reported, "He says nothing would give him greater pleasure."

Our fantastic battle went on for a while longer, until it became apparent that Yartatgurk wasn't up to killing the monster anytime soon, and I called to McCubby to inquire what to do next.

"I'll hang on best I can," he bellowed back, between curses and grunts. "You run for my swag. Get my pistol. Shoot the bugger."

I went, but with misgivings. I feared that we white men—perhaps unconsciously flaunting our superiority—were taking too much of a hand in this ceremony and, by our meddling, might botch whatever mystical significance it held for the natives.

I came back at a run, gripping the revolver in both hands. The python appeared to have recovered from its watery ordeal and was flailing more energetically than ever, occasionally keeping both men in the air simultaneously. In all that confusing uproar, and in my own excitement, nervousness and unfamiliarity with the weapon, I took quaking aim and shot Yartatgurk in the foot.

He did not make any outright complaint (though I think he might have, if he could have), but his eyes were eloquent. I could almost have wept at their glazed expression of disappointment in me. This was a chastening thing to see, but I suppose even the most divinely inspired spiritual leader encounters it at least once in his career. None of us is perfect.

Meanwhile McCubby had disengaged himself from the melee.

He snatched the pistol from me and emptied it into the serpent's ugly head. For a long time, then, he and I leaned against each other and panted wearily, while the blackfellow and the python lay side by side and twitched.

Yartatgurk's injury, I am relieved to say, was not a serious one. Actually, he had suffered more from his stay underwater. McCubby pumped his flaccid arms up and down, disgorging quite an astonishing quantity of water, mud, weeds and polliwogs, while I bound up the hole in his foot with a strip torn from my own bandages.

A .22, it seems, fires a triflingly small pellet, and this one had passed cleanly through Yartatgurk's foot without so much as nicking a tendon. As the lead did not remain in the wound, and as it bled freely, there appeared to be little cause for agonizing —though this he did, at great and vociferous length, when he regained consciousness.

I decided to let the fellow enjoy a short rest and the commiserations of his clucking tribemates. Besides, I was by now so implicated in the ceremony that I figured a little more intervention could do no harm. So I went myself to perform the next step in the rite: to set up the "mimic rainbow" of grass over the defunct snake.

After fumbling unsuccessfully at this project for a considerable while, I came back and said despairingly to McCubby, "Every time I try to bend the grass into a bow it just crumbles into powder."

"Whajjer expect," he said with some acerbity, "after eight buggery months of drought?"

Here was another verity—like the dried-up billalong—which I couldn't reconcile with Frazer's account. If the grass was dry enough to warrant rainmaking, it was too dry to be bent.

Then I had an inspiration and went to look at the muck of our recent dam-site pool. As I'd hoped, there was a sparse growth of grass there, nicely waterlogged by its night's immersion. I plucked all I could find and tied it into a frazzled rainbow with my bootlaces. The horseshoe-shaped object I propped up around the dead python's neck, making him look as jaunty as a racehorse in the winner's circle.

Feeling very pleased with myself, I returned to McCubby. He, like the Anulas, was sympathetically regarding Yartatgurk, who I gathered was relating the whole history of his wounded foot from the day it was born.

"Now tell him," I said, "all he has to do is sing."

For the first time, McCubby seemed disinclined to relay my instructions. He gave me a long look. Then he clasped his hands behind his back and took a contemplative turn up and down the billabong bank, muttering to himself. Finally he shrugged, gave a sort of bleak little laugh, and knelt down to interrupt the nattering Yartatgurk.

As McCubby outlined the next and final step, Yartatgurk's face gradually assumed the expression of a hamstrung horse being asked to perform its own *coup de grace*. After what seemed to me an unnecessarily long colloquy between the two, McCubby said:

"Yartatgurk begs to be excused, Rev. He says he's just had too much to think about, these past few days. First he had to meditate on the nature of them beads you fed him. Then he had to mull over the Bingbingas' burning of his beard, which cost him three years to cultivate and got glazed off in three winks. Then there was being half squoze to a pulp, and then three-quarters drownded, and then nine-tenths bludged to death, and then having his hoof punctuated. He says his poor inferior black brain is just so full of meat for study that it's clean druv out the words of all the songs."

"He doesn't have to sing words," I said. "I gather that any sprightly tune will do, crooned heavenward in a properly beseeching manner."

There was a short silence.

"In all this empty woop-woop," said McCubby under his breath, "one-eighth of a human bean to a square mile, and *you* have to be the one-eighth I cobber up with."

"McCubby," I said patiently, "this is the most important part of the entire ritual."

"Ah, well. Here goes the last of me Hex-lax."

He handed the chocolate to the blackfellow and launched into a long and seductive argument. At last, with a red-eyed glare at me, and so suddenly that I and the Anulas all jumped, Yartatgurk barked viciously into a clamorous chant. The other natives looked slightly uneasy and began to drift back toward camp.

"My word, you're hearing something that not many white coves ever do," said McCubby. "The age-old Anula death song."

"Nonsense," I said. "He's not going to die."

"Not him. You."

I shook my head reprovingly and said, "I've no time for levity. I must get to work on the sermon I'll preach at the conclusion of all this."

As you can appreciate, Dean Dismey, I had set myself quite a task. I had to be ready with two versions, depending on whether the rainmaking was or was not successful. But the sermons had certain similarities—for example, in both of them I referred to Prayer as "a Checkbook on the Bank of God." And this, of course, posed the problem of explaining a checkbook in terms that an Outback aborigine could comprehend.

While I worked in the seclusion of my tent, I yet kept an ear cocked to Yartatgurk's conscientious keening. As night came down, he began to get hoarse, and several times seemed on the verge of flagging in his endeavor. Each time, I would lay aside my pencil and go down to wave encouragingly at him across the billabong. And each time, this indication of my continued interest did not fail to inspire him to a redoubled output of chanting.

The rest of the Anulas remained quietly in their camp this night, without any moans of indigestion, combat fatigue, or other distress. I was grateful that no extraneous clamor disturbed my concentration on the sermons, and even remarked on it to McCubby:

"The natives seem restful tonight."

"T'ain't often the poor buggers come the bounce on a bellyful of good python meat."

I cried, "They've eaten the ceremonial snake?!"

"Don't matter," he said consolingly. "The whole skelington is still down there under your wicker wicket."

Oh, well, I thought. There was nothing I could do about it now. And, as McCubby implied, the skeleton ought to represent as potent a symbol as the entire carcass.

It was well after mdinight, and I had just finished the notes for my next day's services, when a deputation of tribal elders came calling.

"They say you'd oblige 'em, Rev, either to hurry up and die as warranted, or else to placate Yartatgurk someway. They can't git to sleep with him caterwauling."

"Tell them," I said, with a magisterial wave of my hand, "it will all soon be over."

I knew not how truly I had spoken, until I was violently awakened some hours later by my tent folding up like an umbrella—*thwack!*—and disappearing into the darkness.

Then, just as violently, the darkness was riven and utterly abolished by the most brilliant, writhing, forking, jagging, snarling cascade of lightning I ever hope to see. It was instantly succeeded by an even blacker darkness, the acrid stench of ozone, and a roiling cannonade of thunder that simply picked up the whole Never Never land and shook it like a blanket.

When I could hear again, I discerned McCubby's voice, whimpering in stark horror out of the darkness, "Gawd strike me blind." It seemed more than likely. I was admonishing him to temper his impiety with prudence, when a second cosmic uproar, even more impressive than the first, raged through the echoing dome of heaven.

I had not yet recovered from its numbing fury when a wind like a driving piston took me in the back, balled me up, and sent me tumbling end over end across the countryside. I caromed painfully off numerous eucalyptuses and acacias and unidentifiable other obstacles until I collided with another human body. We grabbed onto each other, but kept on traveling until the wind died for a moment.

By great good fortune, it was McCubby I had encountered—though I must say he seemed unaware of any good fortune in this. "What in buggery have you gone and done?" he demanded, in a quaver.

"What hath *God* wrought?" I corrected him. Oh, it would make an ineradicable impression on the Anulas, when I explained that this was not really the doing of their dollar-bird. "Now," I couldn't help exclaiming, "if it will only pour down rain!"

The words were no sooner spoken than McCubby and I were flattened again. The rain had come down like God's boot-heel.

It continued mercilessly to stamp on my back, grinding me into the solid earth so that I could barely expand my chest to breathe. This, I thought in my agony, is really more than I meant to ask for.

After an incalculable while, I was able to inch my mouth over beside McCubby's ear and bellow loud enough for him to hear, "We've got to find my sermon notes before the rain ruins them!"

"Your bloody notes are in Fiji by now!" he shouted back. "And so will we be if we don't do a bleeding bunk in a bleeding hurry!"

I tried to remonstrate that we couldn't leave the Anulas now, when everything was proceeding so well, and when I had such a God-given opportunity to make a splendid conversion of the whole tribe.

"Can't you get it through your googly skull?" he bellowed. "This is the Cockeye Bob—come early and worse than I ever seen it! This whole land will be underwater, and us with it, *if* we don't get blew a thousand mile and tore to rags in the bush!"

"But my entire mission will have been in vain," I protested, between the peals of thunder. "And the poor Anulas deprived of—"

"Bugger the bloody black barstids!" he howled. "They waved mummuk hours ago. We got to get to the lorry—if it ain't flew away. Make the high ground by the Speriment Station."

Clinging fast together, we were just able to blunder our way through what seemed a solid wall of water. The lightning and thunder were simultaneous now, blinding and deafening us at the same time. Torn-off branches, uprooted bushes and trees of increasingly larger size careened like dark meteors across the Never Never land. Once we ducked the weirdest missile of all— the eerily airborne skeleton of Yartatgurk's python, still sporting its natty grass collar.

I thought it odd that we encountered none of the blackfellows. But we did find the truck at last, jostling anxiously on its springs and squeaking in every rivet as if for help. Wind-blasted water streamed *up* its weather side and smoked off its top like the spindrift from a hurricane sea. I really think that only the dead weight of the remaining beads, which still filled three-quarters of the van, prevented the truck's being overturned.

McCubby and I fought our way to the lee door and opened it, to have it nearly blown off the hinges as the wind clawed at it. The inside of the cab was no quieter than outdoors, what with the thunder still headsplittingly audible and the rain practically denting the metal, but the stiller air inside was easier to breathe.

When he stopped panting, McCubby wrung another minor cloudburst out of his whiskers and then started the engine. I laid a restraining hand on his arm. "We can't abandon the Anulas to this," I said. "Could we dump the beads and crowd in the women and pickaninnies?"

"I toldjer, they all took a ball of chalk hours ago!"

"Does that mean they've gone?"

"Soon as you sacked out. They were well clear of the low ground by the time the Cockeye Bob came down."

"Hm," I said, a little hurt. "Rather ungrateful of them, to desert their spiritual adviser without notice."

"Oh, they're *grateful*, Rev," McCubby hastened to assure me. "That's why they waved mummuk—you made 'em wealthy. My word, they're reg'lar plutes now. Nicked off to Darwin, to peddle that python skin to a shoe-manufactory."

I could only wheeze, "The Lord works in mysterious ways . . ."

"Anyhow, that was the reason they guv me," said McCubby, as the truck began to roll. "But now I suspicion they smelled the blow coming and bunked out, like bandicoots before a bush fire."

"Without warning us?"

"Well, that Yartatgurk *had* put the debbil-debbil on you with that death-song of his." After a moment, McCubby added darkly, "I didn't savvy the boong bugger had narked me, too."

With that, he headed the truck for the Experimental Station. Neither the windshield wipers nor the headlights were of any use. There was no road, and the faint track we'd followed coming out here was now obliterated. The air was still thick with flying debris. The truck jolted now and then to the resounding blow of a hurtling eucalyptus bole, or chunk of rock, or kangaroo, for all I know. Miraculously, none of them came through the windshield.

Gradually we inched upward from the low country, along the

gently rising slope of a plateau. When we achieved its level top, we knew we were safe from the rising waters. And when we nosed down its farther slope, the rackety violence of the weather abated somewhat, cut off from us by the intervening highland.

As the noise subsided behind us, I broke the silence to ask McCubby what would become of the Anulas now. I ventured the hope that they would spend their new-found wealth on implements and appliances to raise their living standards. "Perhaps build a rustic church," I mused, "and engage a circuit preacher . . ."

McCubby snorted. "Wealth to them, Rev, is a couple of quid, which is all they'll get for that skin. And they'll blow it all in one cranky shivoo. Buy a few bottles of the cheapest plonk they can find, and stay shikkered for a week. Wake up sober in the Compound calaboose, most likely, with the jumping Joe Blakes for comp'ny."

This was most discouraging. It appeared that I had accomplished nothing whatsoever by my coming, and I said so.

"Why, they'll never forget you, Rev," McCubby said through clenched teeth. "No more will every other bloke in the territory that you caught with his knickers down. Here you've brought on the Wet nearly two months early, and brought it with a vengeance. Prob'ly drownded every jumbuck in the Never Never, washed out the railroad perway, bankrupted every ringer, flooded out the peanut farmers and the cotton planters—"

"Please," I implored. "Don't go on."

There was another long and gloomy silence. Then McCubby took pity on me. He lifted my spirits somewhat—and encapsulated my mission—with a sort of subjunctive consolation.

"If you came out here," he said, "mainly to break the Bingis of conjuring up heathen debbil-debbils to make rain, well, you can bet your best Bible they'll never do *that* again."

And on that optimistic note, I shall hasten this history towards its happy conclusion.

Several days later, McCubby and I arrived at Brunette Downs. He had the truckloads of beads transferred into a caravan of Land Rovers and headed Outback once more. I doubt not at all that he has since become a multimillionaire "plute" by cornering the market in dingo scalps. I was able to engage another driver, and the two of us returned the rented trucks to Sydney.

By the time I got back to the city, I was absolutely penniless, and looking picturesquely, not to say revoltingly, squalid. I hied myself at once to the English-Speaking Union in search of PrimPro BisPac Shagnasty. It was my intention to apply for some temporary underling job in the Sydney church organization and to beg a small salary advance. But it became immediately apparent when I found Bishop Shagnasty, that he was in no charitable mood.

"I keep getting these *dunning* letters," he said peevishly, "from the Port of Sydney Authority. A freight consignment of some sort is there in your name. I can't sign for it, can't even find out what it *is,* but they keep sending me fantastic bills for its storage."

I said I was just as much in the dark as he, but the Bishop interrupted:

"I wouldn't advise that you hang about here, Mobey. Deputy Protector Mashworm may come in at any minute, and he's after your hide. He's already flayed a goodly portion of mine."

"Mine, too," I couldn't forbear muttering.

"*He* keeps getting letters of reproach from the Resident Commissioner of the Northern Territory, inquiring why in blazes you were ever let loose to corrupt the blackfellows. Seems a whole tribe descended en masse on Darwin, got vilely intoxicated and tore up half the city before they could be corralled. When they were sober enough to be questioned, they said a new young Bush Brother—unmistakably you—had provided the money for their binge."

I tried to bleat an explanation, but he overrode me.

"That wasn't all. One of the blacks claimed the Bush Brother had shot and wounded him. Others said that the missionary had provoked an intertribal war. Still others claimed he danced naked before them and then fed them poison, but that part wasn't too clear."

I whinnied again, and was again overridden.

"I don't know exactly *what* you did up there, Mobey, and frankly I don't care to be told. I would be everlastingly grateful, though, for one word from you."

"What's that, your reverence?" I asked huskily.

He stuck out his hand. "Good-by."

Having not much else to do, I drifted down to the Wool-loomooloo docks to inquire about this mysterious freight consignment. It turned out to have been sent by dear old SoPrim's Overseas Mission Board and consisted of one Westinghouse two-seater electric golf cart, seven gross of Lightolier lampshades—that's 1,008 lampshades—and a number of cartons of Old Crone Brand burley snuff.

I was too benumbed and disheartened, by this time, even to evince surprise. I signed a receipt and was given a voucher. I carried the voucher to the sailors' low quarter of the town, where I was approached by shifty-eyed men. One of them, the master of a rusty trawler engaged in smuggling Capitalist luxuries to the underadvantaged Communists of Red China, bought my entire consignment, sight unseen. I have no doubt that I was bilked on the transaction, but I was satisfied to be able to pay off the accumulated storage fees on the stuff and have enough left over to buy steerage passage on the first tramp ship leaving for the good old U.S.A.

The only landfall in this country was New York, so that's where I debarked, about a fortnight ago. Hence the postmark on this letter, because I am still here. I was penniless again by the time I landed. But through fortuitous coincidence I visited the local Natural History Museum (because admission was free) at just the time they were preparing a new aborigine tableau in the Australian wing. When I mentioned my recent stay among the Anulas, I was at once engaged as a technical consultant.

The salary was modest, but I managed to put away a bit, in hopes of soon returning to Virginia and to dear old Southern Primitive, to find out what my next mission was to be. Just recently, however, I have discovered that a mission calls me right here.

The artist painting the backdrop of the aborigine tableau—an Italian chap, I take him to be; he is called Daddio—has introduced me to what he calls his "in-group": habitants of an homogeneous village within the very confines of New York City. He led me into a dim, smoky cellar room (a "pad") full of these people—bearded, smelly, inarticulate—and I felt almost transported back to the abos.

Daddio nudged me and whispered, "Go on, say it. Loud, and just the way I coached you, man."

So I declaimed to the room at large the peculiar introduction he had made me rehearse in advance: "I am Crispin Mobey, boy Bush Brother! I have just been circumcised and I learned my Pitjantjatjara from a defrocked priest named Krapp!"

The people in the room, who had been desultorily chatting among themselves, were instantly silent. Then one said, in a hushed and reverent murmur: "This Mobey is so far in *we're* out . . ."

"Like all of a sudden," breathed another, "*Howl* is the square root of Peale . . ."

A lank-haired girl arose from a squat and scrawled on the wall with her green eyebrow pencil, "Leary, no. Larry Welk, si."

Naked Lunch is, like, Easter brunch," said someone else.

"Like, man," said several people at once, "our leader has been taken to *us!*

None of this conveyed any more to me than had the arcane utterances of McCubby and Yartatgurk. But I have been accepted here as I never was even among the Anulas. Nowadays they wait with bearded lips agape for my tritest pronouncement and listen, as avidly as no other congregation I have ever known, to my most recondite sermons. (The one about Prayer being a Checkbook, etc., I have recited on several occasions in the tribe's coffeehouses, to an accompaniment of tribal string music.)

And so, Dean Dismey, I have been divinely guided—all unwittingly but unswervingly—to the second mission of my career. The more I learn of these villagers and their poor deluded idolatries, the more I feel certain that, sooner or later, I can be of Help.

I have applied to the mission headquarters of the local synod of the Primitive Protestant Church for proper accreditation and have taken the liberty of listing you, reverend sir, and Bishop Shagnasty as references. Any good word that you may be kind enough to vouchsafe in my behalf will be more than appreciated by.

Yours for Humility Rampant,
Crispin Mobey